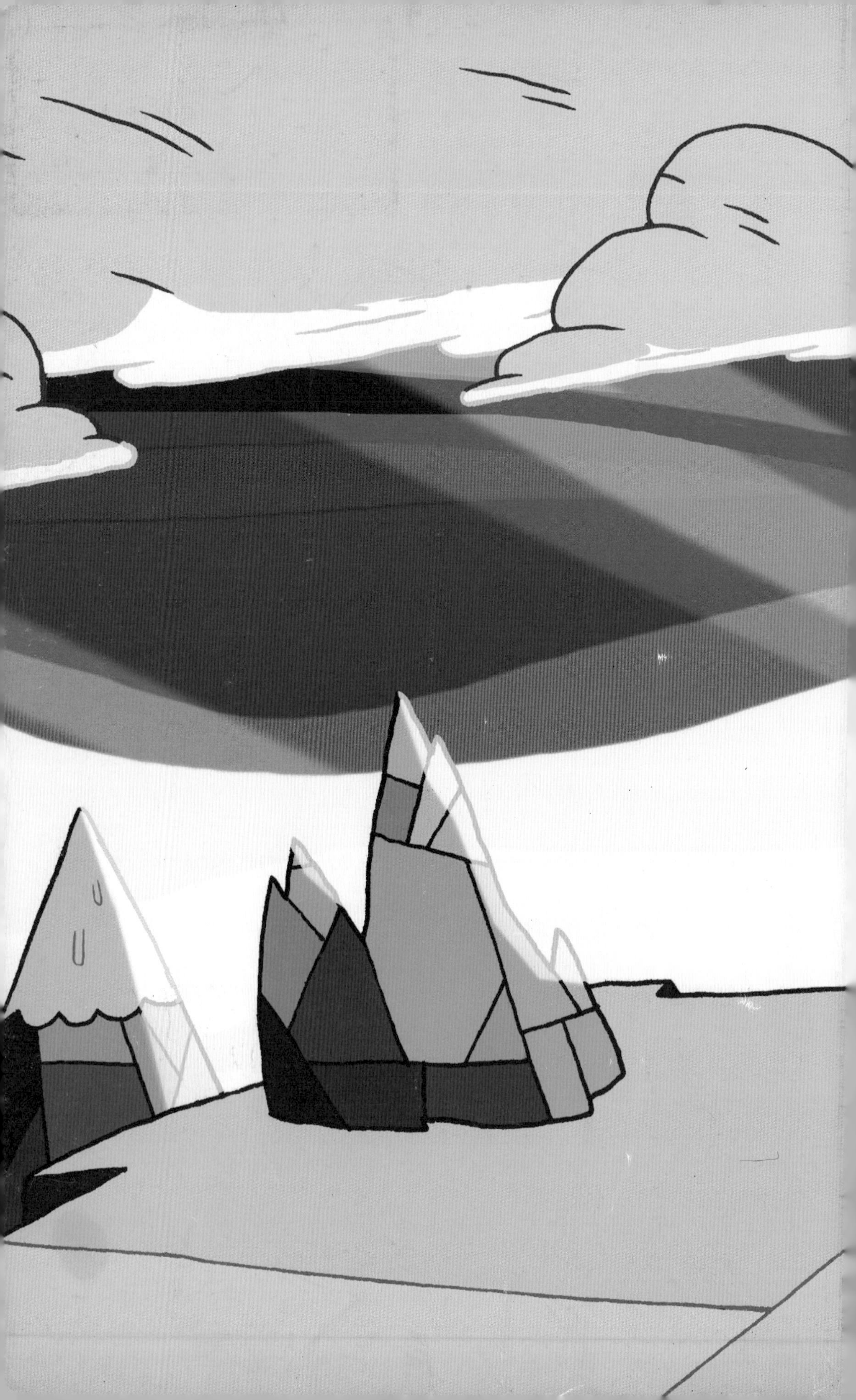

ADVENTURE TIME™

VOLUME 6

WITHDRAWN

ROSS RICHIE CEO & Founder • MARK SMYLIE Founder of Archaia • MATT GAGNON Editor-in-Chief • FILIP SABLIK President of Publishing & Marketing • STEPHEN CHRISTY President of Development
LANCE KREITER VP of Licensing & Merchandising • PHIL BARBARO VP of Finance • BRYCE CARLSON Managing Editor • MEL CAYLO Marketing Manager • SCOTT NEWMAN Production Design Manager
IRENE BRADISH Operations Manager • CHRISTINE DINH Brand Communications Manager • DAFNA PLEBAN Editor • SHANNON WATTERS Editor • ERIC HARBURN Editor • REBECCA TAYLOR Editor
IAN BRILL Editor • CHRIS ROSA Assistant Editor • ALEX GALER Assistant Editor • WHITNEY LEOPARD Assistant Editor • JASMINE AMIRI Assistant Editor • CAMERON CHITTOCK Assistant Editor
KELSEY DIETERICH Production Designer • JILLIAN CRAB Production Designer • KARA LEOPARD Production Designer • DEVIN FUNCHES E-Commerce & Inventory Coordinator • ANDY LIEGL Event Coordinator
AARON FERRARA Operations Assistant • JOSÉ MEZA Sales Assistant • MICHELLE ANKLEY Sales Assistant • ELIZABETH LOUGHRIDGE Accounting Assistant • STEPHANIE HOCUTT PR Assistant

ADVENTURE TIME Volume Six, March 2015. Published by KaBOOM!, a division of Boom Entertainment, Inc. ADVENTURE TIME, CARTOON NETWORK, the logos, and all related characters and elements are trademarks of and © Cartoon Network. (S15) Originally published in single magazine form as ADVENTURE TIME 25-29. © Cartoon Network. (S14) All rights reserved. KaBOOM!™ and the KaBOOM! logo are trademarks of Boom Entertainment, Inc., registered in various countries and categories. All characters, events, and institutions depicted herein are fictional. Any similarity between any of the names, characters, persons, events, and/or institutions in this publication to actual names, characters, and persons, whether living or dead, events, and/or institutions is unintended and purely coincidental. KaBOOM! does not read or accept unsolicited submissions of ideas, stories, or artwork.

A catalog record of this book is available from OCLC and from the KaBOOM! website, www.kaboom-studios.com, on the Librarians Page.

BOOM! Studios, 5670 Wilshire Boulevard, Suite 450, Los Angeles, CA 90036-5679. Printed in China. First Printing.
ISBN: 978-1-60886-482-9, eISBN: 978-1-61398-336-2

CREATED BY
Pendleton Ward

WRITTEN BY
Ryan North

ISSUE 25 ILLUSTRATED BY
Dustin Nguyen, Jess Fink, Jeffrey Brown, Jim Rugg, Shelli Paroline & Braden Lamb
WITH ADDITIONAL COLORS BY
Whitney Cogar and Chris O'Neill

ISSUES 26-29 ILLUSTRATED BY
Jim Rugg

ISSUES 26-28 COLORS BY
Chris O'Neill

ISSUE 29 COLORS BY
Whitney Cogar

LETTERS BY
Steve Wands

COVER BY
Luke Pearson

DESIGNER
Jillian Crab

ASSISTANT EDITOR
Whitney Leopard

EDITOR
Shannon Watters

With special thanks to
Marisa Marionakis, Rick Blanco, Jeff Parker, Laurie Halal-Ono, Nicole Rivera, Conrad Montgomery, Meghan Bradley, Curtis Lelash and the wonderful folks at Cartoon Network.

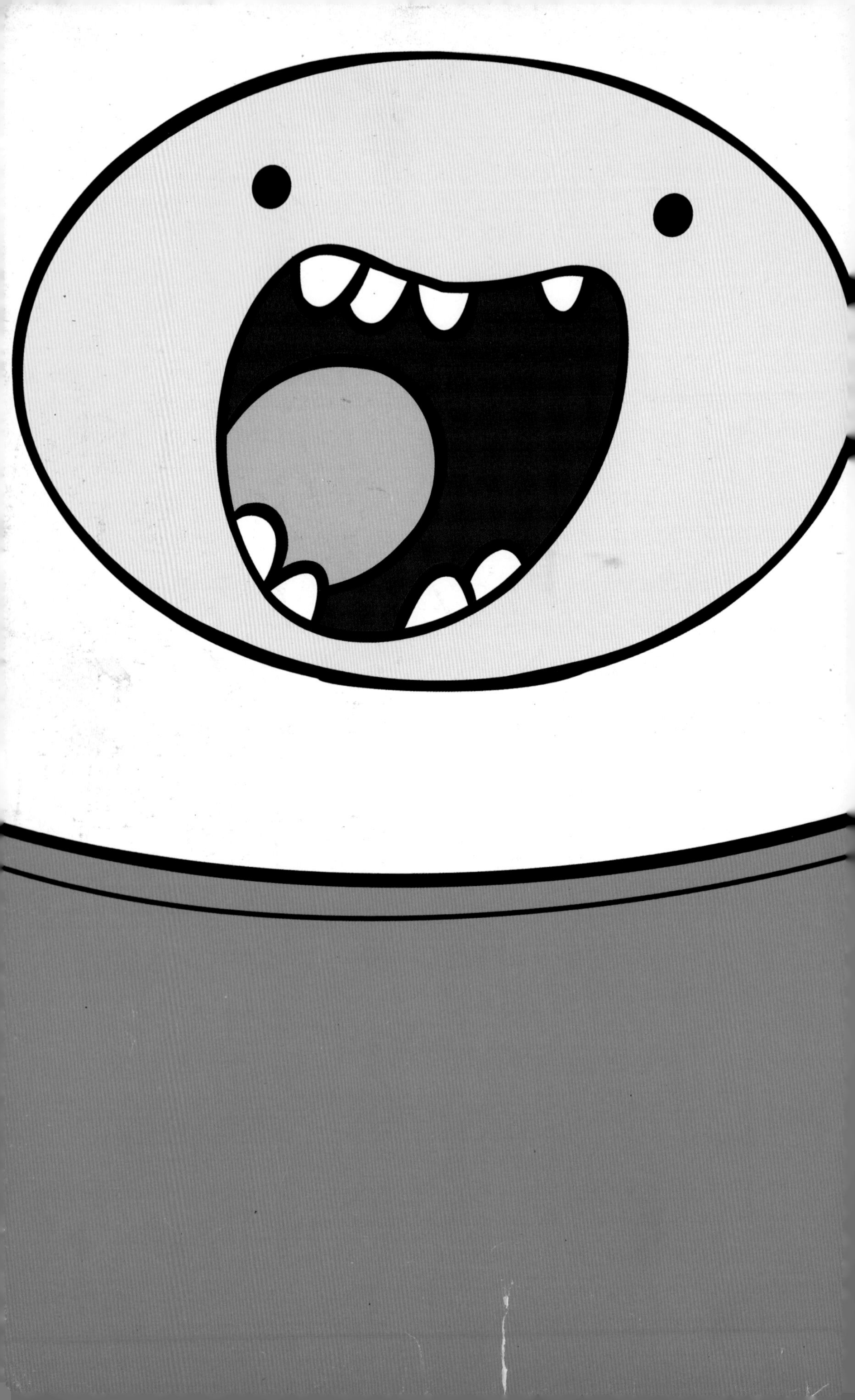

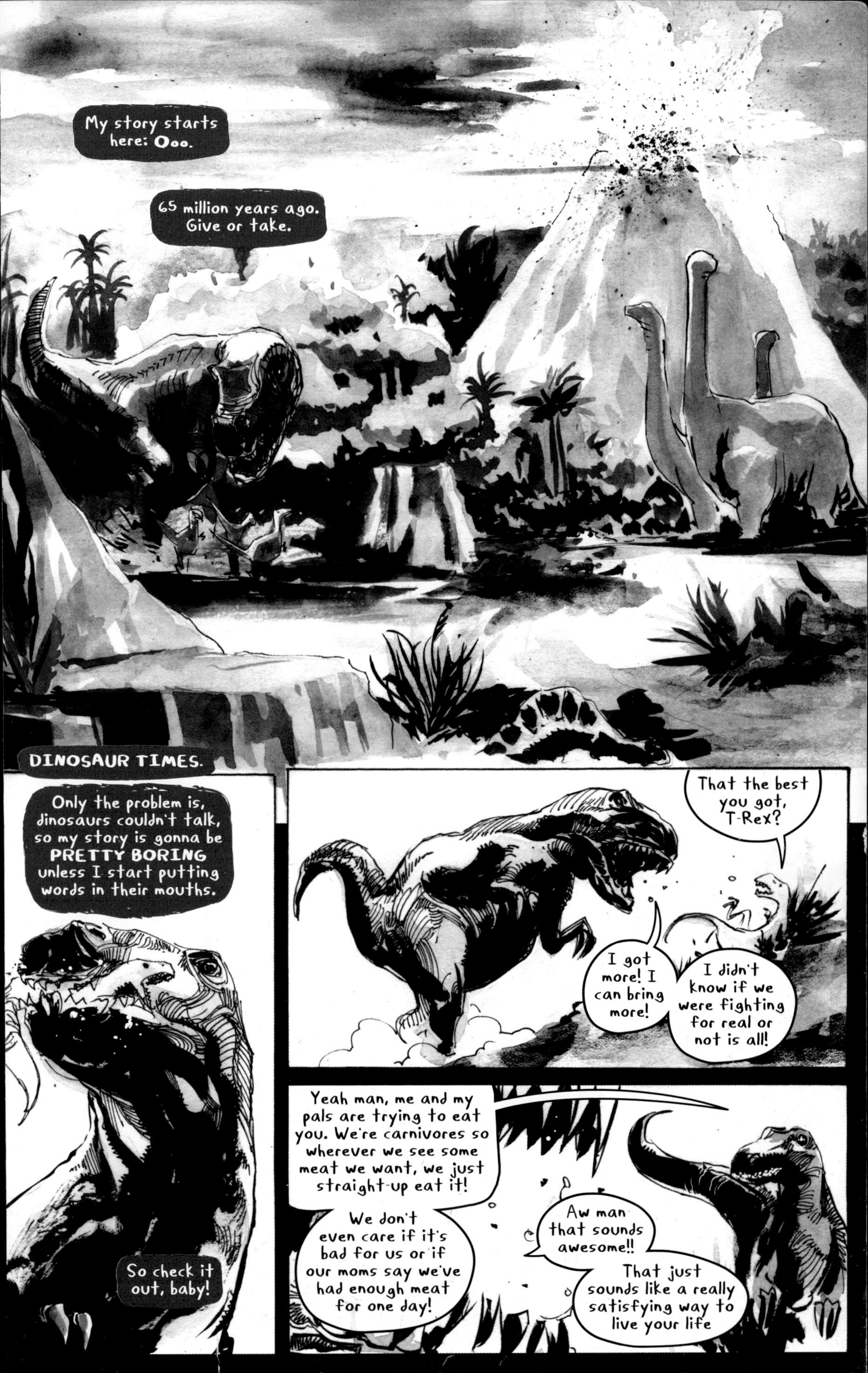
My story starts here: Ooo.
65 million years ago. Give or take.
DINOSAUR TIMES.
Only the problem is, dinosaurs couldn't talk, so my story is gonna be PRETTY BORING unless I start putting words in their mouths.
So check it out, baby!
That the best you got, T-Rex?
I got more! I can bring more!
I didn't know if we were fighting for real or not is all!
Yeah man, me and my pals are trying to eat you. We're carnivores so wherever we see some meat we want, we just straight-up eat it!
We don't even care if it's bad for us or if our moms say we've had enough meat for one day!
Aw man that sounds awesome!!
That just sounds like a really satisfying way to live your life

Moms: what do they know? A lot? Oh, okay, nevermind then I guess

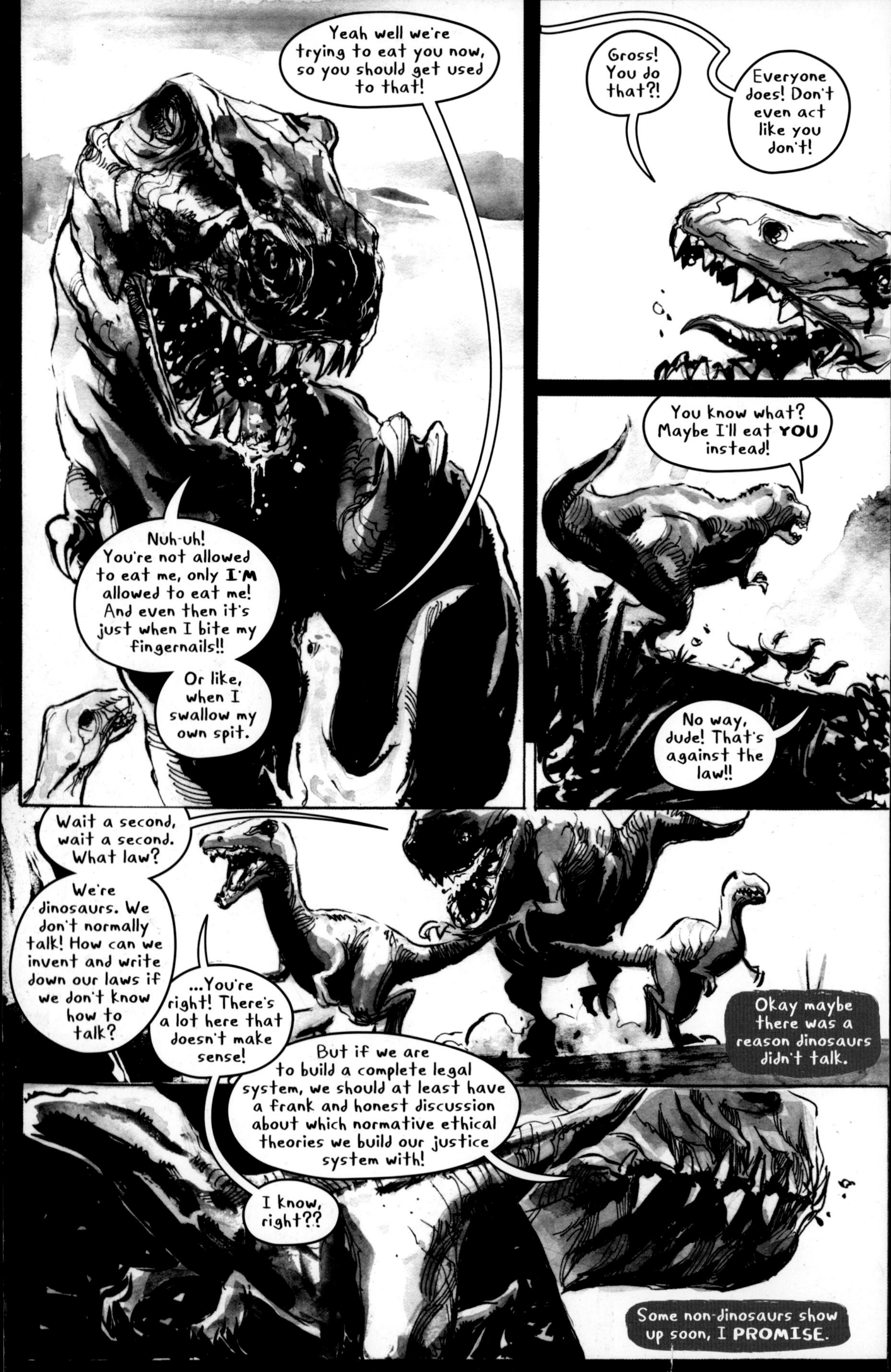

Yeah well we're trying to eat you now, so you should get used to that!
Nuh-uh! You're not allowed to eat me, only I'M allowed to eat me! And even then it's just when I bite my fingernails!!
Or like, when I swallow my own spit.
Gross! You do that?!
Everyone does! Don't even act like you don't!
You know what? Maybe I'll eat YOU instead!
No way, dude! That's against the law!!
Wait a second, wait a second. What law?
We're dinosaurs. We don't normally talk! How can we invent and write down our laws if we don't know how to talk?
...You're right! There's a lot here that doesn't make sense!
Okay maybe there was a reason dinosaurs didn't talk.
But if we are to build a complete legal system, we should at least have a frank and honest discussion about which normative ethical theories we build our justice system with!
I know, right??
Some non-dinosaurs show up soon, I PROMISE.

Sorry for making everyone aware of all that saliva that's floating around inside your mouth RIGHT NOW :(

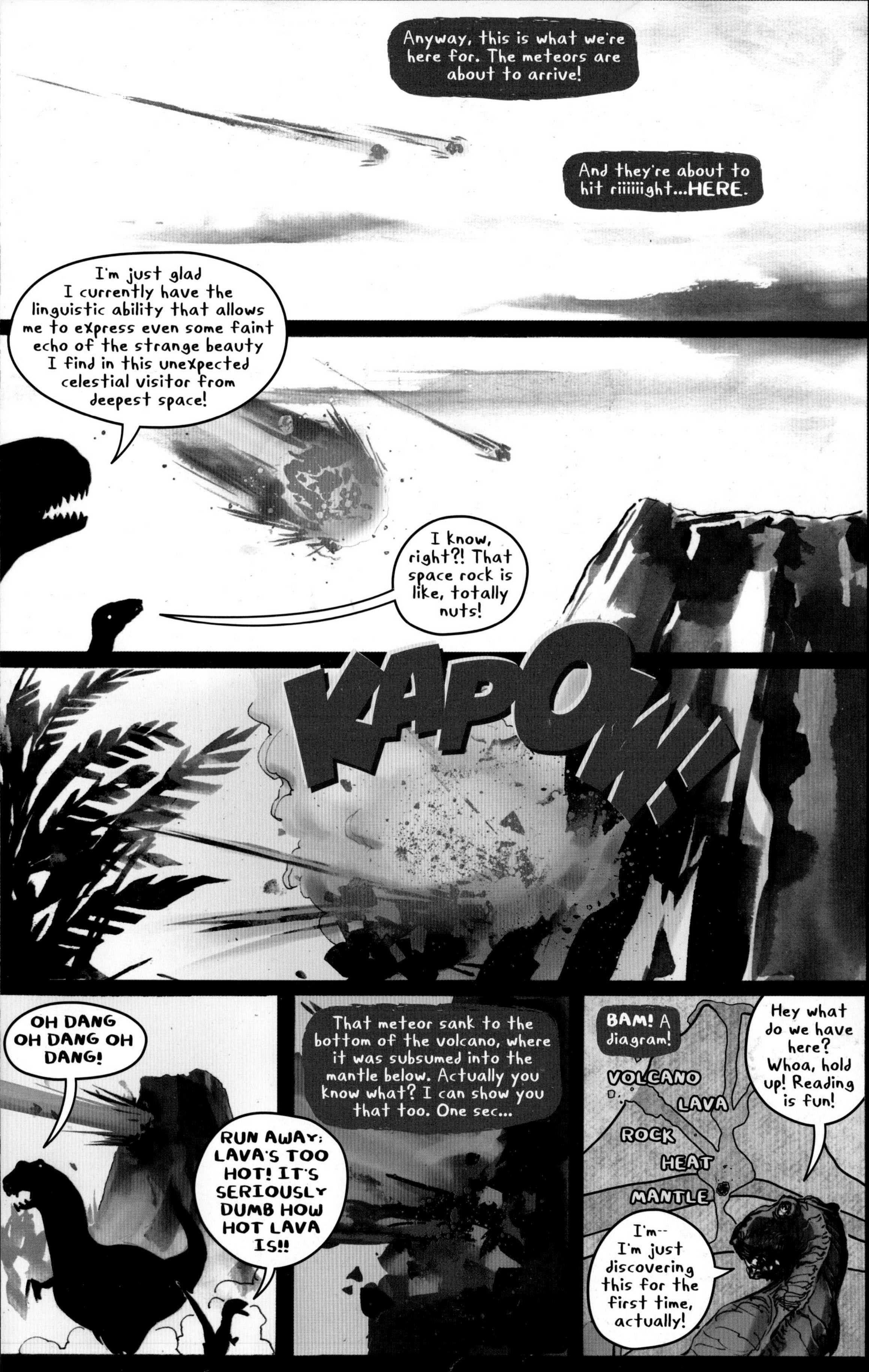
Anyway, this is what we're here for. The meteors are about to arrive!
And they're about to hit riiiiiight...HERE.
I'm just glad I currently have the linguistic ability that allows me to express even some faint echo of the strange beauty I find in this unexpected celestial visitor from deepest space!
I know, right?! That space rock is like, totally nuts!
KAPOW!!
OH DANG OH DANG OH DANG!
RUN AWAY: LAVA'S TOO HOT! IT'S SERIOUSLY DUMB HOW HOT LAVA IS!!
That meteor sank to the bottom of the volcano, where it was subsumed into the mantle below. Actually you know what? I can show you that too. One sec...
BAM! A diagram!
VOLCANO
LAVA
ROCK
HEAT
MANTLE
Hey what do we have here? Whoa, hold up! Reading is fun!
I'm-- I'm just discovering this for the first time, actually!

But you, you knew all along! You are officially smarter than a fictional dinosaur. Hooray!!

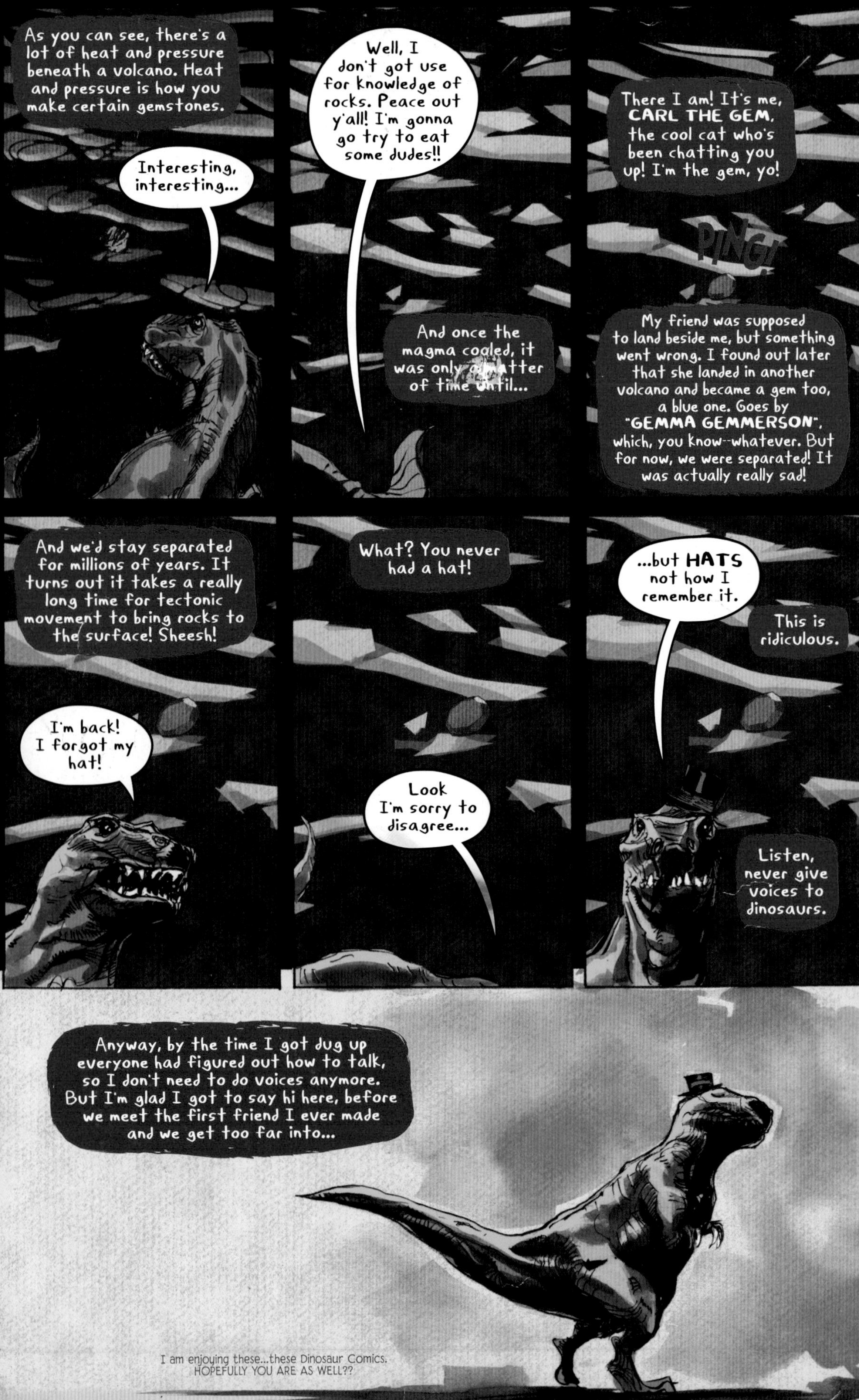
As you can see, there's a lot of heat and pressure beneath a volcano. Heat and pressure is how you make certain gemstones.
Interesting, interesting...
Well, I don't got use for knowledge of rocks. Peace out y'all! I'm gonna go try to eat some dudes!!
And once the magma cooled, it was only a matter of time until...
There I am! It's me, CARL THE GEM, the cool cat who's been chatting you up! I'm the gem, yo!
PING!
My friend was supposed to land beside me, but something went wrong. I found out later that she landed in another volcano and became a gem too, a blue one. Goes by "GEMMA GEMMERSON", which, you know--whatever. But for now, we were separated! It was actually really sad!
And we'd stay separated for millions of years. It turns out it takes a really long time for tectonic movement to bring rocks to the surface! Sheesh!
I'm back! I forgot my hat!
What? You never had a hat!
Look I'm sorry to disagree...
...but HATS not how I remember it.
This is ridiculous.
Listen, never give voices to dinosaurs.
Anyway, by the time I got dug up everyone had figured out how to talk, so I don't need to do voices anymore. But I'm glad I got to say hi here, before we meet the first friend I ever made and we get too far into...
I am enjoying these...these Dinosaur Comics. HOPEFULLY YOU ARE AS WELL??

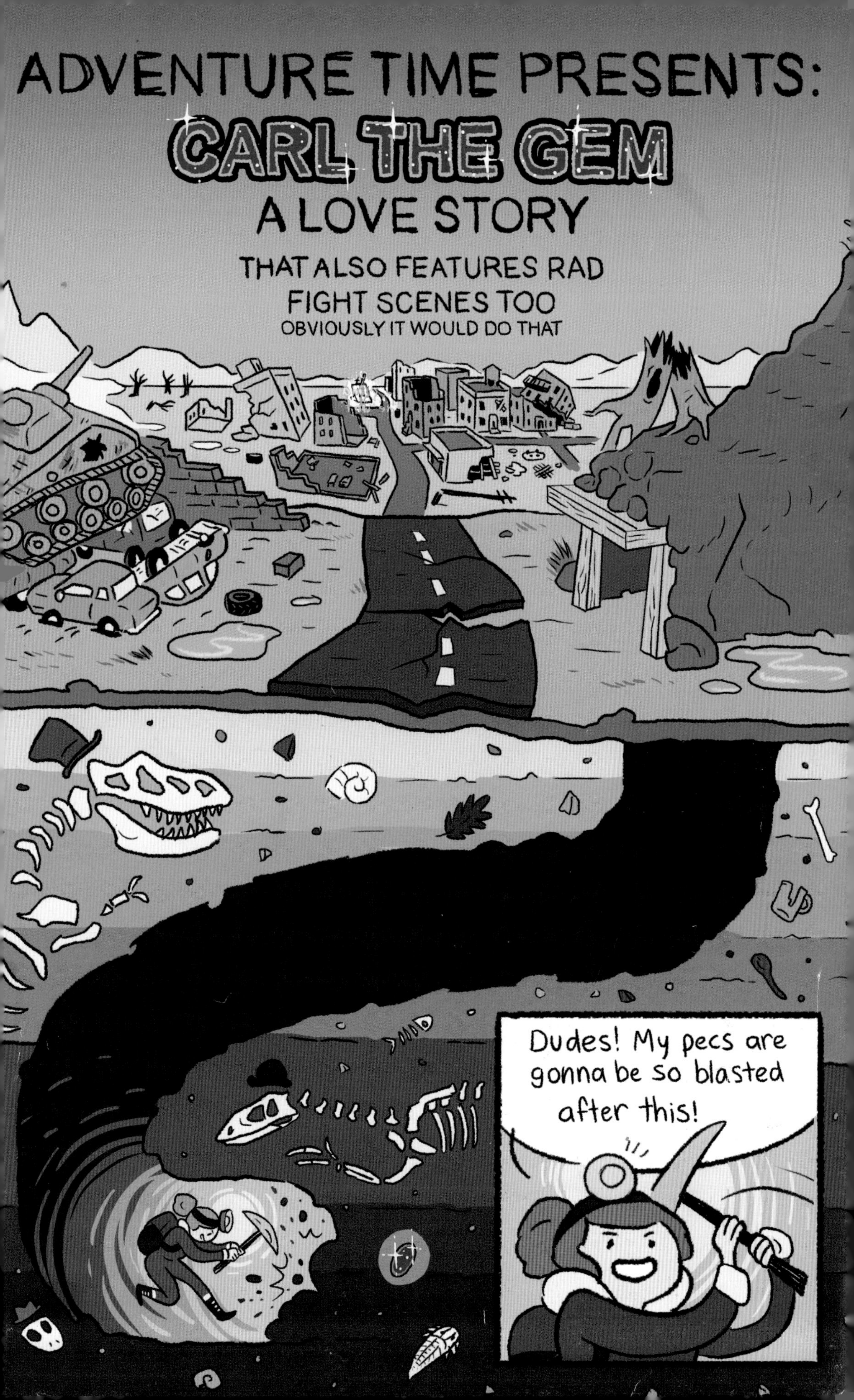
ADVENTURE TIME PRESENTS:
CARL THE GEM
A LOVE STORY
THAT ALSO FEATURES RAD FIGHT SCENES TOO
OBVIOUSLY IT WOULD DO THAT
Dudes! My pecs are gonna be so blasted after this!

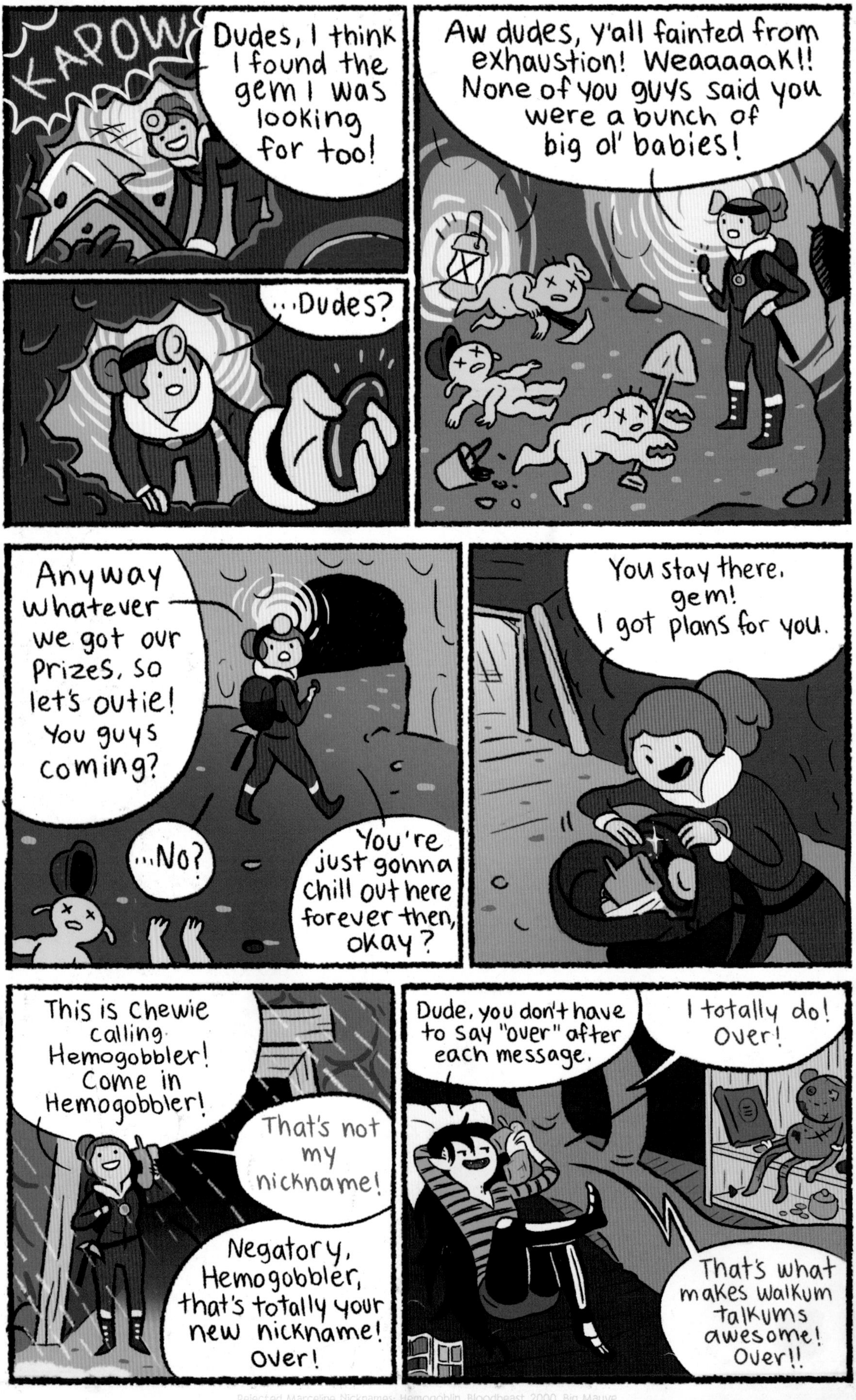
KAPOW
Dudes, I think I found the gem I was looking for too!
...Dudes?
Aw dudes, y'all fainted from exhaustion! Weaaaaak!! None of you guys said you were a bunch of big ol' babies!
Anyway whatever we got our prizes, so let's outie! You guys coming?
...No?
You're just gonna chill out here forever then, okay?
You stay there, gem! I got plans for you.
This is Chewie calling Hemogobbler! Come in Hemogobbler!
That's not my nickname!
Negatory, Hemogobbler, that's totally your new nickname! Over!
Dude, you don't have to say "over" after each message.
I totally do! Over!
That's what makes walkum talkums awesome! Over!!

Rejected Marceline Nicknames: Hemogoblin. Bloodbeast 2000. Big Mauve

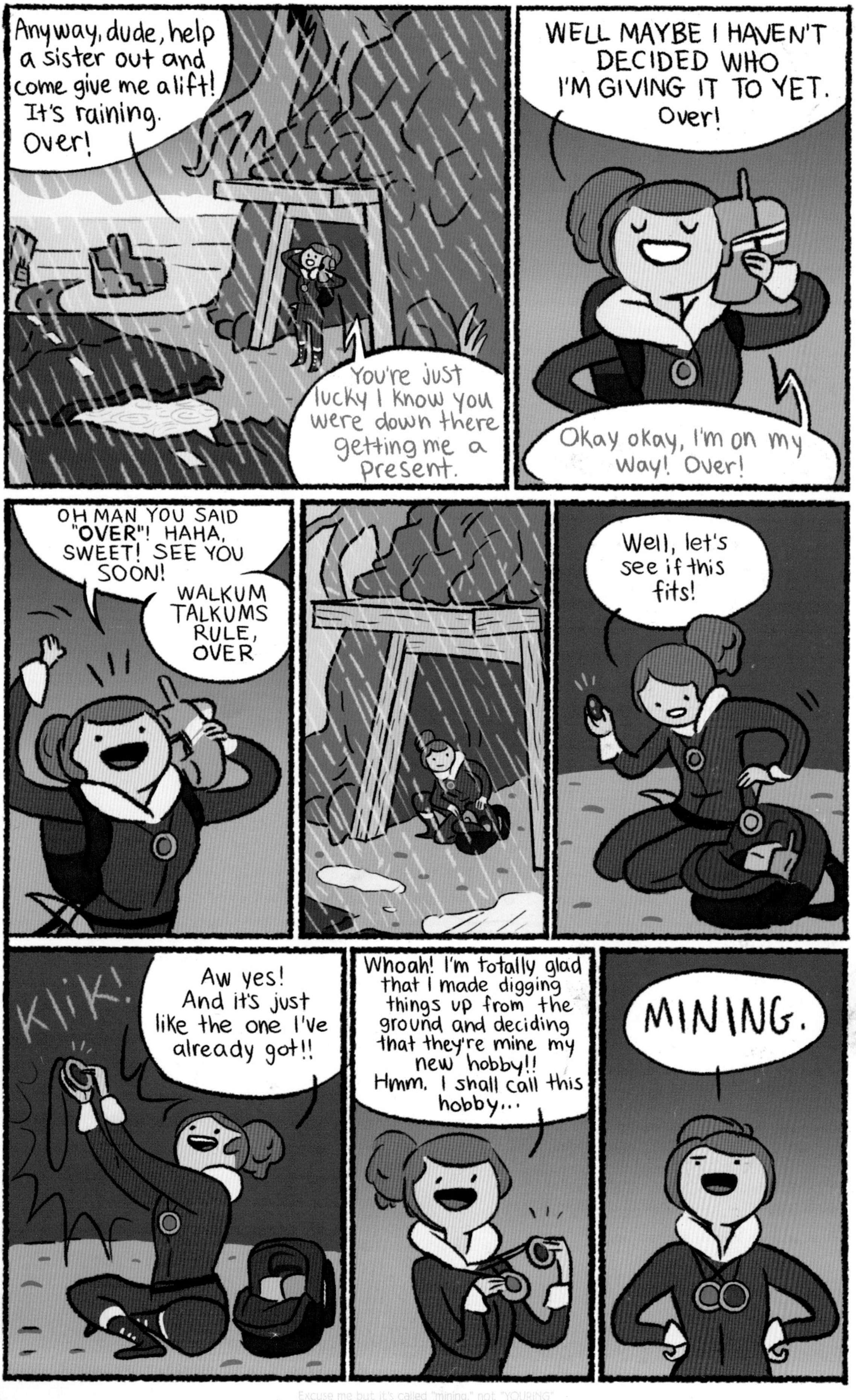

Anyway, dude, help a sister out and come give me a lift! It's raining. Over!
You're just lucky I know you were down there getting me a present.
WELL MAYBE I HAVEN'T DECIDED WHO I'M GIVING IT TO YET. Over!
Okay okay, I'm on my way! Over!
OH MAN YOU SAID "OVER"! HAHA, SWEET! SEE YOU SOON!
WALKUM TALKUMS RULE, OVER
Well, let's see if this fits!
KLIK!
Aw yes! And it's just like the one I've already got!!
Whoah! I'm totally glad that I made digging things up from the ground and deciding that they're mine my new hobby!! Hmm. I shall call this hobby...
MINING.

Excuse me but it's called "mining," not "YOURING"

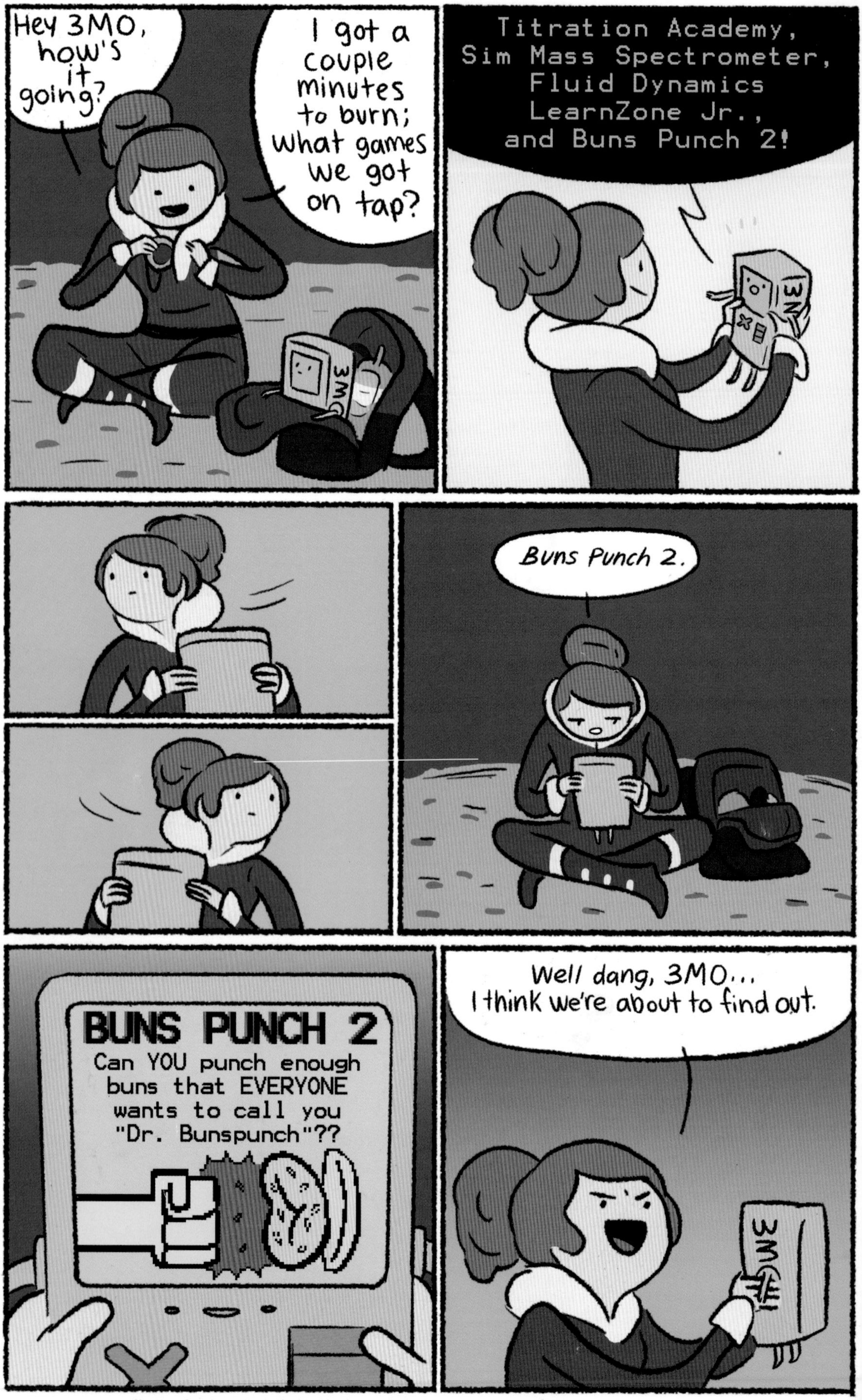
Hey 3MO, how's it going?
I got a couple minutes to burn; what games we got on tap?
Titration Academy, Sim Mass Spectrometer, Fluid Dynamics LearnZone Jr., and Buns Punch 2!
Buns Punch 2.
BUNS PUNCH 2
Can YOU punch enough buns that EVERYONE wants to call you "Dr. Bunspunch"??
Well dang, 3MO... I think we're about to find out.

Sim Mass Spectrometer is the blockbuster sequel to Sim Dumas Method of Molecular Weight Determination

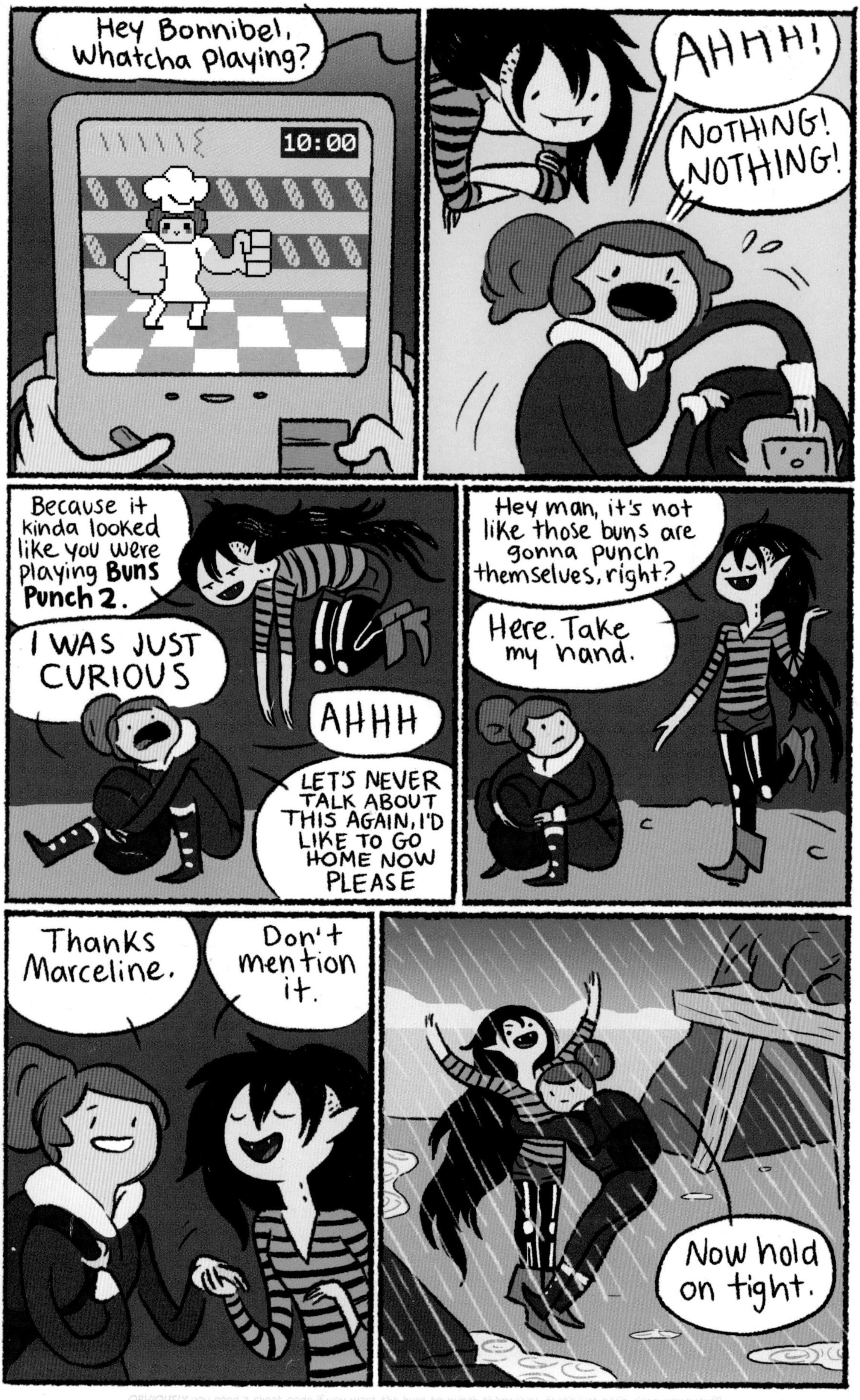
Hey Bonnibel, Whatcha playing?
10:00
AHHH!
NOTHING! NOTHING!
Because it kinda looked like you were playing **Buns Punch 2**.
I WAS JUST CURIOUS
AHHH
LET'S NEVER TALK ABOUT THIS AGAIN, I'D LIKE TO GO HOME NOW PLEASE
Hey man, it's not like those buns are gonna punch themselves, right?
Here. Take my hand.
Thanks Marceline.
Don't mention it.
Now hold on tight.

OBVIOUSLY you need a cheat code if you want the buns to punch themselves, that's just basic video game stuff!

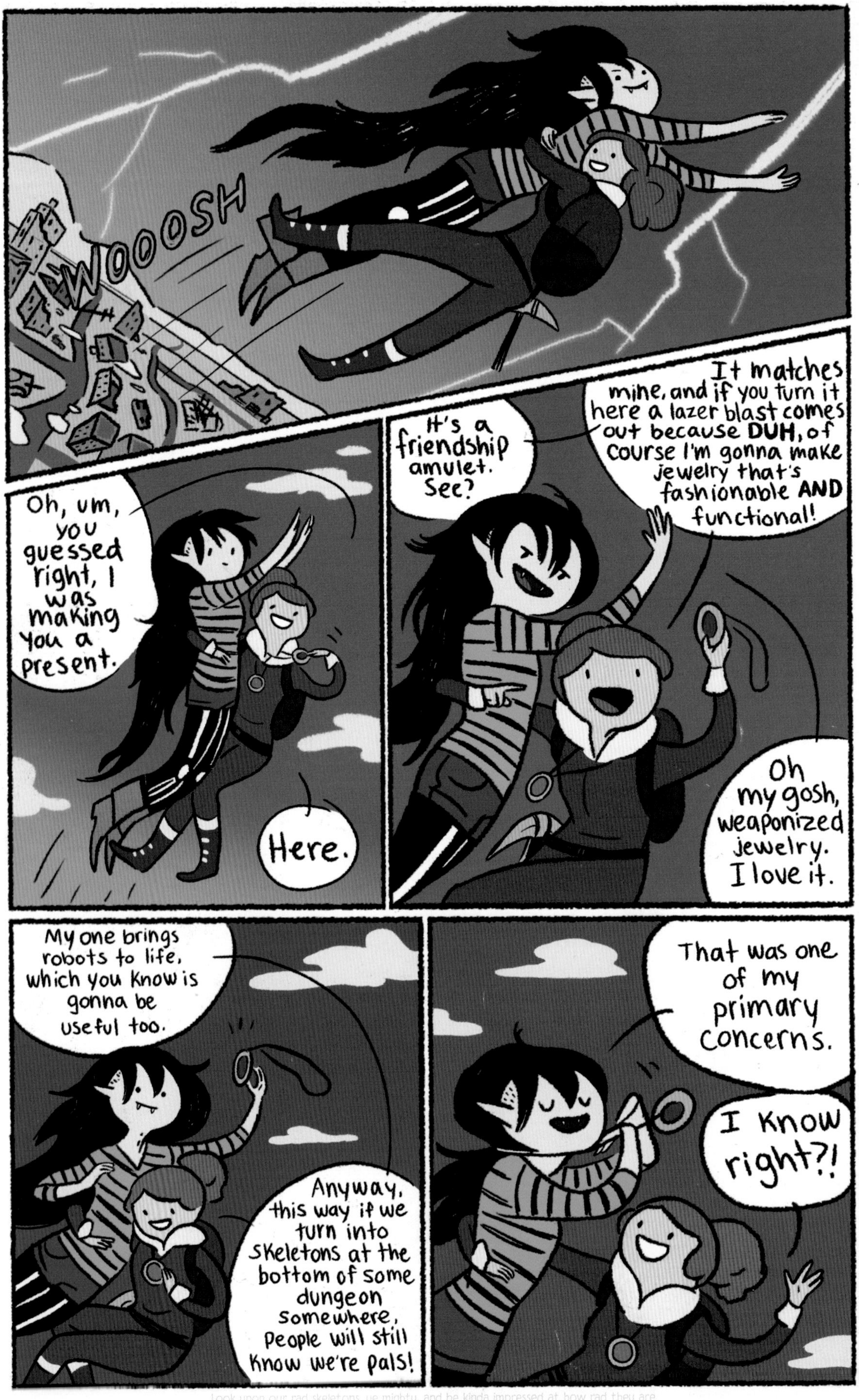
WOOOSH
Oh, um, you guessed right, I was making you a present.
Here.
It's a friendship amulet. See?
It matches mine, and if you turn it here a lazer blast comes out because DUH, of course I'm gonna make jewelry that's fashionable AND functional!
Oh my gosh, weaponized jewelry. I love it.
My one brings robots to life, which you know is gonna be useful too.
Anyway, this way if we turn into skeletons at the bottom of some dungeon somewhere, people will still know we're pals!
That was one of my primary concerns.
I know right?!

Look upon our rad skeletons, ye mighty, and be kinda impressed at how rad they are

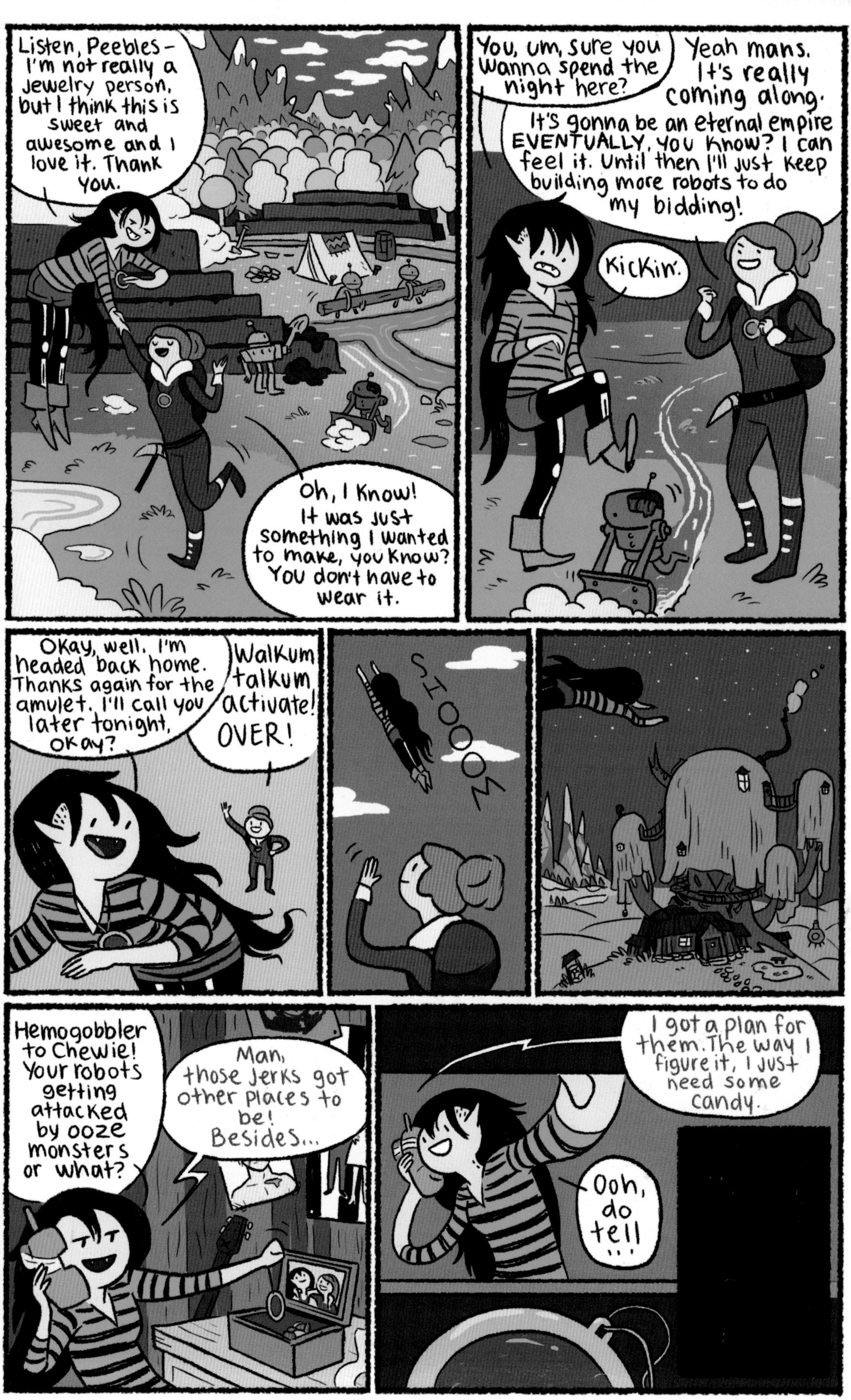
Listen, Peebles- I'm not really a jewelry person, but I think this is sweet and awesome and I love it. Thank you.
Oh, I know! It was just something I wanted to make, you know? You don't have to wear it.
You, um, sure you wanna spend the night here?
Yeah mans. It's really coming along.
It's gonna be an eternal empire EVENTUALLY, you know? I can feel it. Until then I'll just keep building more robots to do my bidding!
Kickin'.
Okay, well. I'm headed back home. Thanks again for the amulet. I'll call you later tonight, okay?
Walkum talkum activate! OVER!
SHOOOOM
Hemogobbler to Chewie! Your robots getting attacked by ooze monsters or what?
Man, those jerks got other places to be! Besides...
I got a plan for them. The way I figure it, I just need some candy.
Ooh, do tell...

Rejected Bonnibel Nicknames: Stretch, Robotmaster 3000, Big Red

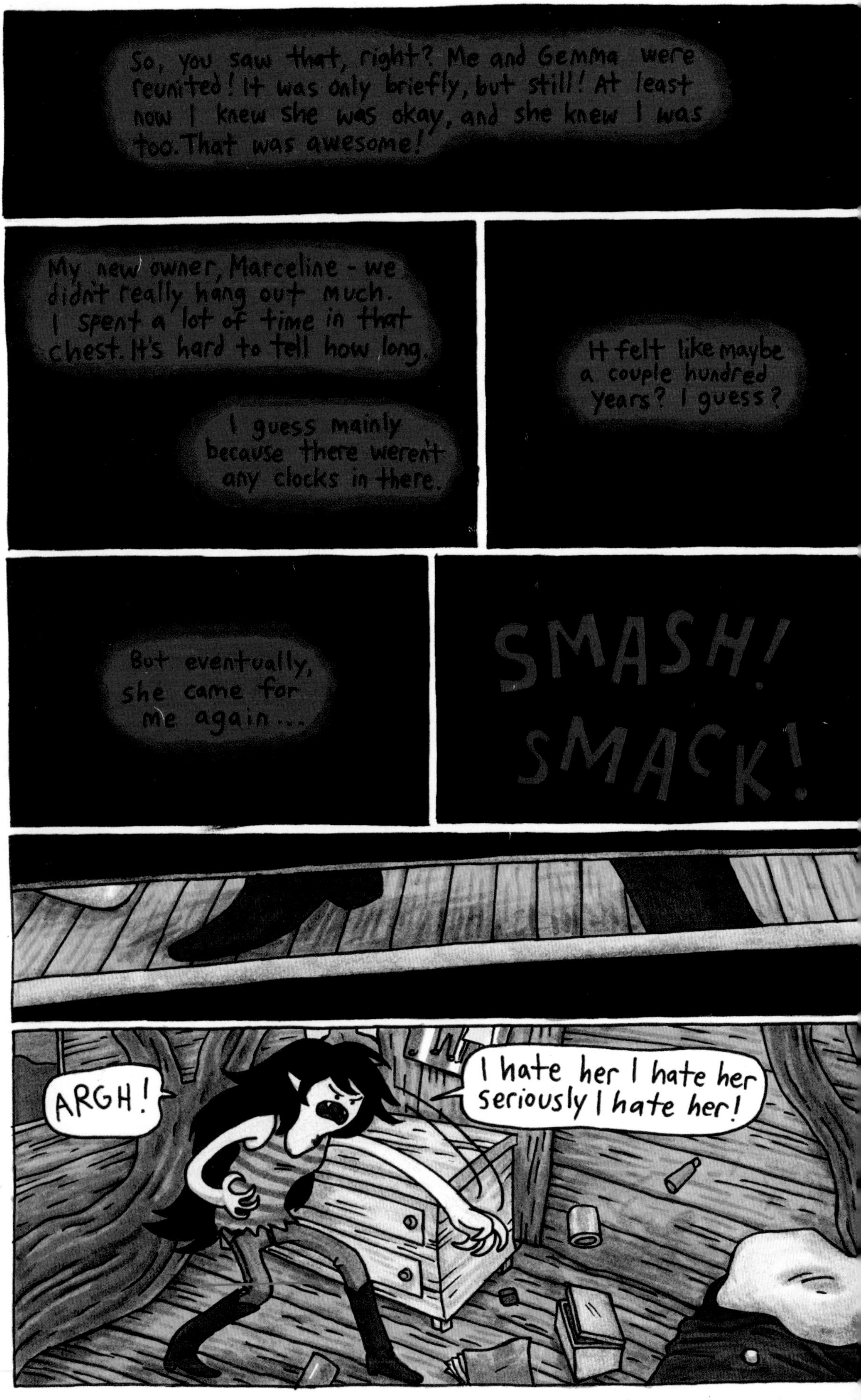
So, you saw that, right? Me and Gemma were reunited! It was only briefly, but still! At least now I knew she was okay, and she knew I was too. That was awesome!
My new owner, Marceline - we didn't really hang out much. I spent a lot of time in that chest. It's hard to tell how long.
I guess mainly because there weren't any clocks in there.
It felt like maybe a couple hundred years? I guess?
But eventually, she came for me again...
SMASH!
SMACK!
ARGH!
I hate her I hate her seriously I hate her!

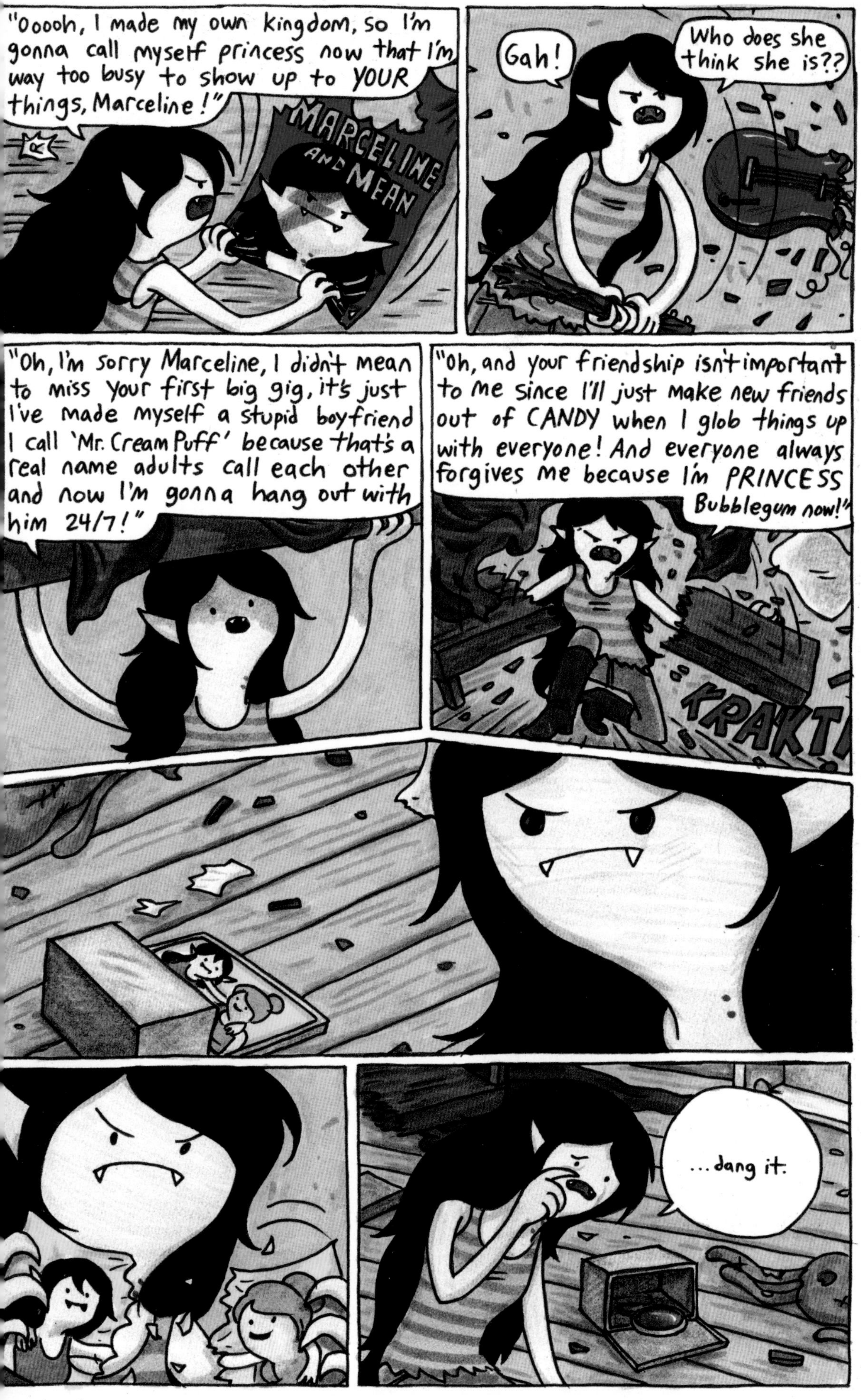
"Ooooh, I made my own kingdom, so I'm gonna call myself princess now that I'm way too busy to show up to YOUR things, Marceline!"
MARCELINE AND MEAN
Gah!
Who does she think she is??
"Oh, I'm sorry Marceline, I didn't mean to miss your first big gig, it's just I've made myself a stupid boyfriend I call 'Mr. Cream Puff' because that's a real name adults call each other and now I'm gonna hang out with him 24/7!"
"Oh, and your friendship isn't important to me since I'll just make new friends out of CANDY when I glob things up with everyone! And everyone always forgives me because I'm PRINCESS Bubblegum now!"
KRAKT
...dang it.

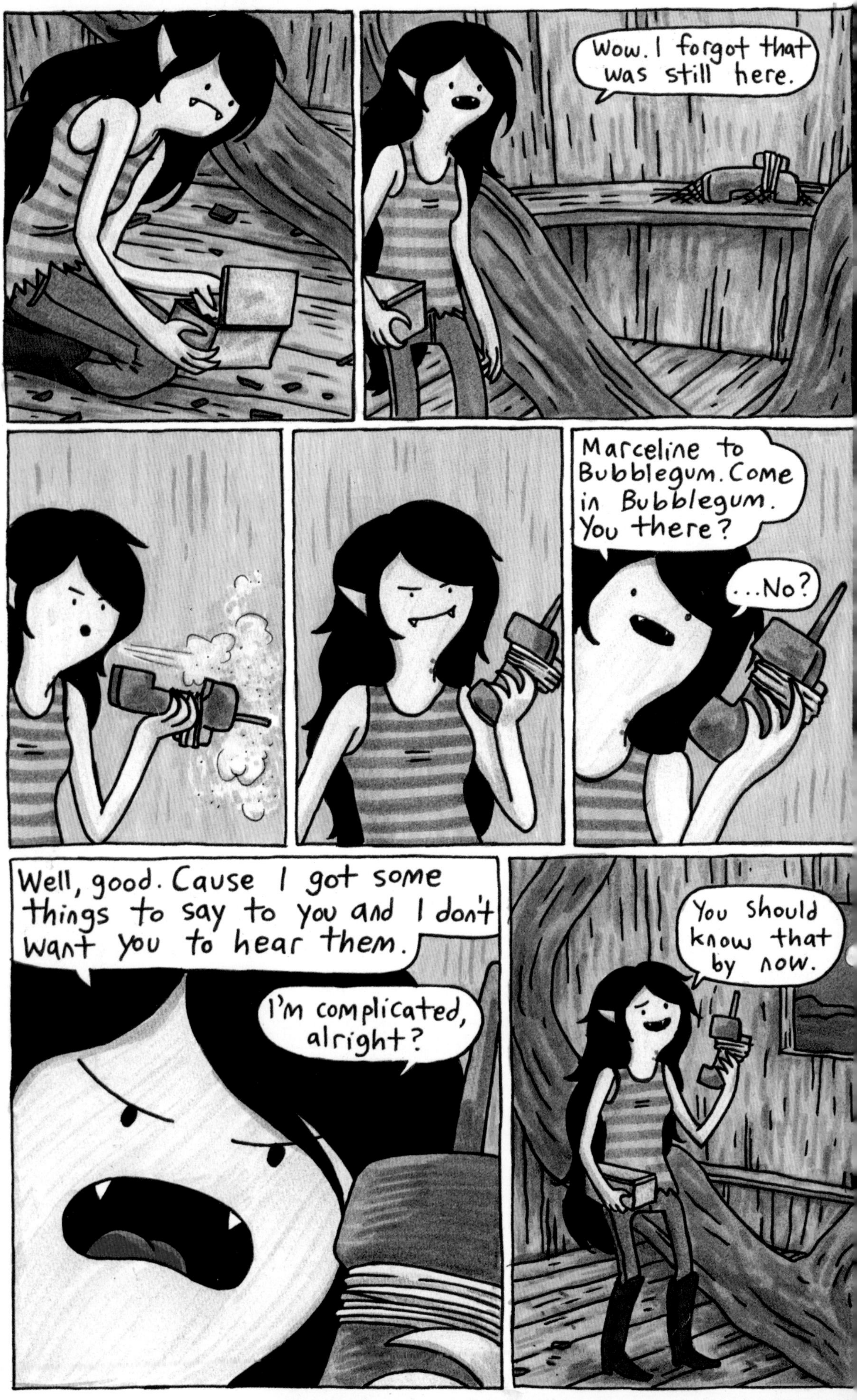
Wow. I forgot that was still here.
Marceline to Bubblegum. Come in Bubblegum. You there?
...No?
Well, good. Cause I got some things to say to you and I don't want you to hear them.
I'm complicated, alright?
You should know that by now.

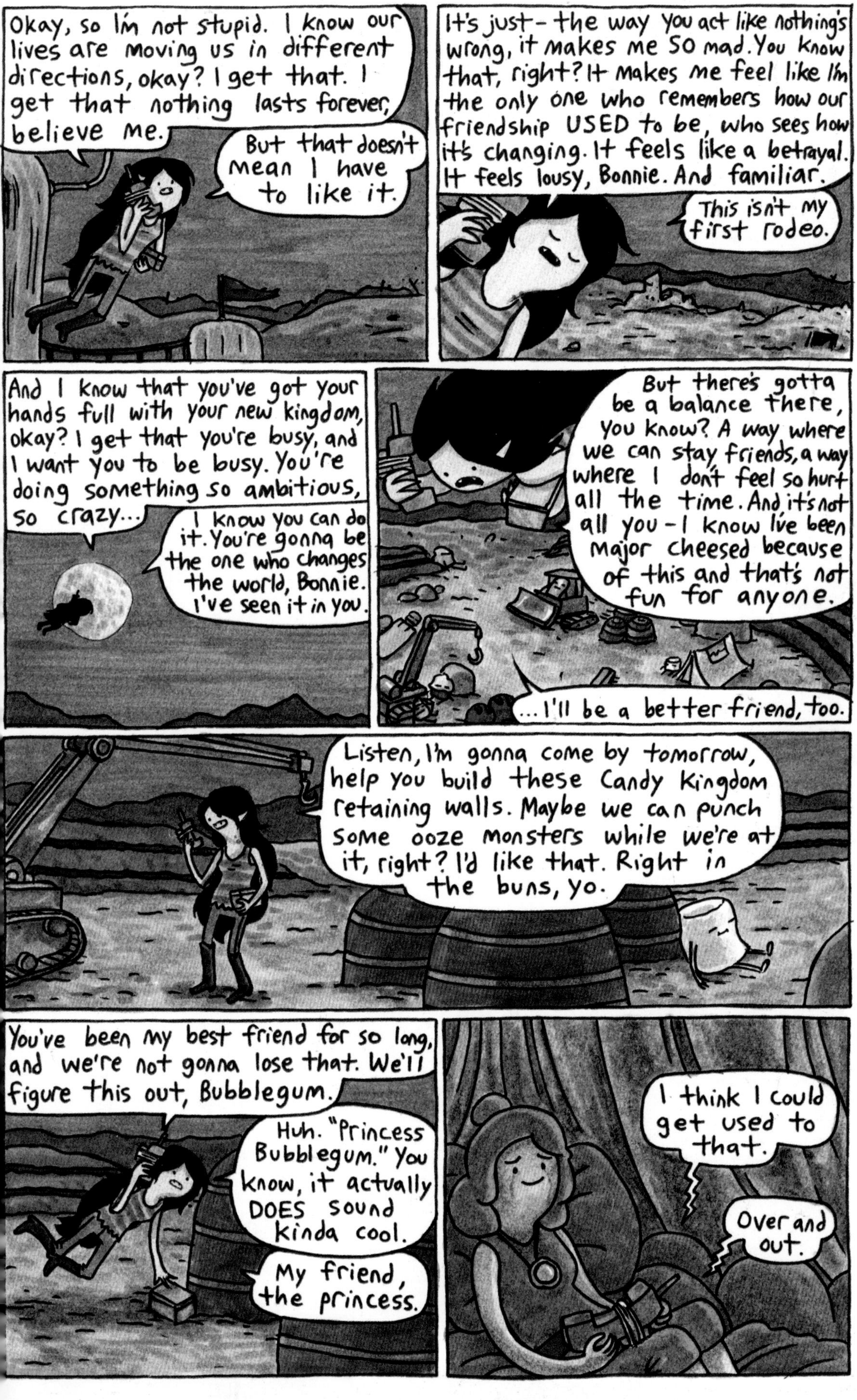

Okay, so I'm not stupid. I know our lives are moving us in different directions, okay? I get that. I get that nothing lasts forever, believe me.
But that doesn't mean I have to like it.
It's just- the way you act like nothing's wrong, it makes me SO mad. You know that, right? It makes me feel like I'm the only one who remembers how our friendship USED to be, who sees how it's changing. It feels like a betrayal. It feels lousy, Bonnie. And familiar.
This isn't my first rodeo.
And I know that you've got your hands full with your new kingdom, okay? I get that you're busy, and I want you to be busy. You're doing something so ambitious, so crazy...
I know you can do it. You're gonna be the one who changes the world, Bonnie. I've seen it in you.
But there's gotta be a balance there, you know? A way where we can stay friends, a way where I don't feel so hurt all the time. And it's not all you - I know I've been major cheesed because of this and that's not fun for anyone.
...I'll be a better friend, too.
Listen, I'm gonna come by tomorrow, help you build these Candy Kingdom retaining walls. Maybe we can punch some ooze monsters while we're at it, right? I'd like that. Right in the buns, yo.
You've been my best friend for so long, and we're not gonna lose that. We'll figure this out, Bubblegum.
Huh. "Princess Bubblegum." You know, it actually DOES sound kinda cool.
My friend, the princess.
I think I could get used to that.
Over and out.

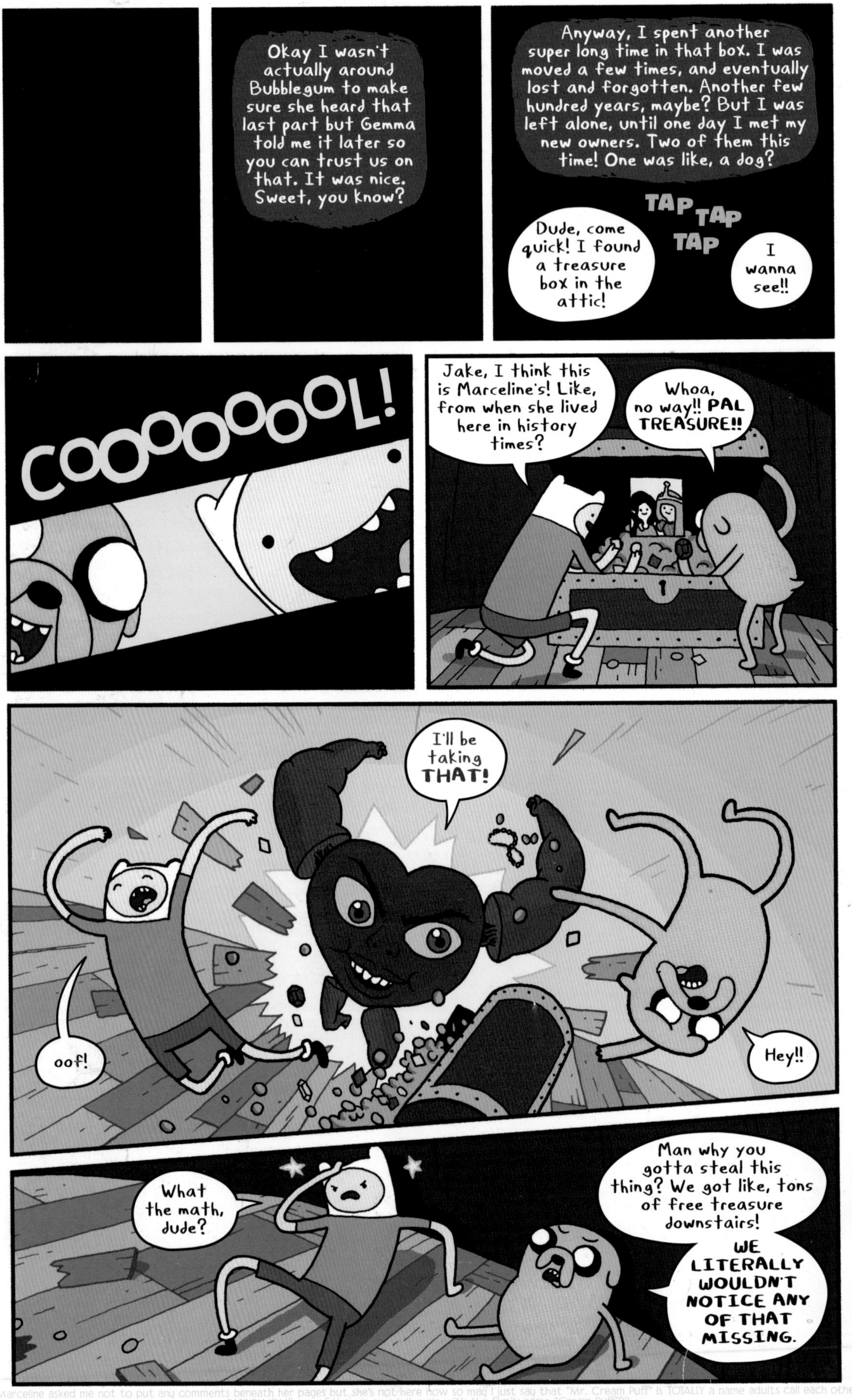
Okay I wasn't actually around Bubblegum to make sure she heard that last part but Gemma told me it later so you can trust us on that. It was nice. Sweet, you know?
Anyway, I spent another super long time in that box. I was moved a few times, and eventually lost and forgotten. Another few hundred years, maybe? But I was left alone, until one day I met my new owners. Two of them this time! One was like, a dog?
Dude, come quick! I found a treasure box in the attic!
TAP TAP TAP
I wanna see!!
COOOOOOOL!
Jake, I think this is Marceline's! Like, from when she lived here in history times?
Whoa, no way!! PAL TREASURE!!
I'll be taking THAT!
oof!
Hey!!
What the math, dude?
Man why you gotta steal this thing? We got like, tons of free treasure downstairs!
WE LITERALLY WOULDN'T NOTICE ANY OF THAT MISSING.

Marceline asked me not to put any comments beneath her pages but she's not here now so may I just say that "Mr. Cream Puff" is TOTALLY a name adults call each othe ESPECIALLY if one of them is an adult male with the family name "Cream Puff"??

THAT treasure is just stuff. But **THIS** treasure...**THIS** treasure is suffused with the **POWER OF PALTIMES**. Once I crack them open and extract their **PAL ESSENCE**, Princess Bubblegum will want to hang out with **ME** instead!

Ricardio, your plan is dumb and made of problems!

Hey, that doesn't belong to you! It doesn't even belong to us really!

Hey, what's the deal? I thought Princess Bubblegum totally broke you the last time you got all up in our pineapples!

One thing you should know about broken hearts, Jake...

...give them a little time, and they always get better.

I'm pretty sure that's a metaphor for feelings, not actual dude's hearts that come alive.

Yeah seriously!

Nobody asked you!

Finn, how come bad guys never hug us instead of punching us or lazering us or whatever??

I KNOW RIGHT??

Marceline's amulet fires a lazer. You wanna see what PB's does?

Wait. Is that the one that Shok--

UM OBVIOUSLY I DON'T CARE IF YOU RECOGNIZE IT OR NOT, I JUST WANT YOU TO KNOW THAT IT BRINGS ROBOTS TO LIFE.

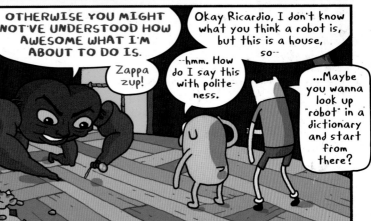

OTHERWISE YOU MIGHT NOT'VE UNDERSTOOD HOW AWESOME WHAT I'M ABOUT TO DO IS.

Zappa zup!

--hmm. How do I say this with polite-ness.

Okay Ricardio, I don't know what you think a robot is, but this is a house, so--

...Maybe you wanna look up "robot" in a dictionary and start from there?

Uh oh.

Aw glob this is either gonna be extremely bad or extremely awesome!

Come ooooooon, extremely awesome!!

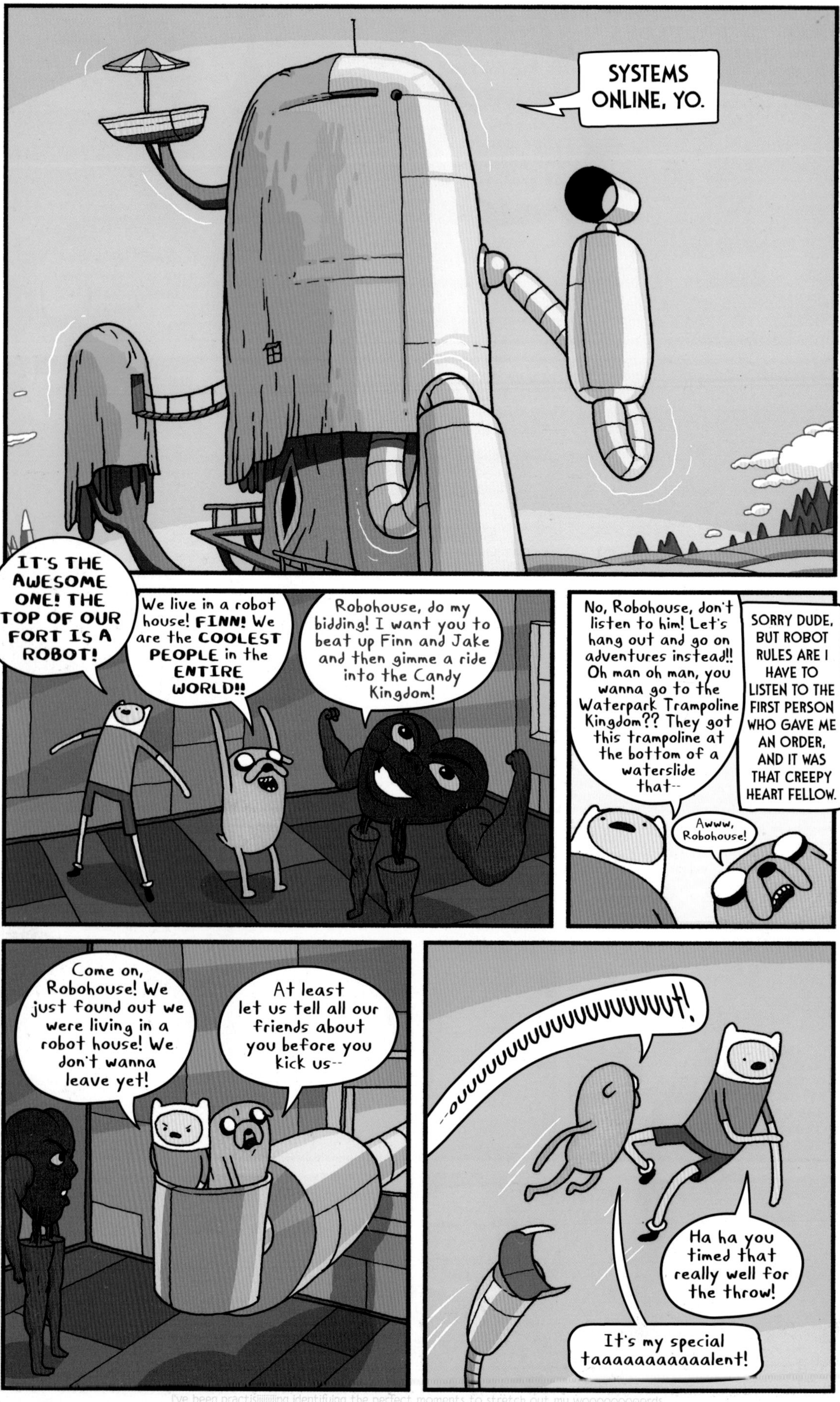
SYSTEMS ONLINE, YO.
IT'S THE AWESOME ONE! THE TOP OF OUR FORT IS A ROBOT!
We live in a robot house! FINN! We are the COOLEST PEOPLE in the ENTIRE WORLD!!
Robohouse, do my bidding! I want you to beat up Finn and Jake and then gimme a ride into the Candy Kingdom!
No, Robohouse, don't listen to him! Let's hang out and go on adventures instead!! Oh man oh man, you wanna go to the Waterpark Trampoline Kingdom?? They got this trampoline at the bottom of a waterslide that--
SORRY DUDE, BUT ROBOT RULES ARE I HAVE TO LISTEN TO THE FIRST PERSON WHO GAVE ME AN ORDER, AND IT WAS THAT CREEPY HEART FELLOW.
Awww, Robohouse!
Come on, Robohouse! We just found out we were living in a robot house! We don't wanna leave yet!
At least let us tell all our friends about you before you kick us--
--ouuuuuuuuuuuuuuuuuuuuuuut!
Ha ha you timed that really well for the throw!
It's my special taaaaaaaaaaalent!

I've been practisiiiiiiing identifying the perfect moments to stretch out my wooooooooords

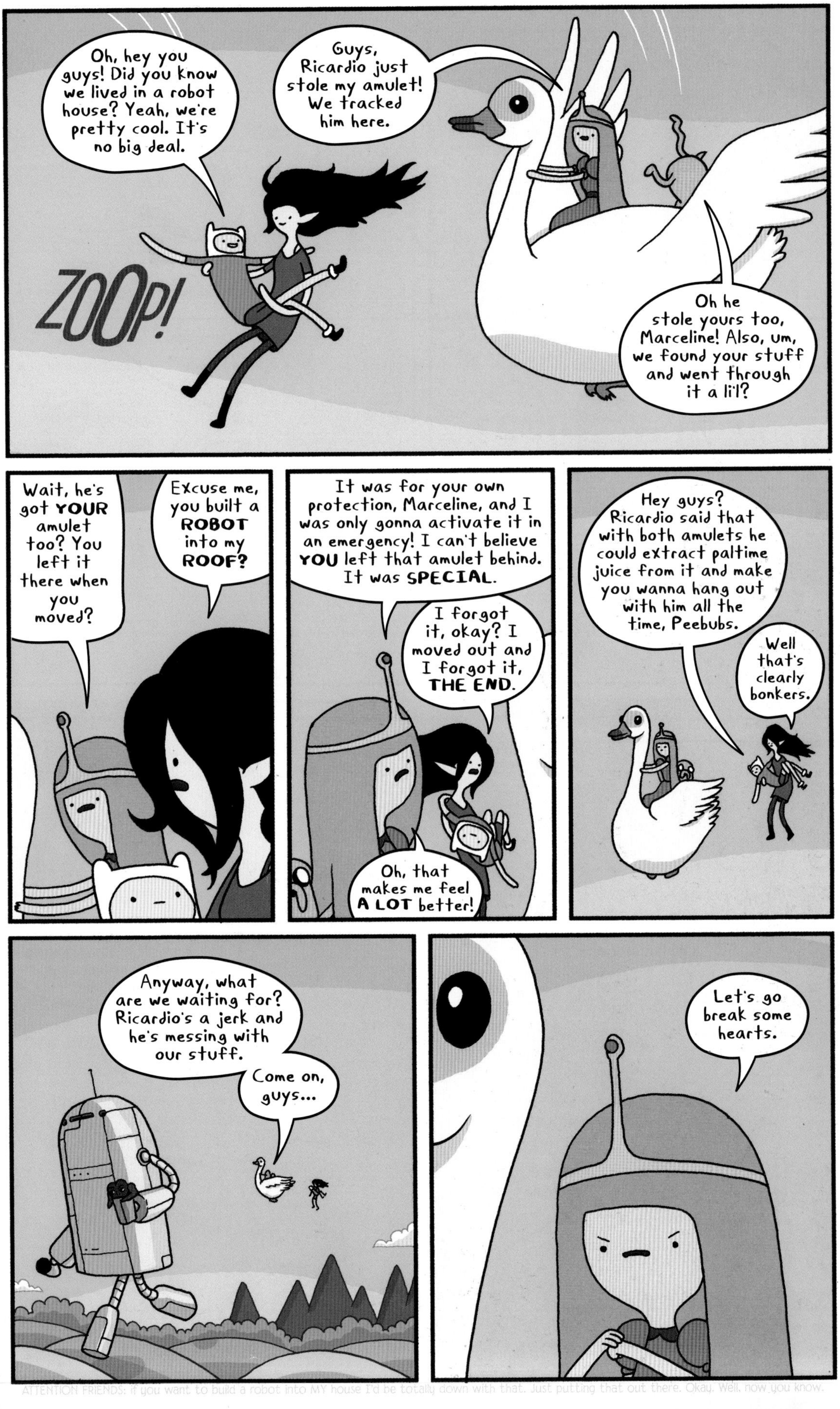
Oh, hey you guys! Did you know we lived in a robot house? Yeah, we're pretty cool. It's no big deal.
Guys, Ricardio just stole my amulet! We tracked him here.
ZOOP!
Oh he stole yours too, Marceline! Also, um, we found your stuff and went through it a li'l?
Wait, he's got YOUR amulet too? You left it there when you moved?
Excuse me, you built a ROBOT into my ROOF?
It was for your own protection, Marceline, and I was only gonna activate it in an emergency! I can't believe YOU left that amulet behind. It was SPECIAL.
I forgot it, okay? I moved out and I forgot it, THE END.
Oh, that makes me feel A LOT better!
Hey guys? Ricardio said that with both amulets he could extract paltime juice from it and make you wanna hang out with him all the time, Peebubs.
Well that's clearly bonkers.
Anyway, what are we waiting for? Ricardio's a jerk and he's messing with our stuff.
Come on, guys...
Let's go break some hearts.

ATTENTION FRIENDS: if you want to build a robot into MY house I'd be totally down with that. Just putting that out there. Okay. Well. now you know.

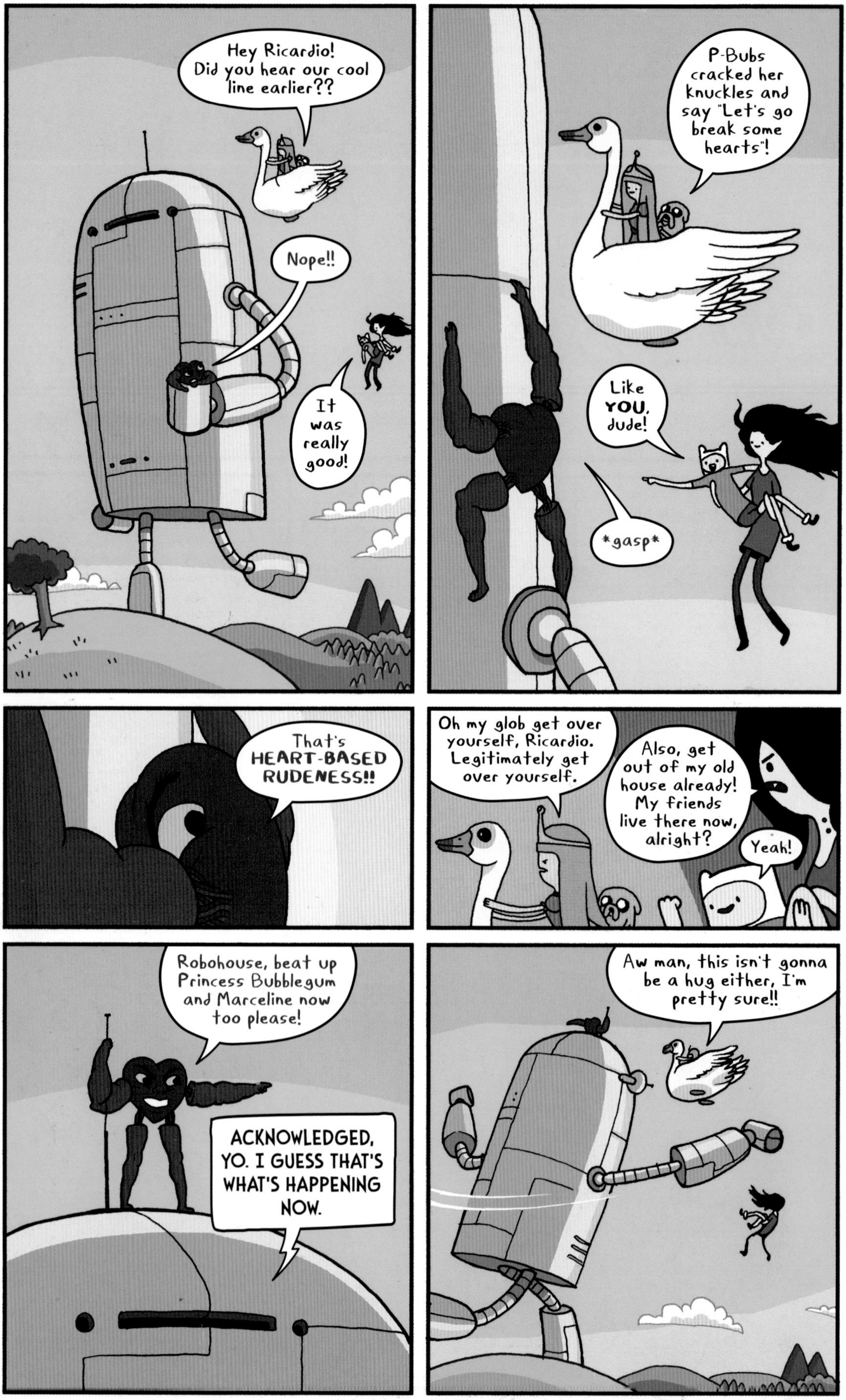
Hey Ricardio! Did you hear our cool line earlier??
Nope!!
It was really good!
P-Bubs cracked her knuckles and say "Let's go break some hearts"!
Like YOU, dude!
gasp
That's HEART-BASED RUDENESS!!
Oh my glob get over yourself, Ricardio. Legitimately get over yourself.
Also, get out of my old house already! My friends live there now, alright?
Yeah!
Robohouse, beat up Princess Bubblegum and Marceline now too please!
ACKNOWLEDGED, YO. I GUESS THAT'S WHAT'S HAPPENING NOW.
Aw man, this isn't gonna be a hug either, I'm pretty sure!!

And yet, hope springs eternal??

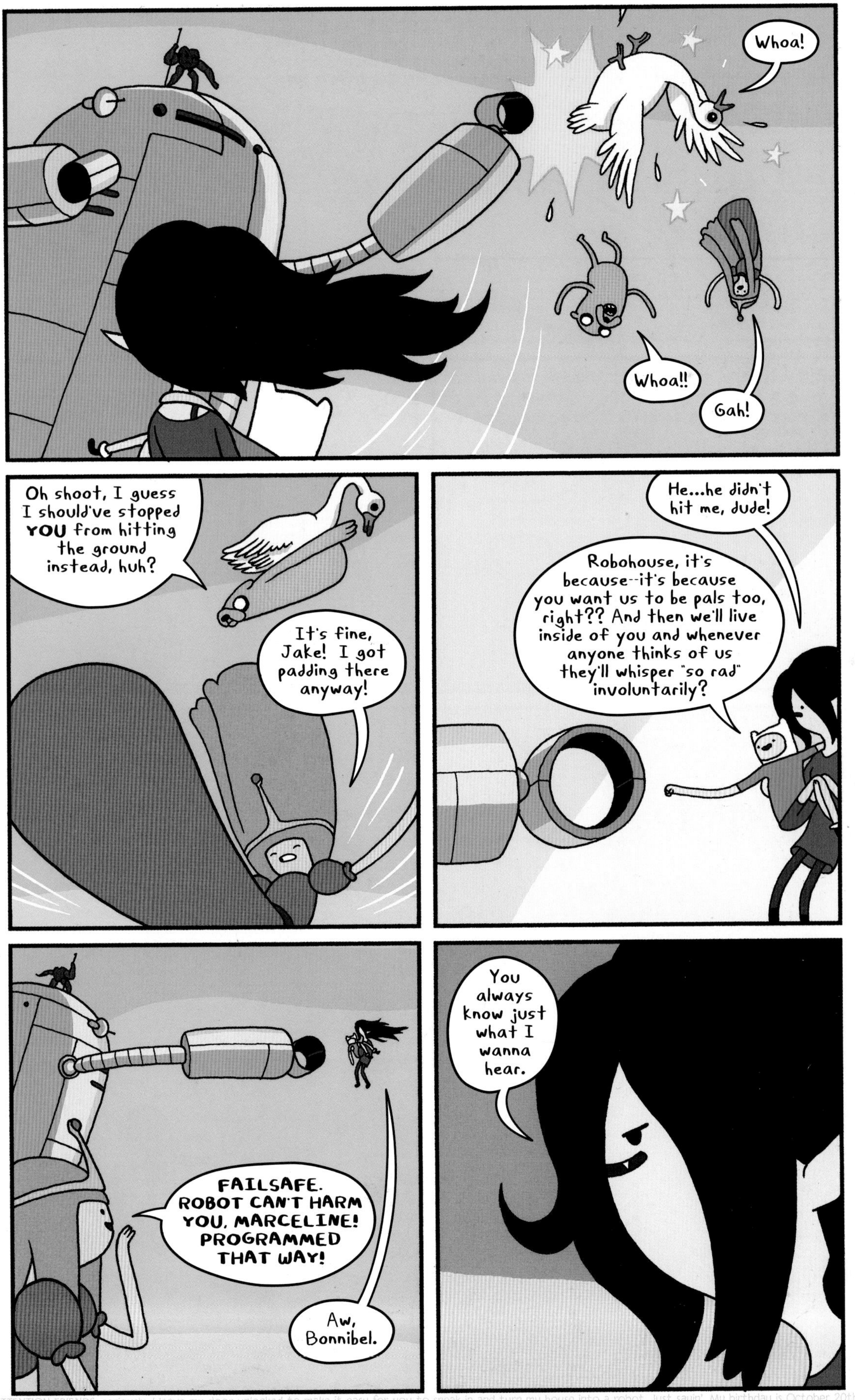
Whoa!
Whoa!!
Gah!
Oh shoot, I guess I should've stopped YOU from hitting the ground instead, huh?
It's fine, Jake! I got padding there anyway!
He...he didn't hit me, dude!
Robohouse, it's because--it's because you want us to be pals too, right?? And then we'll live inside of you and whenever anyone thinks of us they'll whisper "so rad" involuntarily?
FAILSAFE. ROBOT CAN'T HARM YOU, MARCELINE! PROGRAMMED THAT WAY!
Aw, Bonnibel.
You always know just what I wanna hear.

ATTENTION FRIENDS: seriously, I leave my door unlocked to make it easy for you to sneak in and turn my house into a robot. Just sayin'. My birthday is October 20th.

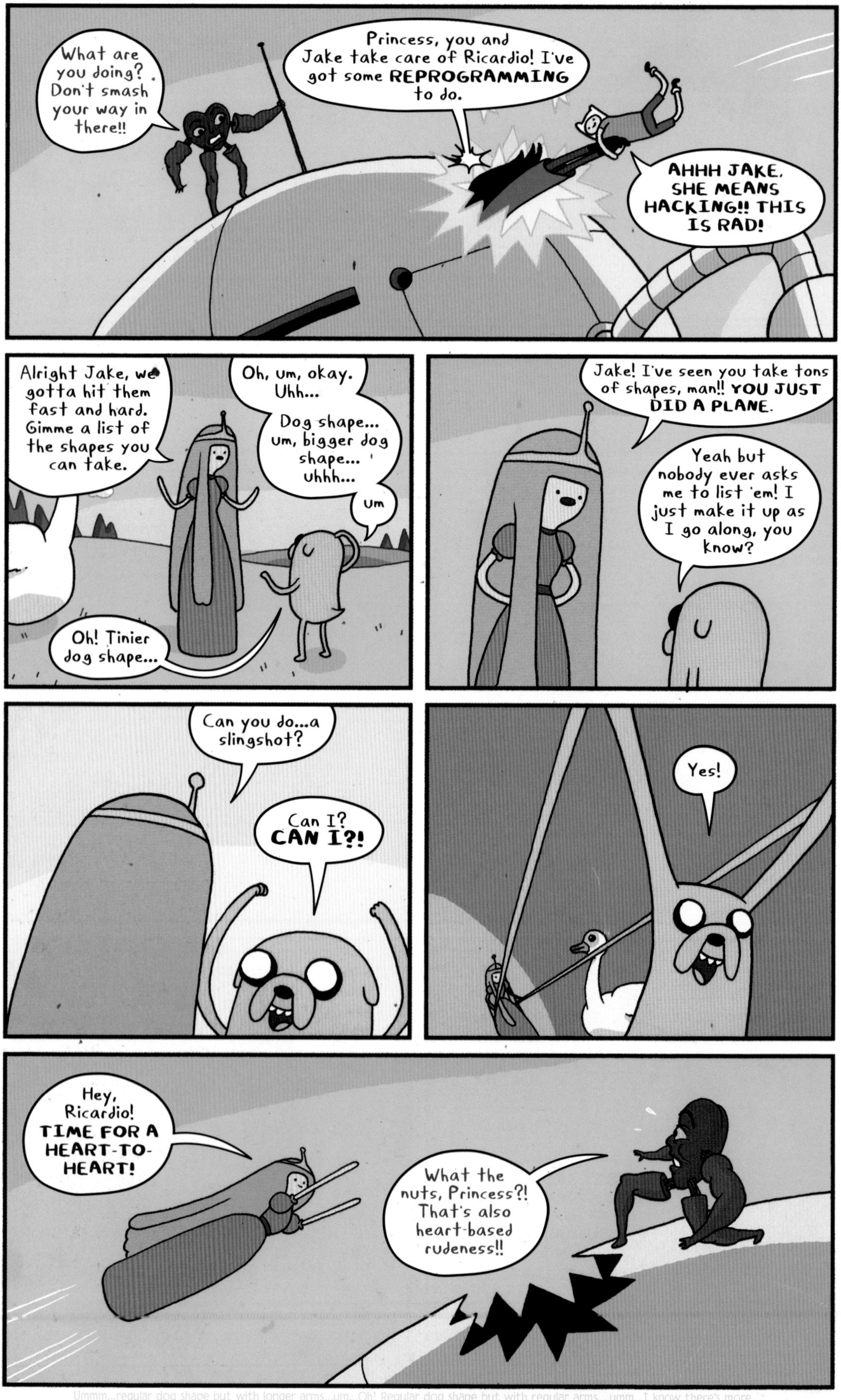
What are you doing? Don't smash your way in there!!
Princess, you and Jake take care of Ricardio! I've got some REPROGRAMMING to do.
AHHH JAKE, SHE MEANS HACKING!! THIS IS RAD!
Alright Jake, we gotta hit them fast and hard. Gimme a list of the shapes you can take.
Oh, um, okay. Uhh...
Dog shape... um, bigger dog shape... uhhh...
um
Oh! Tinier dog shape...
Jake! I've seen you take tons of shapes, man!! YOU JUST DID A PLANE.
Yeah but nobody ever asks me to list 'em! I just make it up as I go along, you know?
Can you do...a slingshot?
Can I? CAN I?!
Yes!
Hey, Ricardio! TIME FOR A HEART-TO-HEART!
What the nuts, Princess?! That's also heart-based rudeness!!

Ummm...regular dog shape but with longer arms...um...Oh! Regular dog shape but with regular arms....umm...I know there's more...

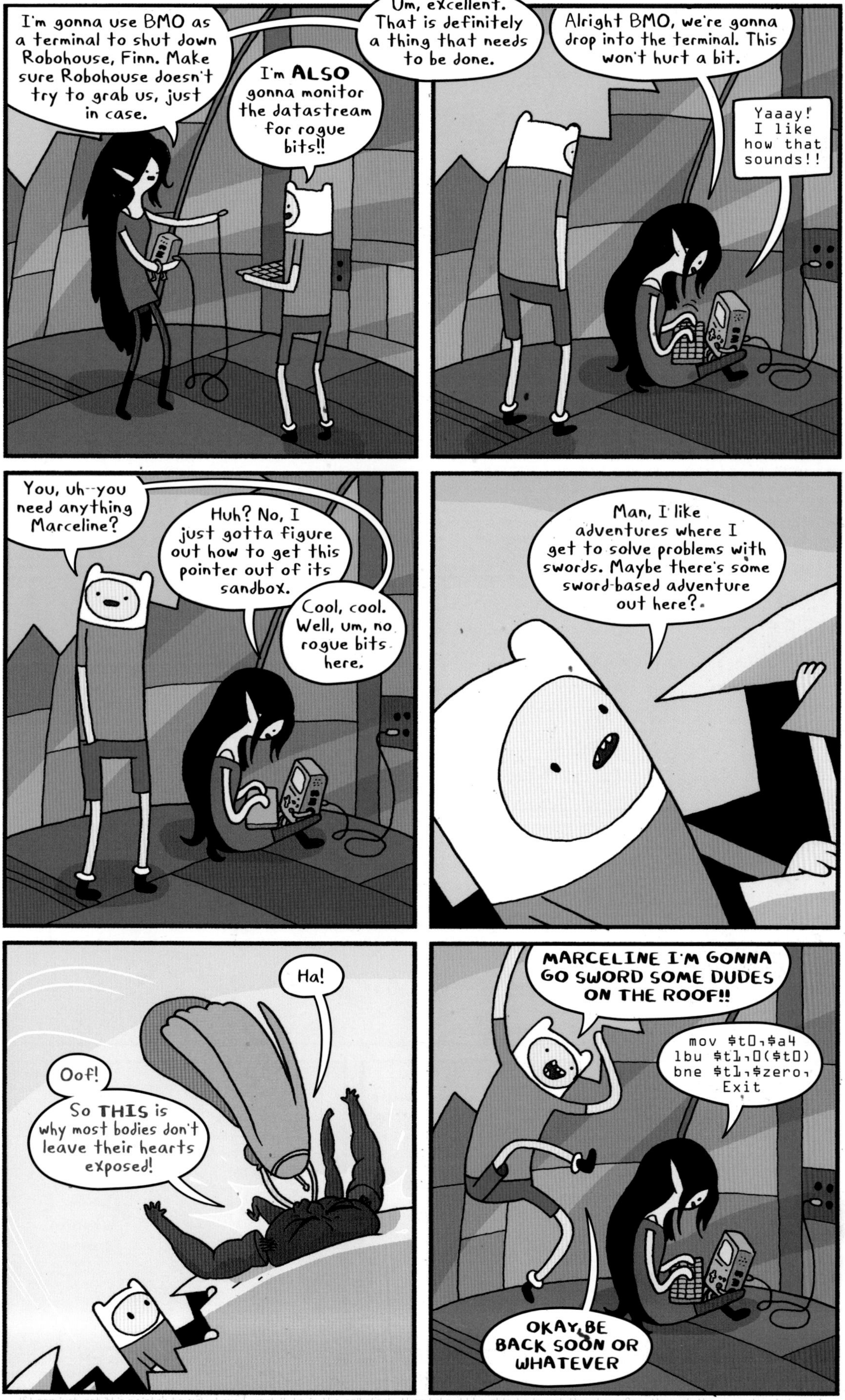
I'm gonna use BMO as a terminal to shut down Robohouse, Finn. Make sure Robohouse doesn't try to grab us, just in case.
Um, excellent. That is definitely a thing that needs to be done.
I'm ALSO gonna monitor the datastream for rogue bits!!
Alright BMO, we're gonna drop into the terminal. This won't hurt a bit.
Yaaay! I like how that sounds!!
You, uh--you need anything Marceline?
Huh? No, I just gotta figure out how to get this pointer out of its sandbox.
Cool, cool. Well, um, no rogue bits here.
Man, I like adventures where I get to solve problems with swords. Maybe there's some sword-based adventure out here?
Ha!
Oof!
So THIS is why most bodies don't leave their hearts exposed!
MARCELINE I'M GONNA GO SWORD SOME DUDES ON THE ROOF!!
mov $t0,$a4
lbu $t1,0($t0)
bne $t1,$zero,
Exit
OKAY, BE BACK SOON OR WHATEVER

If I can just get this pointer to go where I want it to in the call stack, then I should be able to invert the phase flow through the secondary inducers!

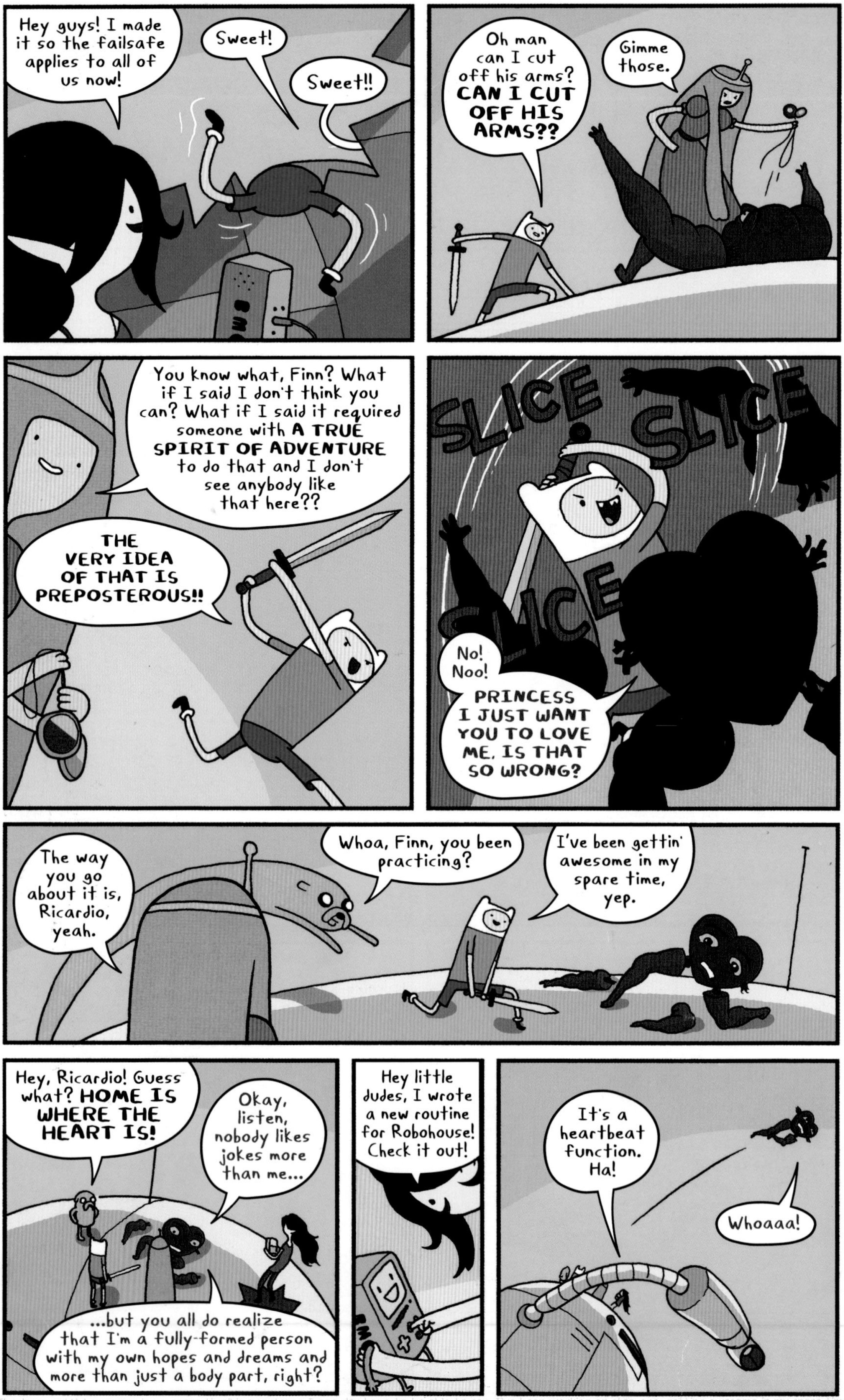
Hey guys! I made it so the failsafe applies to all of us now!
Sweet!
Sweet!!
Oh man can I cut off his arms? **CAN I CUT OFF HIS ARMS??**
Gimme those.
You know what, Finn? What if I said I don't think you can? What if I said it required someone with **A TRUE SPIRIT OF ADVENTURE** to do that and I don't see anybody like that here??
THE VERY IDEA OF THAT IS PREPOSTEROUS!!
SLICE
SLICE
SLICE
No! Noo! **PRINCESS I JUST WANT YOU TO LOVE ME. IS THAT SO WRONG?**
The way you go about it is, Ricardio, yeah.
Whoa, Finn, you been practicing?
I've been gettin' awesome in my spare time, yep.
Hey, Ricardio! Guess what? **HOME IS WHERE THE HEART IS!**
Okay, listen, nobody likes jokes more than me...
...but you all do realize that I'm a fully-formed person with my own hopes and dreams and more than just a body part, right?
Hey little dudes, I wrote a new routine for Robohouse! Check it out!
It's a heartbeat function. Ha!
Whoaaa!

"I've been gettin' awesome in my spare time" is a sentence I one day hope to be able to say. I've been working on step one: getting awesome in my spare time!

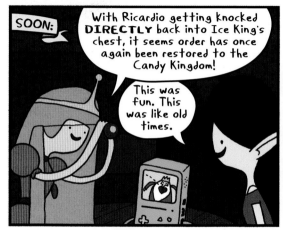

SOON:
With Ricardio getting knocked DIRECTLY back into Ice King's chest, it seems order has once again been restored to the Candy Kingdom!
This was fun. This was like old times.
Listen, Marceline...do you want your amulet back? Because if you don't it's no big deal, I just--
Bonny. Of course I want it back. And I'm sorry I left it behind.
But you know what? It wasn't just you and me who did this. It was all four of us. OUR friendship.
I like that. We could all SHARE ownership of the amulets! Like, PALTIME ARTIFACTS.
Why don't you hold onto these for now, guys? There'll be a symbol of our awesome friendship. Something to remind us of, you know, ourselves!
Can we keep the chest it came in too?
Yeah dudes.
AHHH IT'LL BE A TREASURE CHEST!
Dude we need to make our own AMAZING DUNGEON to put this in!
HEROES ONLY! YES!!
I'd be down helping to build that.
Yeah man.
And now if we're attacked we can go in our own dungeon to bring the house to life again!
And we can shoot our enemies with lazers!! Man!
It's probably WAY more fun to be on the other side of the lazer amulet!!

ATTENTION FRIENDS: Listen. I'm not sure if this is clear or not since nothing has changed, so one last time: I Just Want To Live Inside A Robot House.

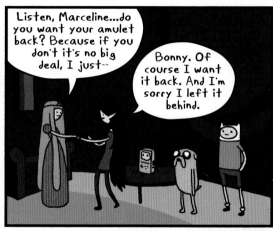

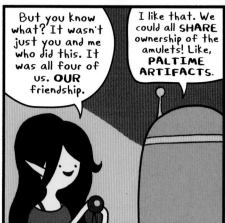

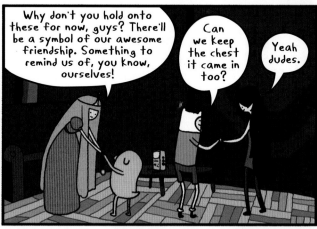

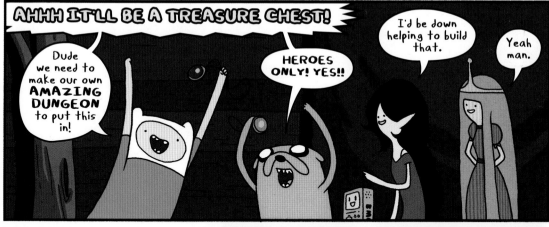

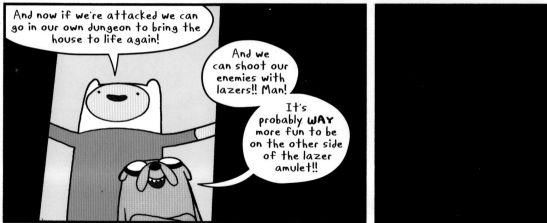

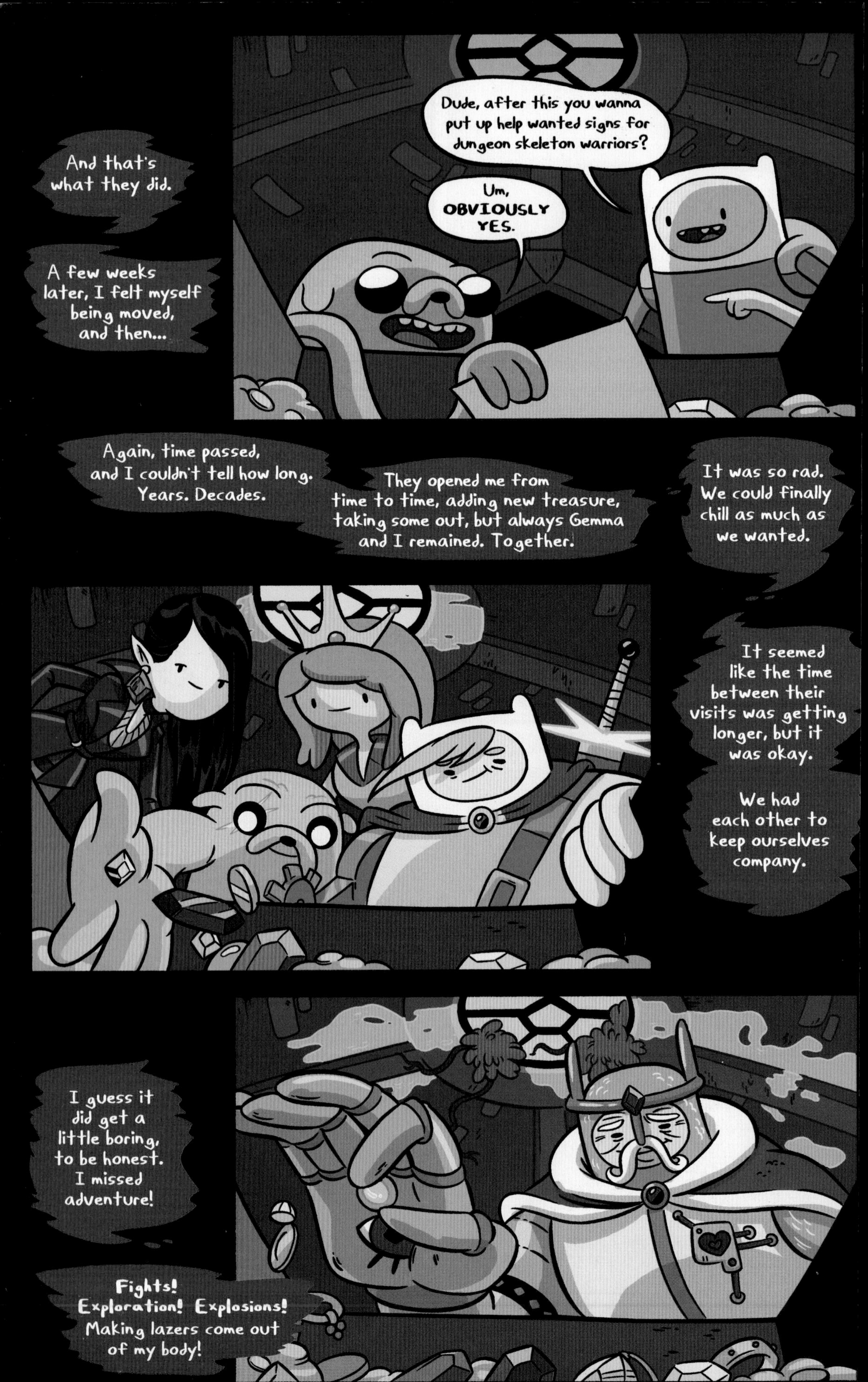
And that's what they did.
Dude, after this you wanna put up help wanted signs for dungeon skeleton warriors?
Um, OBVIOUSLY YES.
A few weeks later, I felt myself being moved, and then...
Again, time passed, and I couldn't tell how long. Years. Decades.
They opened me from time to time, adding new treasure, taking some out, but always Gemma and I remained. Together.
It was so rad. We could finally chill as much as we wanted.
It seemed like the time between their visits was getting longer, but it was okay.
We had each other to keep ourselves company.
I guess it did get a little boring, to be honest. I missed adventure!
Fights! Exploration! Explosions! Making lazers come out of my body!

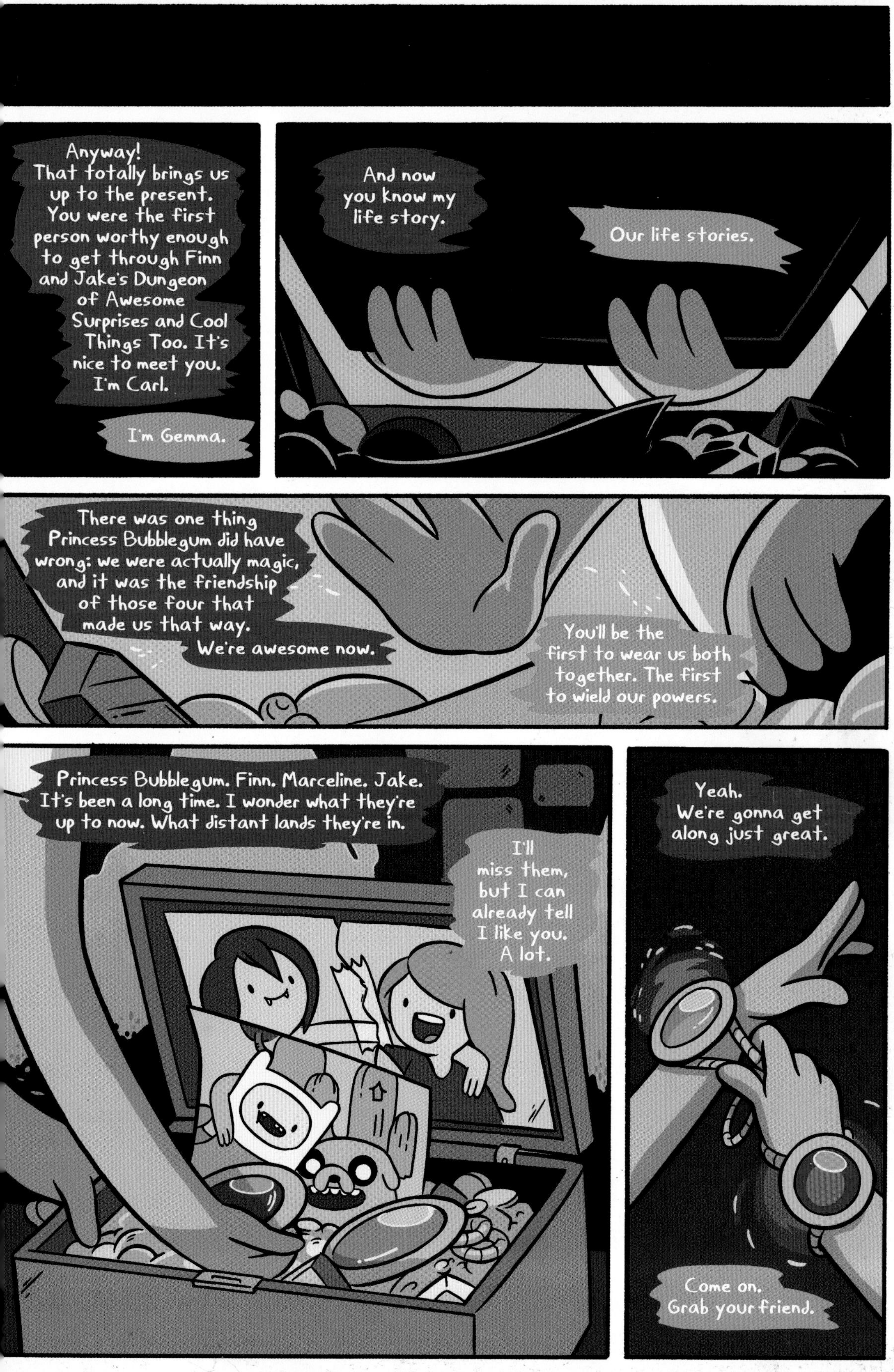
Anyway! That totally brings us up to the present. You were the first person worthy enough to get through Finn and Jake's Dungeon of Awesome Surprises and Cool Things Too. It's nice to meet you. I'm Carl.
I'm Gemma.
And now you know my life story.
Our life stories.
There was one thing Princess Bubblegum did have wrong: we were actually magic, and it was the friendship of those four that made us that way.
We're awesome now.
You'll be the first to wear us both together. The first to wield our powers.
Princess Bubblegum. Finn. Marceline. Jake. It's been a long time. I wonder what they're up to now. What distant lands they're in.
I'll miss them, but I can already tell I like you. A lot.
Yeah. We're gonna get along just great.
Come on. Grab your friend.

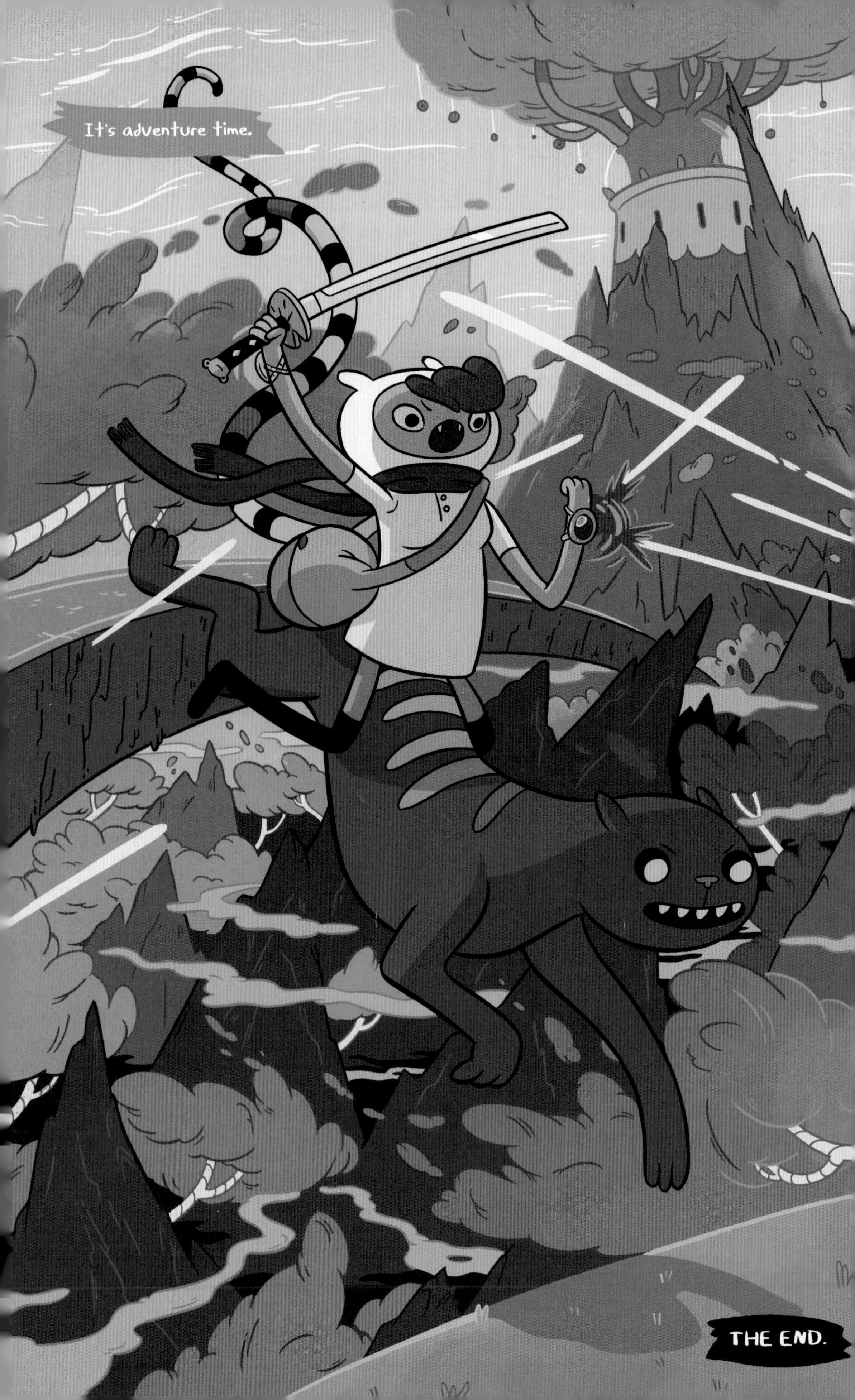
It's adventure time.
THE END.

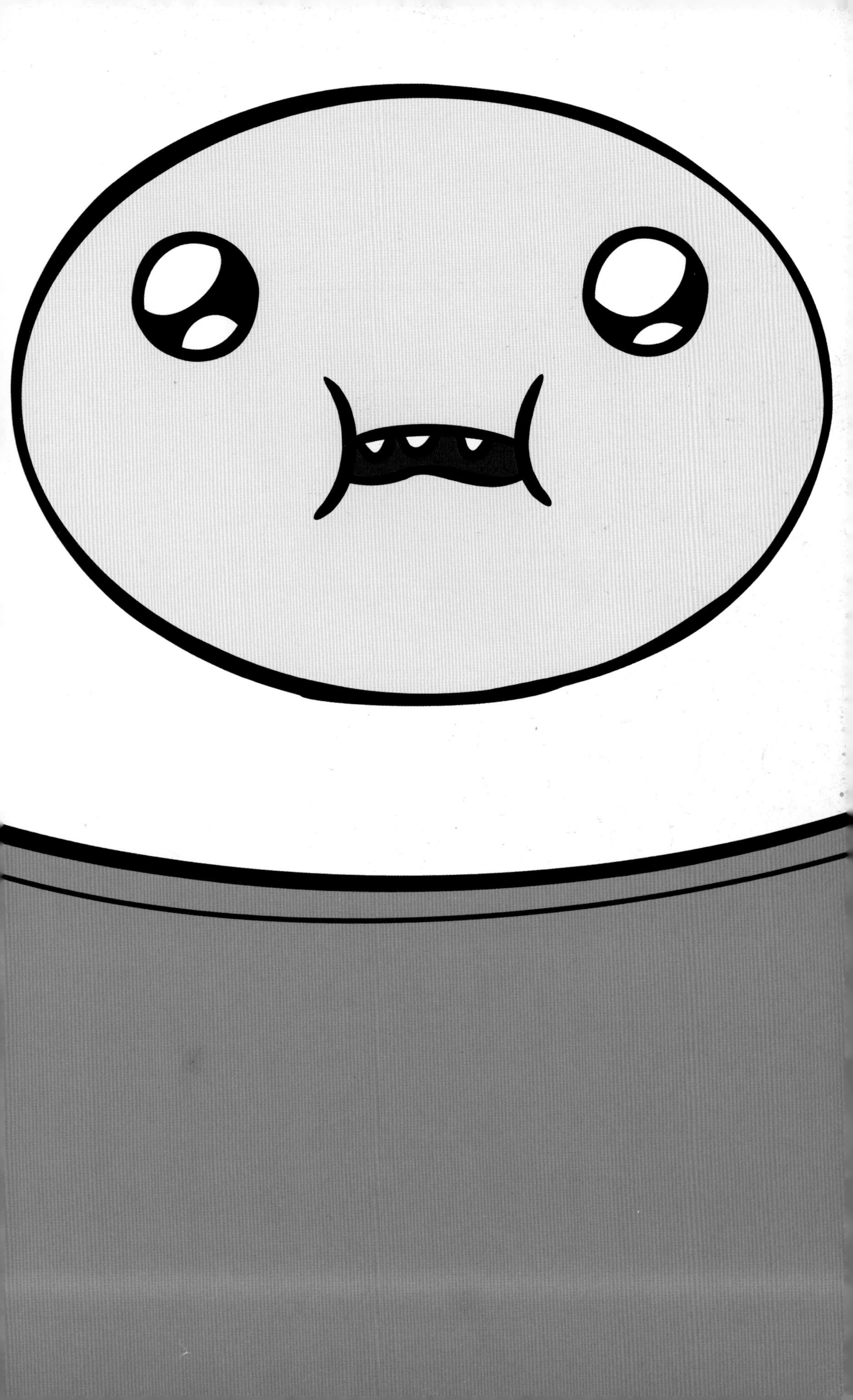

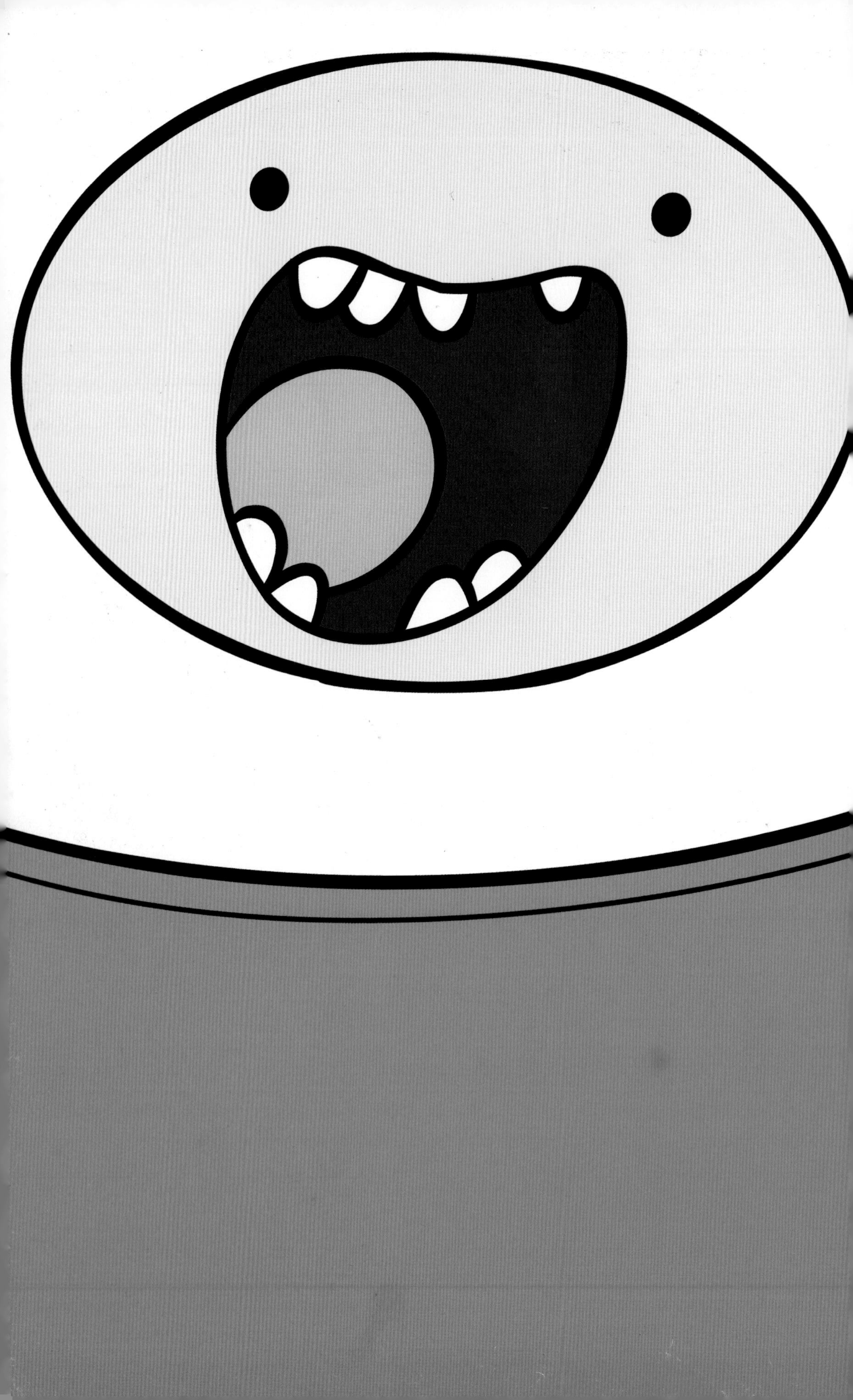

Oooooh! Good morning everybody! I dreamed I had gum in my mouth, but when I pulled it out, it took all my teeth with it!
Also, I dreamed I had teeth!
But the good news was I had way too many teeth in my mouth anyway, and that's not even counting the ones that weren't coming out of my mouth! It was super fun!!
Finn? Jake?
Don't you want to hear about my cool dreams?
Where are you, buddies?
...buddies?
Awesome old Dungeon we found - Finn
TOP SECRET MILITARY FACTORY KEEPOUT
Seriously There's tons of rad Stuff in here, Y'all should check it out, we're about to -Jake

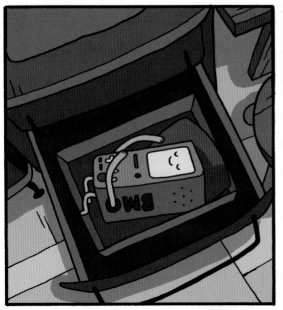

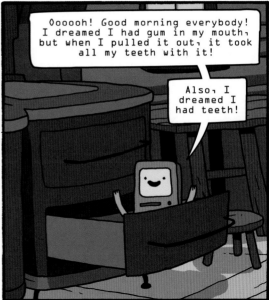

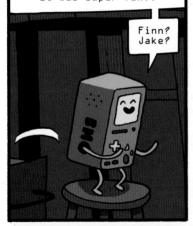

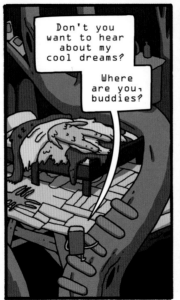

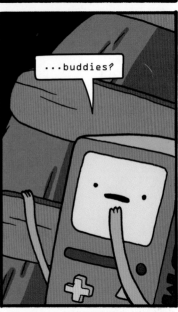

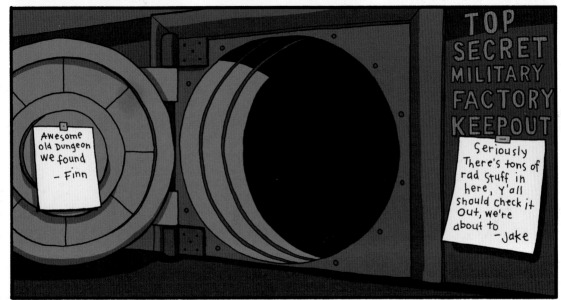

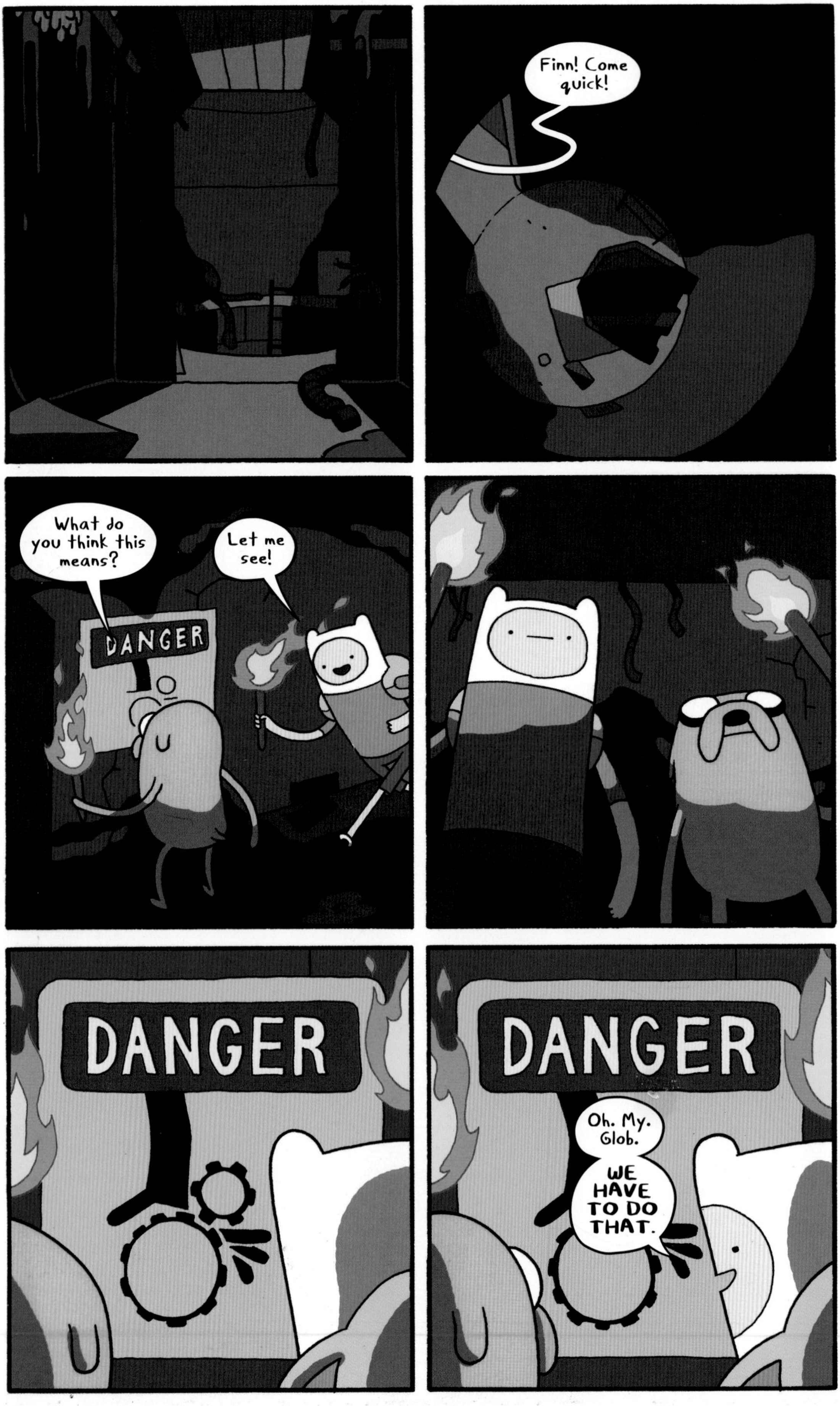
Finn! Come quick!
What do you think this means?
DANGER
Let me see!
DANGER
DANGER
Oh. My. Glob.
WE HAVE TO DO THAT.

ATTENTION READERS: Don't actually do that! Also, be sure to read this almost-hidden text for warnings about things not to do! Okay, we're cool!

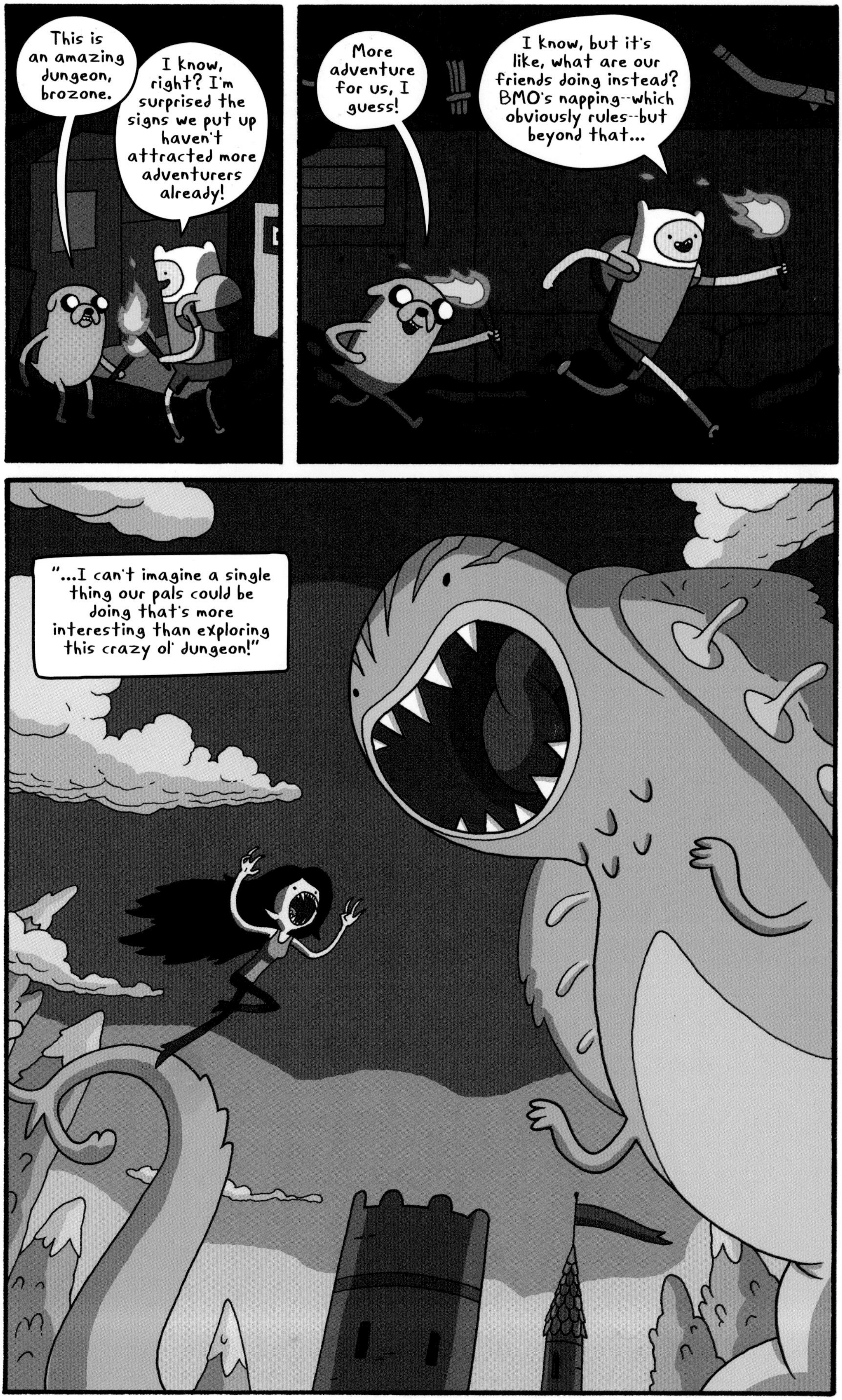
This is an amazing dungeon, brozone.
I know, right? I'm surprised the signs we put up haven't attracted more adventurers already!
More adventure for us, I guess!
I know, but it's like, what are our friends doing instead? BMO's napping--which obviously rules--but beyond that...
"...I can't imagine a single thing our pals could be doing that's more interesting than exploring this crazy ol' dungeon!"

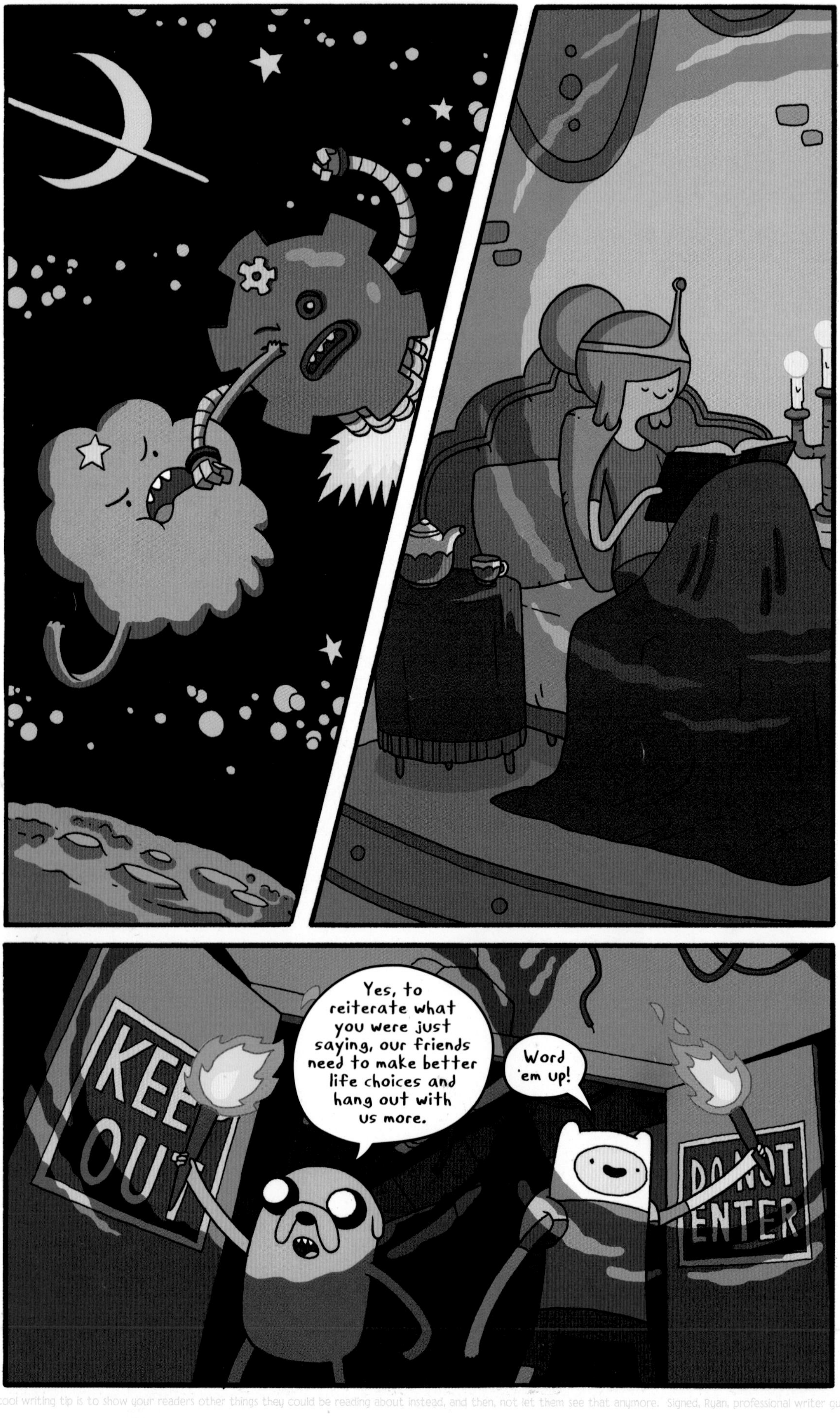
KEEP OUT
Yes, to reiterate what you were just saying, our friends need to make better life choices and hang out with us more.
Word 'em up!
DO NOT ENTER

A cool writing tip is to show your readers other things they could be reading about instead, and then, not let them see that anymore. Signed, Ryan, professional writer guy.

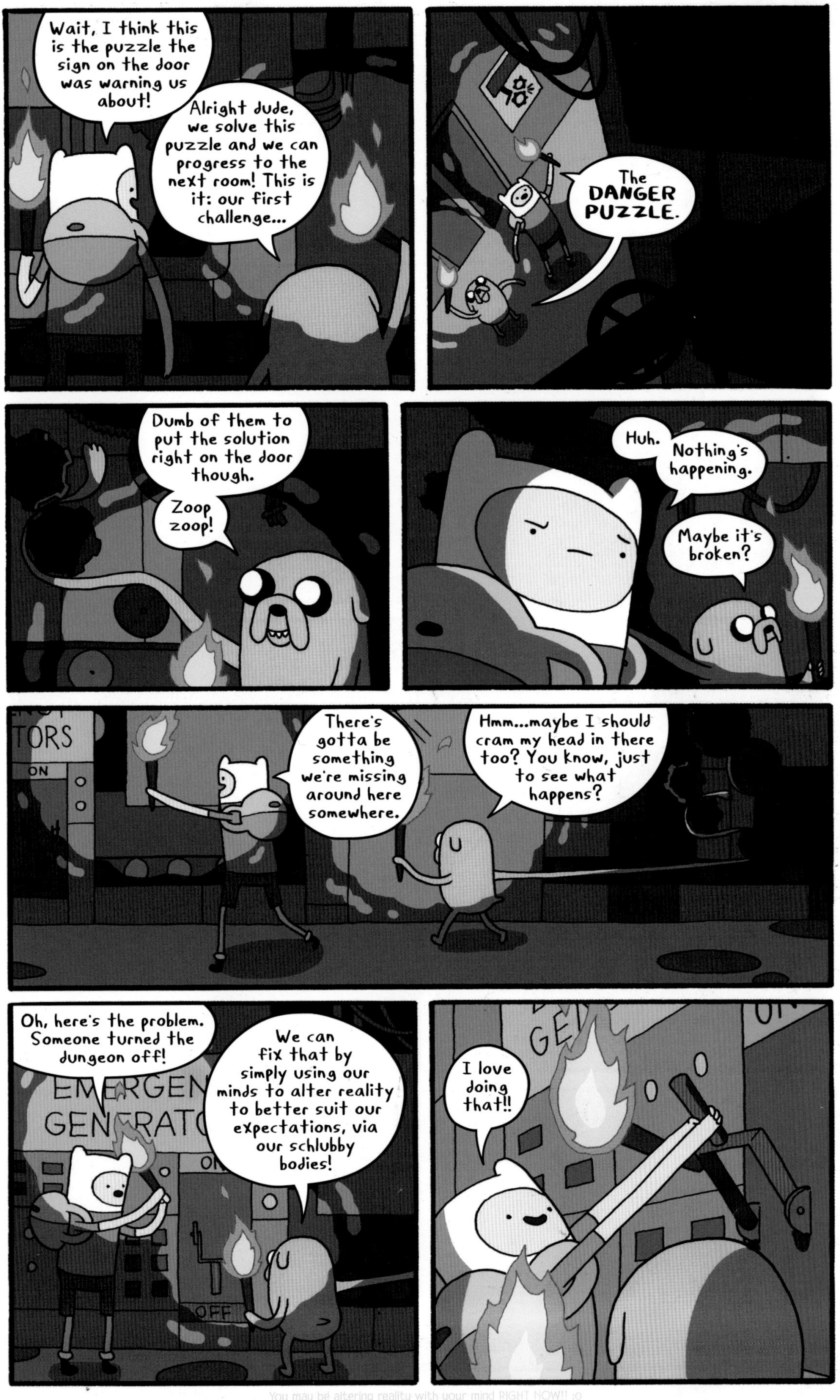
Wait, I think this is the puzzle the sign on the door was warning us about!
Alright dude, we solve this puzzle and we can progress to the next room! This is it: our first challenge...
The DANGER PUZZLE.
Dumb of them to put the solution right on the door though.
Zoop zoop!
Huh.
Nothing's happening.
Maybe it's broken?
TORS
ON
There's gotta be something we're missing around here somewhere.
Hmm...maybe I should cram my head in there too? You know, just to see what happens?
Oh, here's the problem. Someone turned the dungeon off!
EMERGEN
GENERATO
ON
OFF
We can fix that by simply using our minds to alter reality to better suit our expectations, via our schlubby bodies!
I love doing that!!

You may be altering reality with your mind RIGHT NOW!! :o

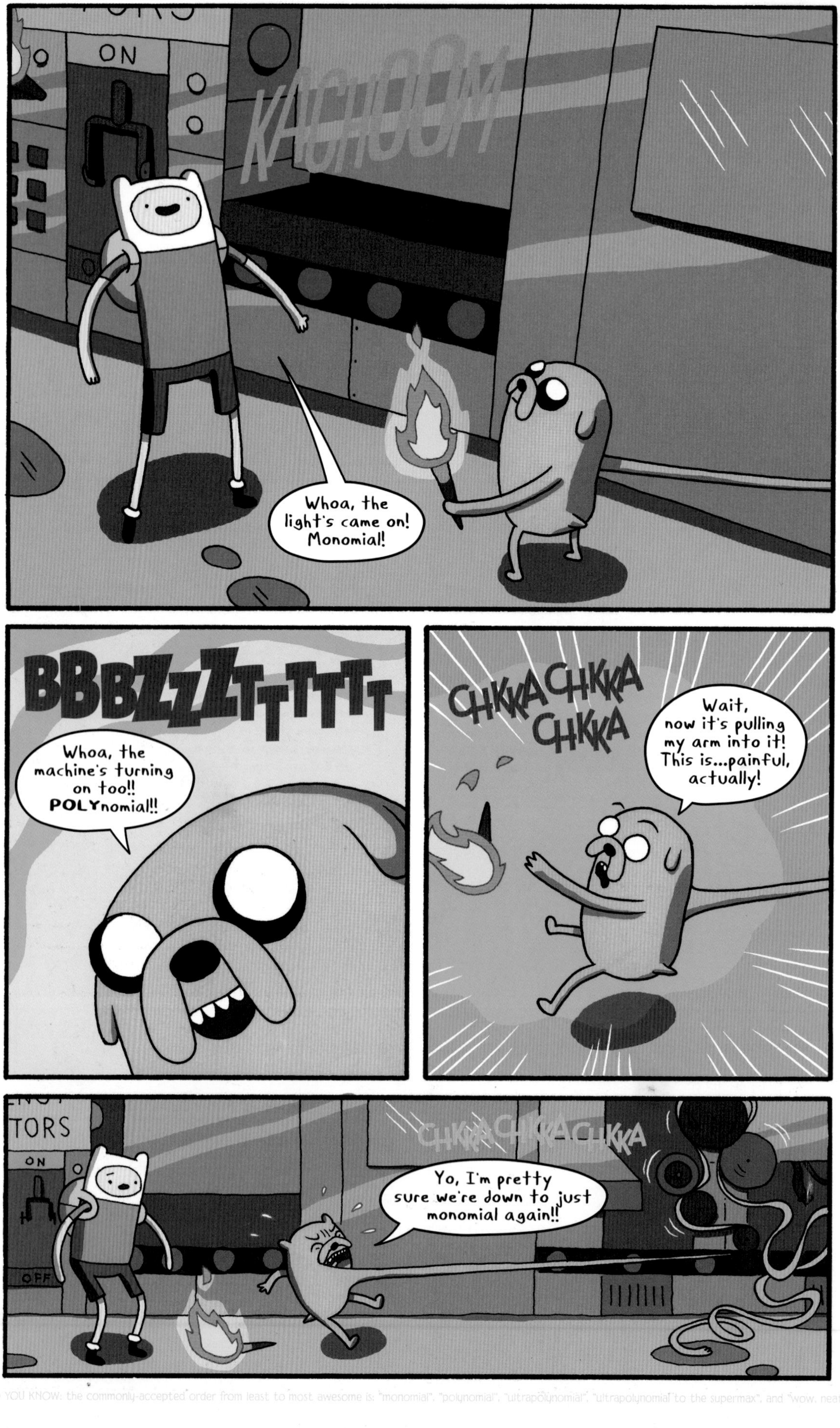
ON
KACHOOM
Whoa, the light's came on! Monomial!
BBBZZZZTTTTTT
Whoa, the machine's turning on too!! POLYnomial!!
CHKKA CHKKA CHKKA
Wait, now it's pulling my arm into it! This is...painful, actually!
TORS
ON
OFF
CHKKA CHKKA CHKKA
Yo, I'm pretty sure we're down to just monomial again!!

DID YOU KNOW: the commonly-accepted order from least to most awesome is: "monomial", "polynomial", "ultrapolynomial", "ultrapolynomial to the supermax", and "wow, neat".

Hey Finn, my stupid body's totally caught in this dumb machine! Help a brother out?
CHKKACHKKA CHKKA
You can't stretch free?
No dice, dude!
Aw dang, now my body's making me experience even MORE pain!
Sheesh!!
EMERG
GENERA S
Okay, I'm turning the dungeon off!
OFF
Seriously though, I'm like "OKAY BODY, THANKS, I TOTALLY AGREE THAT THIS HURTS SO MAYBE YOU CAN STOP MAKING MY BRAIN FEEL PAIN NOW-- you know?"
ENERATORS
KACHOOM
Ow ow ow.
What the--my arm STILL hurts a little even though it's not even in the gears anymore? This is totally bonked!
Attention, world! I hereby take back ALL the good things I said about bodies!!
Even when you said mine looked super awesome in this bear hat?
Okay obviously that still stands.
Your hat ears look like MY ears, only up instead of down!
I can hardly deal!

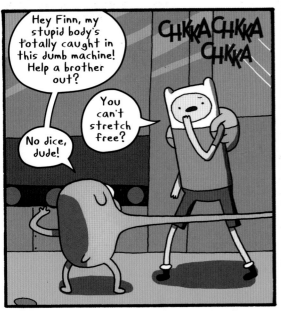

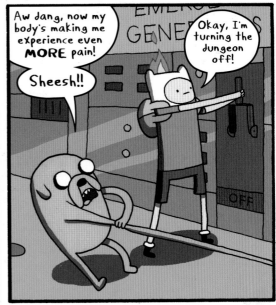

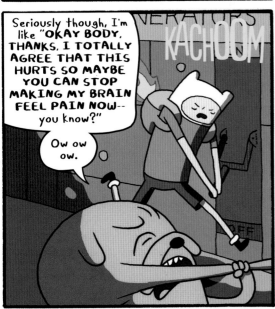

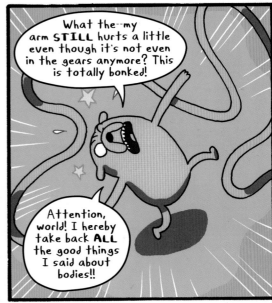

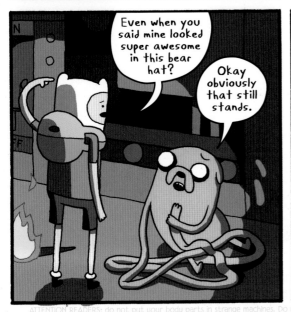

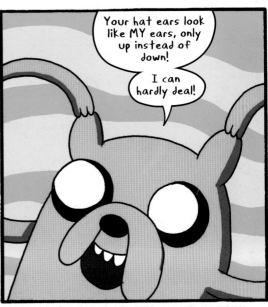

ATTENTION READERS: do not put your body parts in strange machines. Do not take advice from the magical dog in this one specific circumstance.

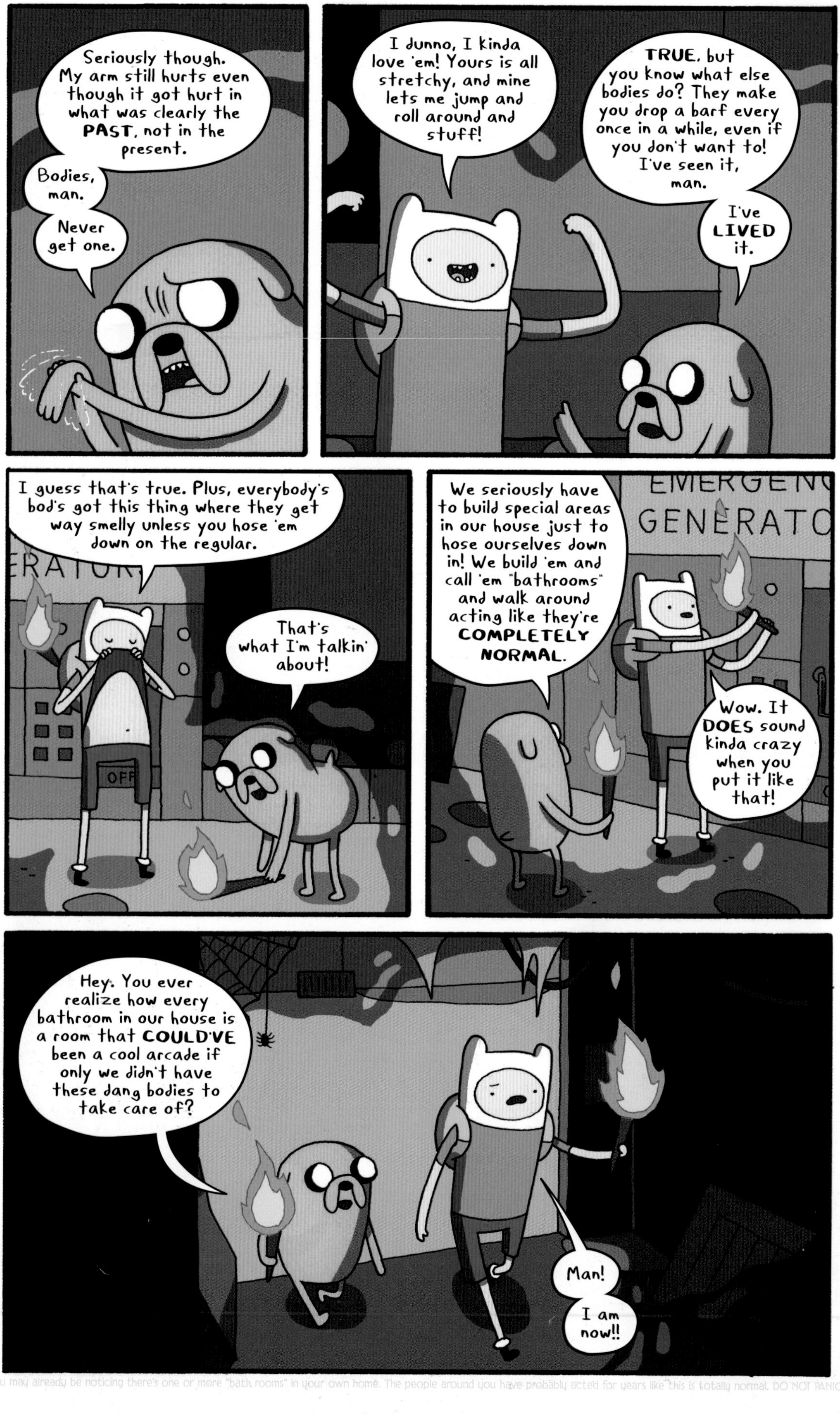
Seriously though. My arm still hurts even though it got hurt in what was clearly the PAST, not in the present.
Bodies, man.
Never get one.
I dunno, I kinda love 'em! Yours is all stretchy, and mine lets me jump and roll around and stuff!
TRUE, but you know what else bodies do? They make you drop a barf every once in a while, even if you don't want to! I've seen it, man.
I've LIVED it.
I guess that's true. Plus, everybody's bod's got this thing where they get way smelly unless you hose 'em down on the regular.
OFF
That's what I'm talkin' about!
We seriously have to build special areas in our house just to hose ourselves down in! We build 'em and call 'em "bathrooms" and walk around acting like they're COMPLETELY NORMAL.
Wow. It DOES sound kinda crazy when you put it like that!
Hey. You ever realize how every bathroom in our house is a room that COULD'VE been a cool arcade if only we didn't have these dang bodies to take care of?
Man!
I am now!!

You may already be noticing there's one or more "bath rooms" in your own home. The people around you have probably acted for years like this is totally normal. DO NOT PANIC.

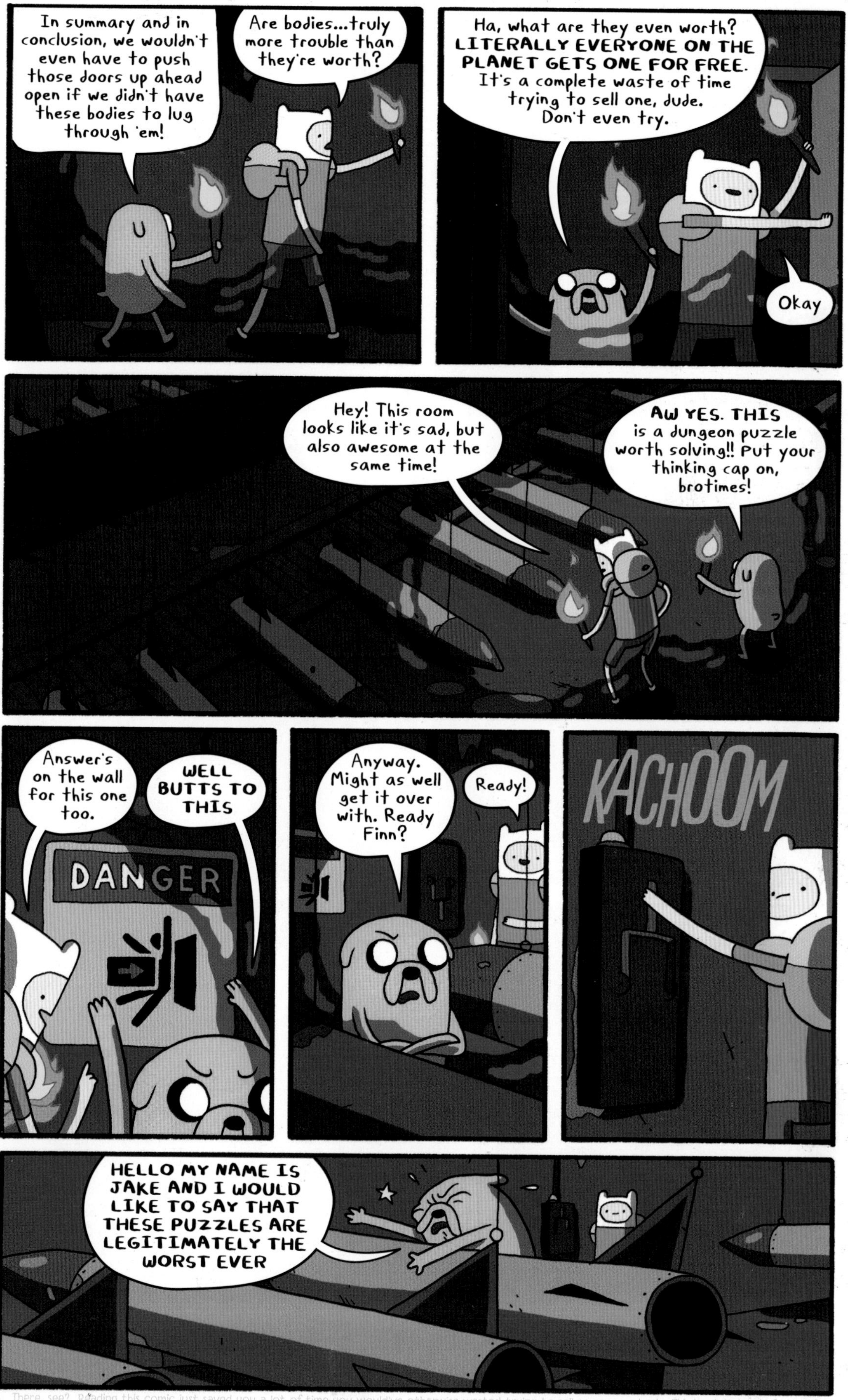
In summary and in conclusion, we wouldn't even have to push those doors up ahead open if we didn't have these bodies to lug through 'em!
Are bodies...truly more trouble than they're worth?
Ha, what are they even worth? LITERALLY EVERYONE ON THE PLANET GETS ONE FOR FREE. It's a complete waste of time trying to sell one, dude. Don't even try.
Okay
Hey! This room looks like it's sad, but also awesome at the same time!
AW YES. THIS is a dungeon puzzle worth solving!! Put your thinking cap on, brotimes!
Answer's on the wall for this one too.
WELL BUTTS TO THIS
DANGER
Anyway. Might as well get it over with. Ready Finn?
Ready!
KACHOOM
HELLO MY NAME IS JAKE AND I WOULD LIKE TO SAY THAT THESE PUZZLES ARE LEGITIMATELY THE WORST EVER

There, see? Reading this comic just saved you a lot of time you would've otherwise wasted trying to sell someone a body. This book just paid for itself!

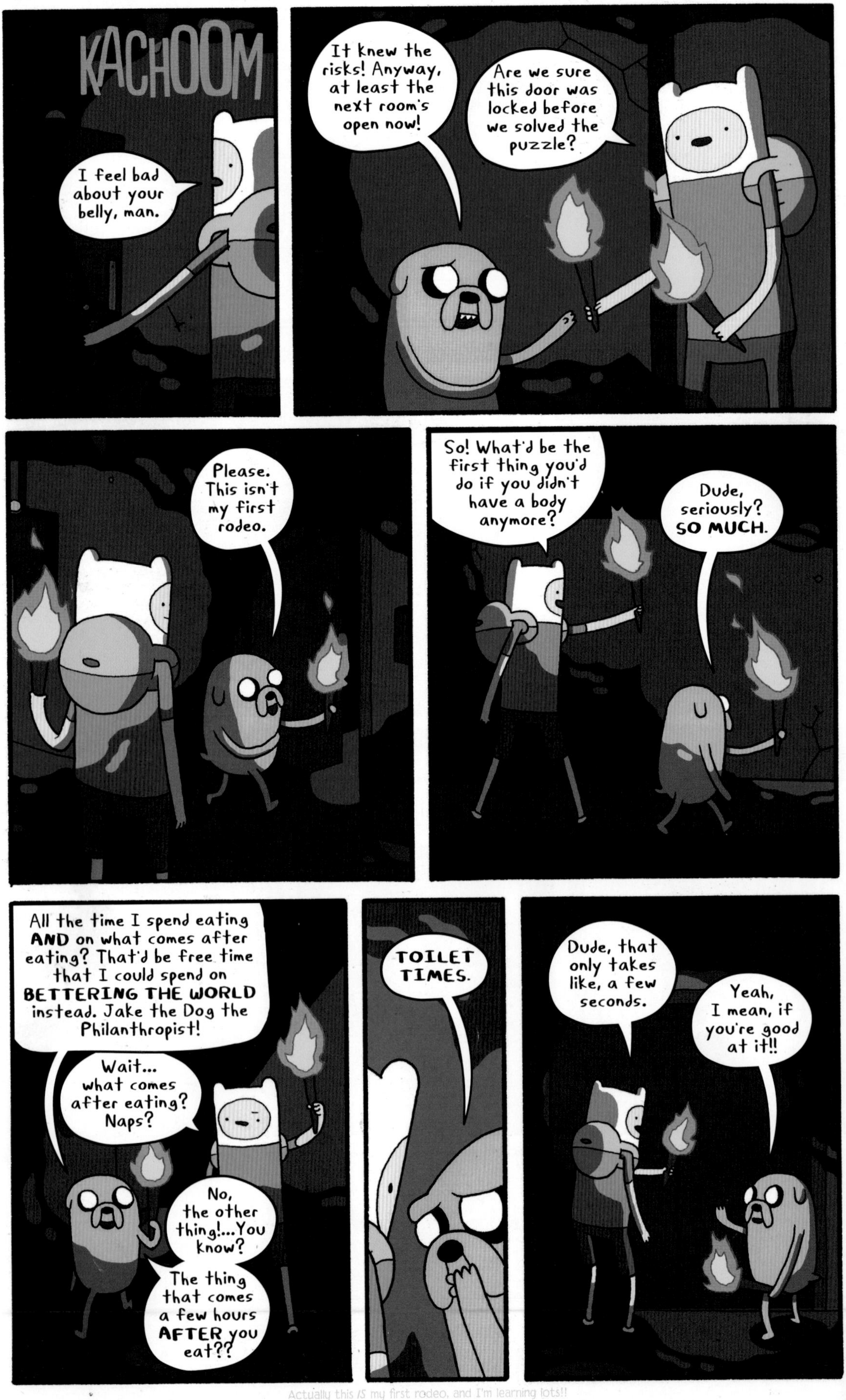
KACHOOM
I feel bad about your belly, man.
It knew the risks! Anyway, at least the next room's open now!
Are we sure this door was locked before we solved the puzzle?
Please. This isn't my first rodeo.
So! What'd be the first thing you'd do if you didn't have a body anymore?
Dude, seriously? SO MUCH.
All the time I spend eating AND on what comes after eating? That'd be free time that I could spend on BETTERING THE WORLD instead. Jake the Dog the Philanthropist!
Wait... what comes after eating? Naps?
No, the other thing!...You know?
The thing that comes a few hours AFTER you eat??
TOILET TIMES.
Dude, that only takes like, a few seconds.
Yeah, I mean, if you're good at it!!

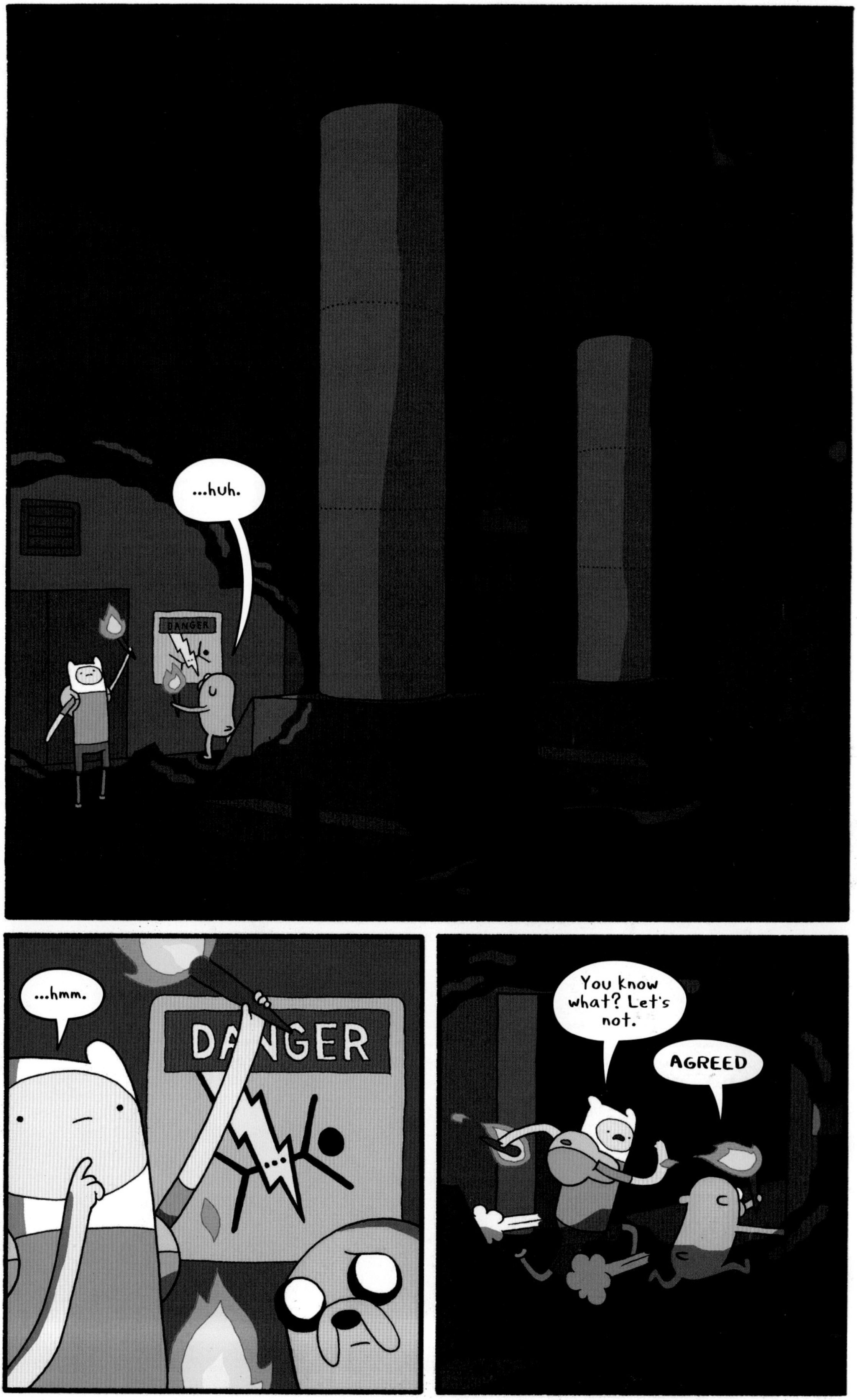
DANGER
...huh.
...hmm.
DANGER
You know what? Let's not.
AGREED

DID YOU KNOW: I feel real bad for whoever has to model for those stick-figure signs.

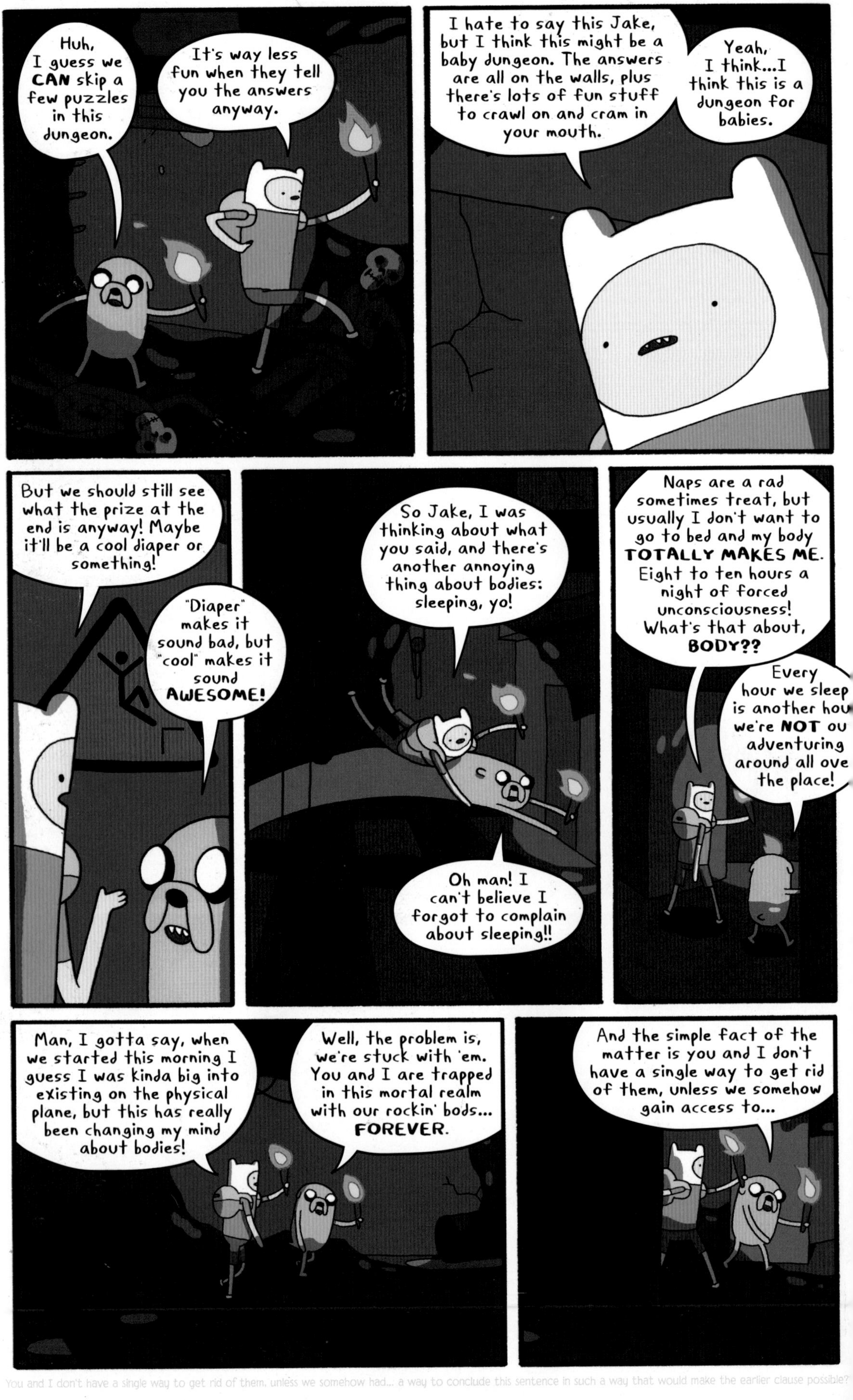
Huh, I guess we CAN skip a few puzzles in this dungeon.
It's way less fun when they tell you the answers anyway.
I hate to say this Jake, but I think this might be a baby dungeon. The answers are all on the walls, plus there's lots of fun stuff to crawl on and cram in your mouth.
Yeah, I think...I think this is a dungeon for babies.
But we should still see what the prize at the end is anyway! Maybe it'll be a cool diaper or something!
"Diaper" makes it sound bad, but "cool" makes it sound AWESOME!
So Jake, I was thinking about what you said, and there's another annoying thing about bodies: sleeping, yo!
Oh man! I can't believe I forgot to complain about sleeping!!
Naps are a rad sometimes treat, but usually I don't want to go to bed and my body TOTALLY MAKES ME. Eight to ten hours a night of forced unconsciousness! What's that about, BODY??
Every hour we sleep is another hou we're NOT ou adventuring around all ove the place!
Man, I gotta say, when we started this morning I guess I was kinda big into existing on the physical plane, but this has really been changing my mind about bodies!
Well, the problem is, we're stuck with 'em. You and I are trapped in this mortal realm with our rockin' bods... FOREVER.
And the simple fact of the matter is you and I don't have a single way to get rid of them, unless we somehow gain access to...

You and I don't have a single way to get rid of them, unless we somehow had... a way to conclude this sentence in such a way that would make the earlier clause possible?

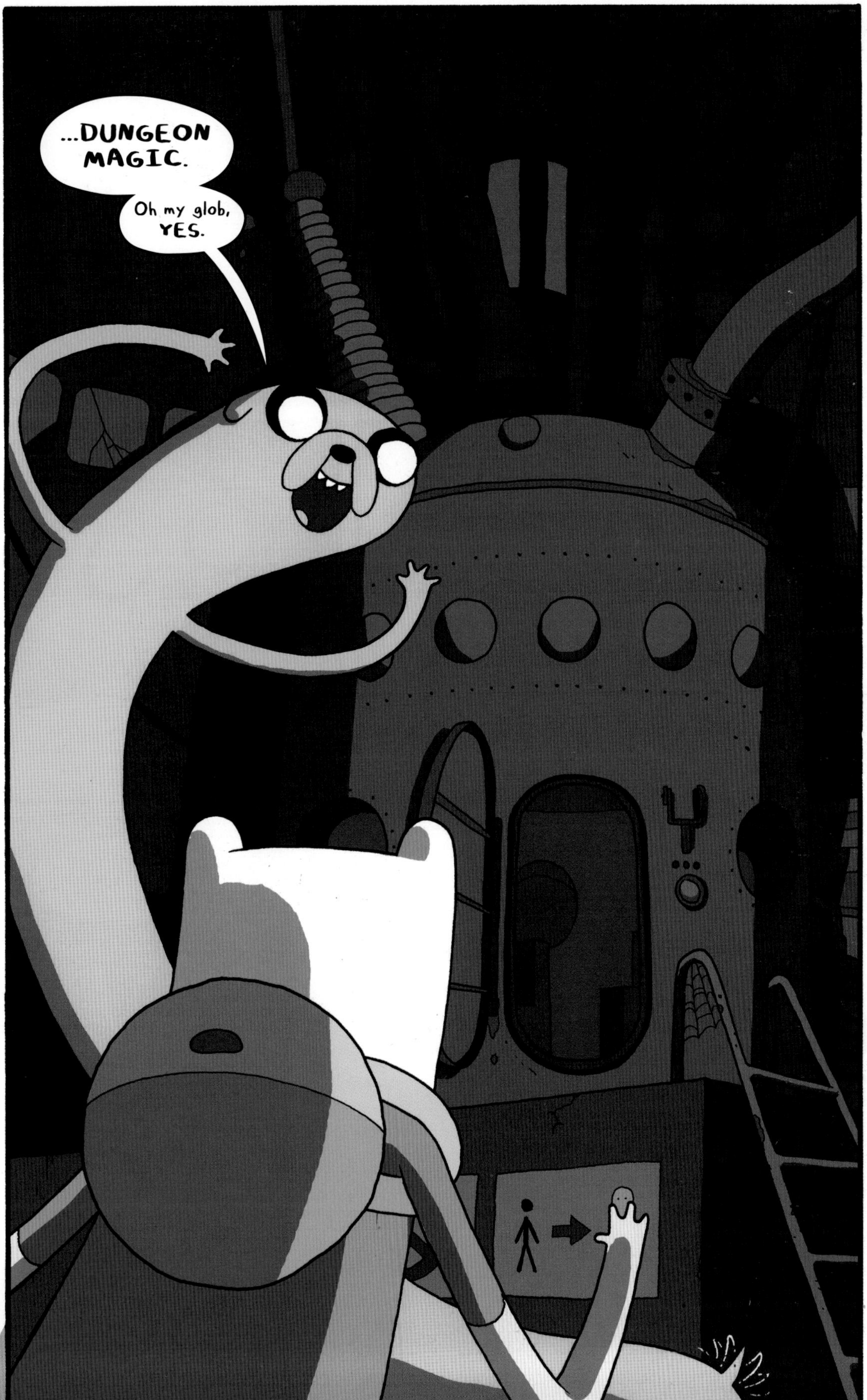
...DUNGEON MAGIC.
Oh my glob, YES.

Oh okay that's good too

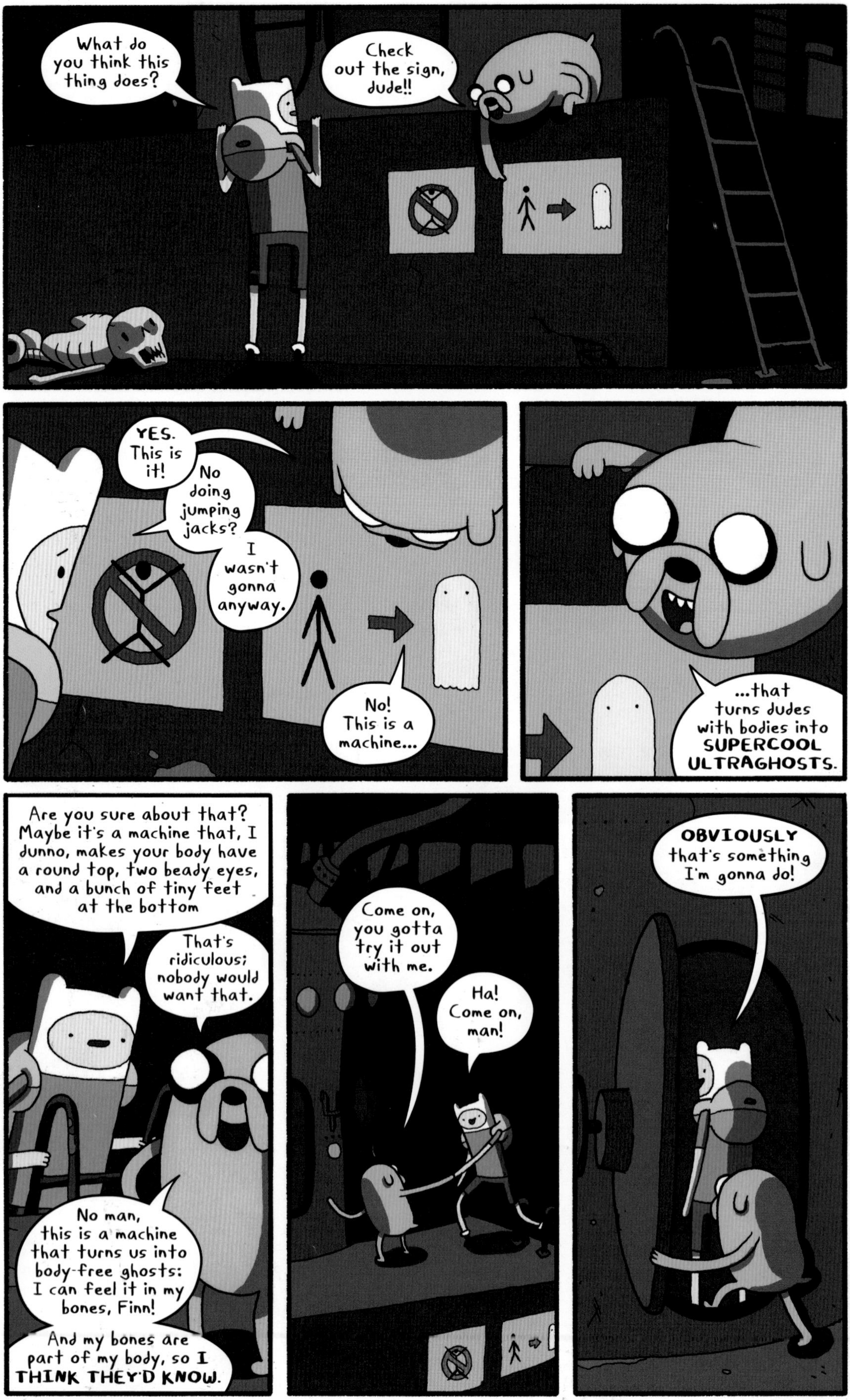
What do you think this thing does?
Check out the sign, dude!!
YES. This is it!
No doing jumping jacks?
I wasn't gonna anyway.
No! This is a machine...
...that turns dudes with bodies into SUPERCOOL ULTRAGHOSTS.
Are you sure about that? Maybe it's a machine that, I dunno, makes your body have a round top, two beady eyes, and a bunch of tiny feet at the bottom
That's ridiculous; nobody would want that.
No man, this is a machine that turns us into body-free ghosts: I can feel it in my bones, Finn!
And my bones are part of my body, so I THINK THEY'D KNOW.
Come on, you gotta try it out with me.
Ha! Come on, man!
OBVIOUSLY that's something I'm gonna do!

Pictured, above: the reason this comic is called "Adventure Time With Finn and Jake" and not "Well-Considered And Viable Decisions With Finn and Jake"

Oh right, power!
One sec.
Mmpht!
Alright! STAYING UP ALL NIGHT WITH MY COOL BEST FRIEND FOR AS LONG AS WE WANT, HERE I COME.
I think it's starting, man! Hurry up!!
No body starts without me, Finn!!
Come on, that was a really appropriate joke, buddy!
Ohhhhhhhh
I get it

Pictured, above: all that remains of my ill-fated "Jake's Hand in: You're A Handy Man To Have Around, Jake" spin-off series. :(

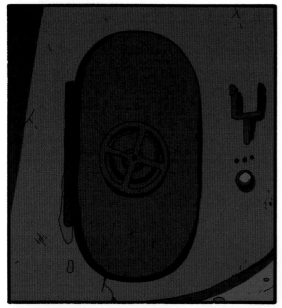

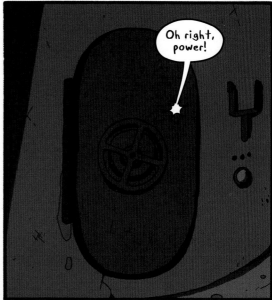

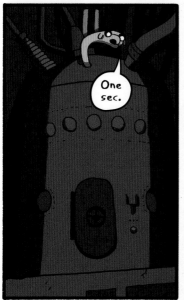

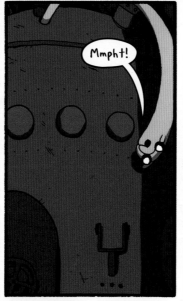

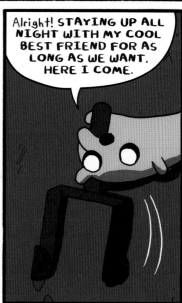

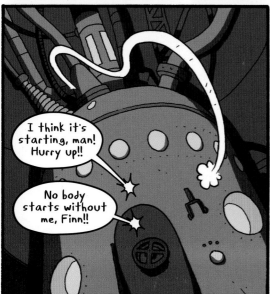

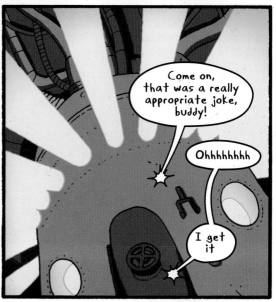

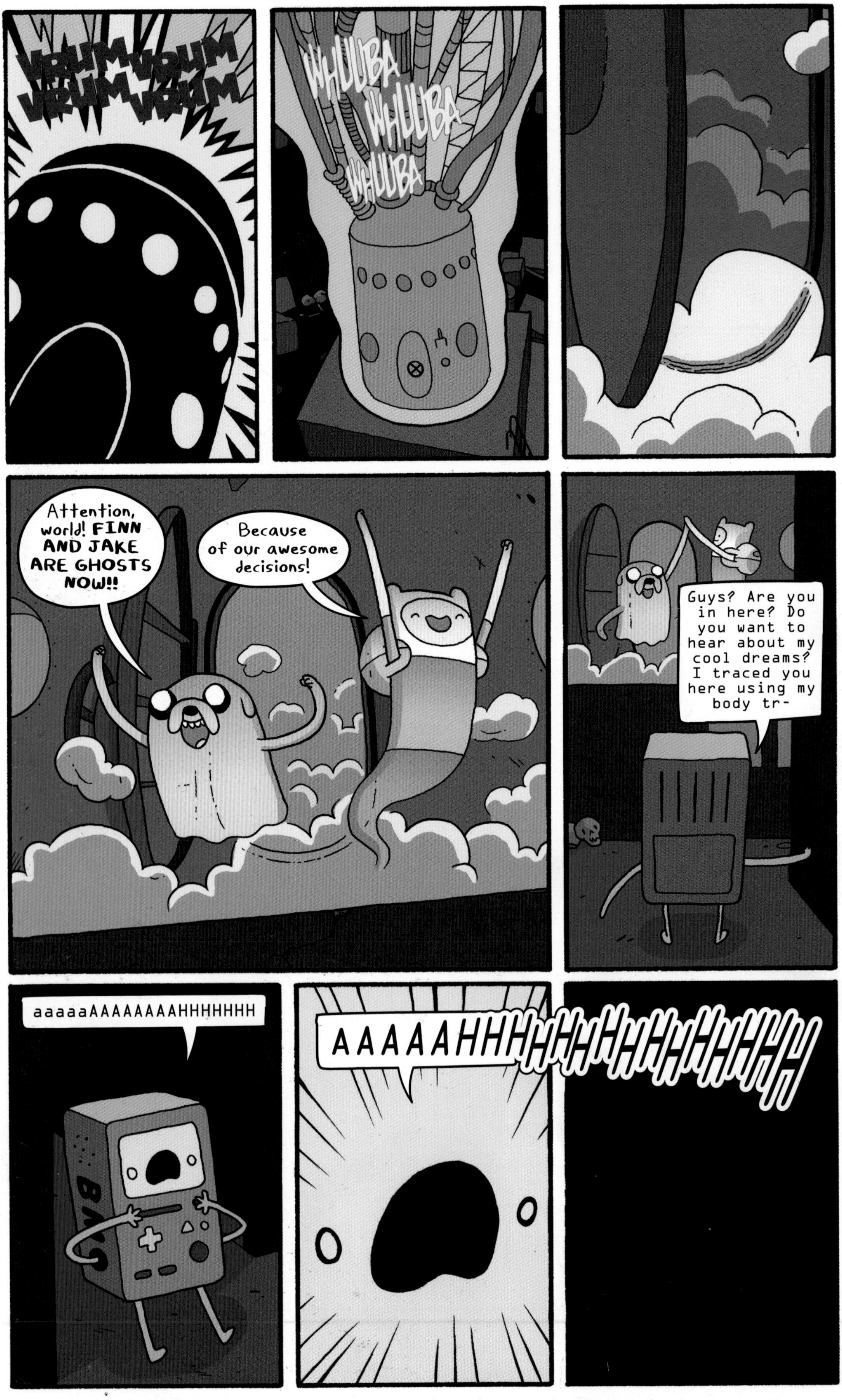
VRUM VRUM
VRUM VRUM
WHUUBA
WHUUBA
WHUUBA
Attention, world! FINN AND JAKE ARE GHOSTS NOW!!
Because of our awesome decisions!
Guys? Are you in here? Do you want to hear about my cool dreams? I traced you here using my body tr-
aaaaaAAAAAAAAHHHHHHH
AAAAAHHHHHHHHHHHHHHH

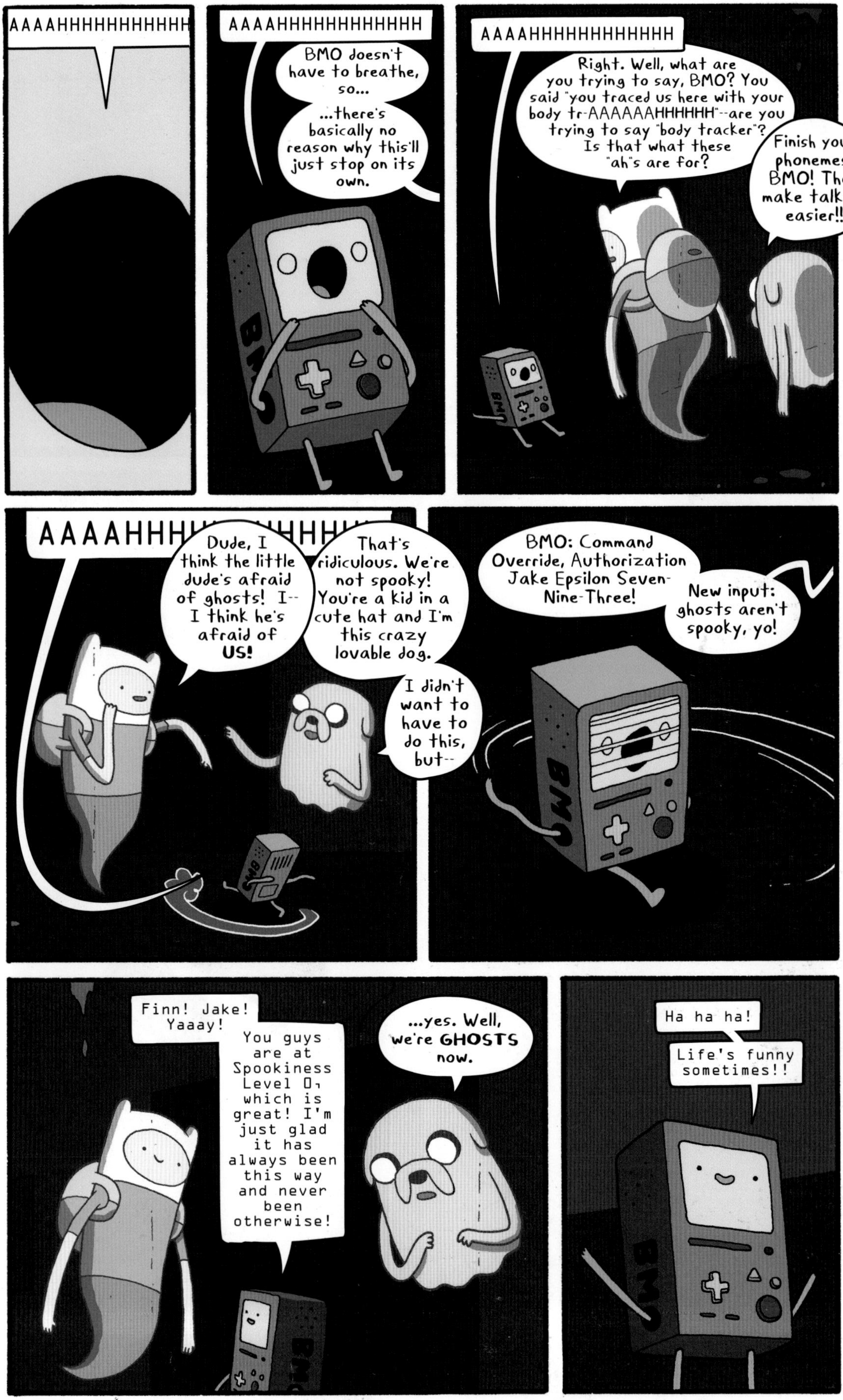
AAAAHHHHHHHHHHH
AAAAHHHHHHHHHHHH
BMO doesn't have to breathe, so...
...there's basically no reason why this'll just stop on its own.
AAAAHHHHHHHHHHHH
Right. Well, what are you trying to say, BMO? You said "you traced us here with your body tr-AAAAAAHHHHHH"--are you trying to say "body tracker"? Is that what these "ah"s are for?
Finish your phonemes, BMO! They make talking easier!!
AAAAHHH HHHHH
Dude, I think the little dude's afraid of ghosts! I-- I think he's afraid of **US!**
That's ridiculous. We're not spooky! You're a kid in a cute hat and I'm this crazy lovable dog.
I didn't want to have to do this, but--
BMO: Command Override, Authorization Jake Epsilon Seven-Nine-Three!
New input: ghosts aren't spooky, yo!
Finn! Jake! Yaaay!
You guys are at Spookiness Level 0, which is great! I'm just glad it has always been this way and never been otherwise!
...yes. Well, we're **GHOSTS** now.
Ha ha ha!
Life's funny sometimes!!

If only there were command overrides authorization Jake Epsilon Seven-Nine-Three for... the human heart??

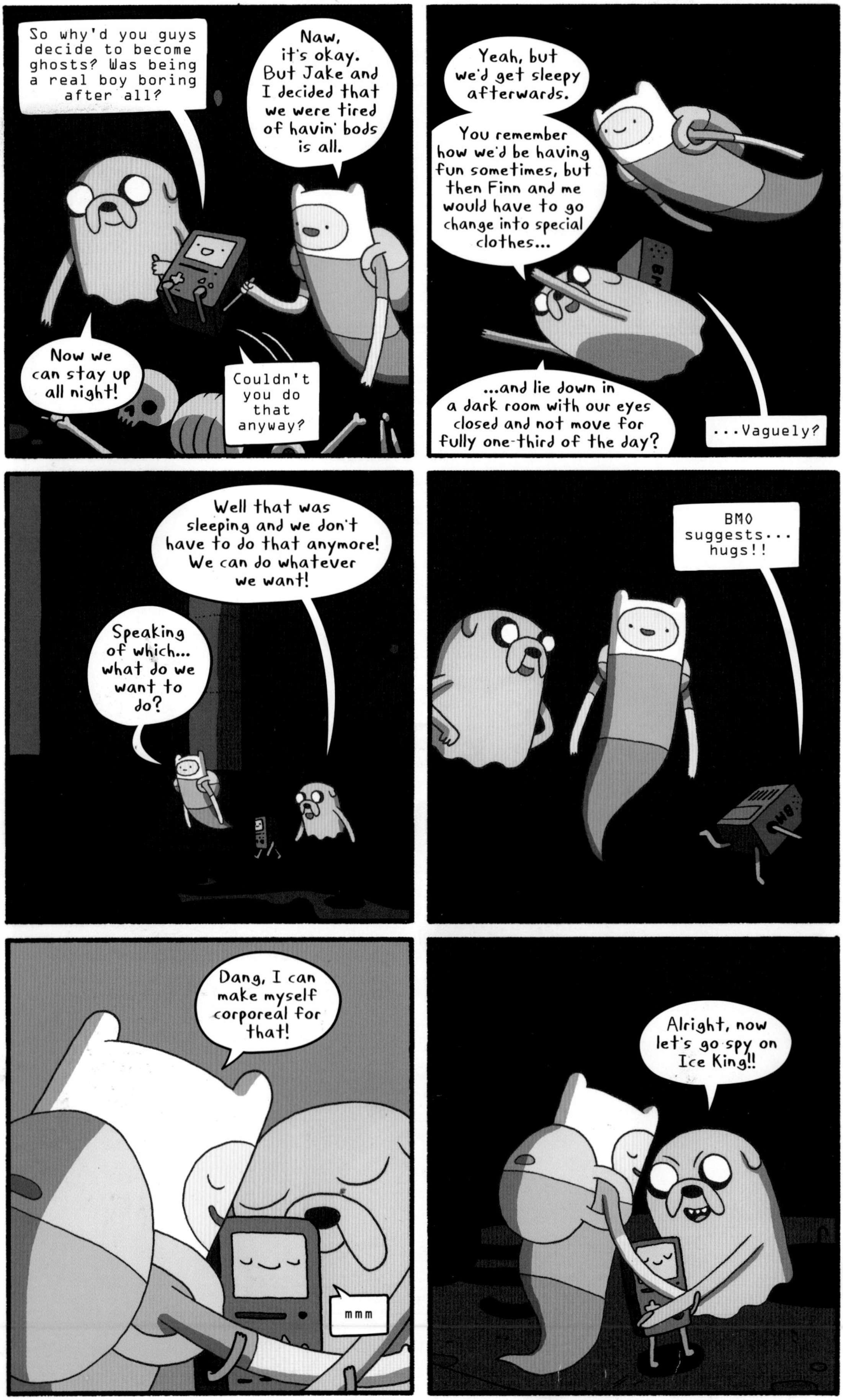

So why'd you guys decide to become ghosts? Was being a real boy boring after all?
Naw, it's okay. But Jake and I decided that we were tired of havin' bods is all.
Now we can stay up all night!
Couldn't you do that anyway?
Yeah, but we'd get sleepy afterwards.
You remember how we'd be having fun sometimes, but then Finn and me would have to go change into special clothes...
...and lie down in a dark room with our eyes closed and not move for fully one-third of the day?
...Vaguely?
Well that was sleeping and we don't have to do that anymore! We can do whatever we want!
Speaking of which... what do we want to do?
BMO suggests... hugs!!
Dang, I can make myself corporeal for that!
mmm
Alright, now let's go spy on Ice King!!

Sometimes being a real boy is actually pretty boring though. I've lived several years as a real boy so I *THINK* I know what I'm talking about.

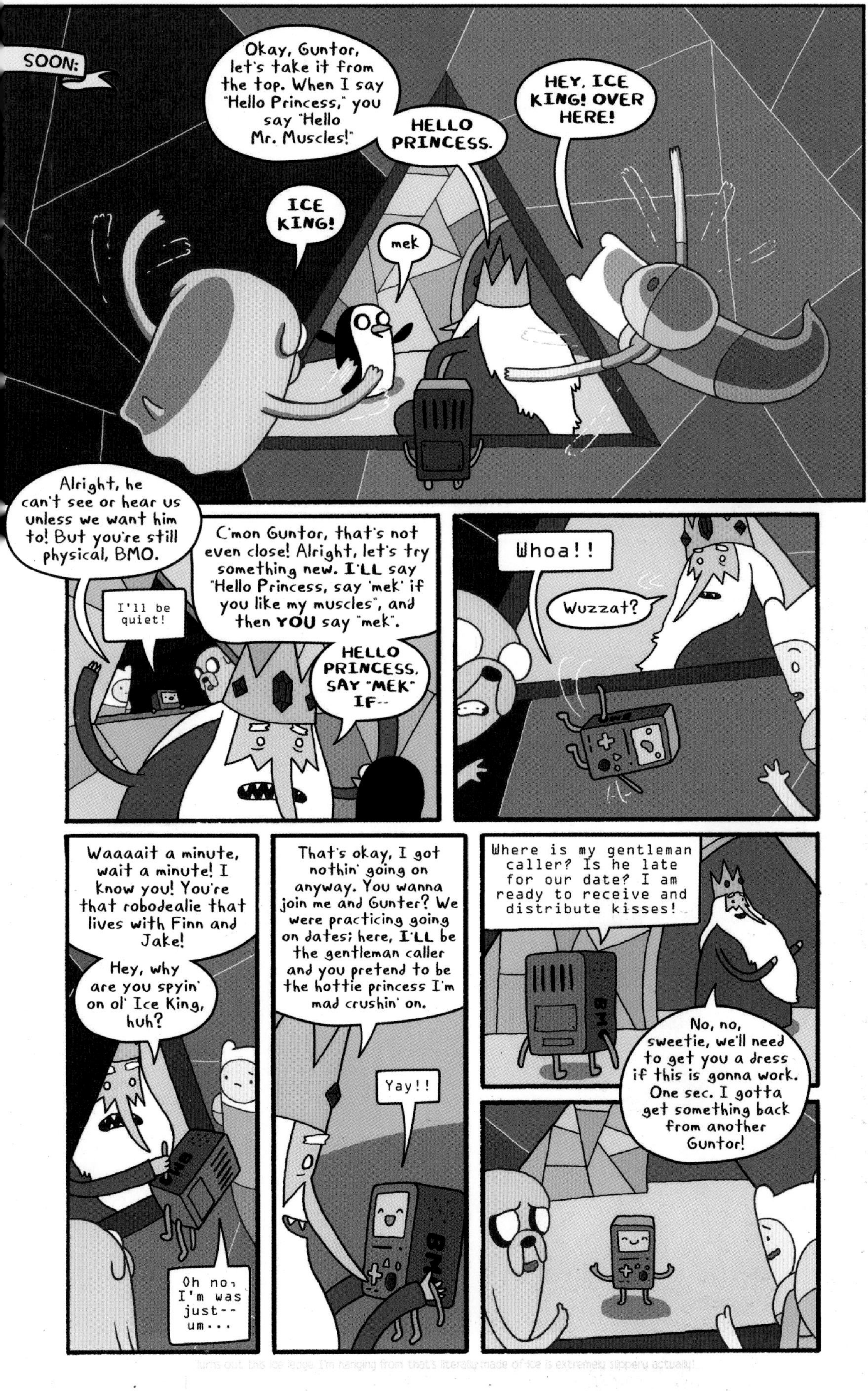
SOON:
Okay, Guntor, let's take it from the top. When I say "Hello Princess," you say "Hello Mr. Muscles!"
HELLO PRINCESS.
HEY, ICE KING! OVER HERE!
ICE KING!
mek
Alright, he can't see or hear us unless we want him to! But you're still physical, BMO.
I'll be quiet!
C'mon Guntor, that's not even close! Alright, let's try something new. I'LL say "Hello Princess, say 'mek' if you like my muscles", and then YOU say "mek".
HELLO PRINCESS, SAY "MEK" IF--
Whoa!!
Wuzzat?
Waaaait a minute, wait a minute! I know you! You're that robodealie that lives with Finn and Jake!
Hey, why are you spyin' on ol' Ice King, huh?
Oh no, I'm was just--um...
That's okay, I got nothin' going on anyway. You wanna join me and Gunter? We were practicing going on dates; here, I'LL be the gentleman caller and you pretend to be the hottie princess I'm mad crushin' on.
Yay!!
Where is my gentleman caller? Is he late for our date? I am ready to receive and distribute kisses!
No, no, sweetie, we'll need to get you a dress if this is gonna work. One sec. I gotta get something back from another Guntor!

Turns out, this Ice ledge I'm hanging from that's literally made of ice is extremely slippery actually!

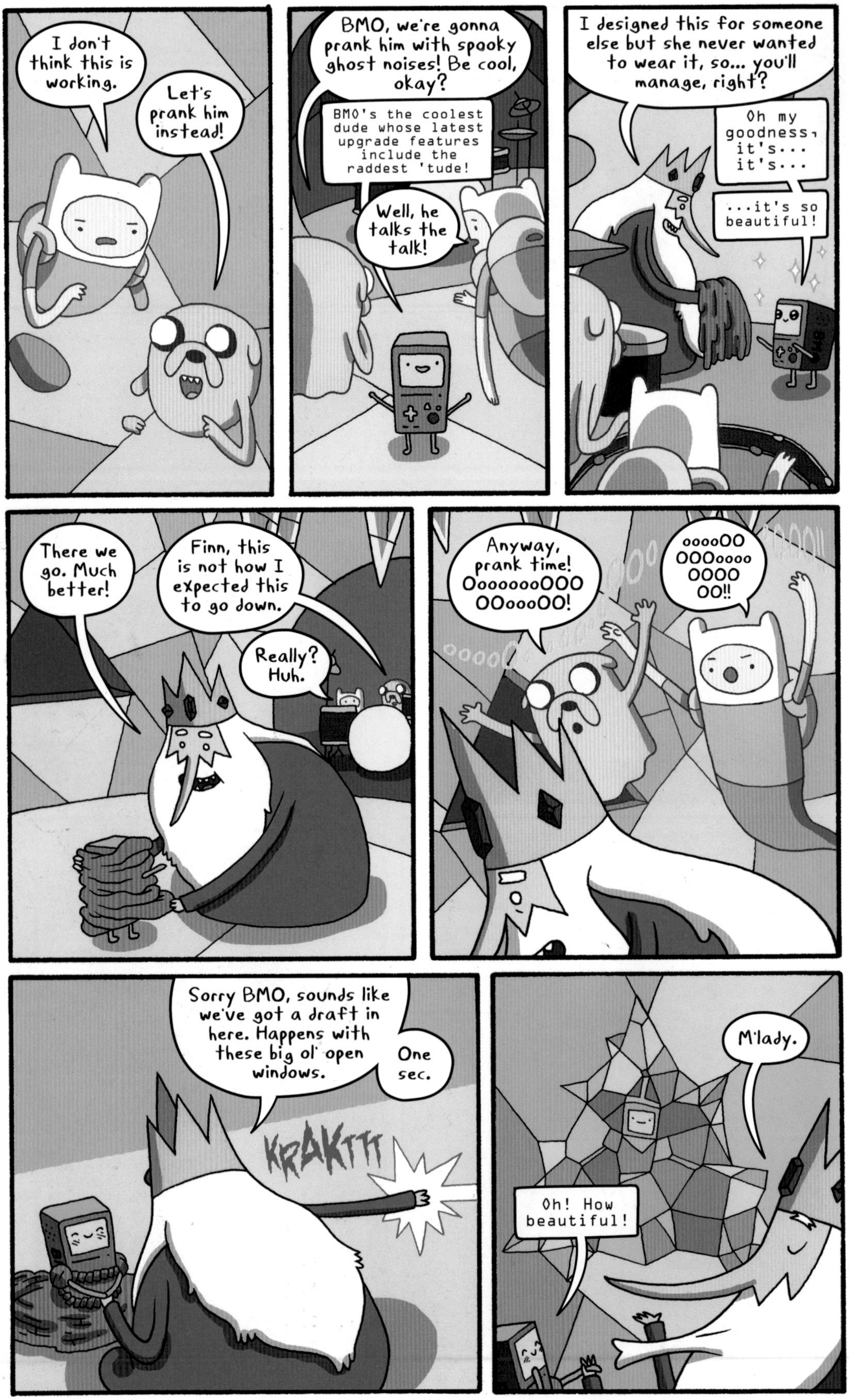
I don't think this is working.
Let's prank him instead!
BMO, we're gonna prank him with spooky ghost noises! Be cool, okay?
BMO's the coolest dude whose latest upgrade features include the raddest 'tude!
Well, he talks the talk!
I designed this for someone else but she never wanted to wear it, so... you'll manage, right?
Oh my goodness, it's... it's...
...it's so beautiful!
There we go. Much better!
Finn, this is not how I expected this to go down.
Really? Huh.
Anyway, prank time! OoooooOOO OOoooOO!
oooOO OOOoooo OOOO OO!!
Sorry BMO, sounds like we've got a draft in here. Happens with these big ol' open windows.
One sec.
KRAKTTT
M'lady.
Oh! How beautiful!

BMO has legs that are unwilling or unable to quit

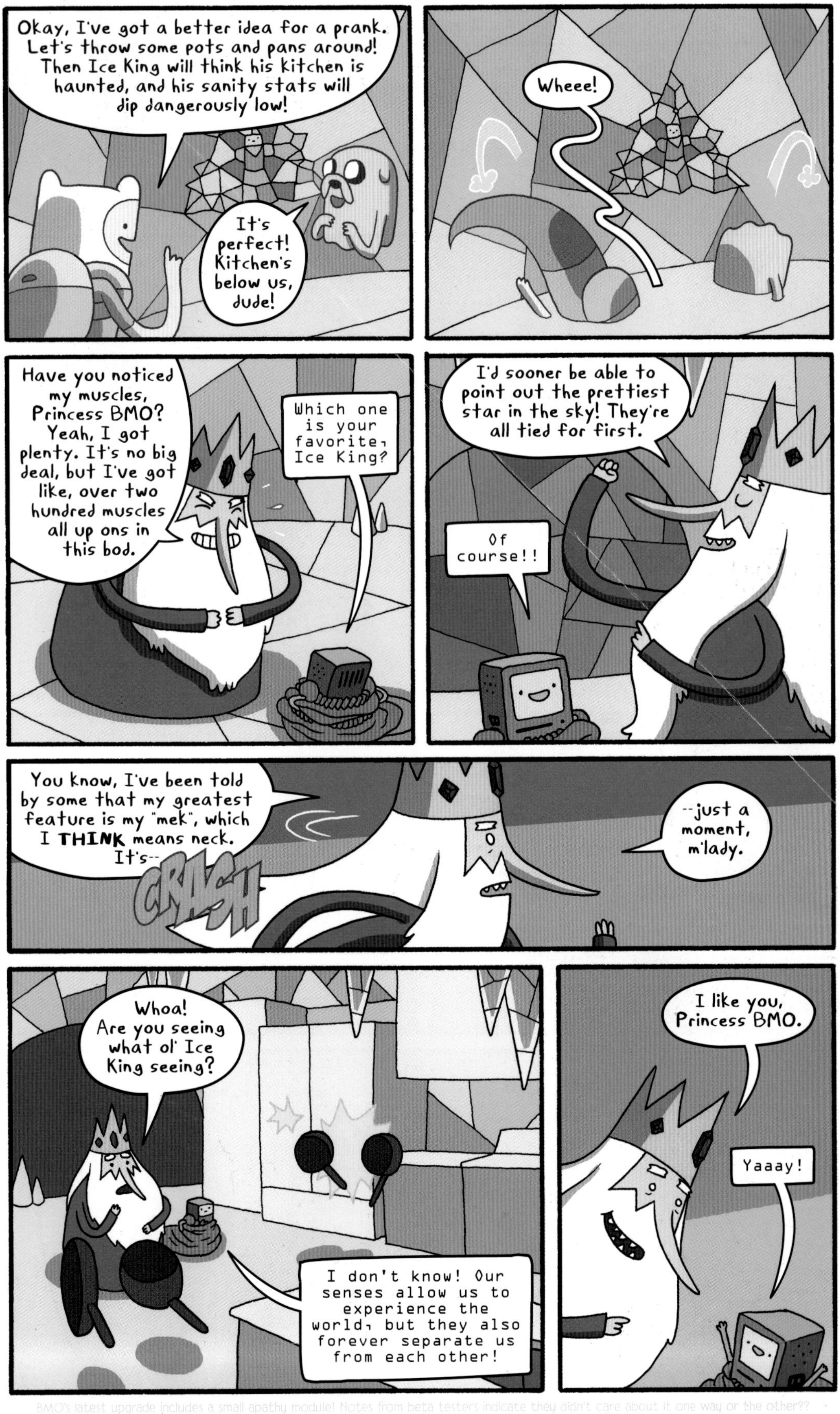
Okay, I've got a better idea for a prank. Let's throw some pots and pans around! Then Ice King will think his kitchen is haunted, and his sanity stats will dip dangerously low!
It's perfect! Kitchen's below us, dude!
Wheee!
Have you noticed my muscles, Princess BMO? Yeah, I got plenty. It's no big deal, but I've got like, over two hundred muscles all up ons in this bod.
Which one is your favorite, Ice King?
I'd sooner be able to point out the prettiest star in the sky! They're all tied for first.
Of course!!
You know, I've been told by some that my greatest feature is my "mek", which I **THINK** means neck. It's--
CRASH
--just a moment, m'lady.
Whoa! Are you seeing what ol' Ice King seeing?
I don't know! Our senses allow us to experience the world, but they also forever separate us from each other!
I like you, Princess BMO.
Yaaay!

BMO's latest upgrade includes a small apathy module! Notes from beta testers indicate they didn't care about it one way or the other??

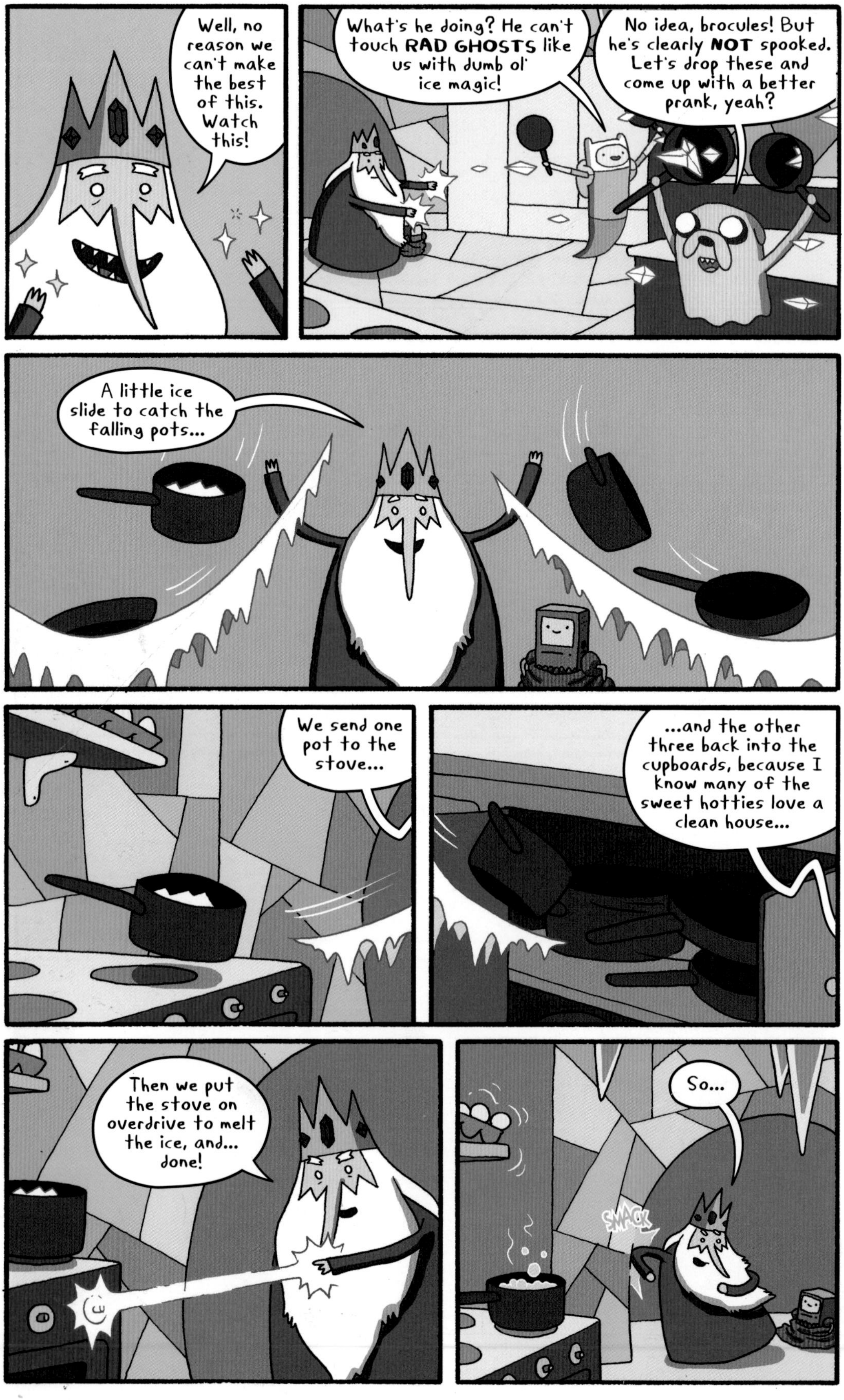
Well, no reason we can't make the best of this. Watch this!
What's he doing? He can't touch RAD GHOSTS like us with dumb ol' ice magic!
No idea, brocules! But he's clearly NOT spooked. Let's drop these and come up with a better prank, yeah?
A little ice slide to catch the falling pots...
We send one pot to the stove...
...and the other three back into the cupboards, because I know many of the sweet hotties love a clean house...
Then we put the stove on overdrive to melt the ice, and... done!
So...
SMACK

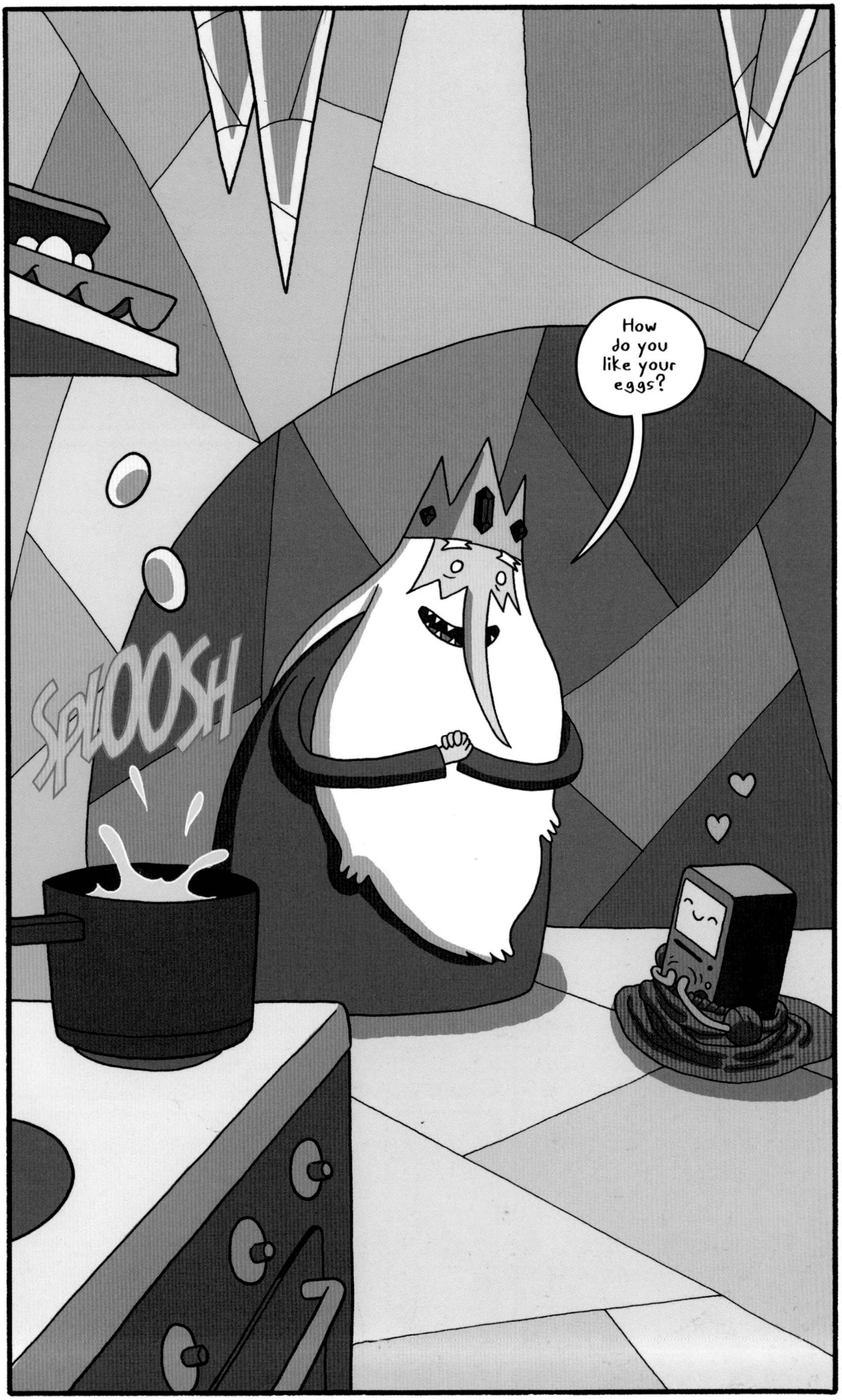
How do you like your eggs?
SPLOOSH

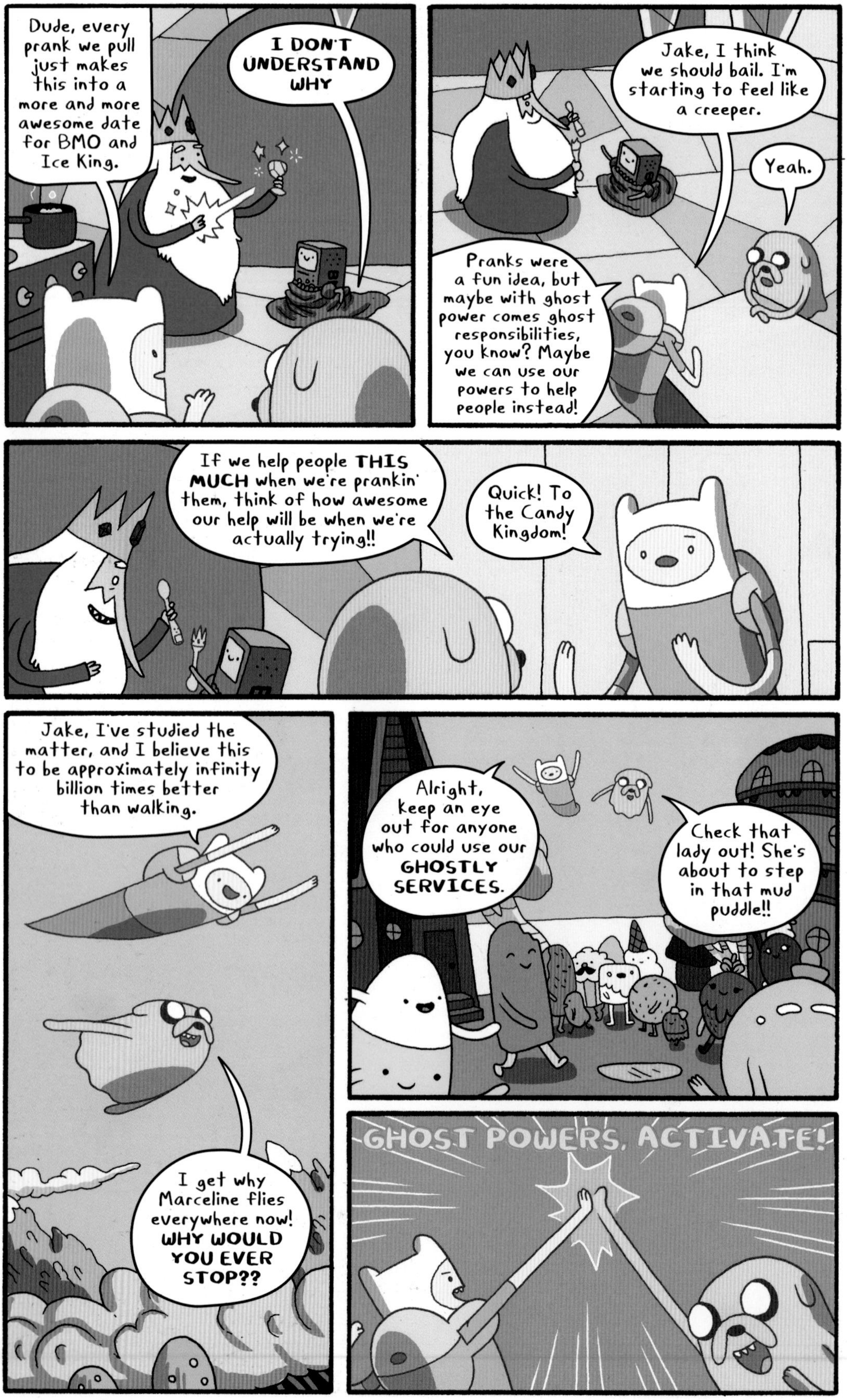
Dude, every prank we pull just makes this into a more and more awesome date for BMO and Ice King.
I DON'T UNDERSTAND WHY
Jake, I think we should bail. I'm starting to feel like a creeper.
Yeah.
Pranks were a fun idea, but maybe with ghost power comes ghost responsibilities, you know? Maybe we can use our powers to help people instead!
If we help people THIS MUCH when we're prankin' them, think of how awesome our help will be when we're actually trying!!
Quick! To the Candy Kingdom!
Jake, I've studied the matter, and I believe this to be approximately infinity billion times better than walking.
I get why Marceline flies everywhere now! WHY WOULD YOU EVER STOP??
Alright, keep an eye out for anyone who could use our GHOSTLY SERVICES.
Check that lady out! She's about to step in that mud puddle!!
GHOST POWERS, ACTIVATE!

Sorry I didn't put stuff here these last two pages! Ice King's smooth moves were working on me, too! I was too busy trying to date him to write anything!! :o

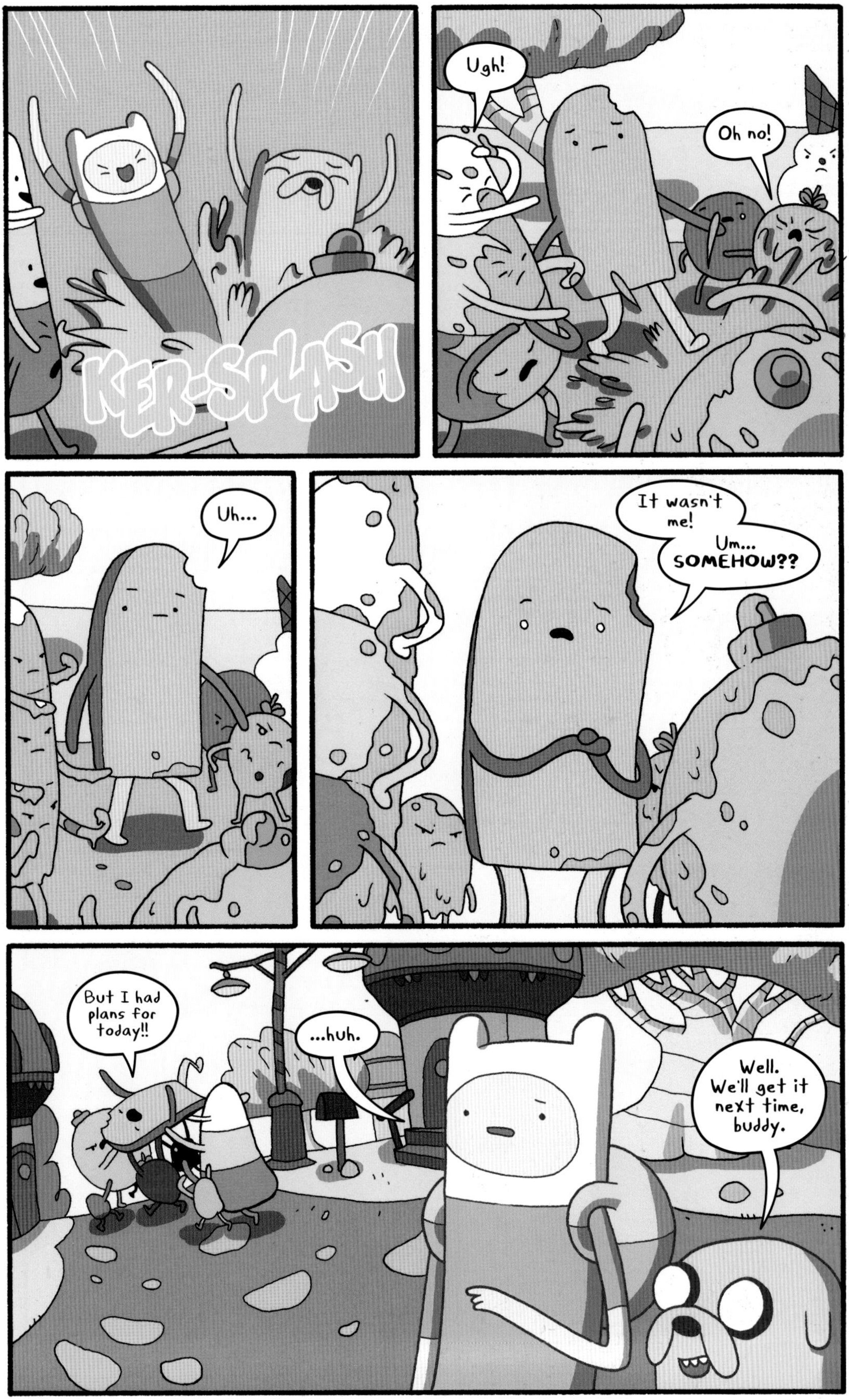
KER-SPLASH
Ugh!
Oh no!
Uh...
It wasn't me!
Um... SOMEHOW??
But I had plans for today!!
...huh.
Well. We'll get it next time, buddy.

Those plans did not involve getting carried over here by strangers! Obviously I am adapting my plans to include that now, but I'd really prefer if I didn't have to!

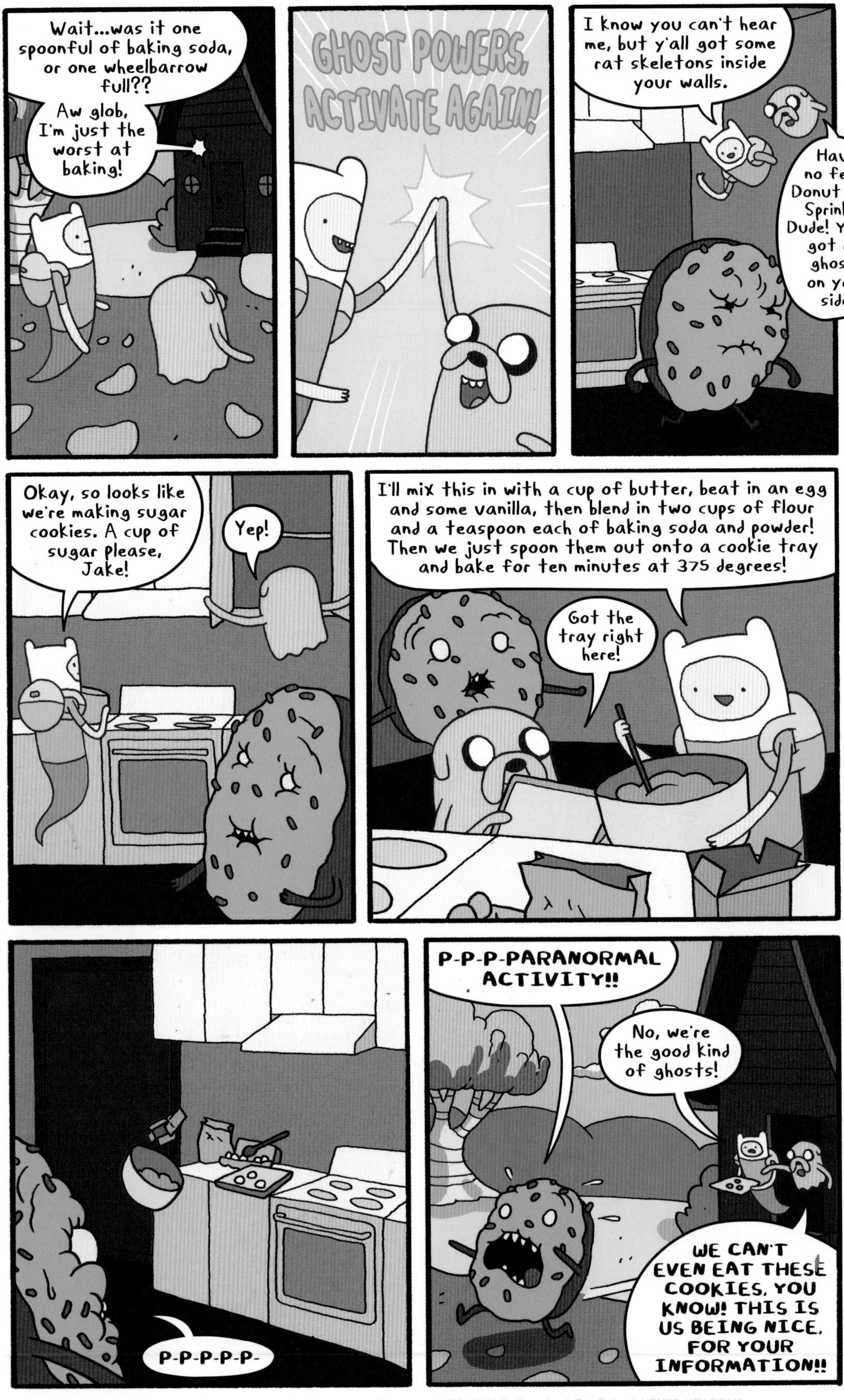
Wait...was it one spoonful of baking soda, or one wheelbarrow full??
Aw glob, I'm just the worst at baking!
GHOST POWERS, ACTIVATE AGAIN!
I know you can't hear me, but y'all got some rat skeletons inside your walls.
Have no fear, Donut With Sprinkles Dude! You've got rad ghosts on your side!
Okay, so looks like we're making sugar cookies. A cup of sugar please, Jake!
Yep!
I'll mix this in with a cup of butter, beat in an egg and some vanilla, then blend in two cups of flour and a teaspoon each of baking soda and powder! Then we just spoon them out onto a cookie tray and bake for ten minutes at 375 degrees!
Got the tray right here!
P-P-P-P-P-
P-P-P-PARANORMAL ACTIVITY!!
No, we're the good kind of ghosts!
WE CAN'T EVEN EAT THESE COOKIES, YOU KNOW! THIS IS US BEING NICE, FOR YOUR INFORMATION!!

That's right. I had Candy Dude all set up to say "Paranormal SNACKtivity", and yet I refrained. YOU'RE WELCOME.

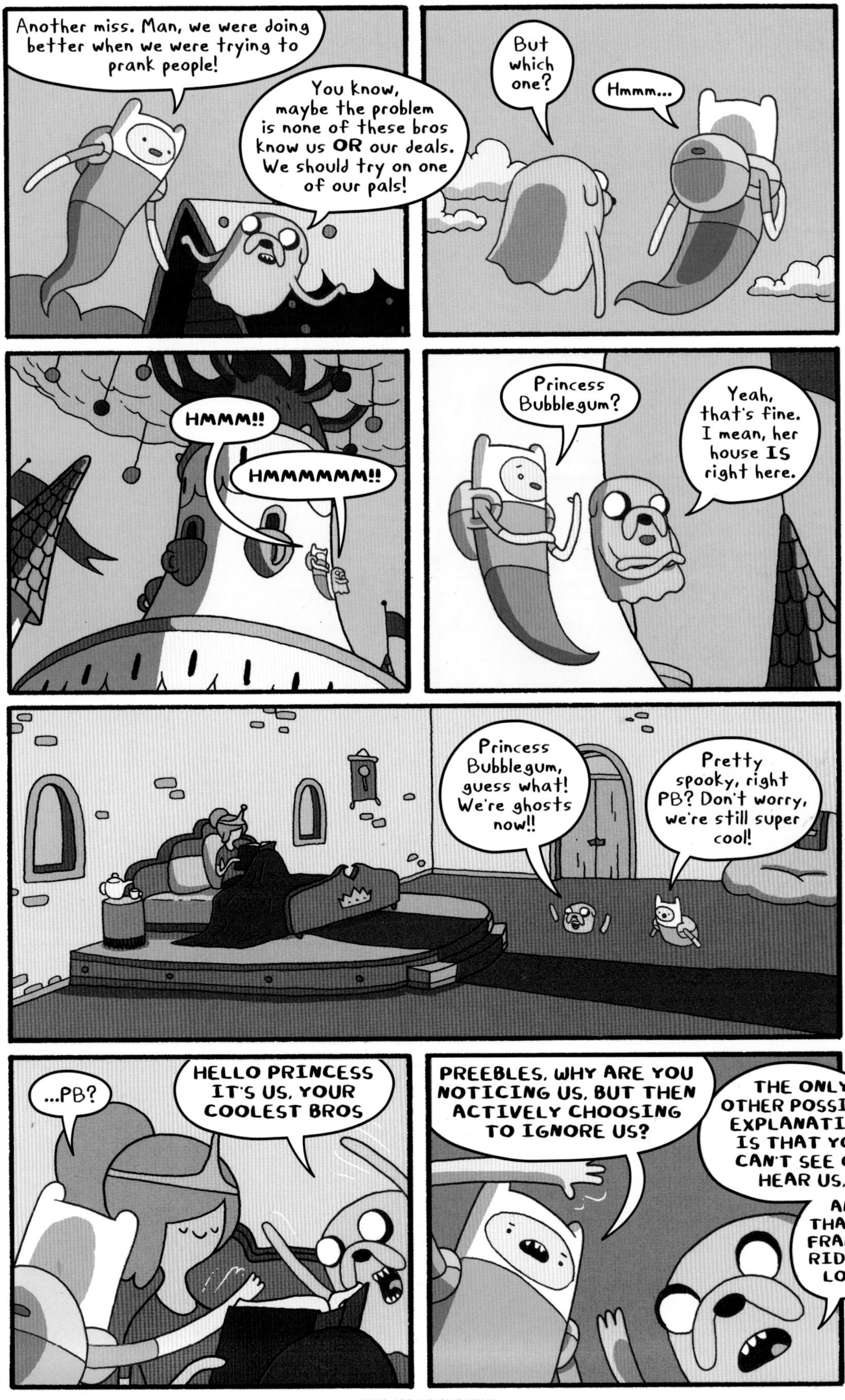
Another miss. Man, we were doing better when we were trying to prank people!
You know, maybe the problem is none of these bros know us **OR** our deals. We should try on one of our pals!
But which one?
Hmmm...
HMMM!!
HMMMMMM!!
Princess Bubblegum?
Yeah, that's fine. I mean, her house **IS** right here.
Princess Bubblegum, guess what! We're ghosts now!!
Pretty spooky, right PB? Don't worry, we're still super cool!
...PB?
HELLO PRINCESS IT'S US, YOUR COOLEST BROS
PREEBLES, WHY ARE YOU NOTICING US, BUT THEN ACTIVELY CHOOSING TO IGNORE US?
THE ONLY OTHER POSSIBLE EXPLANATION IS THAT YOU CAN'T SEE OR HEAR US,
AND THAT IS FRANKLY RIDICU-LOUS.

WHY ARE WE SHOUTING

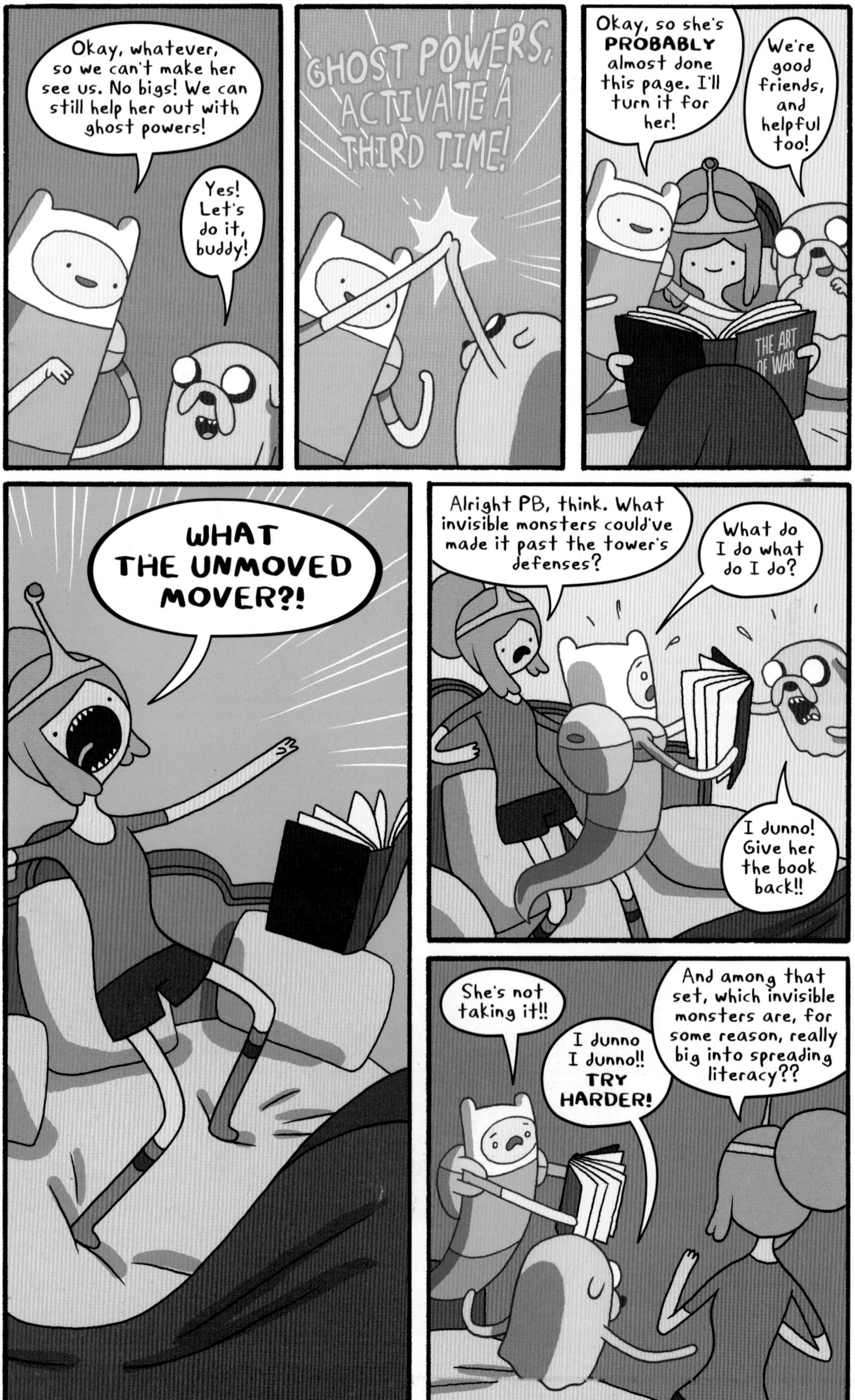
Okay, whatever, so we can't make her see us. No bigs! We can still help her out with ghost powers!
Yes! Let's do it, buddy!
GHOST POWERS, ACTIVATE A THIRD TIME!
Okay, so she's **PROBABLY** almost done this page. I'll turn it for her!
We're good friends, and helpful too!
THE ART OF WAR
WHAT THE UNMOVED MOVER?!
Alright PB, think. What invisible monsters could've made it past the tower's defenses?
What do I do what do I do?
I dunno! Give her the book back!!
She's not taking it!!
I dunno I dunno!! TRY HARDER!
And among that set, which invisible monsters are, for some reason, really big into spreading literacy??

I guess the first thing people notice about me is how I live in a haunted house where ghosts will encourage you to read and expand your horizons

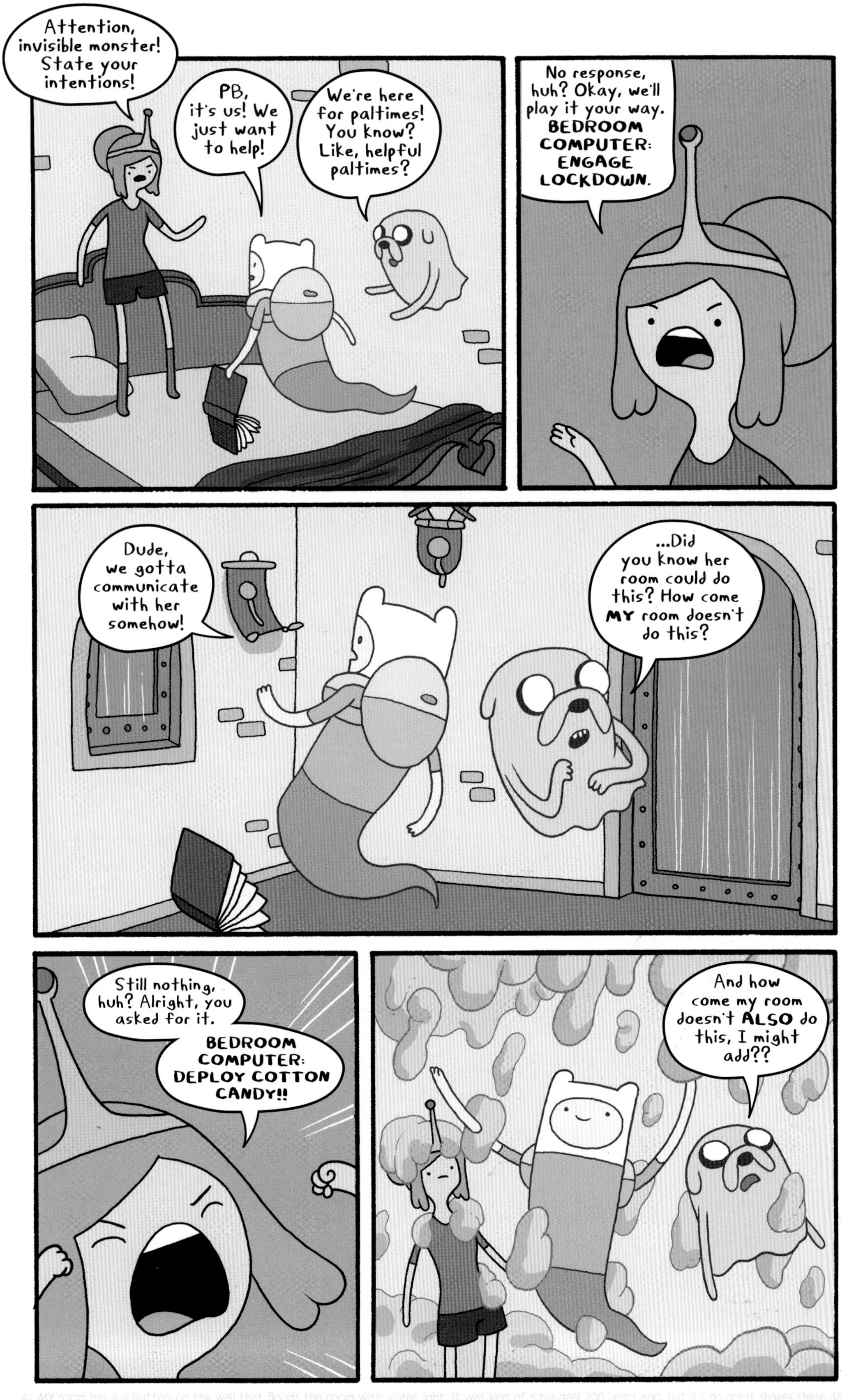

Attention, invisible monster! State your intentions!
PB, it's us! We just want to help!
We're here for paltimes! You know? Like, helpful paltimes?
No response, huh? Okay, we'll play it your way. **BEDROOM COMPUTER: ENGAGE LOCKDOWN.**
Dude, we gotta communicate with her somehow!
...Did you know her room could do this? How come **MY** room doesn't do this?
Still nothing, huh? Alright, you asked for it.
BEDROOM COMPUTER: DEPLOY COTTON CANDY!!
And how come my room doesn't **ALSO** do this, I might add??

All *MY* room has is a button on the wall that floods the room with visible light. It was kind of a big deal 200 years ago, but it's no great shakes these days.

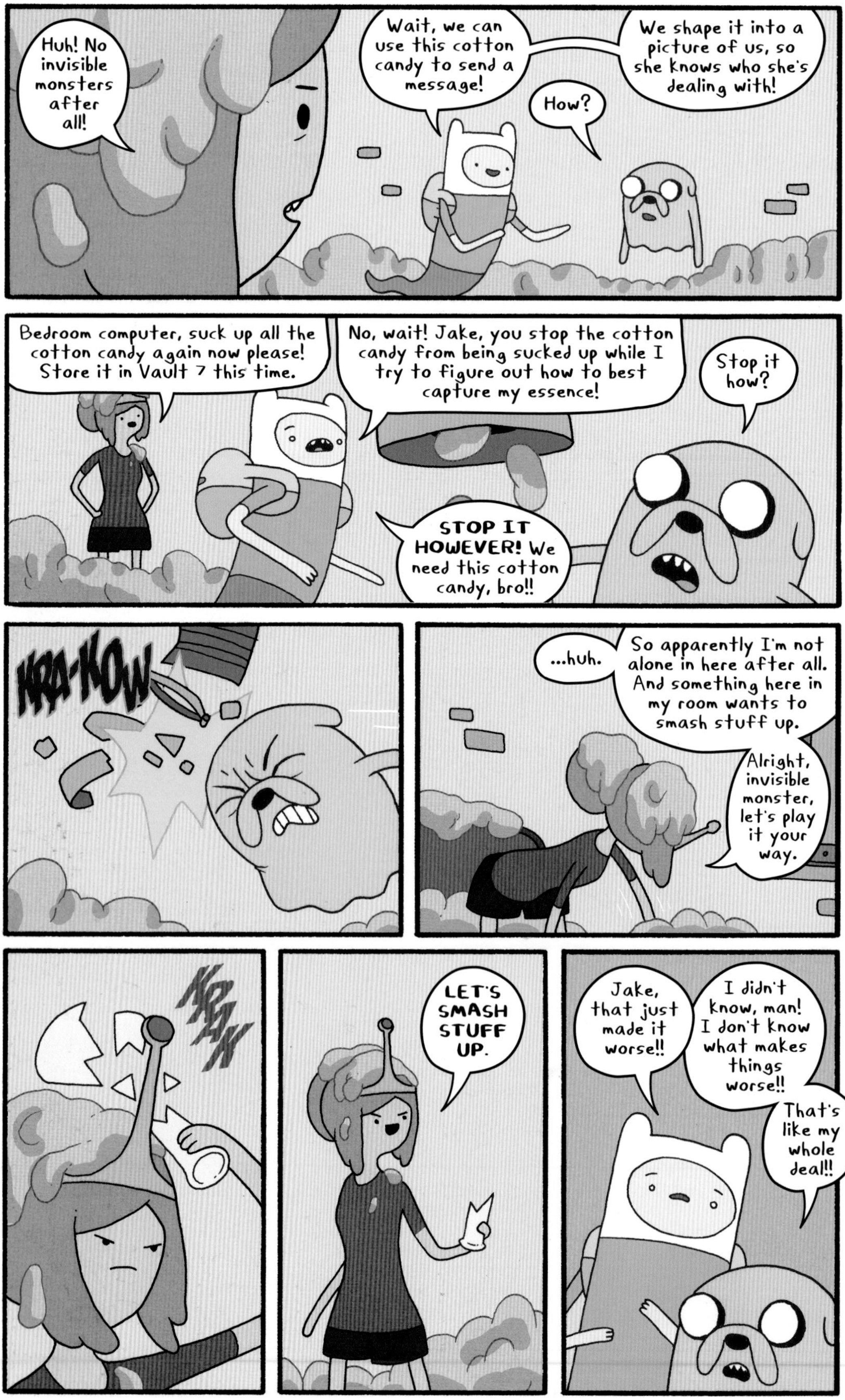
Huh! No invisible monsters after all!
Wait, we can use this cotton candy to send a message!
How?
We shape it into a picture of us, so she knows who she's dealing with!
Bedroom computer, suck up all the cotton candy again now please! Store it in Vault 7 this time.
No, wait! Jake, you stop the cotton candy from being sucked up while I try to figure out how to best capture my essence!
Stop it how?
STOP IT HOWEVER! We need this cotton candy, bro!!
KRA-KOW
...huh.
So apparently I'm not alone in here after all. And something here in my room wants to smash stuff up.
Alright, invisible monster, let's play it your way.
KRAK
LET'S SMASH STUFF UP.
Jake, that just made it worse!!
I didn't know, man! I don't know what makes things worse!!
That's like my whole deal!!

You wanna get crazy in here? Let's get crazy in here. All we need... is some *Bubblegum*.

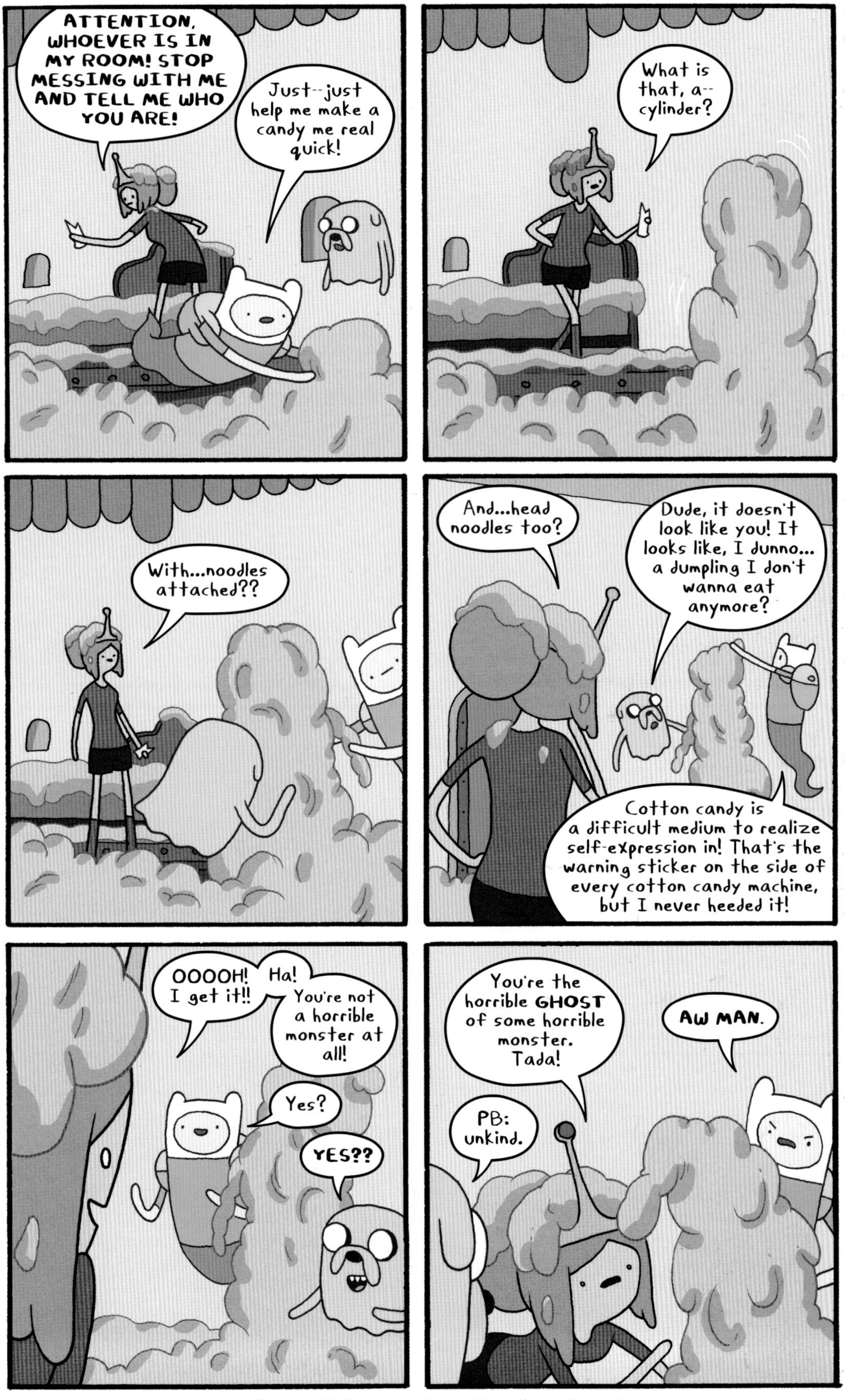
ATTENTION, WHOEVER IS IN MY ROOM! STOP MESSING WITH ME AND TELL ME WHO YOU ARE!
Just--just help me make a candy me real quick!
What is that, a--cylinder?
With...noodles attached??
And...head noodles too?
Dude, it doesn't look like you! It looks like, I dunno... a dumpling I don't wanna eat anymore?
Cotton candy is a difficult medium to realize self-expression in! That's the warning sticker on the side of every cotton candy machine, but I never heeded it!
OOOOH! I get it!!
Ha! You're not a horrible monster at all!
Yes?
YES??
You're the horrible GHOST of some horrible monster. Tada!
AW MAN.
PB: unkind.

You're the ghost with the most... success at interrupting my day recently

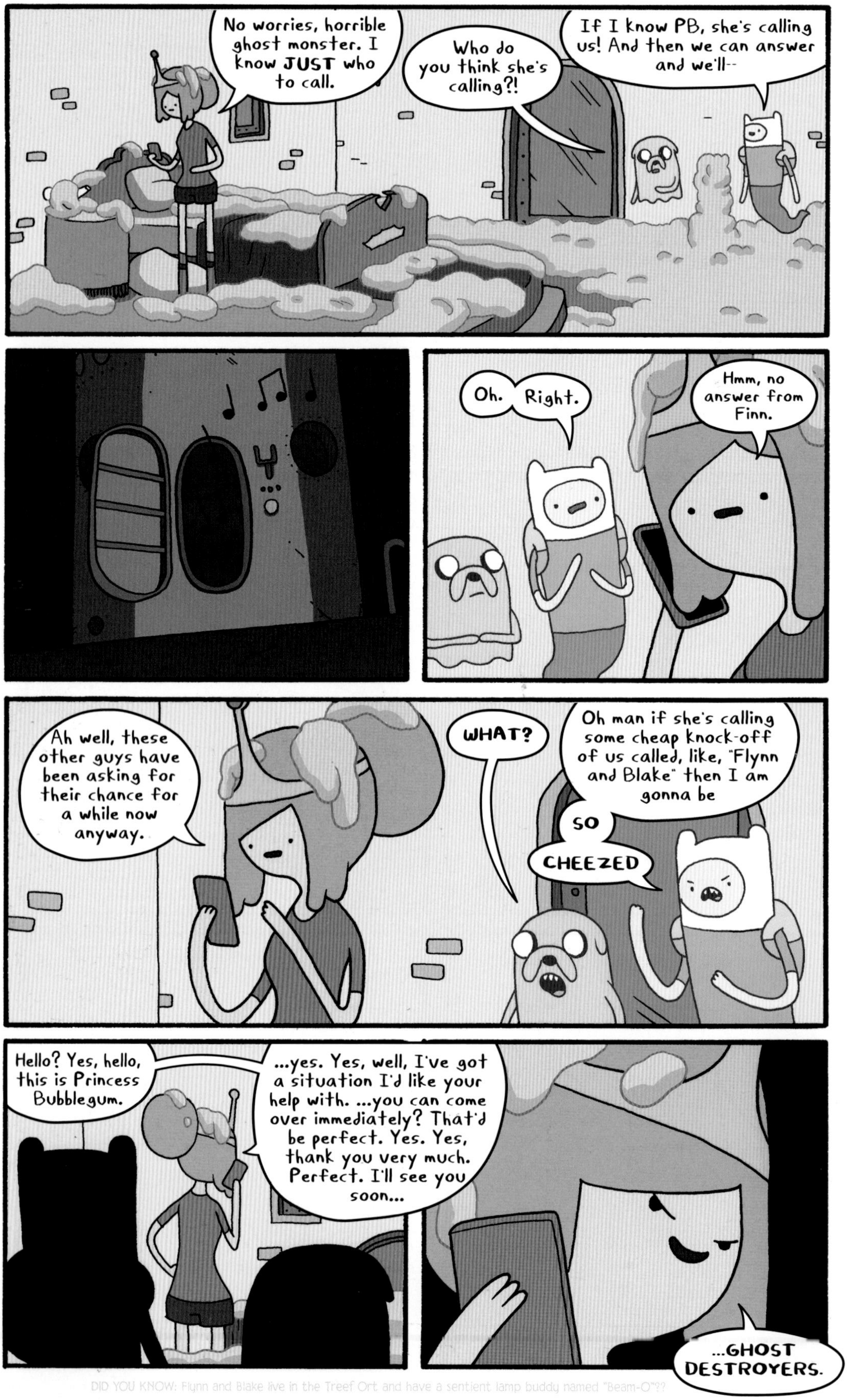
No worries, horrible ghost monster. I know **JUST** who to call.
Who do you think she's calling?!
If I know PB, she's calling us! And then we can answer and we'll--
Oh.
Right.
Hmm, no answer from Finn.
Ah well, these other guys have been asking for their chance for a while now anyway.
WHAT?
Oh man if she's calling some cheap knock-off of us called, like, "Flynn and Blake" then I am gonna be
SO
CHEEZED
Hello? Yes, hello, this is Princess Bubblegum.
...yes. Yes, well, I've got a situation I'd like your help with. ...you can come over immediately? That'd be perfect. Yes. Yes, thank you very much. Perfect. I'll see you soon...
...GHOST DESTROYERS.

DID YOU KNOW: Flynn and Blake live in the Treef Ort and have a sentient lamp buddy named "Beam-O"??

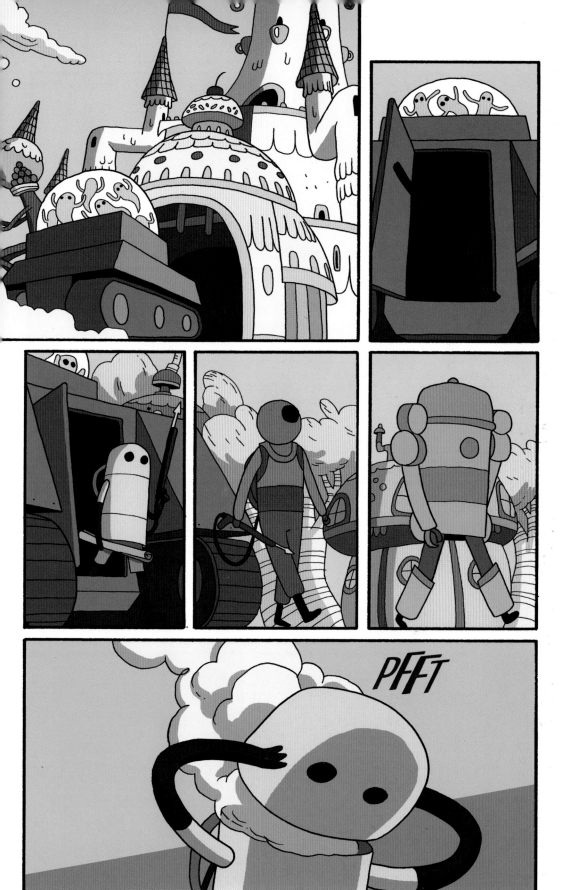

PFFT

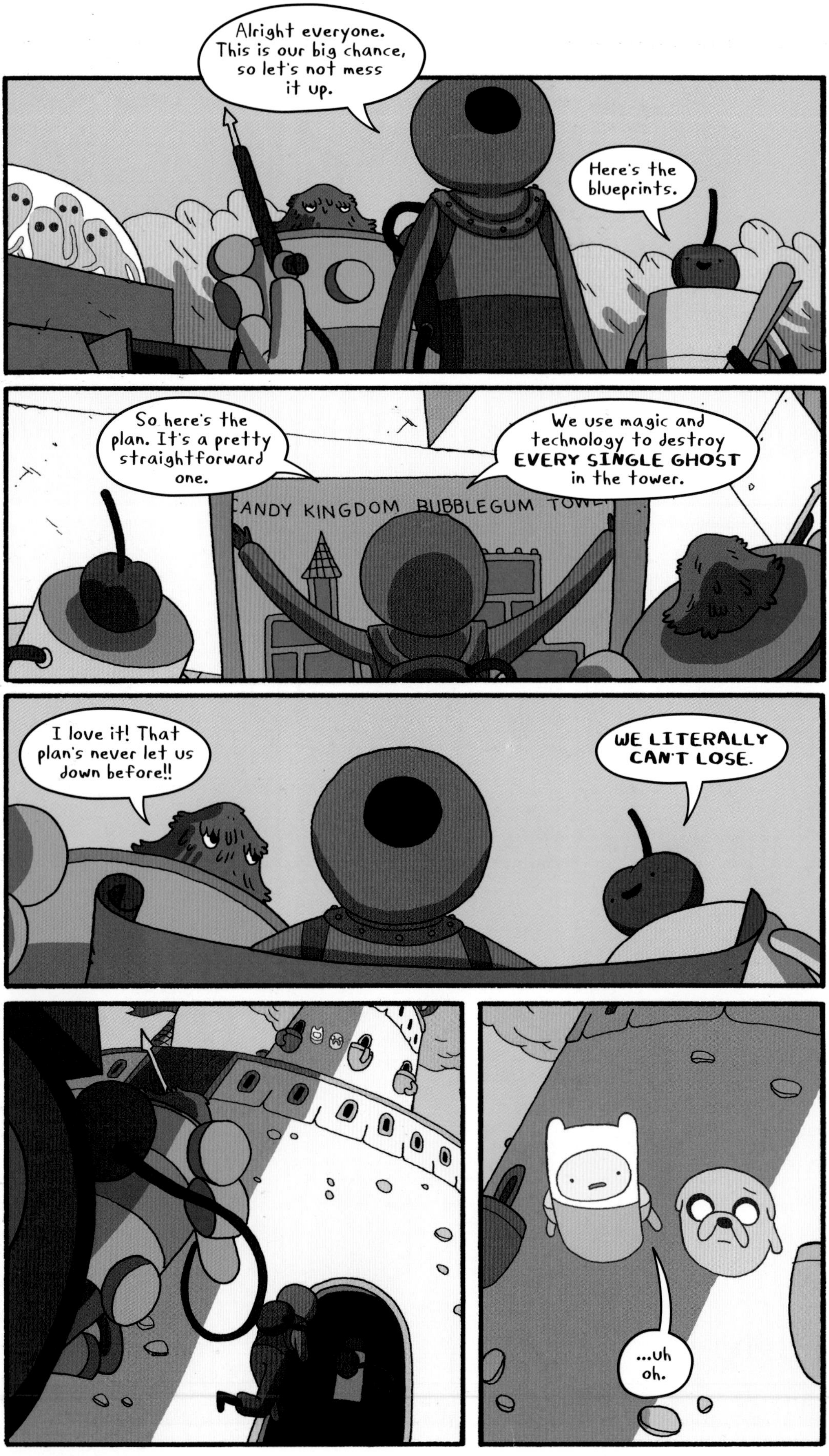

Alright everyone. This is our big chance, so let's not mess it up.
Here's the blueprints.
So here's the plan. It's a pretty straightforward one.
We use magic and technology to destroy **EVERY SINGLE GHOST** in the tower.
I love it! That plan's never let us down before!!
WE LITERALLY CAN'T LOSE.
...uh oh.

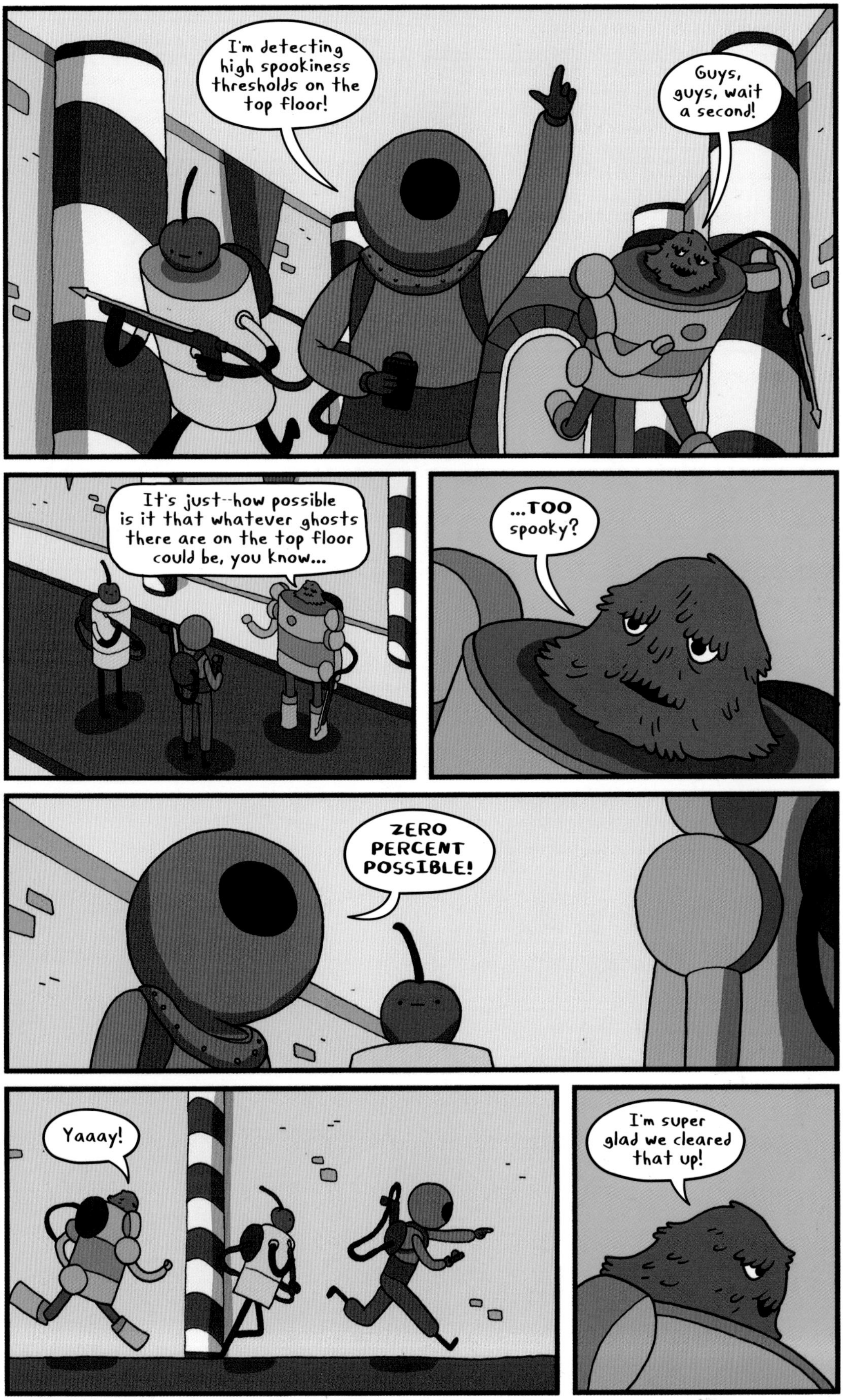

I'm detecting high spookiness thresholds on the top floor!
Guys, guys, wait a second!
It's just--how possible is it that whatever ghosts there are on the top floor could be, you know...
...TOO spooky?
ZERO PERCENT POSSIBLE!
Yaaay!
I'm super glad we cleared that up!

This page merely serves to lull the reader into a false sense of security regarding spookiness levels. Who knows how spooky the following pages will be?? I MEAN, I DO, BUT I'M NOT TELLING

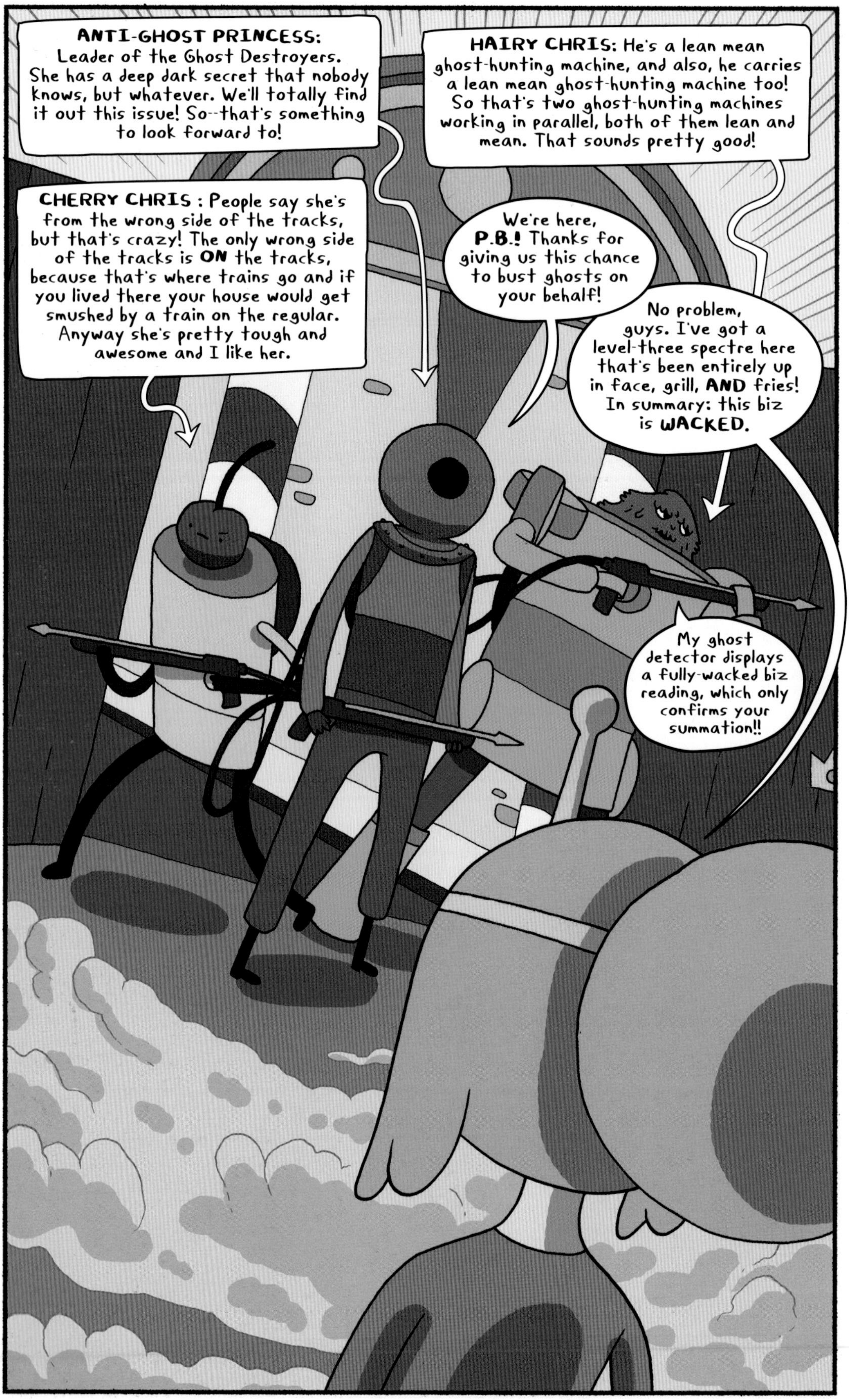
ANTI-GHOST PRINCESS: Leader of the Ghost Destroyers. She has a deep dark secret that nobody knows, but whatever. We'll totally find it out this issue! So--that's something to look forward to!
HAIRY CHRIS: He's a lean mean ghost-hunting machine, and also, he carries a lean mean ghost-hunting machine too! So that's two ghost-hunting machines working in parallel, both of them lean and mean. That sounds pretty good!
CHERRY CHRIS : People say she's from the wrong side of the tracks, but that's crazy! The only wrong side of the tracks is ON the tracks, because that's where trains go and if you lived there your house would get smushed by a train on the regular. Anyway she's pretty tough and awesome and I like her.
We're here, P.B.! Thanks for giving us this chance to bust ghosts on your behalf!
No problem, guys. I've got a level-three spectre here that's been entirely up in face, grill, AND fries! In summary: this biz is WACKED.
My ghost detector displays a fully-wacked biz reading, which only confirms your summation!!

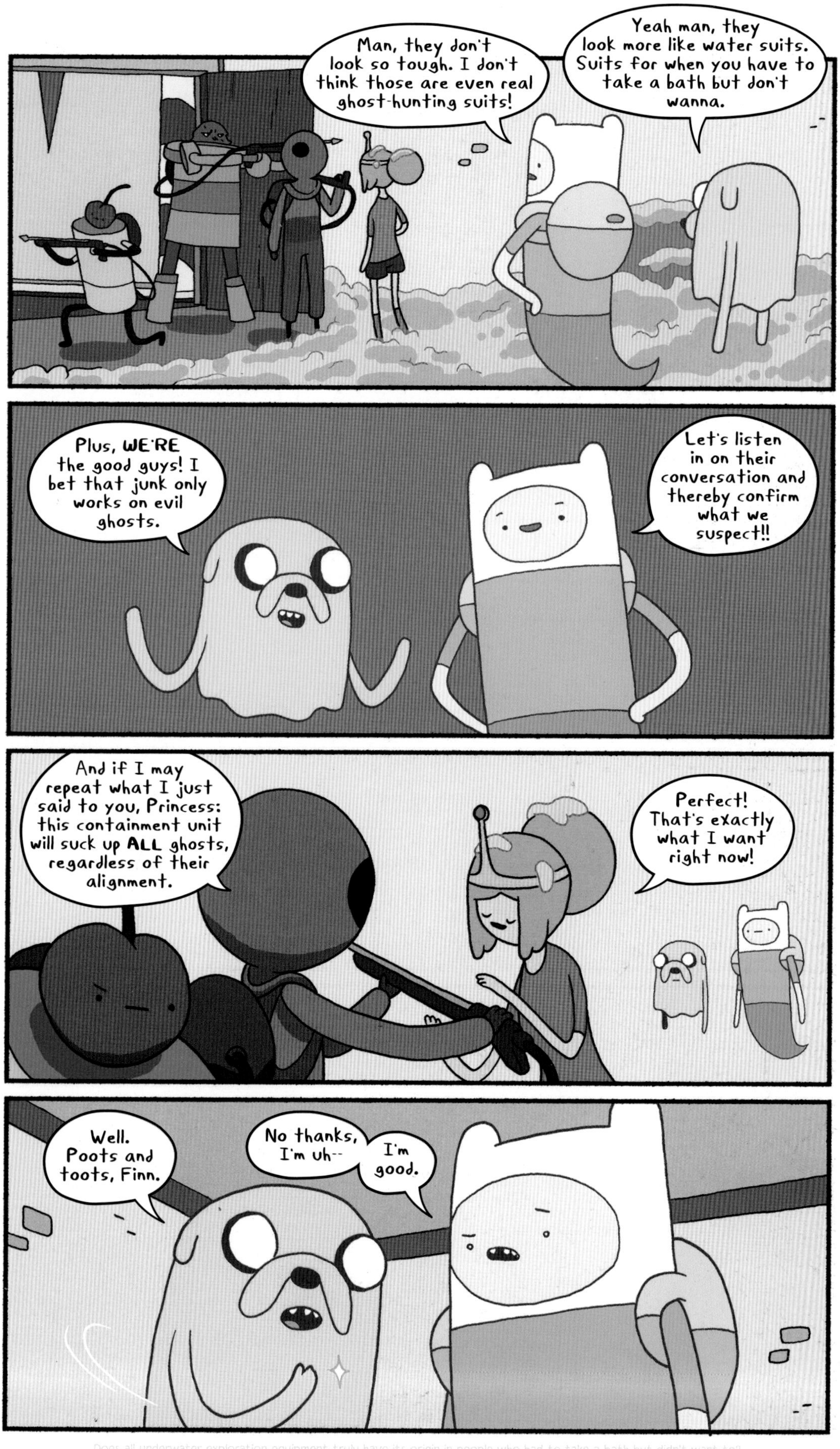
Man, they don't look so tough. I don't think those are even real ghost-hunting suits!
Yeah man, they look more like water suits. Suits for when you have to take a bath but don't wanna.
Plus, WE'RE the good guys! I bet that junk only works on evil ghosts.
Let's listen in on their conversation and thereby confirm what we suspect!!
And if I may repeat what I just said to you, Princess: this containment unit will suck up ALL ghosts, regardless of their alignment.
Perfect! That's exactly what I want right now!
Well. Poots and toots, Finn.
No thanks, I'm uh--
I'm good.

Does all underwater exploration equipment truly have its origin in people who had to take a bath but didn't want to?
Well I looked it up, and the encyclopedia didn't explicitly state the idea was wrong!!

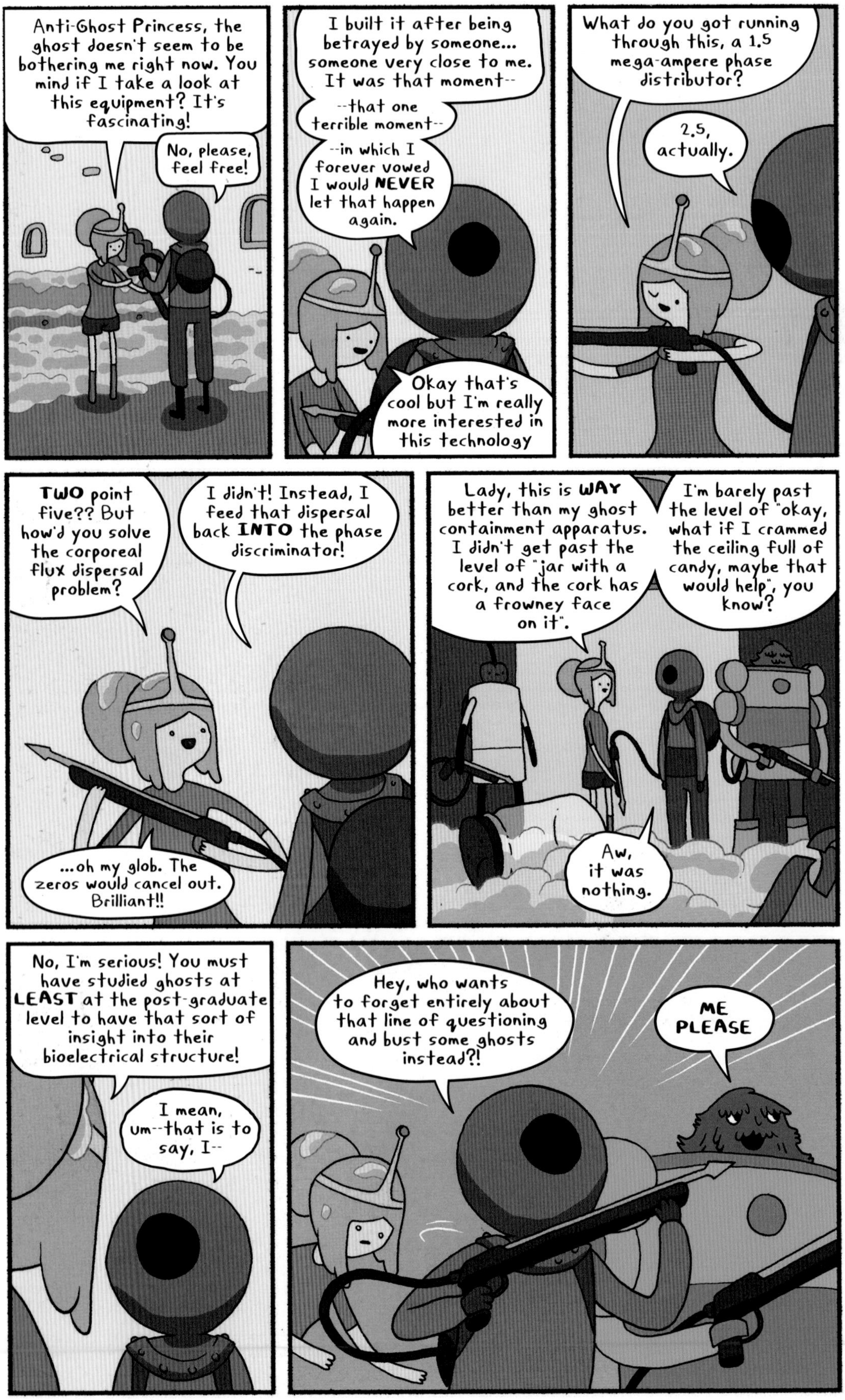

Anti-Ghost Princess, the ghost doesn't seem to be bothering me right now. You mind if I take a look at this equipment? It's fascinating!
No, please, feel free!
I built it after being betrayed by someone... someone very close to me. It was that moment--
--that one terrible moment--
--in which I forever vowed I would NEVER let that happen again.
Okay that's cool but I'm really more interested in this technology
What do you got running through this, a 1.5 mega-ampere phase distributor?
2.5, actually.
TWO point five?? But how'd you solve the corporeal flux dispersal problem?
I didn't! Instead, I feed that dispersal back INTO the phase discriminator!
...oh my glob. The zeros would cancel out. Brilliant!!
Lady, this is WAY better than my ghost containment apparatus. I didn't get past the level of "jar with a cork, and the cork has a frowney face on it".
I'm barely past the level of "okay, what if I crammed the ceiling full of candy, maybe that would help", you know?
Aw, it was nothing.
No, I'm serious! You must have studied ghosts at LEAST at the post-graduate level to have that sort of insight into their bioelectrical structure!
I mean, um--that is to say, I--
Hey, who wants to forget entirely about that line of questioning and bust some ghosts instead?!
ME PLEASE

2.5 mega-ampere is a lot of mega-amperes. And it's like, 2500000 regular-amperes!

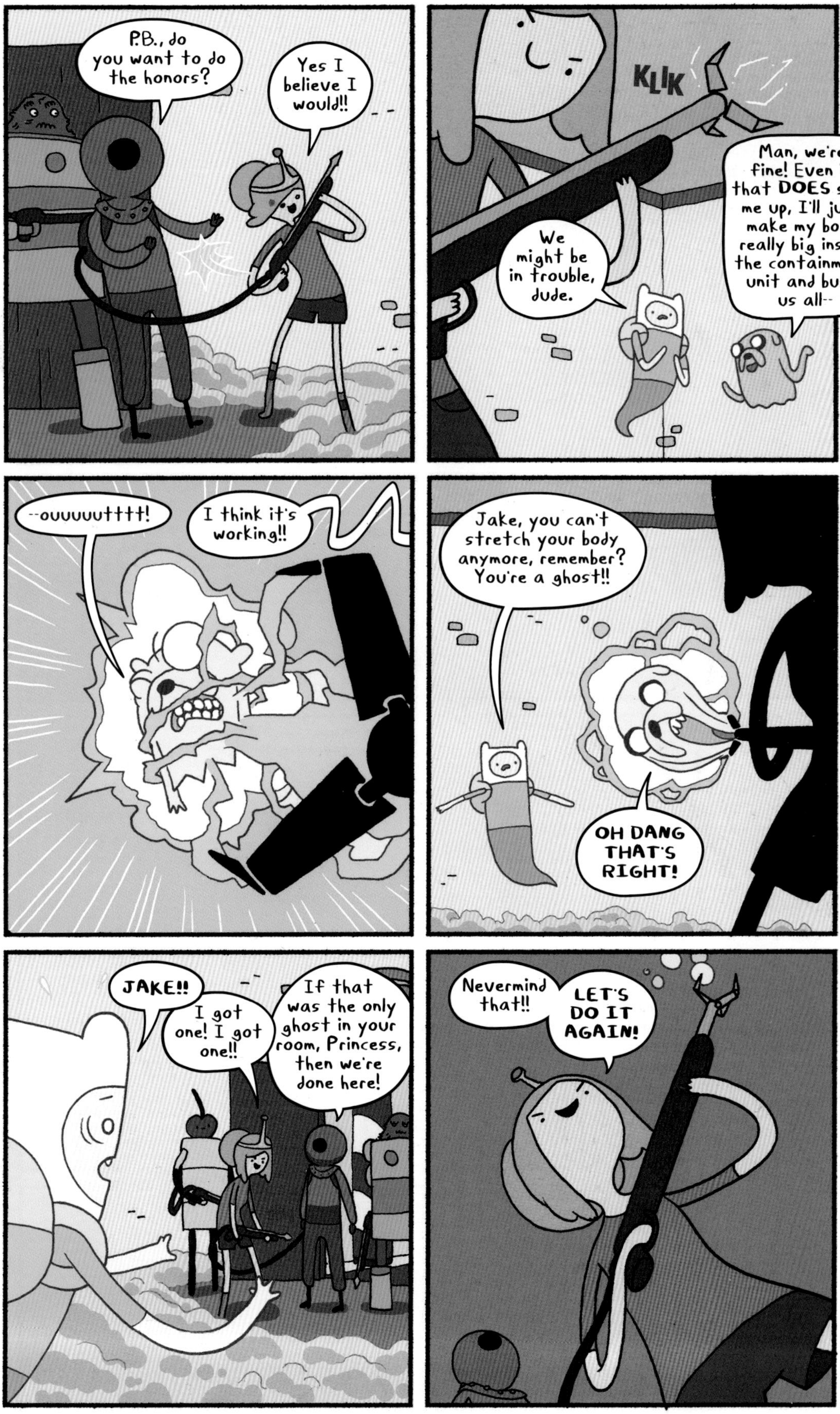
P.B., do you want to do the honors?
Yes I believe I would!!
KLIK
We might be in trouble, dude.
Man, we're fine! Even if that DOES suck me up, I'll just make my body really big inside the containment unit and bust us all--
--ouuuuutttt!
I think it's working!!
Jake, you can't stretch your body anymore, remember? You're a ghost!!
OH DANG THAT'S RIGHT!
JAKE!!
I got one! I got one!!
If that was the only ghost in your room, Princess, then we're done here!
Nevermind that!!
LET'S DO IT AGAIN!

Pfft. Changing your form without a magical body? That's a stretch.

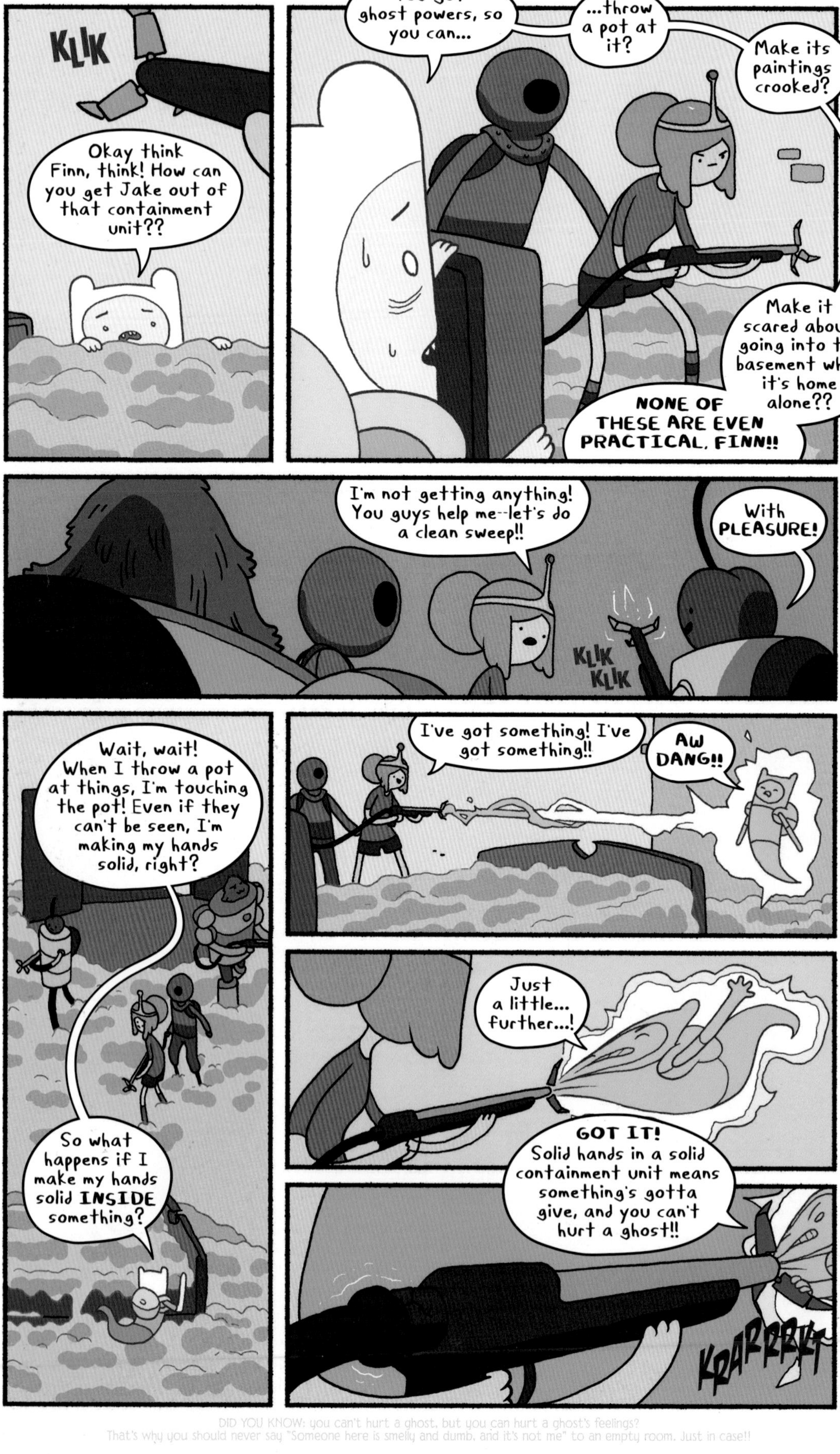
KLIK
Okay think Finn, think! How can you get Jake out of that containment unit??
You got ghost powers, so you can...
...throw a pot at it?
Make its paintings crooked?
Make it scared about going into the basement when it's home alone??
NONE OF THESE ARE EVEN PRACTICAL, FINN!!
I'm not getting anything! You guys help me--let's do a clean sweep!!
With PLEASURE!
KLIK KLIK
Wait, wait! When I throw a pot at things, I'm touching the pot! Even if they can't be seen, I'm making my hands solid, right?
So what happens if I make my hands solid INSIDE something?
I've got something! I've got something!!
AW DANG!!
Just a little... further...!
GOT IT! Solid hands in a solid containment unit means something's gotta give, and you can't hurt a ghost!!
KRARRRKT

DID YOU KNOW: you can't hurt a ghost, but you can hurt a ghost's feelings?
That's why you should never say "Someone here is smelly and dumb, and it's not me" to an empty room. Just in case!!

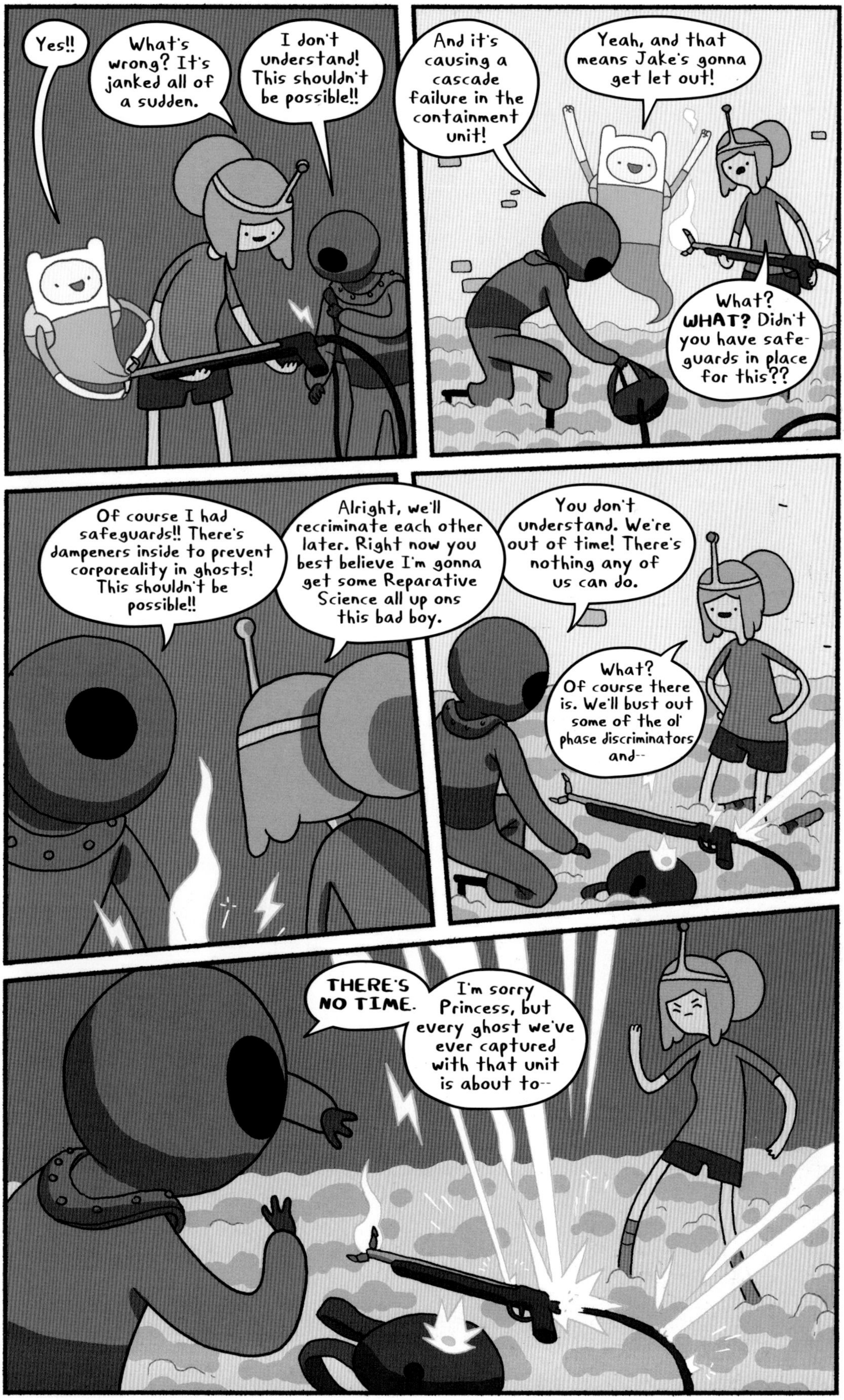
Yes!!
What's wrong? It's janked all of a sudden.
I don't understand! This shouldn't be possible!!
And it's causing a cascade failure in the containment unit!
Yeah, and that means Jake's gonna get let out!
What? WHAT? Didn't you have safe-guards in place for this??
Of course I had safeguards!! There's dampeners inside to prevent corporeality in ghosts! This shouldn't be possible!!
Alright, we'll recriminate each other later. Right now you best believe I'm gonna get some Reparative Science all up ons this bad boy.
You don't understand. We're out of time! There's nothing any of us can do.
What? Of course there is. We'll bust out some of the ol' phase discriminators and--
THERE'S NO TIME.
I'm sorry Princess, but every ghost we've ever captured with that unit is about to--

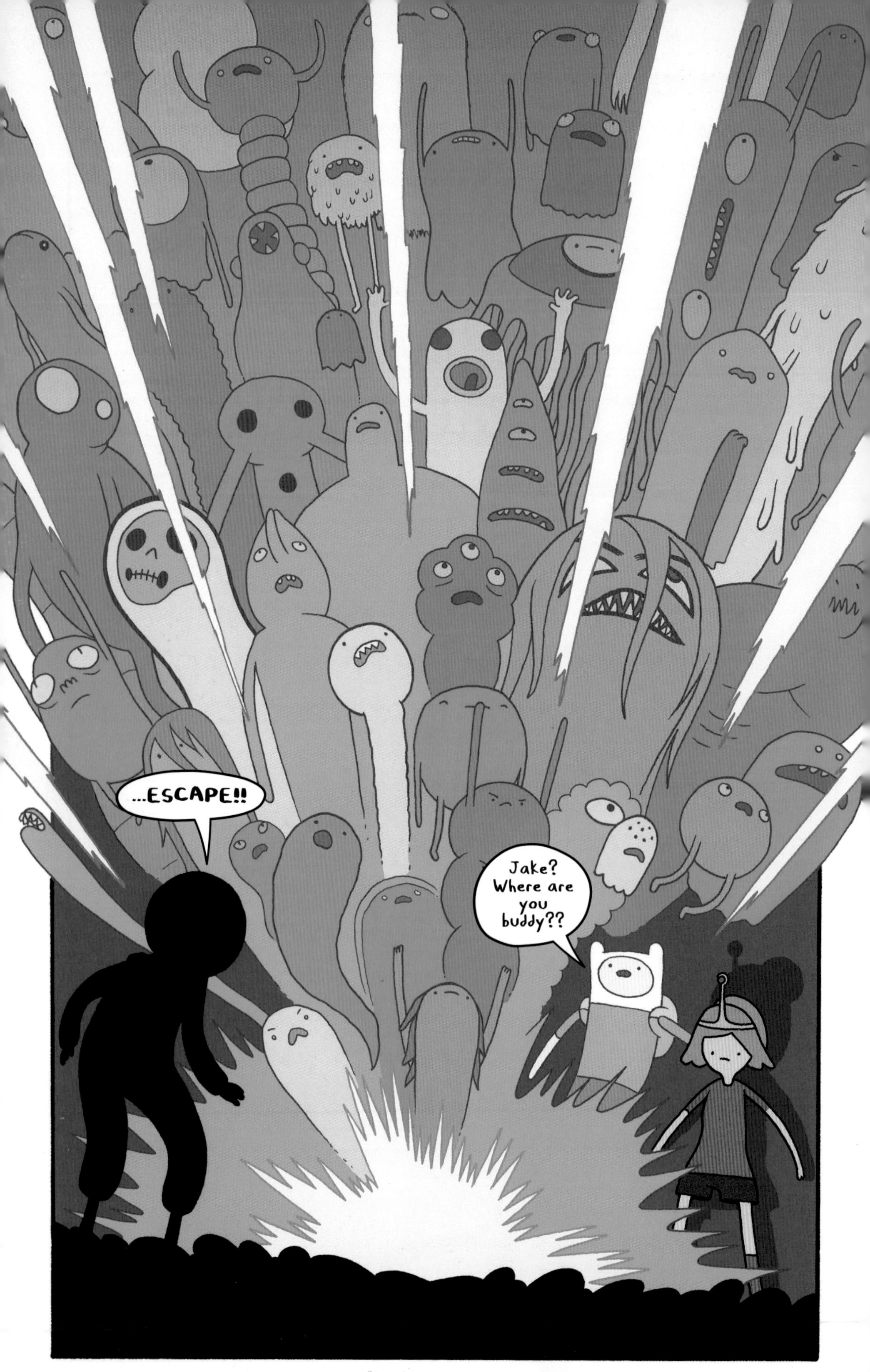

...ESCAPE!!
Jake? Where are you buddy??

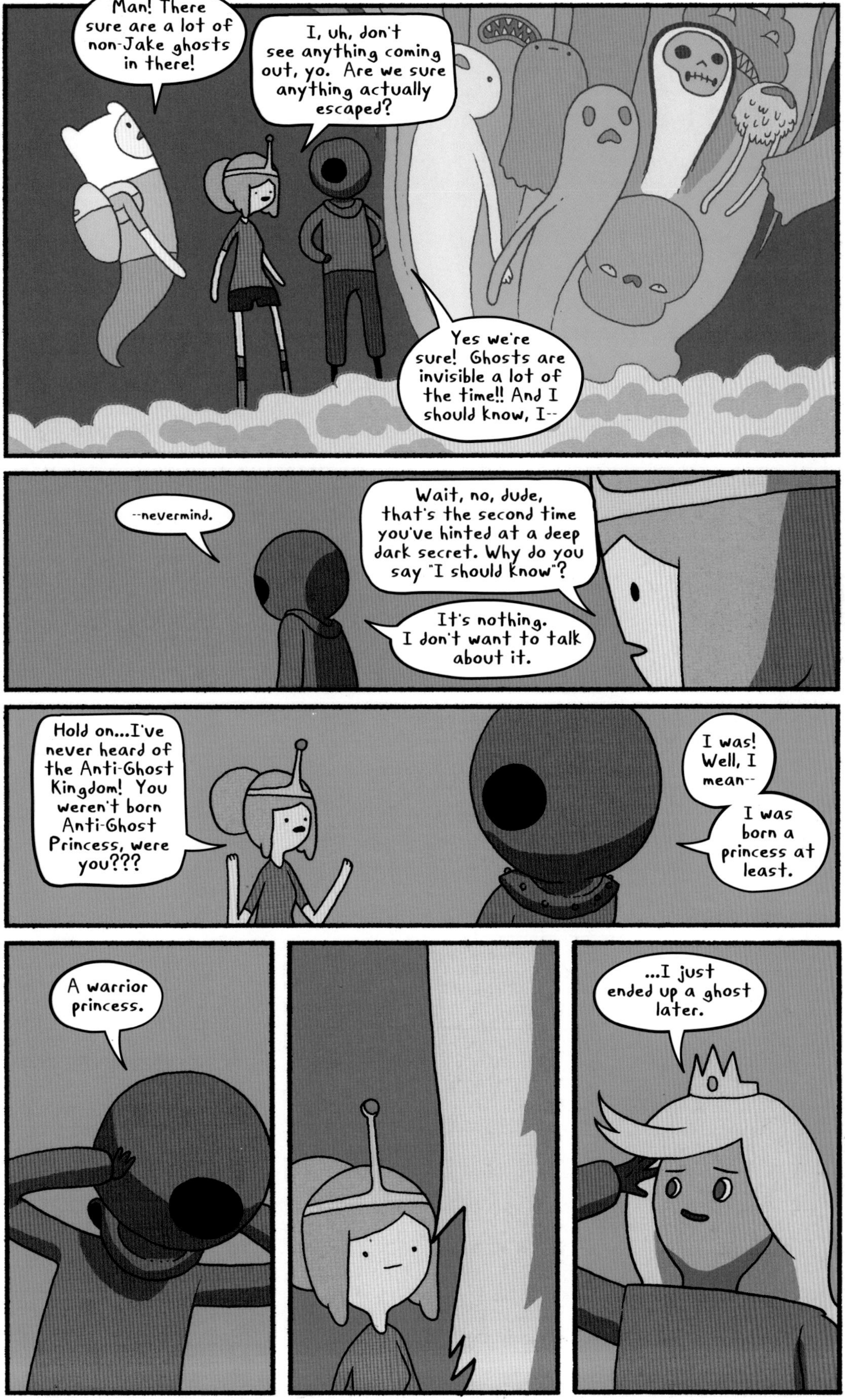

Man! There sure are a lot of non-Jake ghosts in there!
I, uh, don't see anything coming out, yo. Are we sure anything actually escaped?
Yes we're sure! Ghosts are invisible a lot of the time!! And I should know, I--
--nevermind.
Wait, no, dude, that's the second time you've hinted at a deep dark secret. Why do you say "I should know"?
It's nothing. I don't want to talk about it.
Hold on...I've never heard of the Anti-Ghost Kingdom! You weren't born Anti-Ghost Princess, were you???
I was! Well, I mean--
I was born a princess at least.
A warrior princess.
...I just ended up a ghost later.

I say, could this conversation be illustrated somehow??

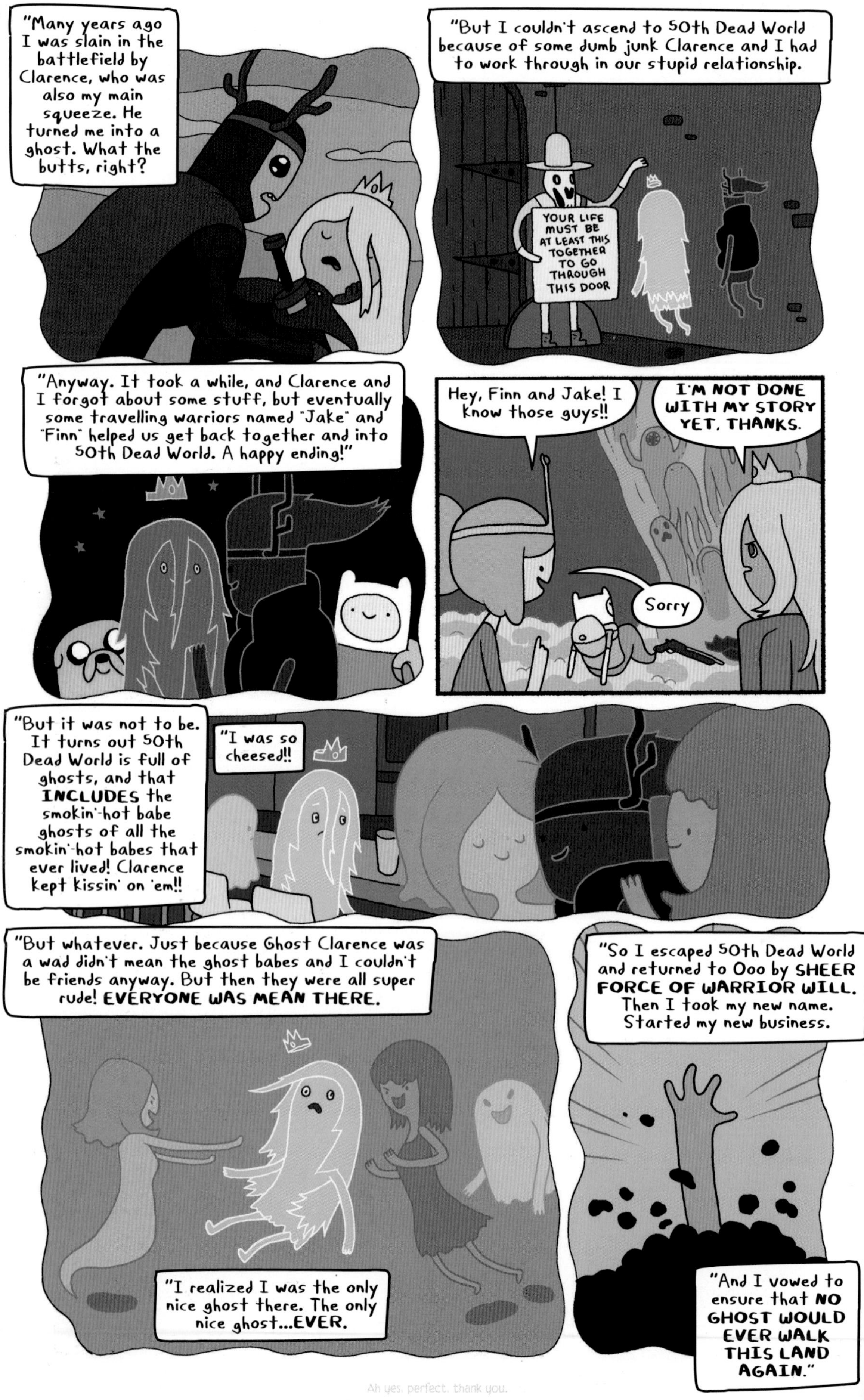
"Many years ago I was slain in the battlefield by Clarence, who was also my main squeeze. He turned me into a ghost. What the butts, right?
"But I couldn't ascend to 50th Dead World because of some dumb junk Clarence and I had to work through in our stupid relationship.
YOUR LIFE MUST BE AT LEAST THIS TOGETHER TO GO THROUGH THIS DOOR
"Anyway. It took a while, and Clarence and I forgot about some stuff, but eventually some travelling warriors named "Jake" and "Finn" helped us get back together and into 50th Dead World. A happy ending!"
Hey, Finn and Jake! I know those guys!!
I'M NOT DONE WITH MY STORY YET, THANKS.
Sorry
"But it was not to be. It turns out 50th Dead World is full of ghosts, and that INCLUDES the smokin'-hot babe ghosts of all the smokin'-hot babes that ever lived! Clarence kept kissin' on 'em!!
"I was so cheesed!!
"But whatever. Just because Ghost Clarence was a wad didn't mean the ghost babes and I couldn't be friends anyway. But then they were all super rude! EVERYONE WAS MEAN THERE.
"I realized I was the only nice ghost there. The only nice ghost...EVER.
"So I escaped 50th Dead World and returned to Ooo by SHEER FORCE OF WARRIOR WILL. Then I took my new name. Started my new business.
"And I vowed to ensure that NO GHOST WOULD EVER WALK THIS LAND AGAIN."

Ah yes, perfect, thank you.

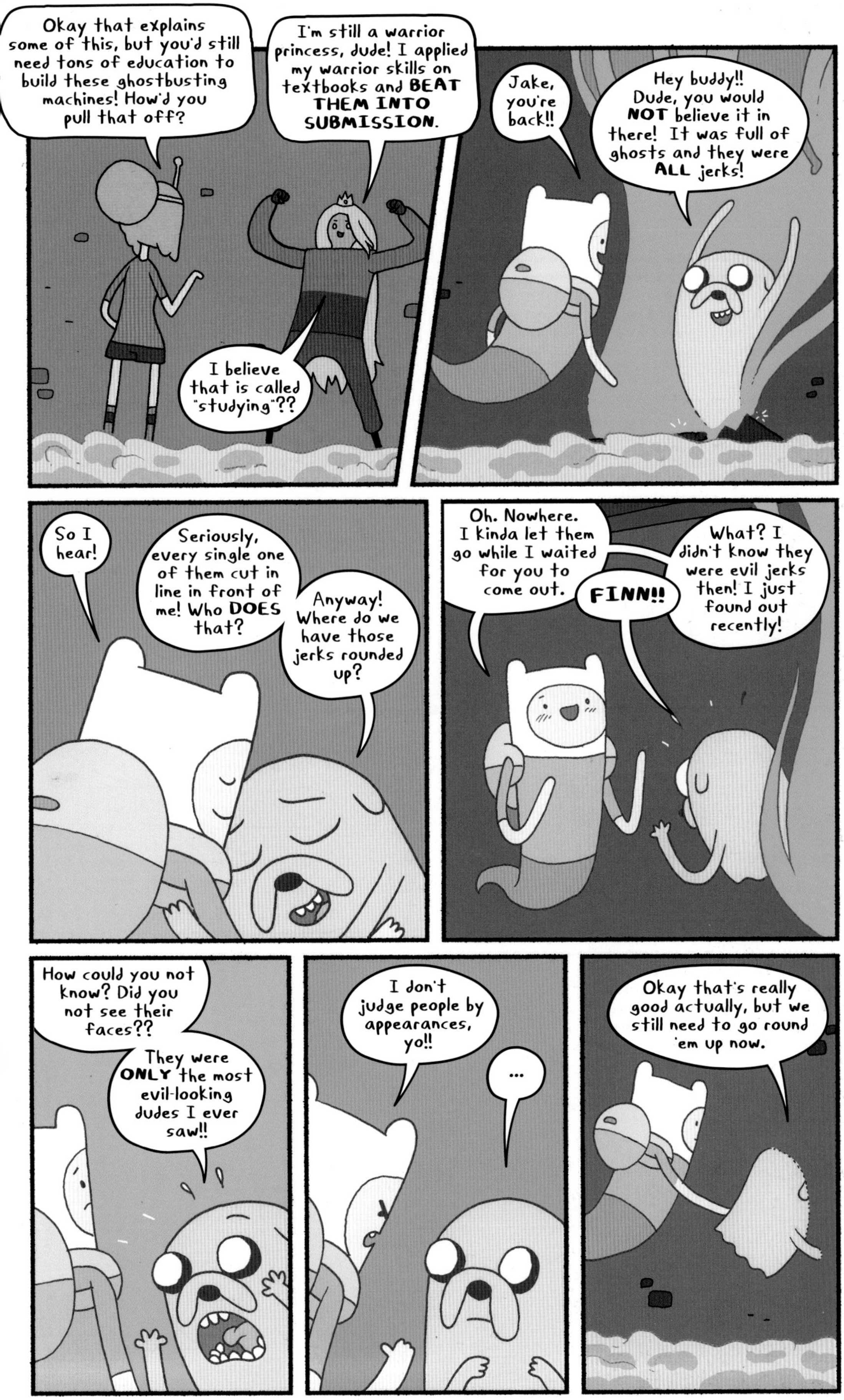
Okay that explains some of this, but you'd still need tons of education to build these ghostbusting machines! How'd you pull that off?
I'm still a warrior princess, dude! I applied my warrior skills on textbooks and **BEAT THEM INTO SUBMISSION**.
I believe that is called "studying"??
Jake, you're back!!
Hey buddy!! Dude, you would **NOT** believe it in there! It was full of ghosts and they were **ALL** jerks!
So I hear!
Seriously, every single one of them cut in line in front of me! Who **DOES** that?
Anyway! Where do we have those jerks rounded up?
Oh. Nowhere. I kinda let them go while I waited for you to come out.
FINN!!
What? I didn't know they were evil jerks then! I just found out recently!
How could you not know? Did you not see their faces??
They were **ONLY** the most evil-looking dudes I ever saw!!
I don't judge people by appearances, yo!!
...
Okay that's really good actually, but we still need to go round 'em up now.

Anyone who says studying isn't cool is just sad that they don't have enough muscles to beat books into submission and then STORE THE ESSENCE OF THESE DEFEATED BOOKS INSIDE THEIR HEAD.

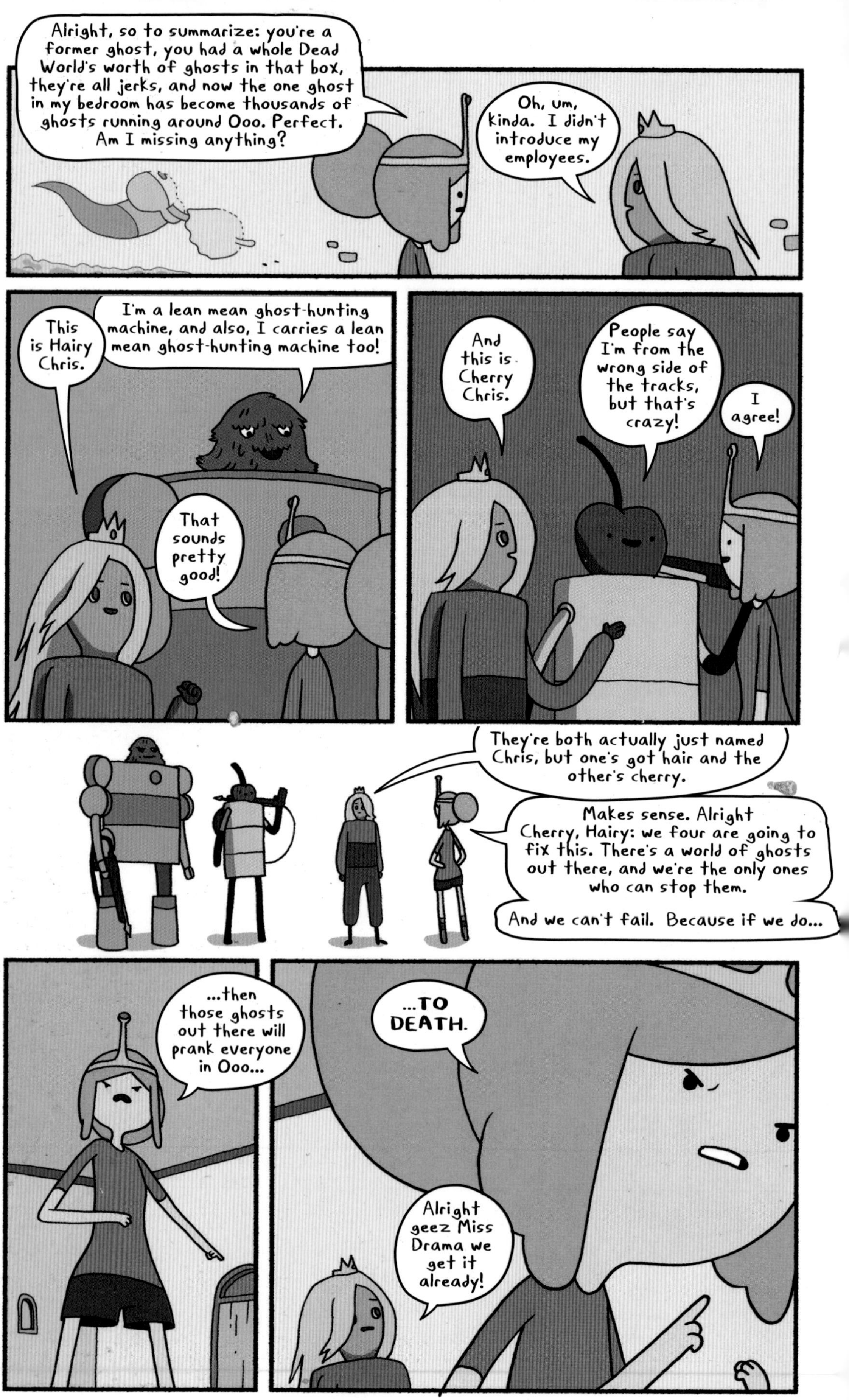
Alright, so to summarize: you're a former ghost, you had a whole Dead World's worth of ghosts in that box, they're all jerks, and now the one ghost in my bedroom has become thousands of ghosts running around Ooo. Perfect. Am I missing anything?
Oh, um, kinda. I didn't introduce my employees.
This is Hairy Chris.
I'm a lean mean ghost-hunting machine, and also, I carries a lean mean ghost-hunting machine too!
That sounds pretty good!
And this is Cherry Chris.
People say I'm from the wrong side of the tracks, but that's crazy!
I agree!
They're both actually just named Chris, but one's got hair and the other's cherry.
Makes sense. Alright Cherry, Hairy: we four are going to fix this. There's a world of ghosts out there, and we're the only ones who can stop them.
And we can't fail. Because if we do...
...then those ghosts out there will prank everyone in Ooo...
...TO DEATH.
Alright geez Miss Drama we get it already!

Imagine naming your baby "Hairy Chris". Imagine how hairy your baby would have to be for that to happen. Wow. WOW.

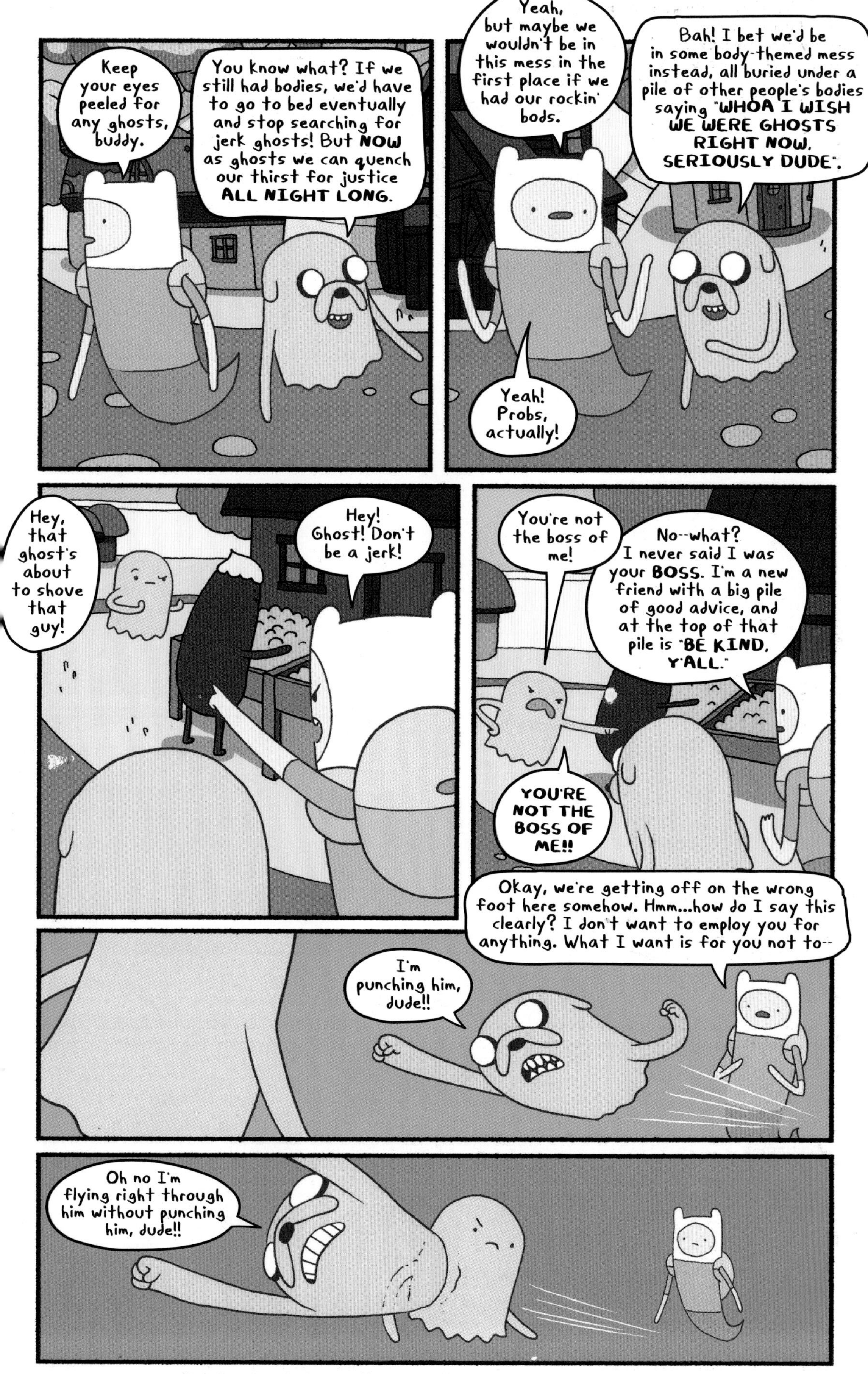
Keep your eyes peeled for any ghosts, buddy.
You know what? If we still had bodies, we'd have to go to bed eventually and stop searching for jerk ghosts! But NOW as ghosts we can quench our thirst for justice ALL NIGHT LONG.
Yeah, but maybe we wouldn't be in this mess in the first place if we had our rockin' bods.
Bah! I bet we'd be in some body-themed mess instead, all buried under a pile of other people's bodies saying "WHOA I WISH WE WERE GHOSTS RIGHT NOW, SERIOUSLY DUDE".
Yeah! Probs, actually!
Hey, that ghost's about to shove that guy!
Hey! Ghost! Don't be a jerk!
You're not the boss of me!
No--what? I never said I was your BOSS. I'm a new friend with a big pile of good advice, and at the top of that pile is "BE KIND, Y'ALL."
YOU'RE NOT THE BOSS OF ME!!
Okay, we're getting off on the wrong foot here somehow. Hmm...how do I say this clearly? I don't want to employ you for anything. What I want is for you not to--
I'm punching him, dude!!
Oh no I'm flying right through him without punching him, dude!!

"Body-themed mess" gets grosser the more you think about it; it may be... the grossest phrase??

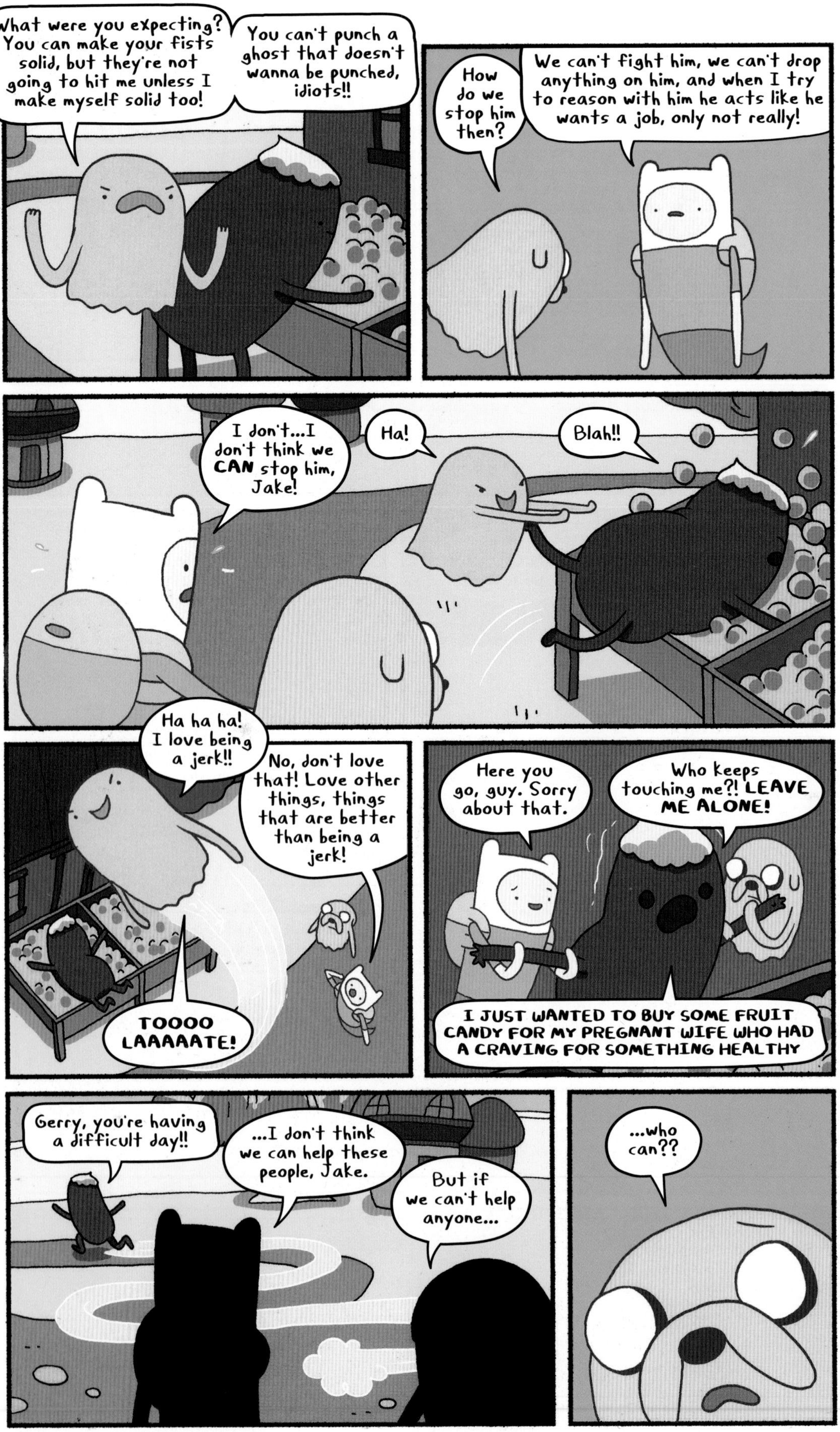
What were you expecting? You can make your fists solid, but they're not going to hit me unless I make myself solid too!
You can't punch a ghost that doesn't wanna be punched, idiots!!
How do we stop him then?
We can't fight him, we can't drop anything on him, and when I try to reason with him he acts like he wants a job, only not really!
I don't...I don't think we CAN stop him, Jake!
Ha!
Blah!!
Ha ha ha! I love being a jerk!!
No, don't love that! Love other things, things that are better than being a jerk!
TOOOO LAAAAATE!
Here you go, guy. Sorry about that.
Who keeps touching me?! LEAVE ME ALONE!
I JUST WANTED TO BUY SOME FRUIT CANDY FOR MY PREGNANT WIFE WHO HAD A CRAVING FOR SOMETHING HEALTHY
Gerry, you're having a difficult day!!
...I don't think we can help these people, Jake.
But if we can't help anyone...
...who can??

Gerry can still pull this off. I believe in Gerry. Globspeed, Gerry.

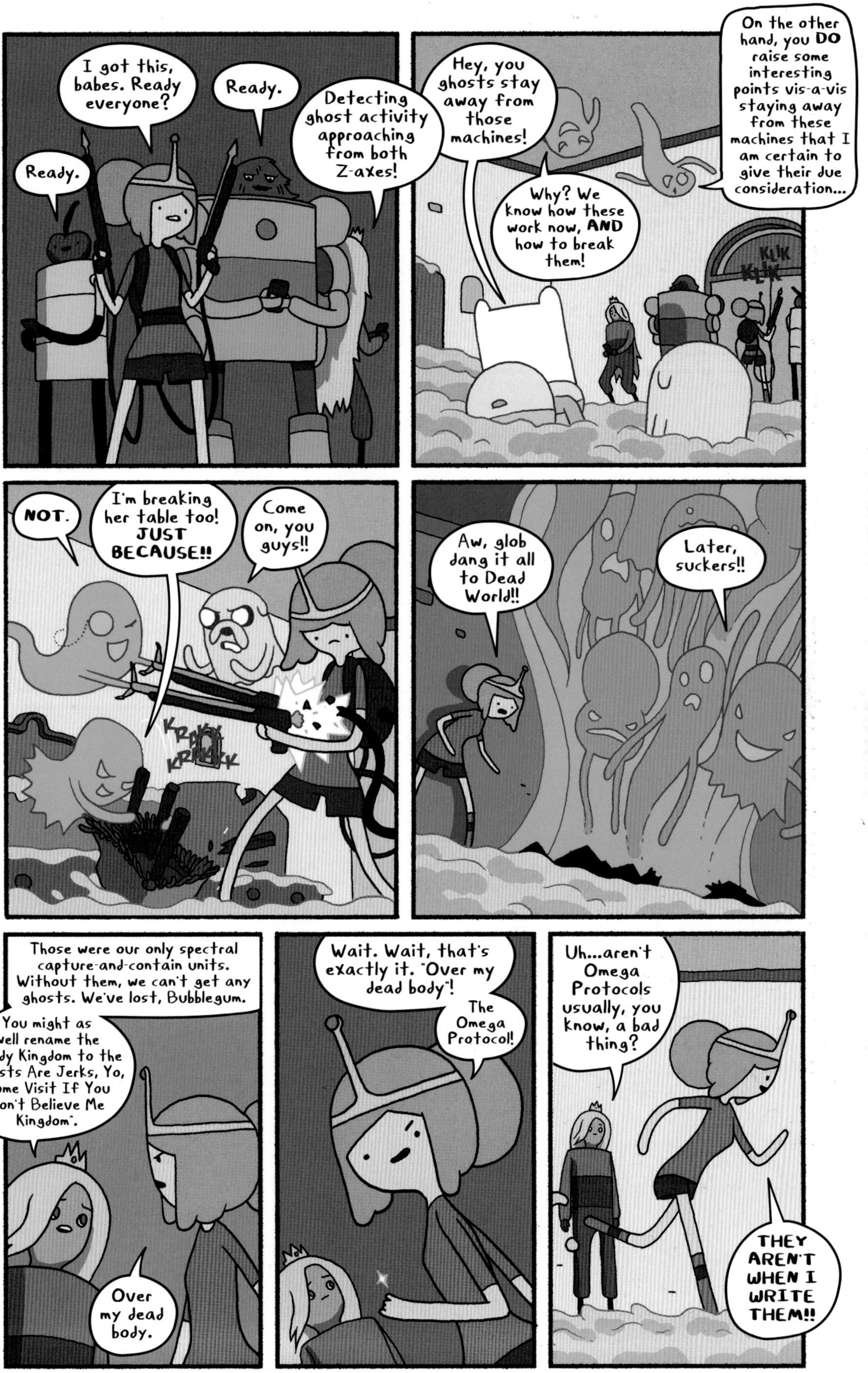
Ready.
I got this, babes. Ready everyone?
Ready.
Detecting ghost activity approaching from both Z-axes!
Hey, you ghosts stay away from those machines!
Why? We know how these work now, AND how to break them!
On the other hand, you DO raise some interesting points vis-a-vis staying away from these machines that I am certain to give their due consideration...
KLIK
KLIK
NOT.
I'm breaking her table too! JUST BECAUSE!!
Come on, you guys!!
Aw, glob dang it all to Dead World!!
Later, suckers!!
Those were our only spectral capture-and-contain units. Without them, we can't get any ghosts. We've lost, Bubblegum.
You might as well rename the Candy Kingdom to the "Ghosts Are Jerks, Yo, Come Visit If You Don't Believe Me Kingdom".
Over my dead body.
Wait. Wait, that's exactly it. "Over my dead body"!
The Omega Protocol!
Uh...aren't Omega Protocols usually, you know, a bad thing?
THEY AREN'T WHEN I WRITE THEM!!

You might as well rename the Candy Kingdom to the "No Wait, Ghosts Are Rad. Don't Listen To People Whose Hair Stands Straight Up When They Say It's Too Scary Kingdom"

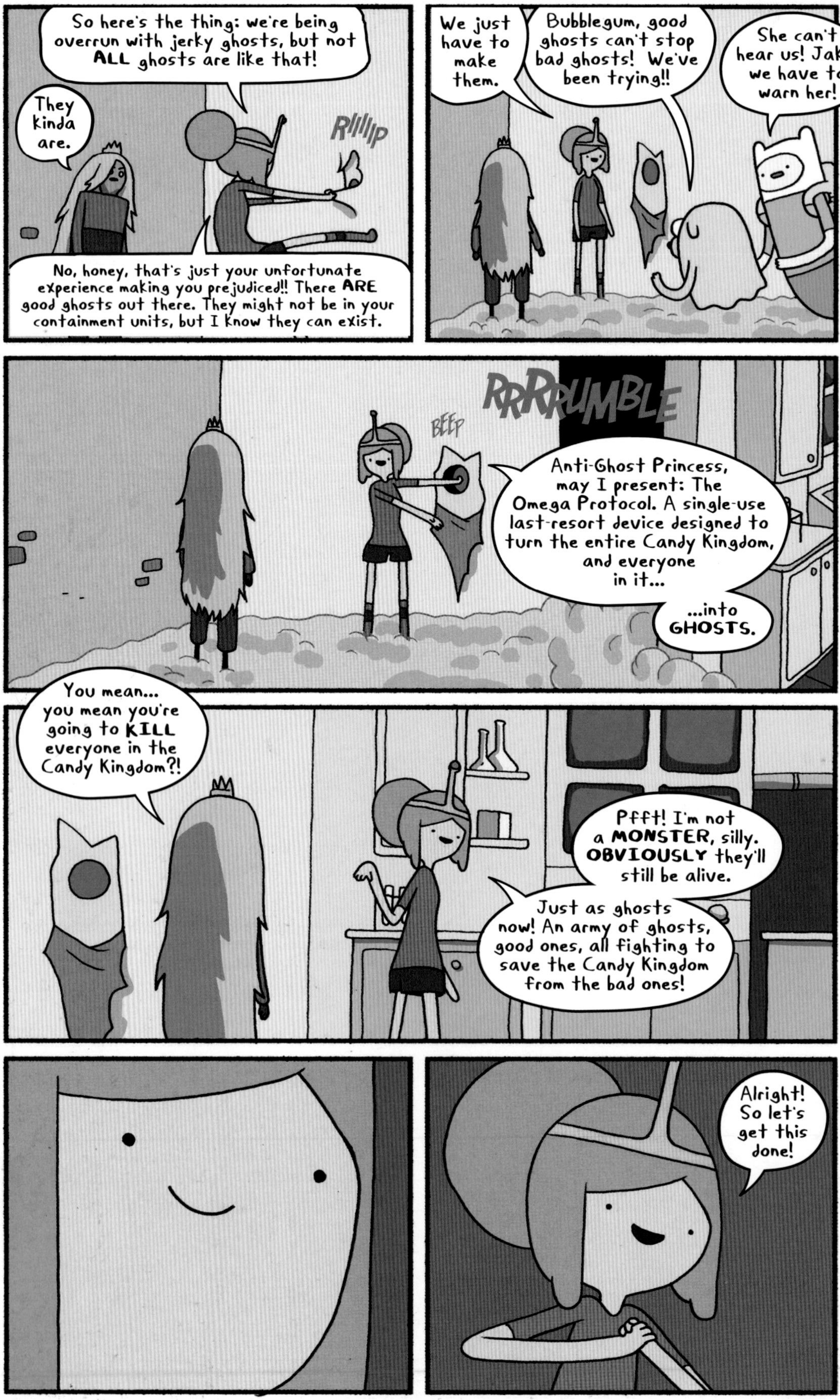
So here's the thing: we're being overrun with jerky ghosts, but not ALL ghosts are like that!
They kinda are.
RIIIIP
No, honey, that's just your unfortunate experience making you prejudiced!! There ARE good ghosts out there. They might not be in your containment units, but I know they can exist.
We just have to make them.
Bubblegum, good ghosts can't stop bad ghosts! We've been trying!!
She can't hear us! Jake, we have to warn her!
RRRRUMBLE
BEEP
Anti-Ghost Princess, may I present: The Omega Protocol. A single-use last-resort device designed to turn the entire Candy Kingdom, and everyone in it...
...into GHOSTS.
You mean... you mean you're going to KILL everyone in the Candy Kingdom?!
Pfft! I'm not a MONSTER, silly. OBVIOUSLY they'll still be alive.
Just as ghosts now! An army of ghosts, good ones, all fighting to save the Candy Kingdom from the bad ones!
Alright! So let's get this done!

PB built the Omega Protocol on evenings and weekends a few years back. It's nice to have hobbies.

Princess, you need to see this!

Ouch, someone's janking up my neck!

Wait, what's this? Writing??

"Yo that won't make a difference". Huh.

If only I could know when this was written, so that I might discern what "that" applies to! **OH WELL!!**

Aw man!!

Hold on Jake, I got this! Make her look again...right...about...

...**NOW!**

IT'S ME FINN AND I'M A GHOST AND... TO KNOW ...N TRYING TO ...D GHOSTS ...WE... STOP ...BUT WE...

It says... Finn's a ghost? How'd you become a ghost, Finn?

Actually, nevermind! We'll be able to talk way easier later once we're **ALL** transformed into ghosts!

But what if I don't want to be a ghost again?

You're not really Anti-Ghost Princess, you know? Not on the inside. There, you're a **WARRIOR** Princess. And if we're gonna fight ghosts, we'll need warriors.

Hmm... I guess I could be down with that, actually.

Alright. We're with you, Princess Bubblegum.

The Candy Kingdom is going to war.

Haha, sweeeeeet.

VRRRRT

KLIK

Our enemy won't stand a ghost of a chance.

KRAKKKTZZZTT

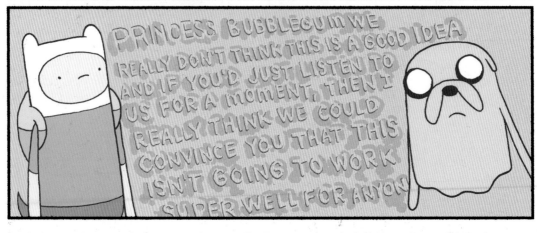

PRINCESS BUBBLEGUM WE REALLY DON'T THINK THIS IS A GOOD IDEA AND IF YOU'D JUST LISTEN TO US FOR A MOMENT, THEN I REALLY THINK WE COULD CONVINCE YOU THAT THIS ISN'T GOING TO WORK SUPER WELL FOR ANYON

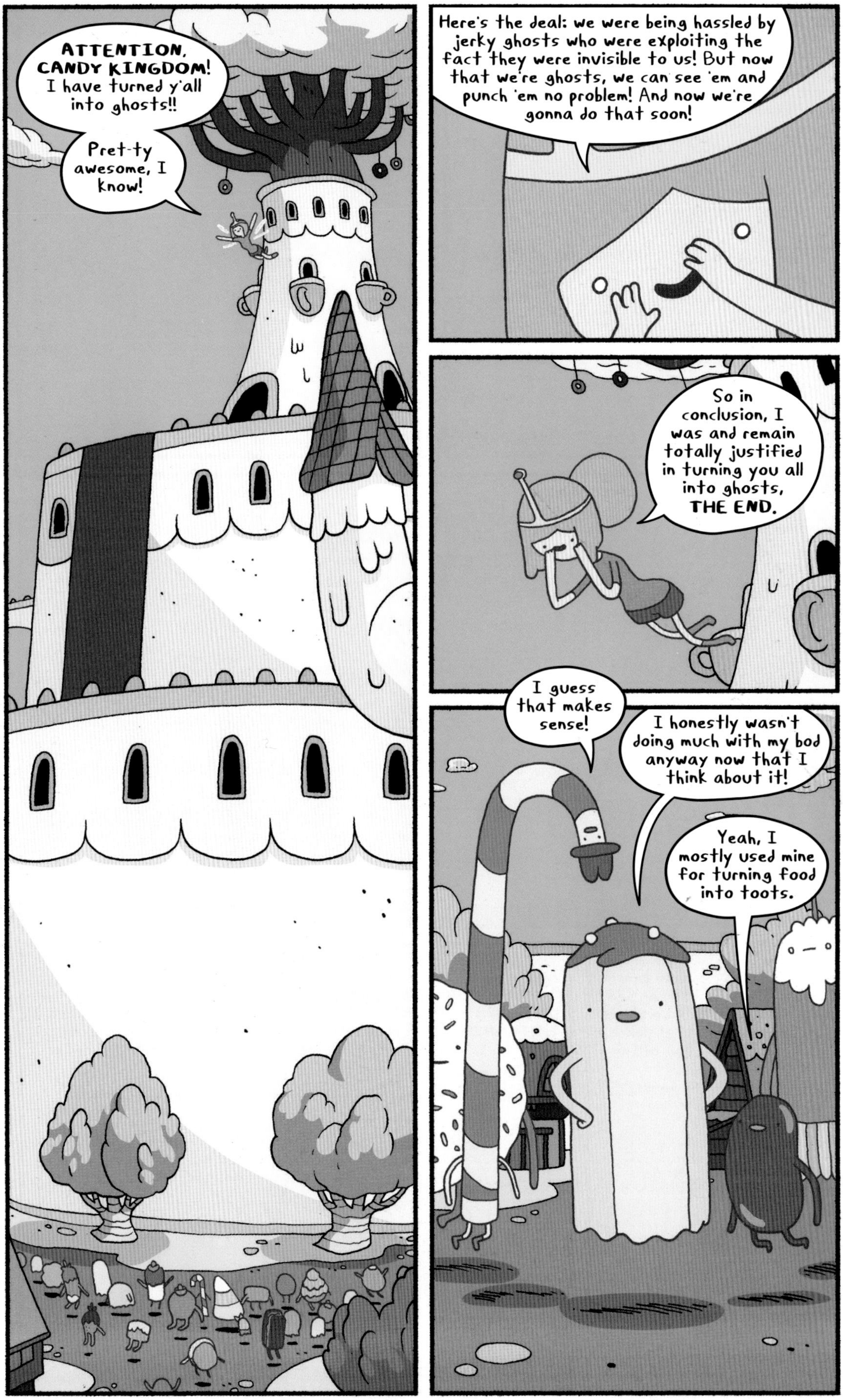
ATTENTION, CANDY KINGDOM! I have turned y'all into ghosts!!
Pret-ty awesome, I know!
Here's the deal: we were being hassled by jerky ghosts who were exploiting the fact they were invisible to us! But now that we're ghosts, we can see 'em and punch 'em no problem! And now we're gonna do that soon!
So in conclusion, I was and remain totally justified in turning you all into ghosts, THE END.
I guess that makes sense!
I honestly wasn't doing much with my bod anyway now that I think about it!
Yeah, I mostly used mine for turning food into toots.

I do that too. NO REGRETS.

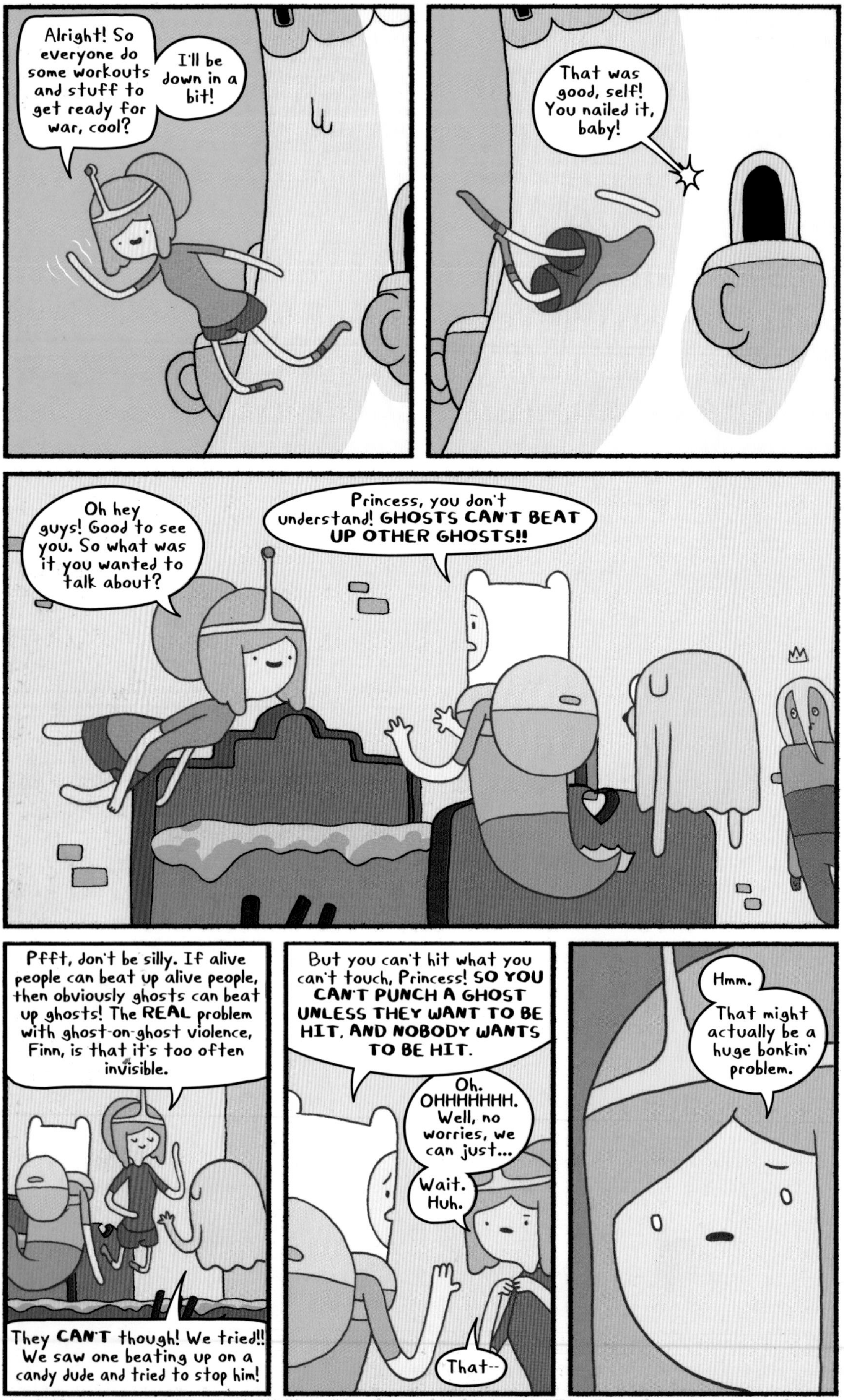
Alright! So everyone do some workouts and stuff to get ready for war, cool?
I'll be down in a bit!
That was good, self! You nailed it, baby!
Oh hey guys! Good to see you. So what was it you wanted to talk about?
Princess, you don't understand! GHOSTS CAN'T BEAT UP OTHER GHOSTS!!
Pfft, don't be silly. If alive people can beat up alive people, then obviously ghosts can beat up ghosts! The REAL problem with ghost-on-ghost violence, Finn, is that it's too often invisible.
They CAN'T though! We tried!! We saw one beating up on a candy dude and tried to stop him!
But you can't hit what you can't touch, Princess! SO YOU CAN'T PUNCH A GHOST UNLESS THEY WANT TO BE HIT, AND NOBODY WANTS TO BE HIT.
Oh. OHHHHHHH. Well, no worries, we can just...
Wait. Huh.
That--
Hmm.
That might actually be a huge bonkin' problem.

I just realized I never warned you that there'd be ghosts in this story!! Sorry if you are afraid of ghosts, and do NOT turn the page if you don't want to be terrified even more!

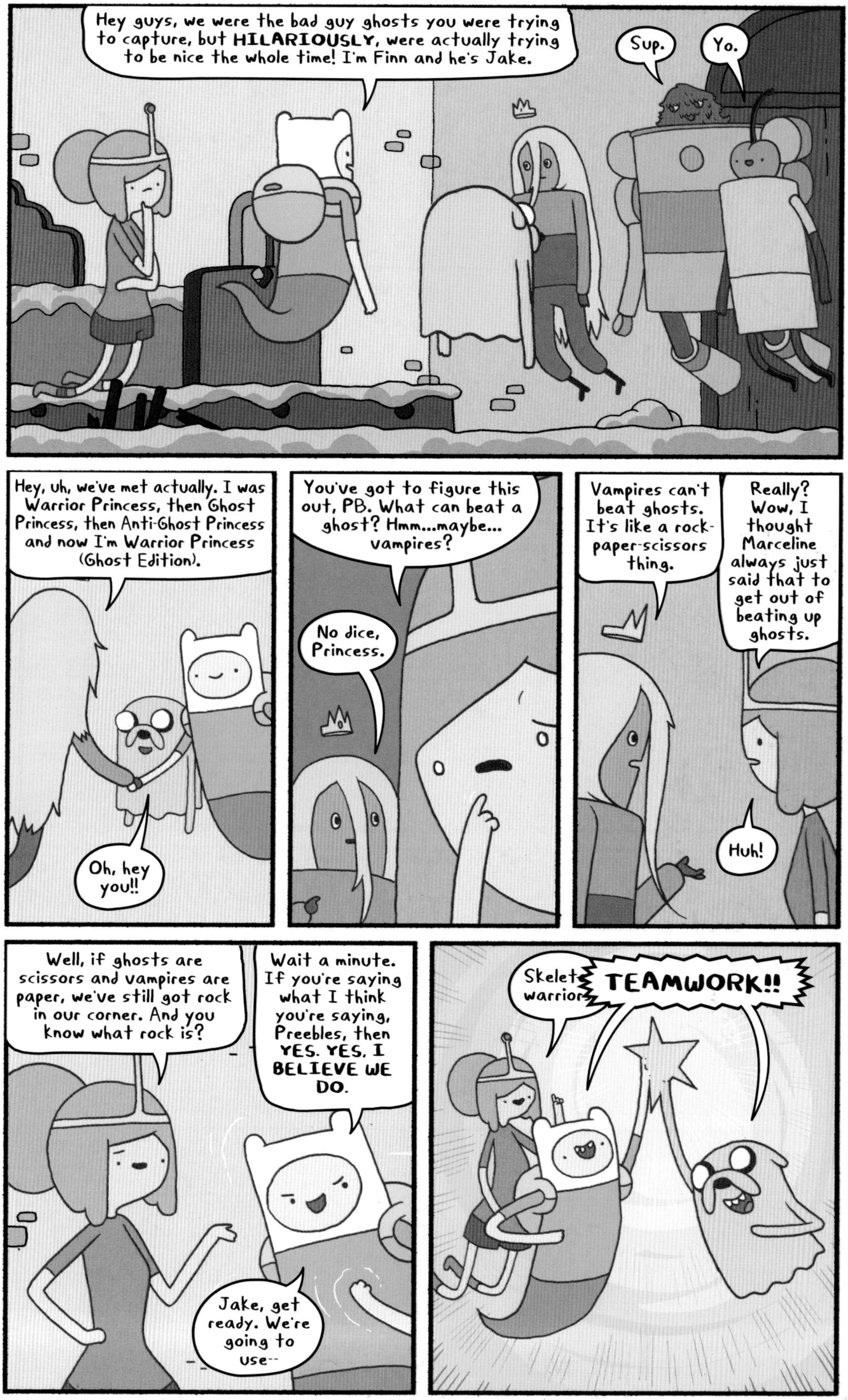
Hey guys, we were the bad guy ghosts you were trying to capture, but **HILARIOUSLY**, were actually trying to be nice the whole time! I'm Finn and he's Jake.
Sup.
Yo.
Hey, uh, we've met actually. I was Warrior Princess, then Ghost Princess, then Anti-Ghost Princess and now I'm Warrior Princess (Ghost Edition).
Oh, hey you!!
You've got to figure this out, PB. What can beat a ghost? Hmm...maybe... vampires?
No dice, Princess.
Vampires can't beat ghosts. It's like a rock-paper-scissors thing.
Really? Wow, I thought Marceline always just said that to get out of beating up ghosts.
Huh!
Well, if ghosts are scissors and vampires are paper, we've still got rock in our corner. And you know what rock is?
Wait a minute. If you're saying what I think you're saying, Preebles, then **YES. YES. I BELIEVE WE DO.**
Jake, get ready. We're going to use--
Skelet warrior
TEAMWORK!!

I warned you! Everyone on this page is a ghost, and the ghosts are now TEAMING UP. Welcome to a new level of terror, easily-scared readers!!

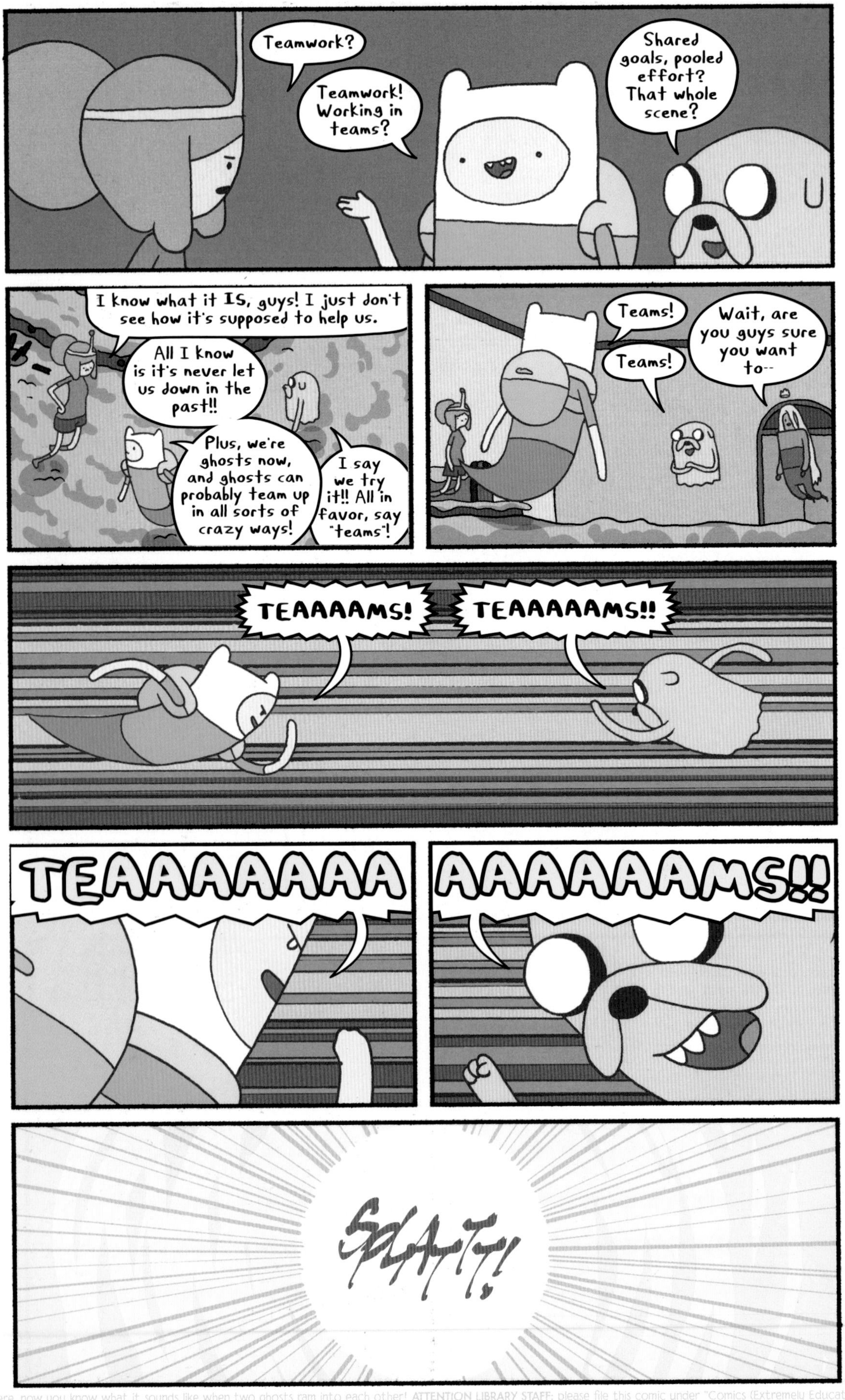
Teamwork?
Teamwork! Working in teams?
Shared goals, pooled effort? That whole scene?
I know what it IS, guys! I just don't see how it's supposed to help us.
All I know is it's never let us down in the past!!
Plus, we're ghosts now, and ghosts can probably team up in all sorts of crazy ways!
I say we try it!! All in favor, say "teams"!
Teams!
Teams!
Wait, are you guys sure you want to--
TEAAAAMS!
TEAAAAAMS!!
TEAAAAAAAA
AAAAAAAMS!!

There, now you know what it sounds like when two ghosts ram into each other! ATTENTION LIBRARY STAFF: please file this comic under "Comics (Extremely Educationa

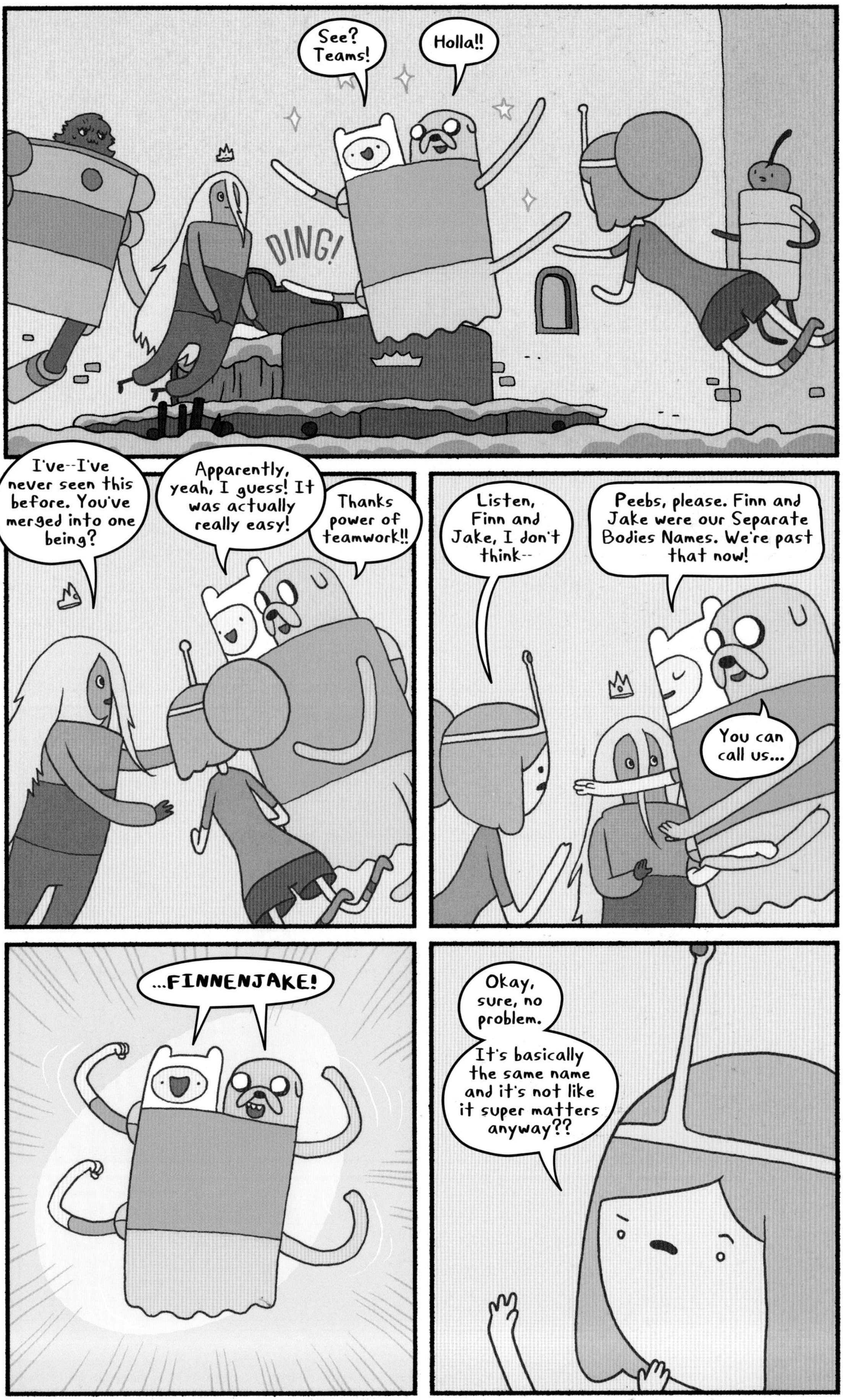
See? Teams!
Holla!!
DING!
I've--I've never seen this before. You've merged into one being?
Apparently, yeah, I guess! It was actually really easy!
Thanks power of teamwork!!
Listen, Finn and Jake, I don't think--
Peebs, please. Finn and Jake were our Separate Bodies Names. We're past that now!
You can call us...
...FINNENJAKE!
Okay, sure, no problem.
It's basically the same name and it's not like it super matters anyway??

No wait, call us Jakenfinn! No wait, Jakenfinnenfinnenjake!

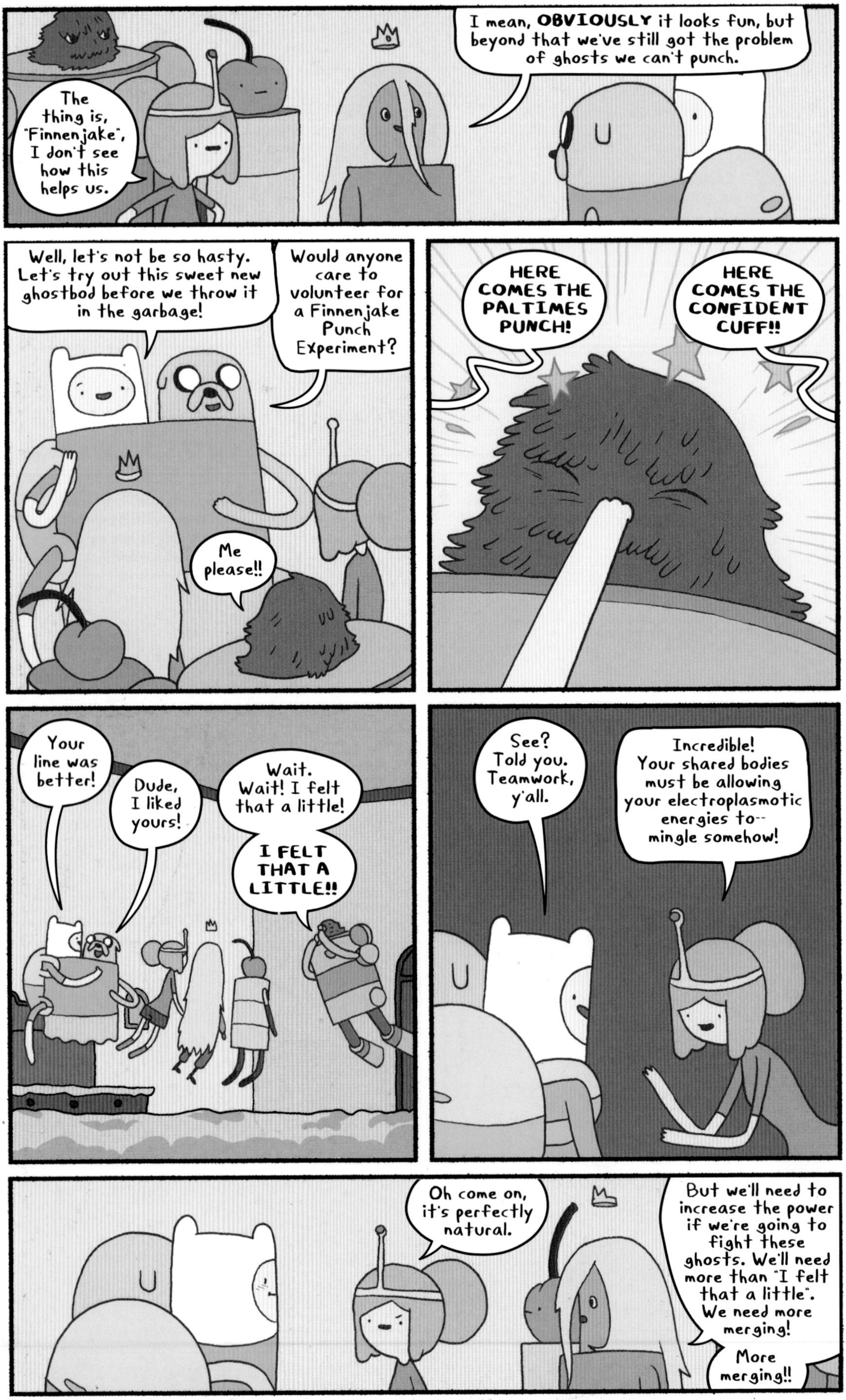
The thing is, "Finnenjake", I don't see how this helps us.
I mean, OBVIOUSLY it looks fun, but beyond that we've still got the problem of ghosts we can't punch.
Well, let's not be so hasty. Let's try out this sweet new ghostbod before we throw it in the garbage!
Would anyone care to volunteer for a Finnenjake Punch Experiment?
Me please!!
HERE COMES THE PALTIMES PUNCH!
HERE COMES THE CONFIDENT CUFF!!
Your line was better!
Dude, I liked yours!
Wait. Wait! I felt that a little!
I FELT THAT A LITTLE!!
See? Told you. Teamwork, y'all.
Incredible! Your shared bodies must be allowing your electroplasmotic energies to-- mingle somehow!
Oh come on, it's perfectly natural.
But we'll need to increase the power if we're going to fight these ghosts. We'll need more than "I felt that a little". We need more merging!
More merging!!

Never be ashamed of your electroplasmotic energies. NEVER.

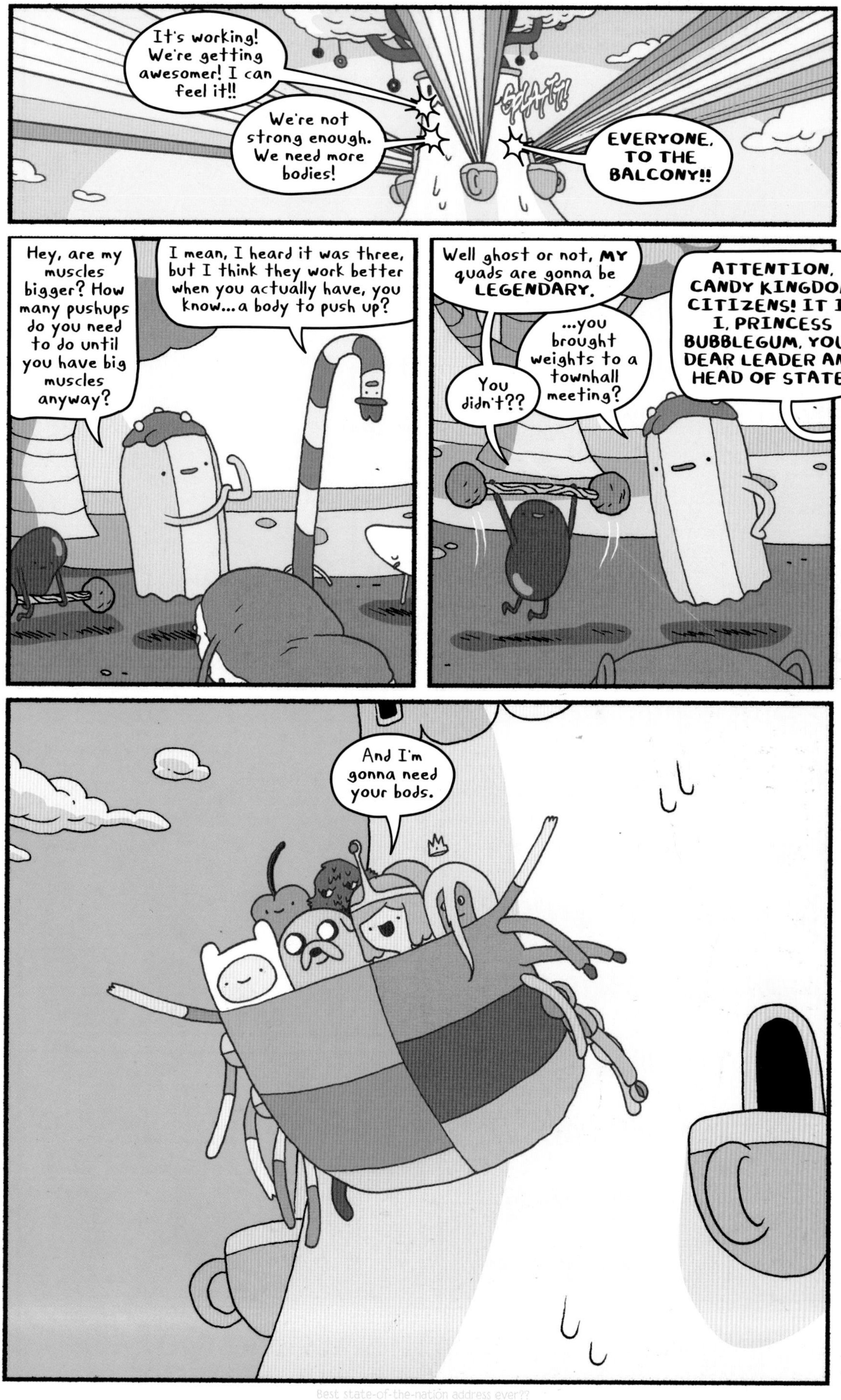
It's working! We're getting awesomer! I can feel it!!
We're not strong enough. We need more bodies!
EVERYONE, TO THE BALCONY!!
Hey, are my muscles bigger? How many pushups do you need to do until you have big muscles anyway?
I mean, I heard it was three, but I think they work better when you actually have, you know...a body to push up?
Well ghost or not, MY quads are gonna be LEGENDARY.
You didn't??
...you brought weights to a townhall meeting?
ATTENTION, CANDY KINGDOM CITIZENS! IT IS I, PRINCESS BUBBLEGUM, YOUR DEAR LEADER AND HEAD OF STATE!
And I'm gonna need your bods.

Best state-of-the-nation address ever??

Princess, I've got some legendary quads here! I therefore volunteer!!
Um...I've got sucky quads right now. Can I still volunteer?
Yes! All bods are acceptable, regardless of how rad or sucky their quads are!
There's more to each and all of you than your quads anyway!
For example, there's your electroplasmic energy levels that **SHOULD** allow us to override the corporeality intentionality of the other ghosts!
And you're **SURE** this'll help us get rid of those bad ghosts?
Yes! The **ONLY** way to win this war is for all y'all to combine with me into one giant bod!
Trust me.
I'm the **PRINCESS**.
Now get in here, everyone!!
Today's not turning out how we expected, huh?
I guess. I kinda saw this coming though.
SPLATTT!
Really. You really saw this coming.
I have some pretty vivid nightmares, okay??
SPLATTT!

Hey, sorry for making you suddenly acutely aware that your own Head of State isn't nearly as rad as PB :(

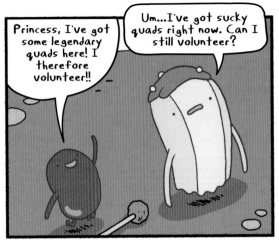

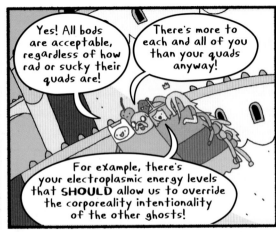

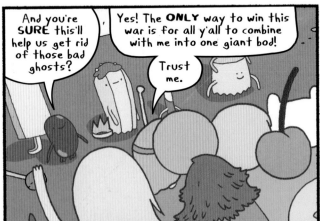

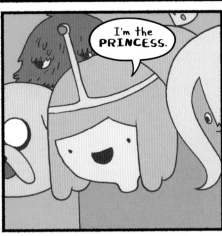

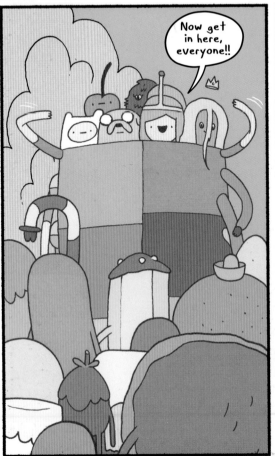

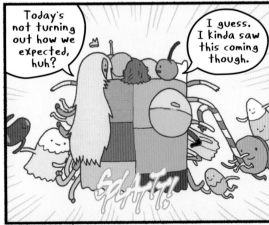

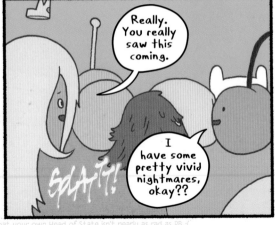

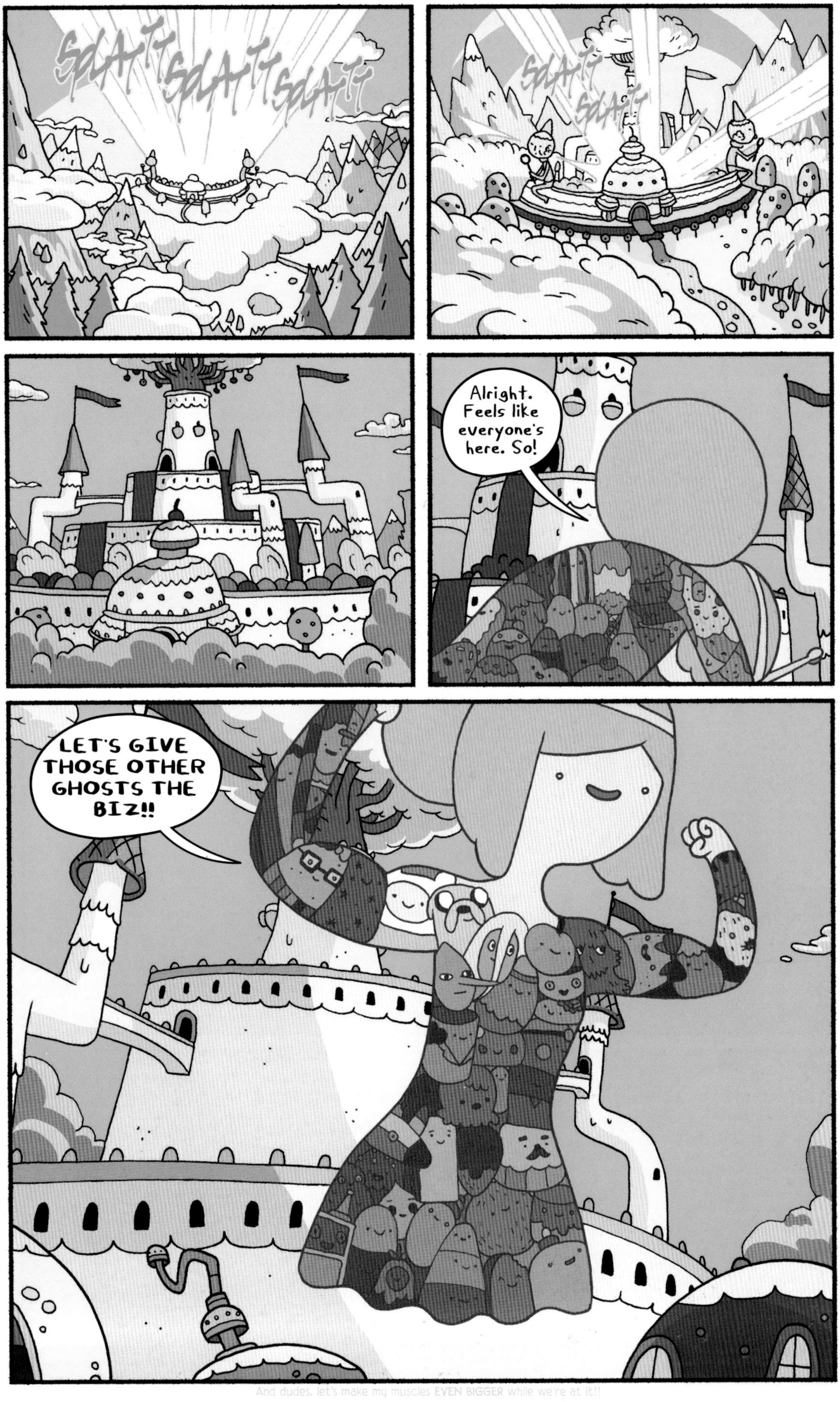
SPLATT SPLATT SPLATT
SPLATT SPLATT
Alright. Feels like everyone's here. So!
LET'S GIVE THOSE OTHER GHOSTS THE BIZ!!

And dudes, let's make my muscles **EVEN BIGGER** while we're at it!!

Princess, we've got a containment unit in our headquarters, over that ridge. If we can get ALL the ghosts in there before any of them can break it, they shouldn't be able to get out.

Perfect. Then this'll be easy! All we need to do...

...is pick up all the evil ghosts here...

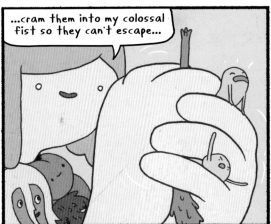

...cram them into my colossal fist so they can't escape...

...do a final pass to make sure we didn't miss any...

...carry them over the ridge...

...and stuff them into containment!

Wow it took you a really long time to say that sentence

But I don't want to go back! It's so boring in there! You don't even know!!

Have pity on me! Please!!

Also, it smells like old socks in there! I'm serious! I think someone might've left an old sock in there or something!!

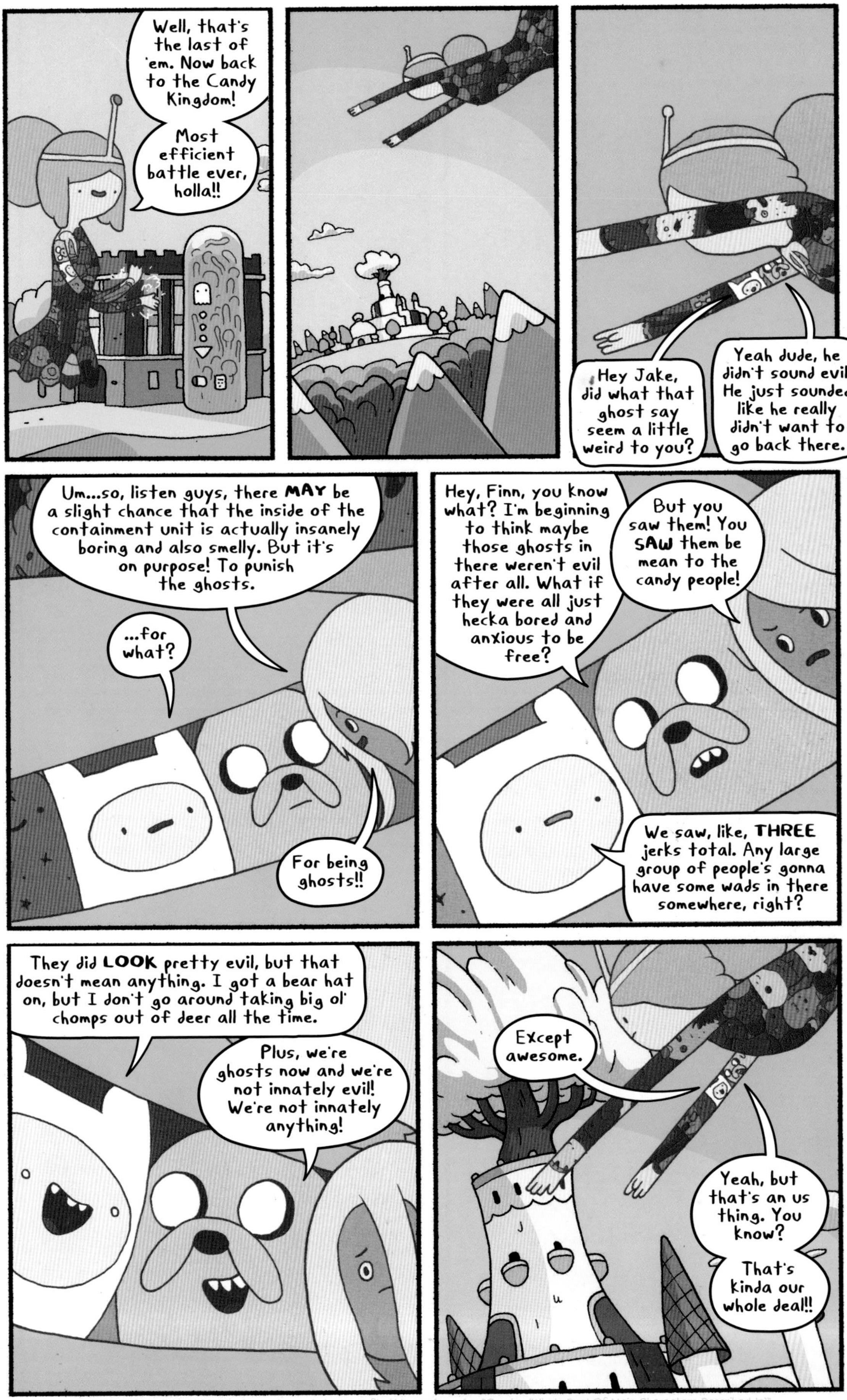

Well, that's the last of 'em. Now back to the Candy Kingdom!
Most efficient battle ever, holla!!
Hey Jake, did what that ghost say seem a little weird to you?
Yeah dude, he didn't sound evil! He just sounded like he really didn't want to go back there.
Um...so, listen guys, there MAY be a slight chance that the inside of the containment unit is actually insanely boring and also smelly. But it's on purpose! To punish the ghosts.
...for what?
For being ghosts!!
Hey, Finn, you know what? I'm beginning to think maybe those ghosts in there weren't evil after all. What if they were all just hecka bored and anxious to be free?
But you saw them! You SAW them be mean to the candy people!
We saw, like, THREE jerks total. Any large group of people's gonna have some wads in there somewhere, right?
They did LOOK pretty evil, but that doesn't mean anything. I got a bear hat on, but I don't go around taking big ol' chomps out of deer all the time.
Plus, we're ghosts now and we're not innately evil! We're not innately anything!
Except awesome.
Yeah, but that's an us thing. You know?
That's kinda our whole deal!!

ATTENTION LIBRARY STAFF: changed my mind, please file this comic under "Comics (Whole Deal Of Main Characters Described In)".

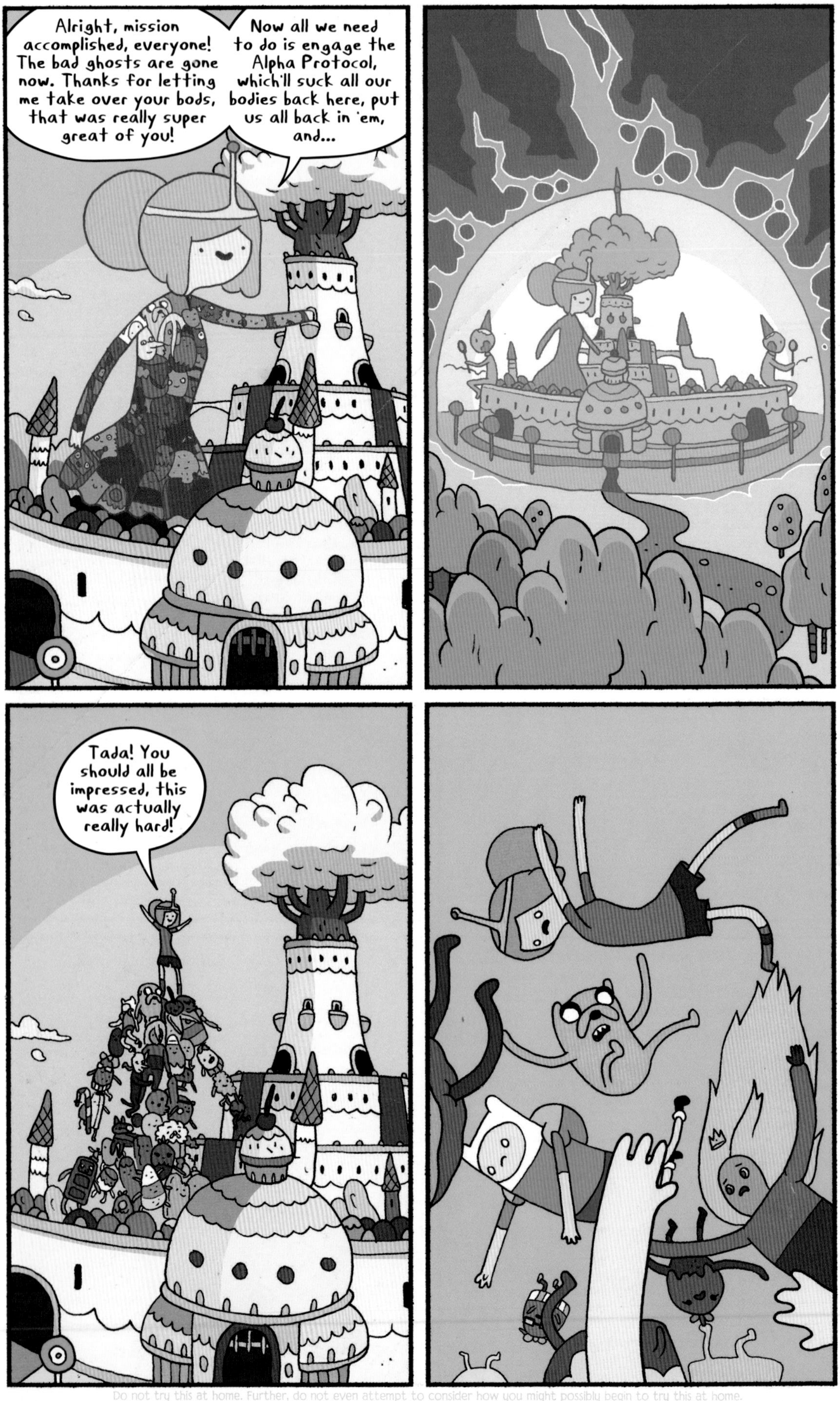
Alright, mission accomplished, everyone! The bad ghosts are gone now. Thanks for letting me take over your bods, that was really super great of you!
Now all we need to do is engage the Alpha Protocol, which'll suck all our bodies back here, put us all back in 'em, and...
Tada! You should all be impressed, this was actually really hard!

Do not try this at home. Further, do not even attempt to consider how you might possibly begin to try this at home.

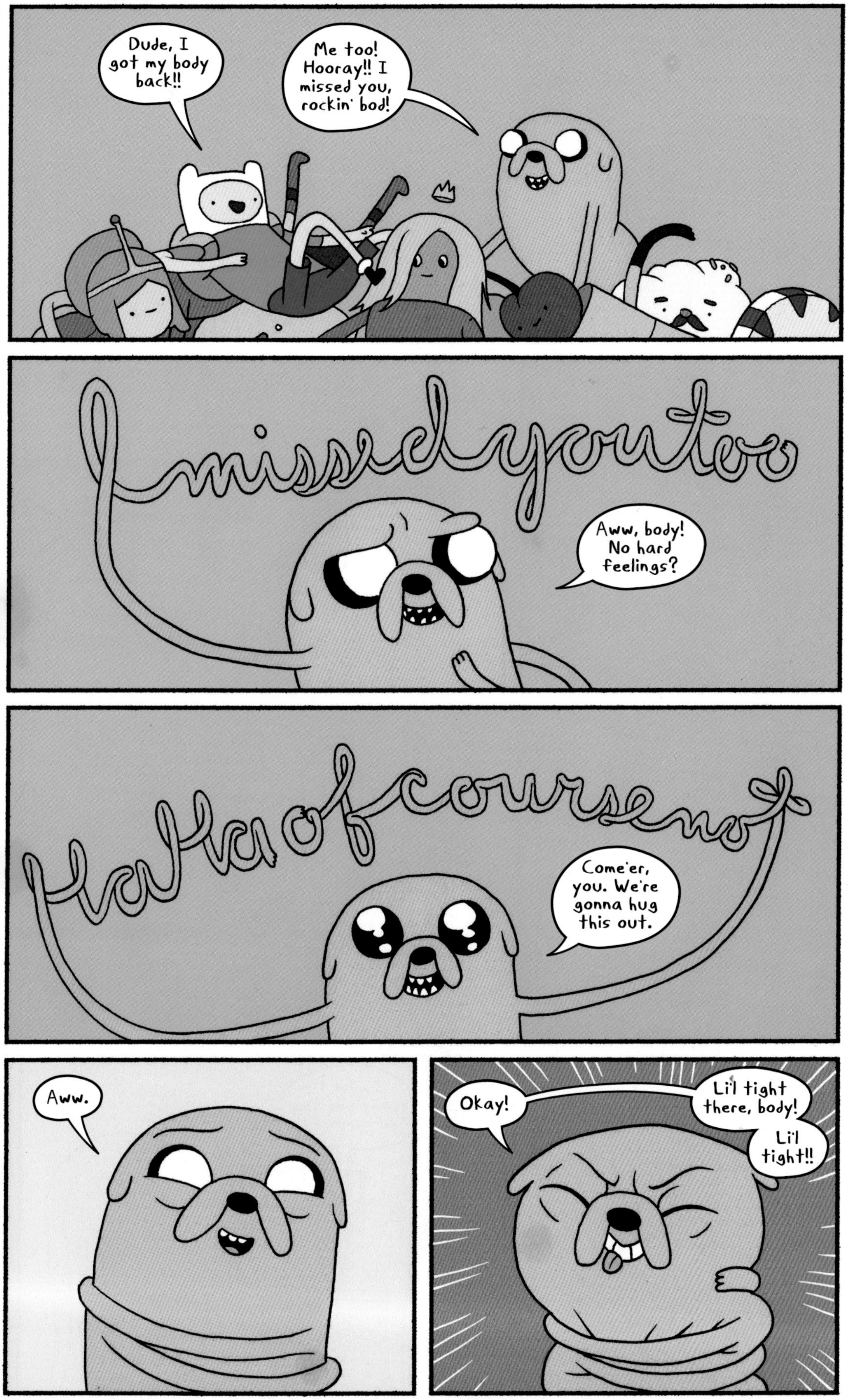
Dude, I got my body back!!
Me too! Hooray!! I missed you, rockin' bod!
Imissedyoutoo
Aww, body! No hard feelings?
Hahaofcoursenot
Come'er, you. We're gonna hug this out.
Aww.
Okay!
Li'l tight there, body!
Li'l tight!!

"Imissedyoutoo"? I'm sorry, Jake's Body, but that's not even a word. I simply can't understand what you're trying to say.

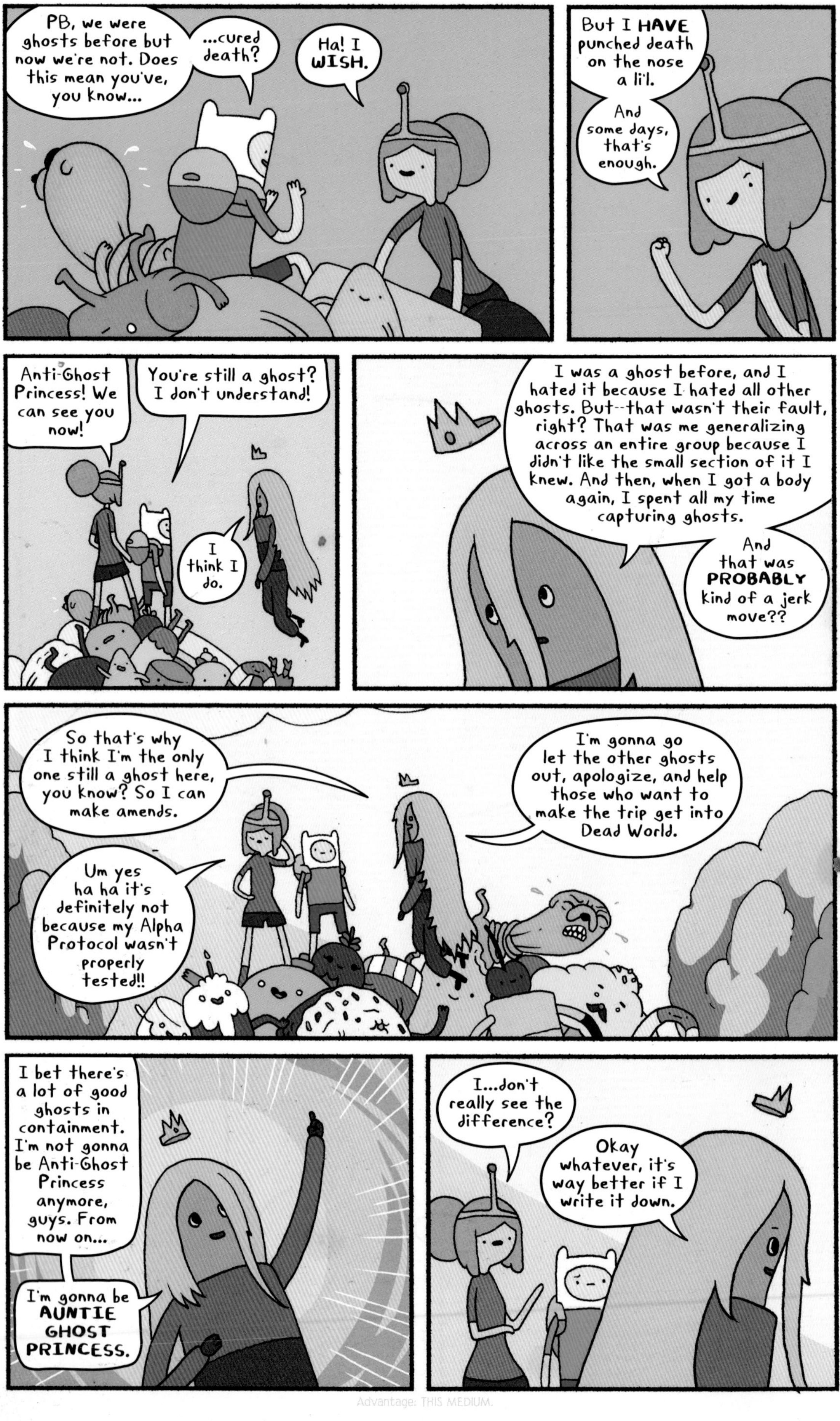
PB, we were ghosts before but now we're not. Does this mean you've, you know...
...cured death?
Ha! I **WISH.**
But I **HAVE** punched death on the nose a li'l.
And some days, that's enough.
Anti-Ghost Princess! We can see you now!
You're still a ghost? I don't understand!
I think I do.
I was a ghost before, and I hated it because I hated all other ghosts. But--that wasn't their fault, right? That was me generalizing across an entire group because I didn't like the small section of it I knew. And then, when I got a body again, I spent all my time capturing ghosts.
And that was **PROBABLY** kind of a jerk move??
So that's why I think I'm the only one still a ghost here, you know? So I can make amends.
I'm gonna go let the other ghosts out, apologize, and help those who want to make the trip get into Dead World.
Um yes ha ha it's definitely not because my Alpha Protocol wasn't properly tested!!
I bet there's a lot of good ghosts in containment. I'm not gonna be Anti-Ghost Princess anymore, guys. From now on...
I'm gonna be **AUNTIE GHOST PRINCESS.**
I...don't really see the difference?
Okay whatever, it's way better if I write it down.

Advantage: THIS MEDIUM.

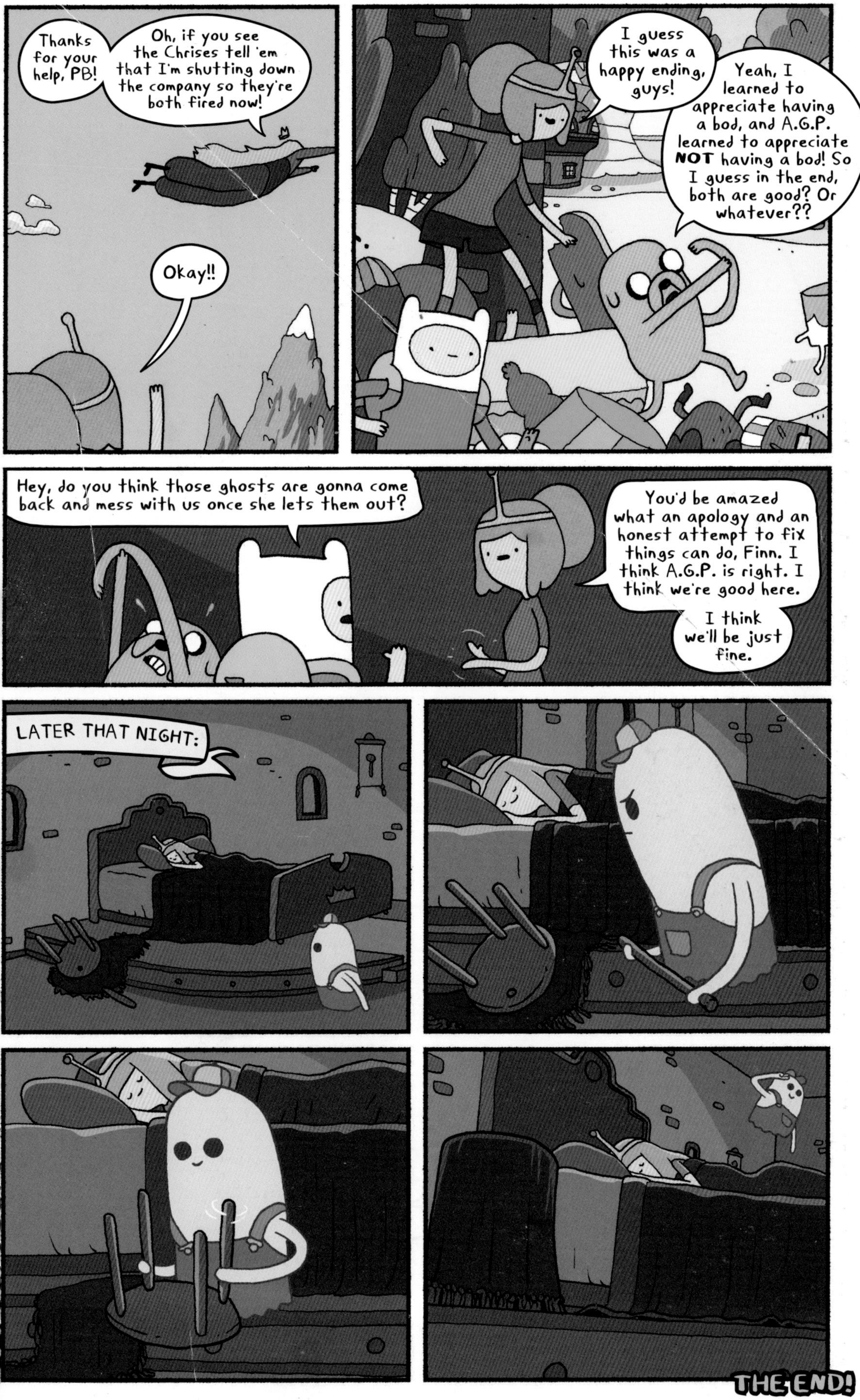
Thanks for your help, PB!
Oh, if you see the Chrises tell 'em that I'm shutting down the company so they're both fired now!
Okay!!
I guess this was a happy ending, guys!
Yeah, I learned to appreciate having a bod, and A.G.P. learned to appreciate NOT having a bod! So I guess in the end, both are good? Or whatever??
Hey, do you think those ghosts are gonna come back and mess with us once she lets them out?
You'd be amazed what an apology and an honest attempt to fix things can do, Finn. I think A.G.P. is right. I think we're good here.
I think we'll be just fine.
LATER THAT NIGHT:
THE END!

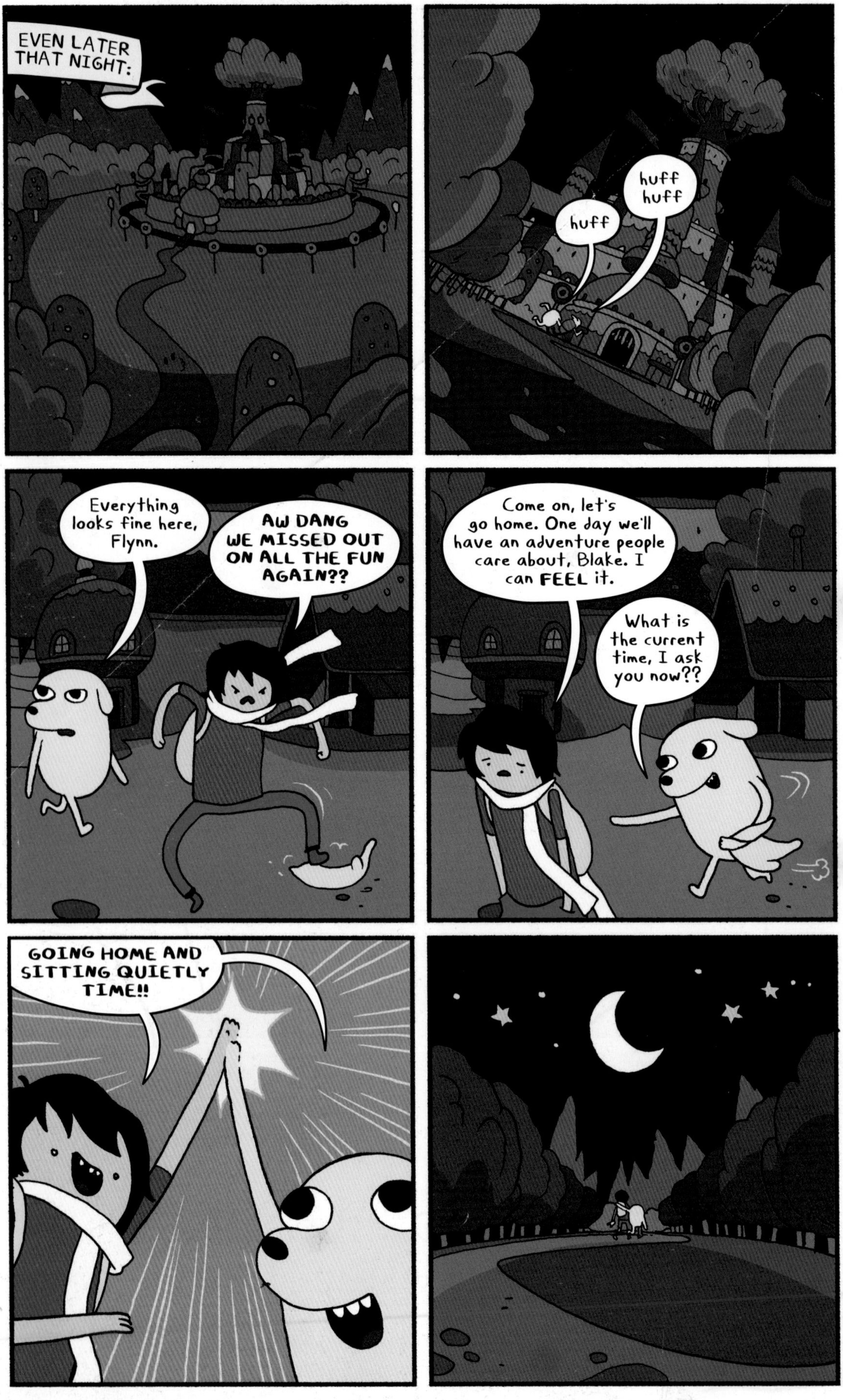
EVEN LATER THAT NIGHT:
huff
huff huff
Everything looks fine here, Flynn.
AW DANG WE MISSED OUT ON ALL THE FUN AGAIN??
Come on, let's go home. One day we'll have an adventure people care about, Blake. I can FEEL it.
What is the current time, I ask you now??
GOING HOME AND SITTING QUIETLY TIME!!

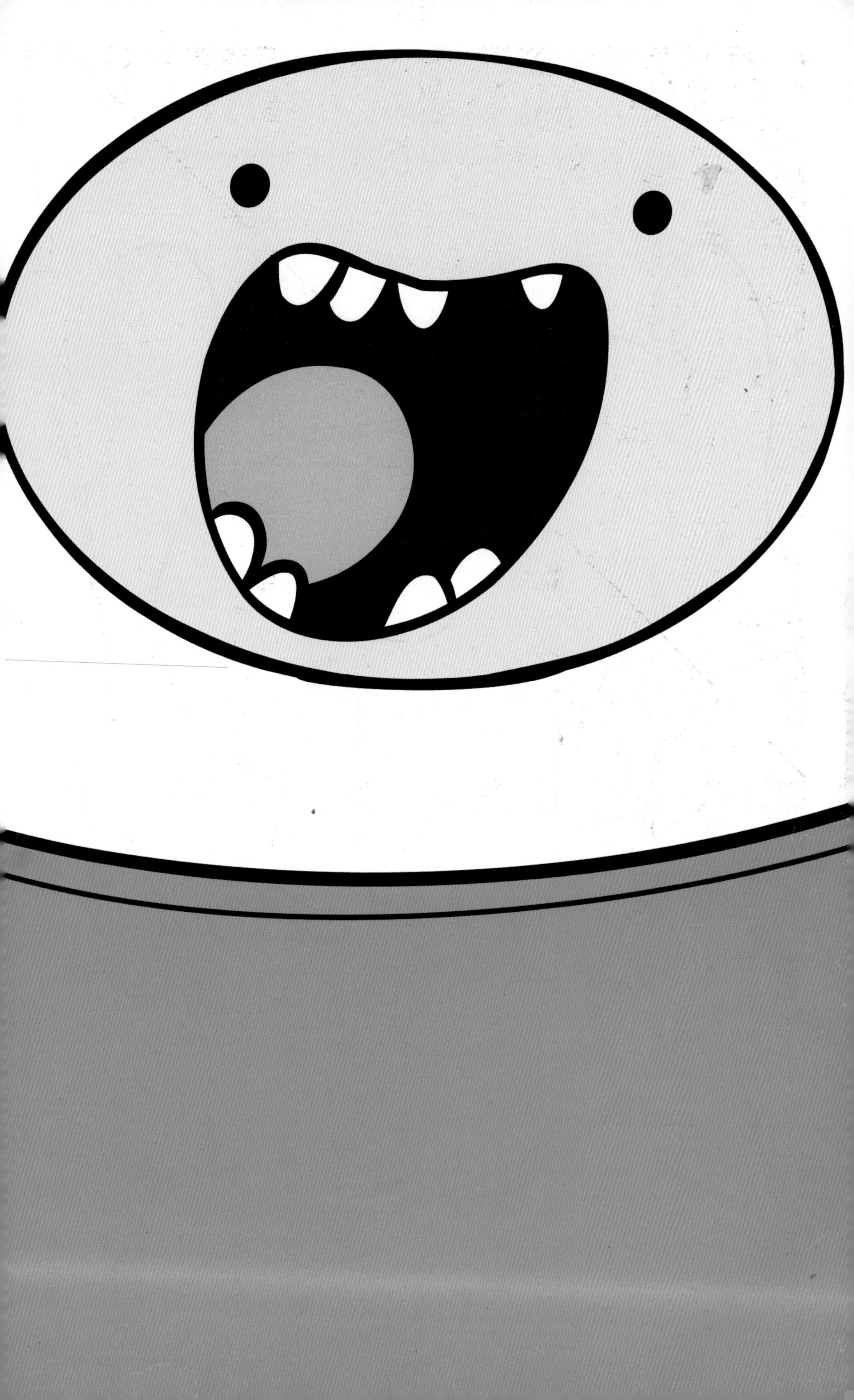

COVER GALLERY

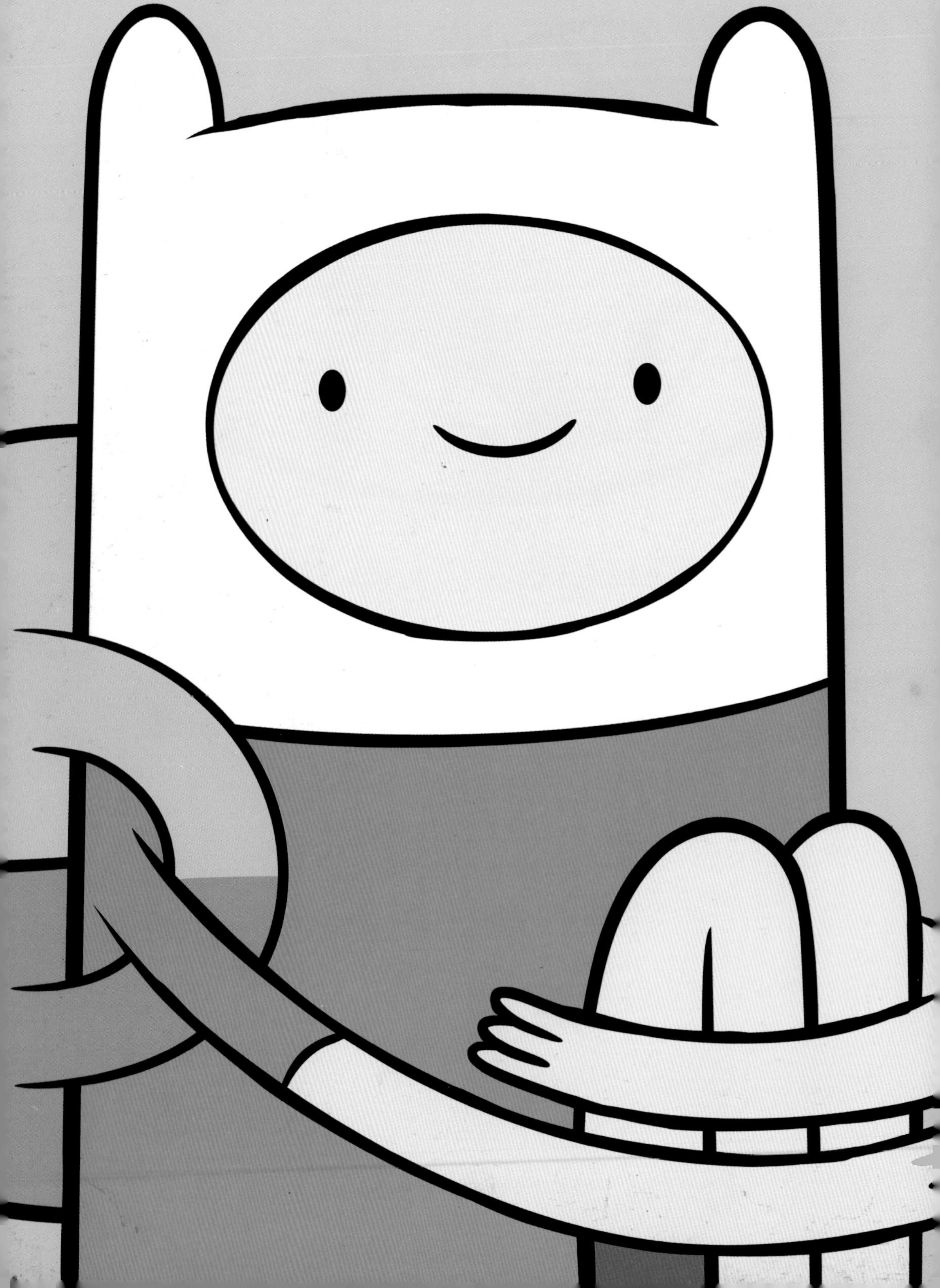

Cover 25A:
Matt Cummings

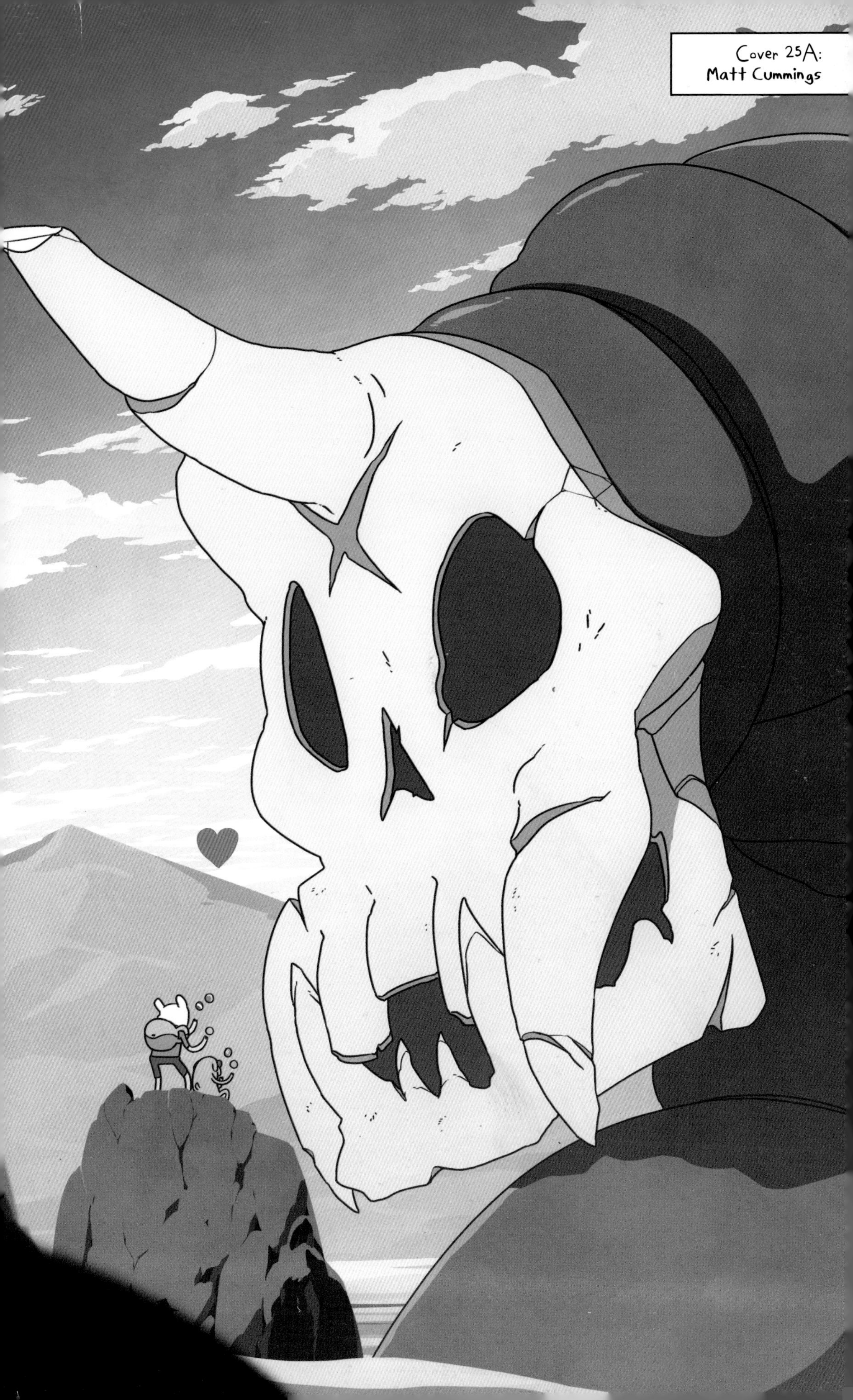

Cover 25B:
Luke Pearson

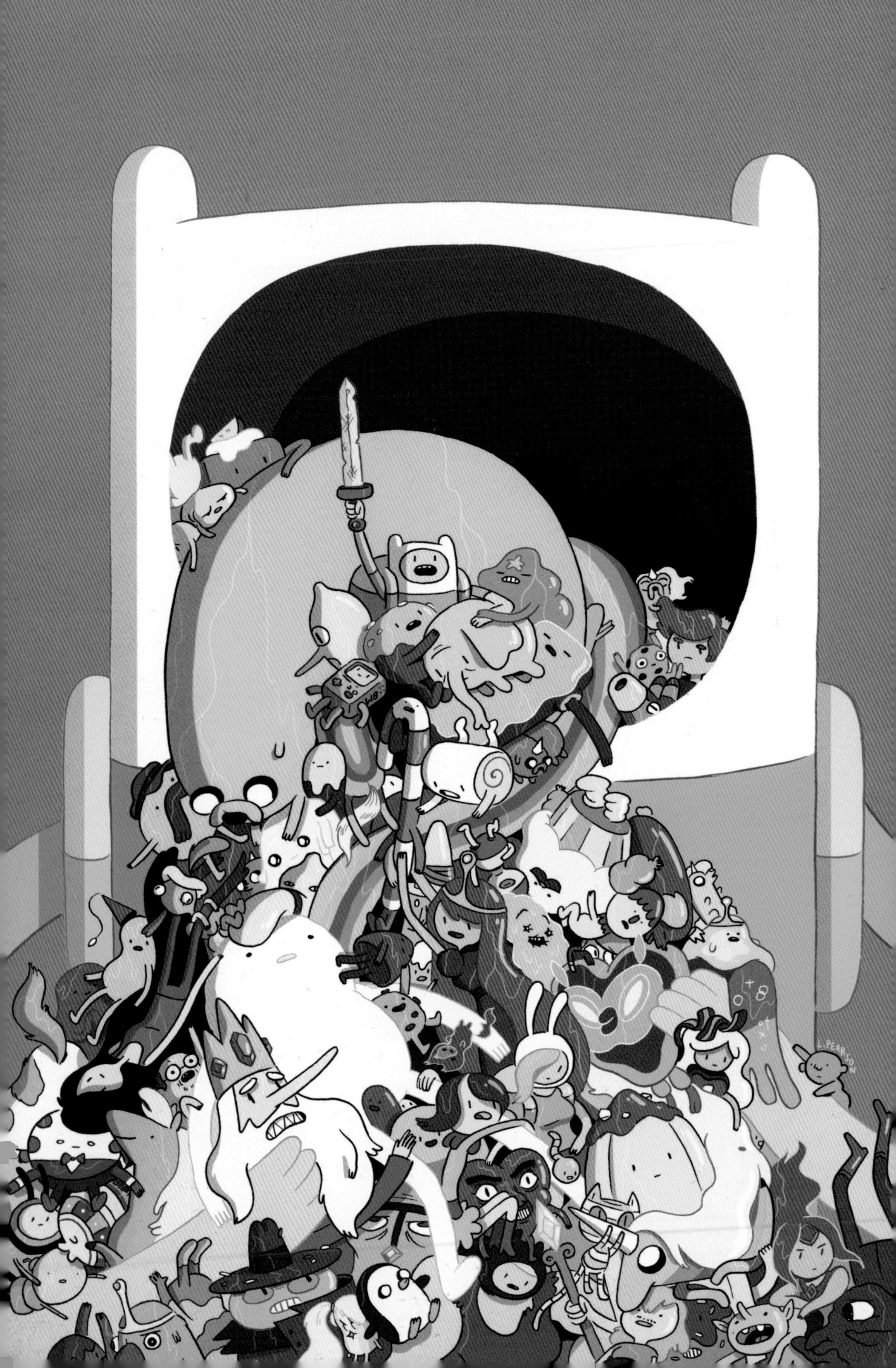
L. PEARSON

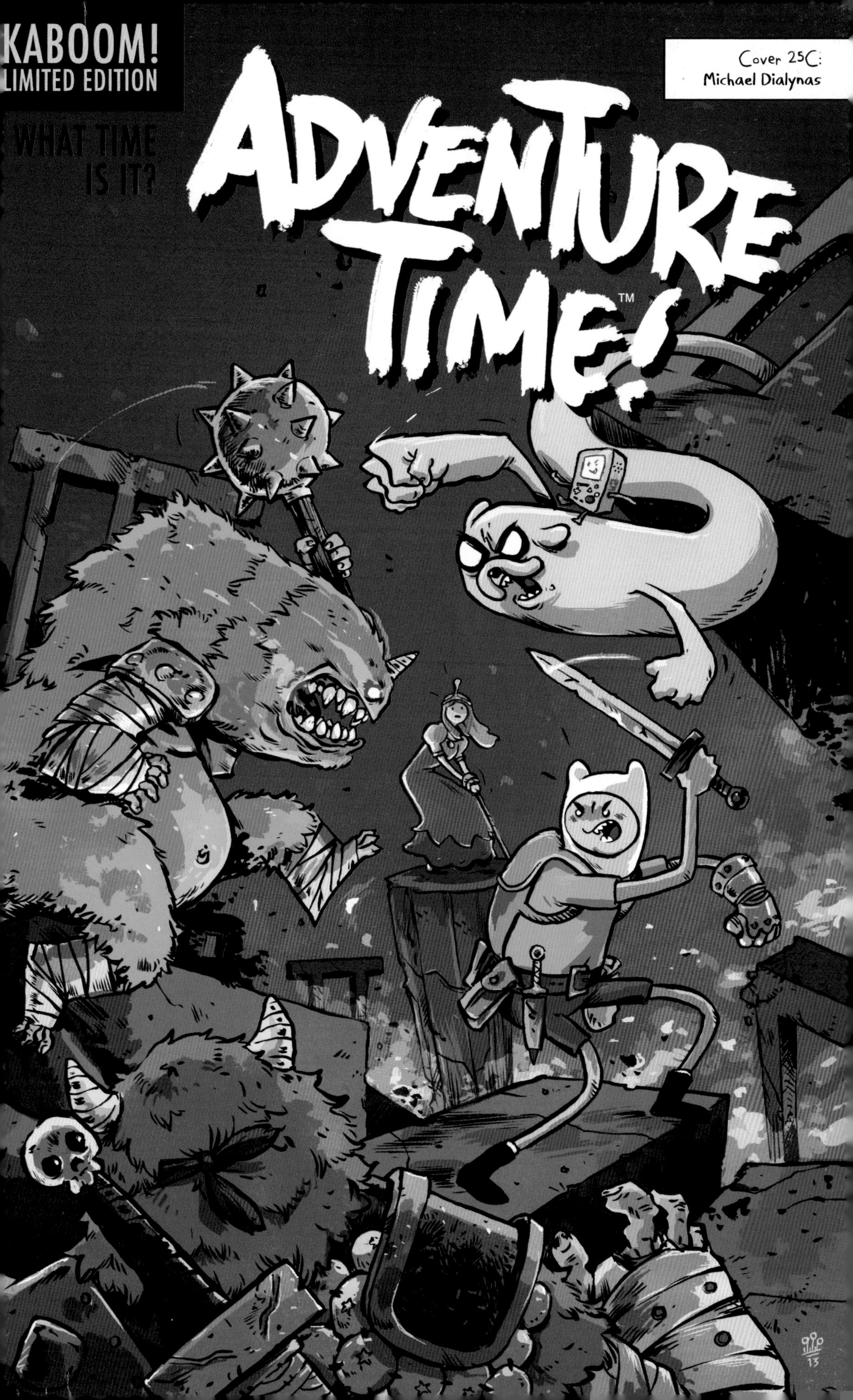

KABOOM!
LIMITED EDITION
WHAT TIME IS IT?
ADVENTURE TIME!™
Cover 25C:
Michael Dialynas

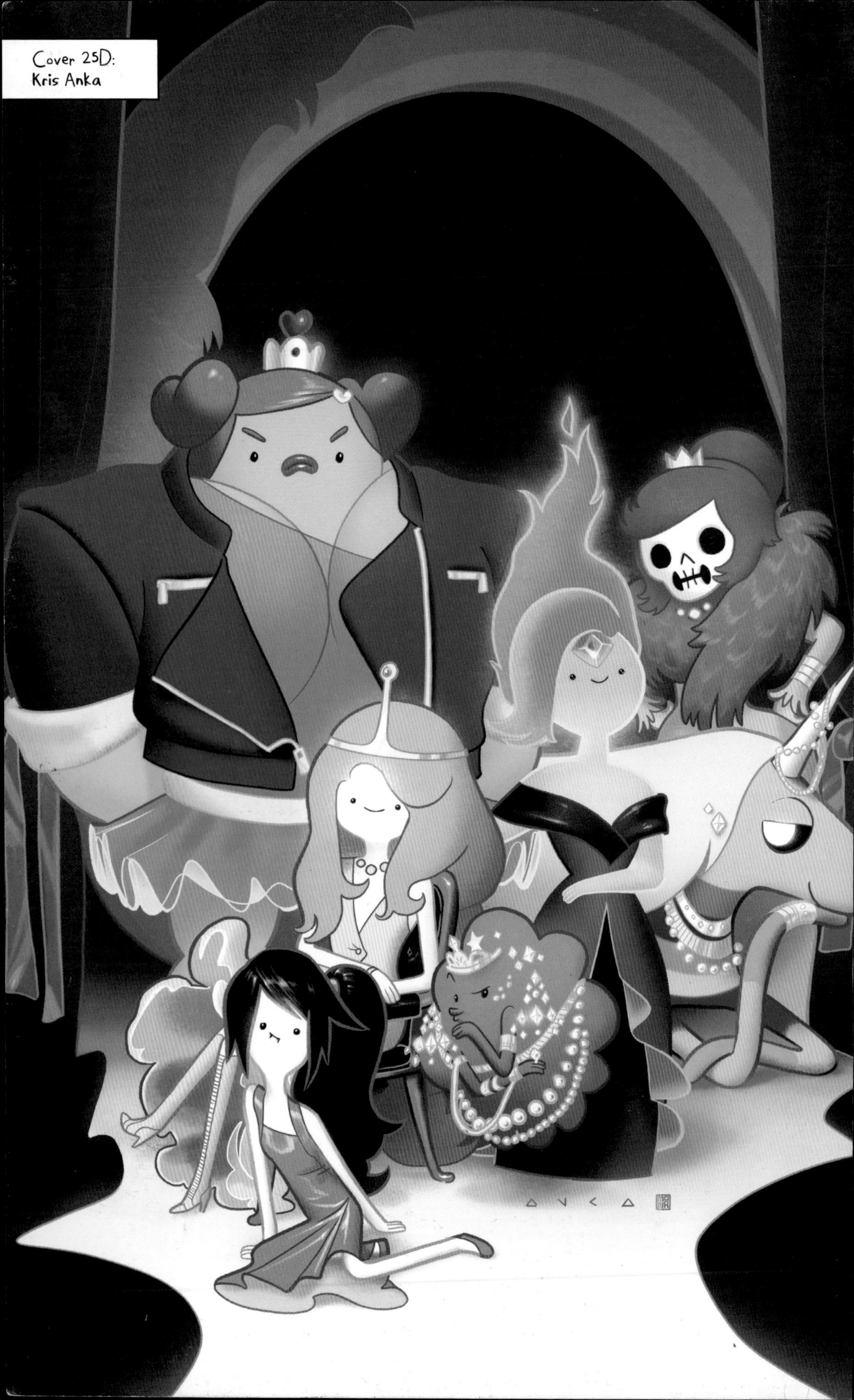

Cover 25D:
Kris Anka

Cover 25E:
Jeffrey Brown

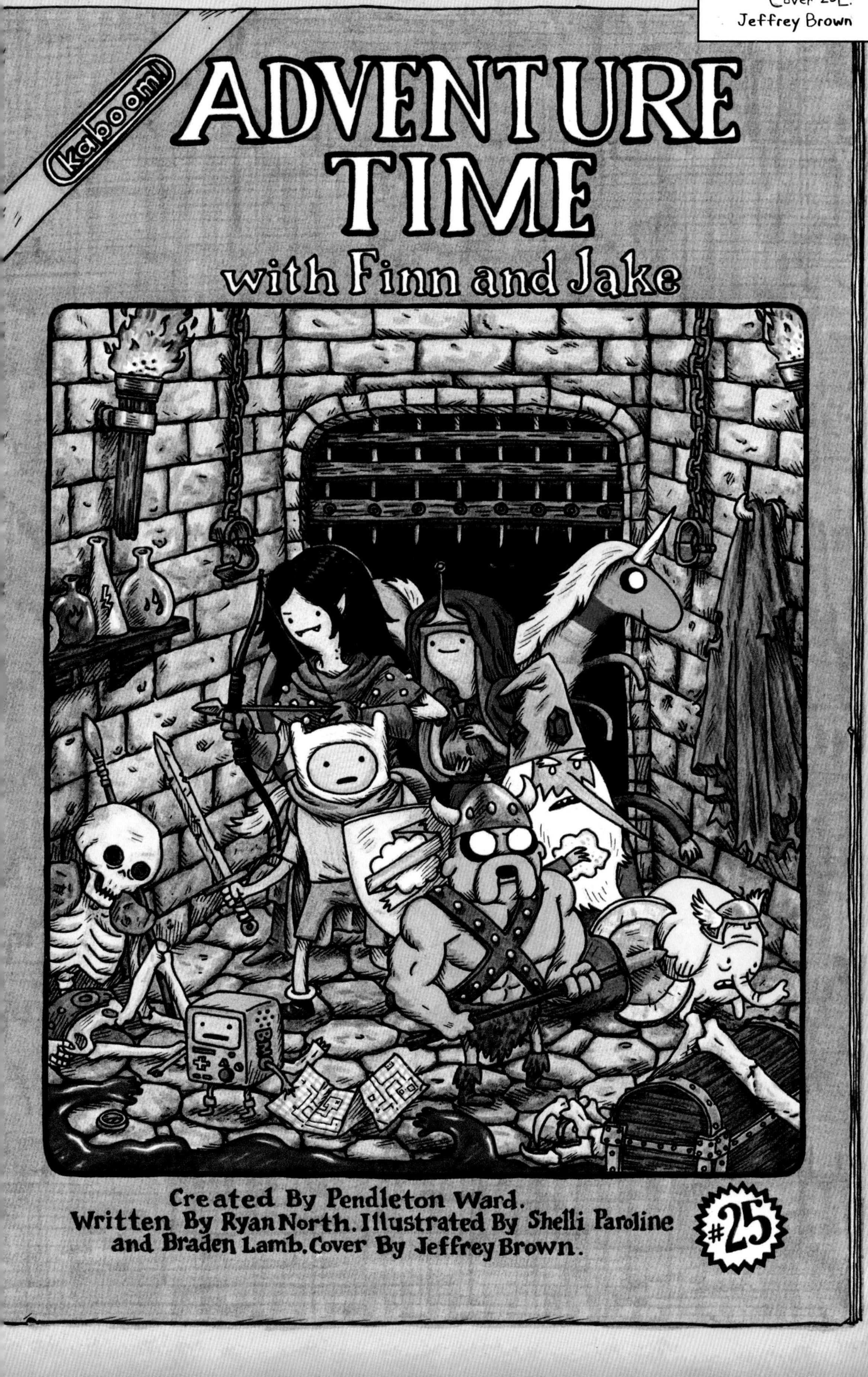
kaboom!
ADVENTURE TIME
with Finn and Jake
Created By Pendleton Ward.
Written By Ryan North. Illustrated By Shelli Paroline and Braden Lamb. Cover By Jeffrey Brown.
#25

Cover 26A:
Hannah Bischak

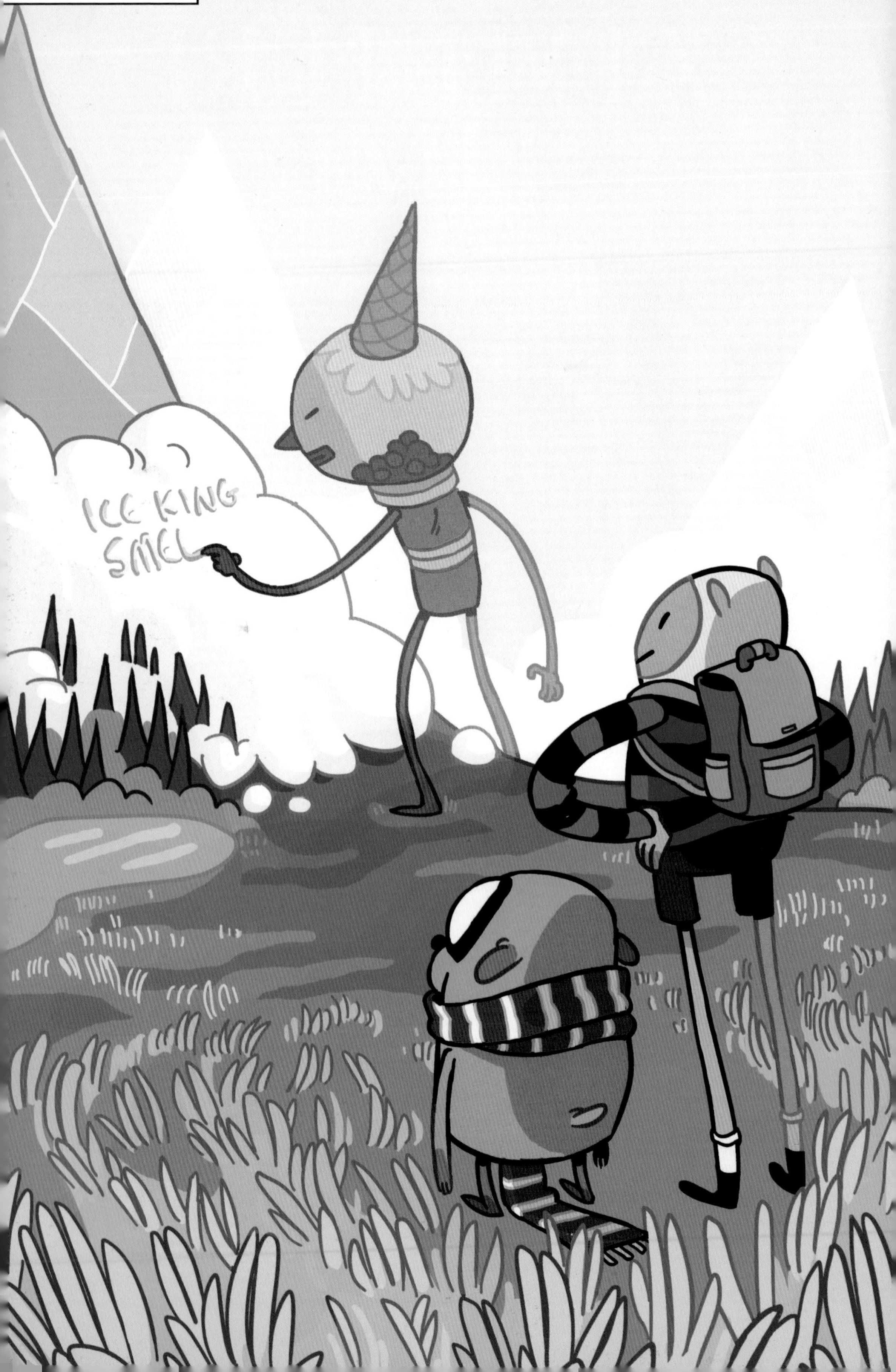
ICE KING
SMEL

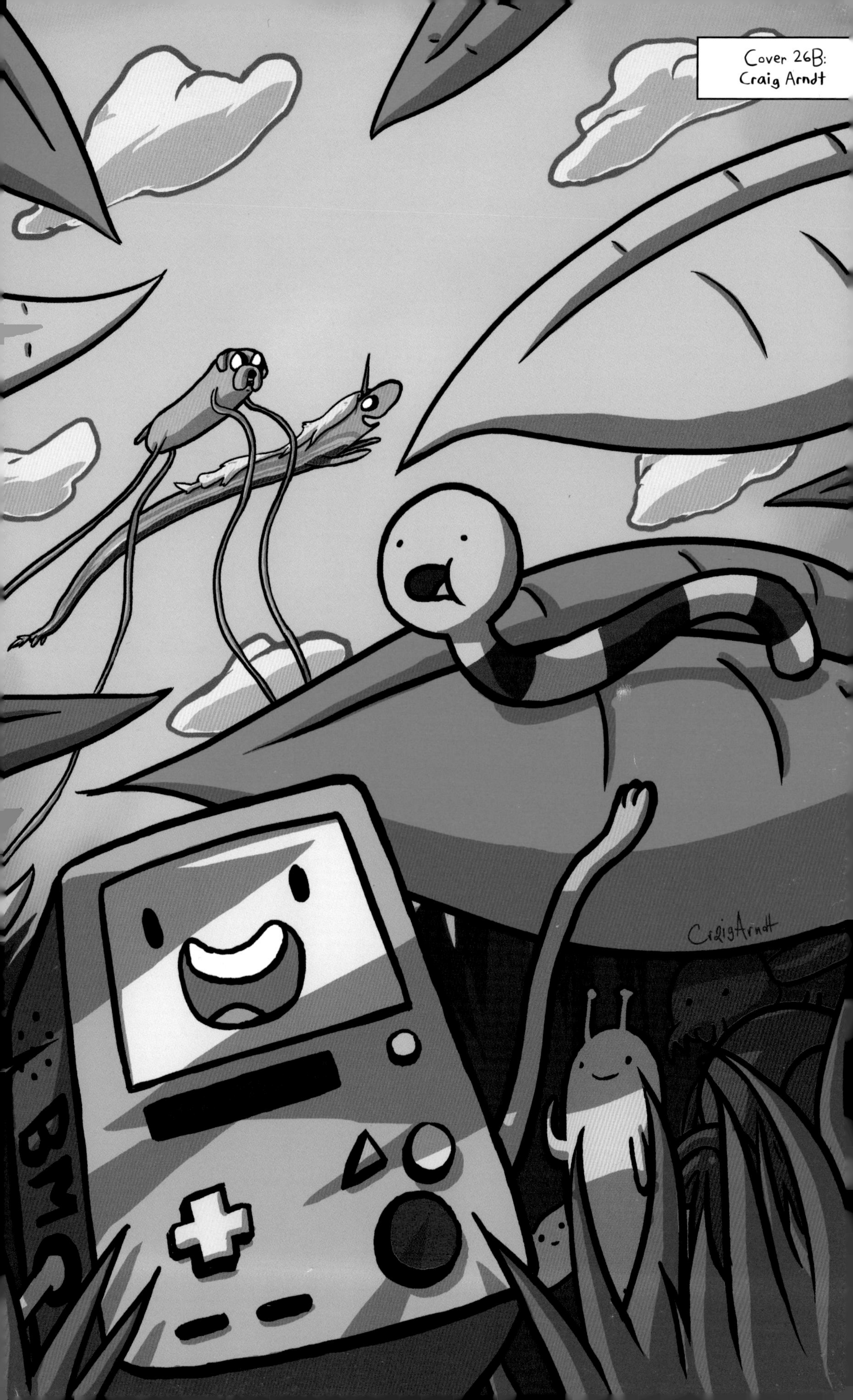
CraigArndt

Cover 26B:
Craig Arndt

Cover 26C:
Emily Hu

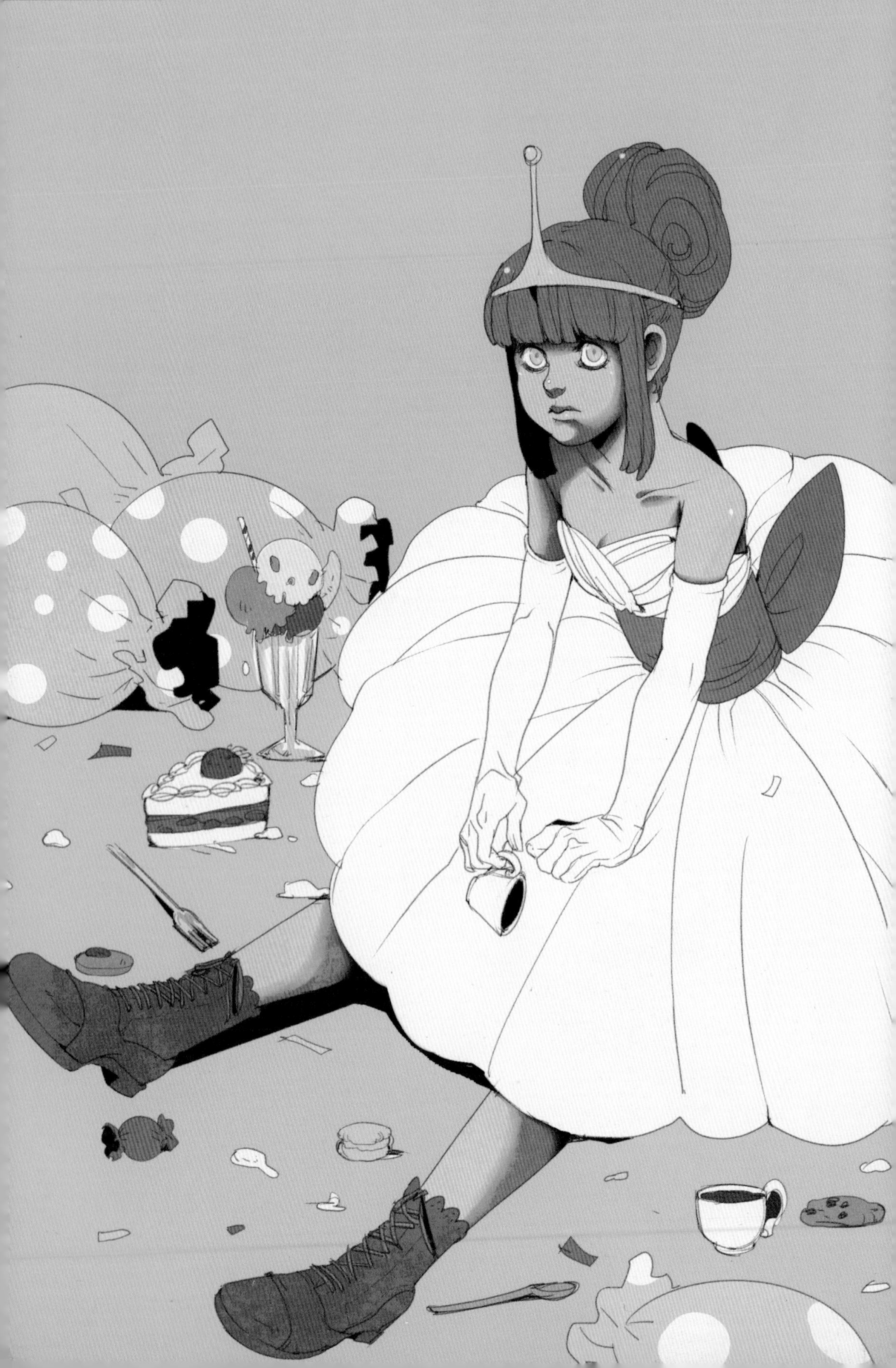

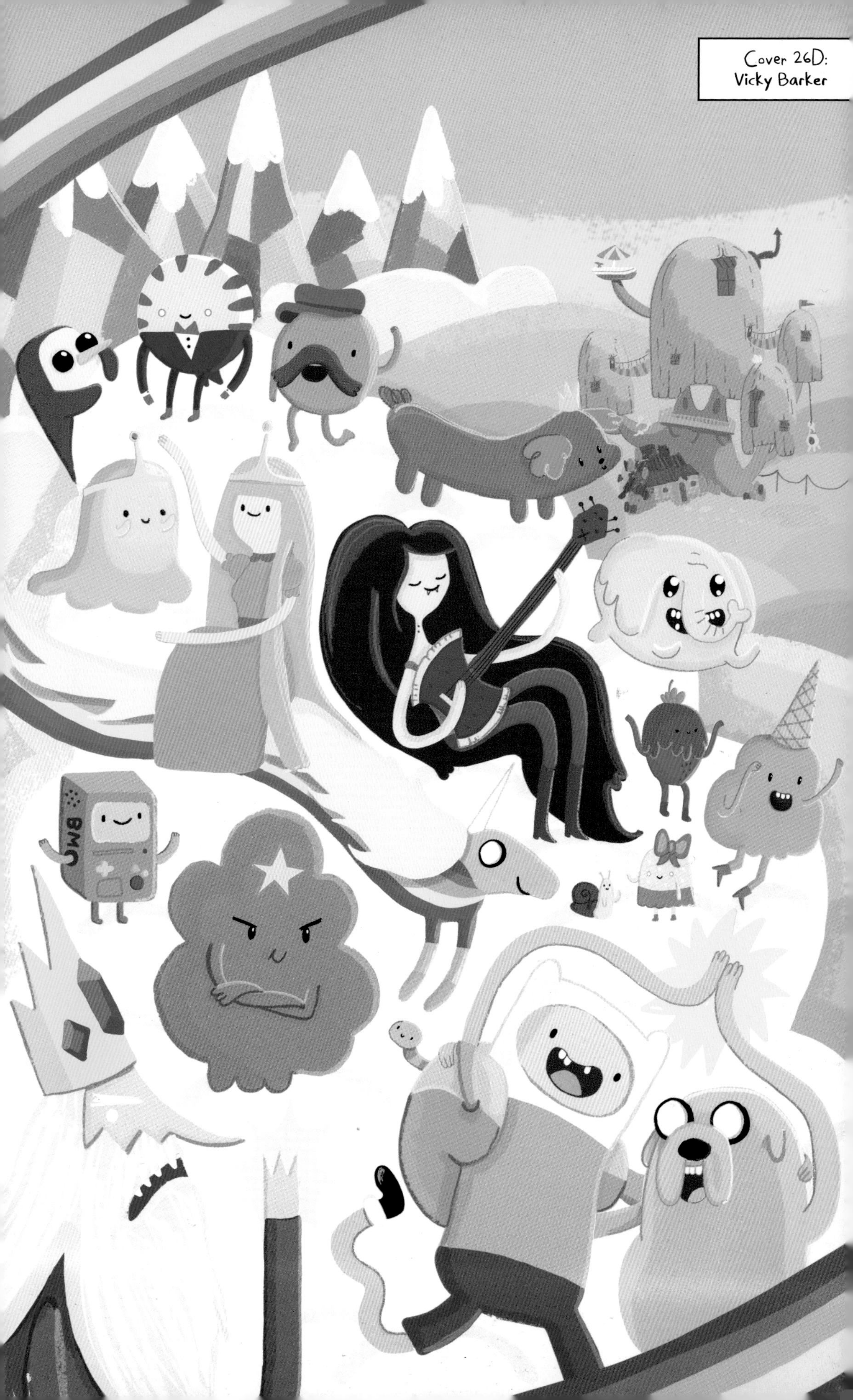
BMO

Cover 26D:
Vicky Barker

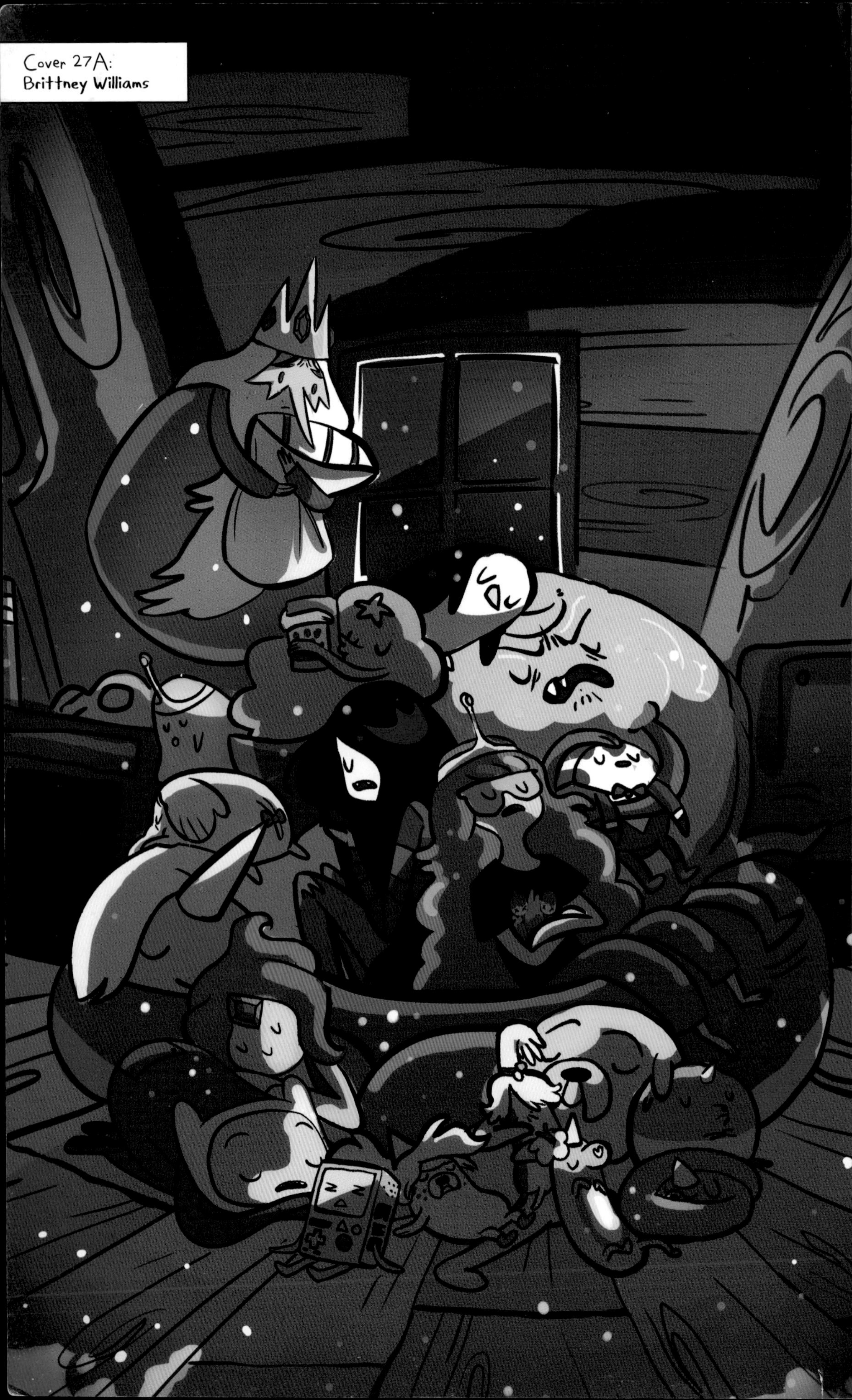

Cover 27A:
Brittney Williams

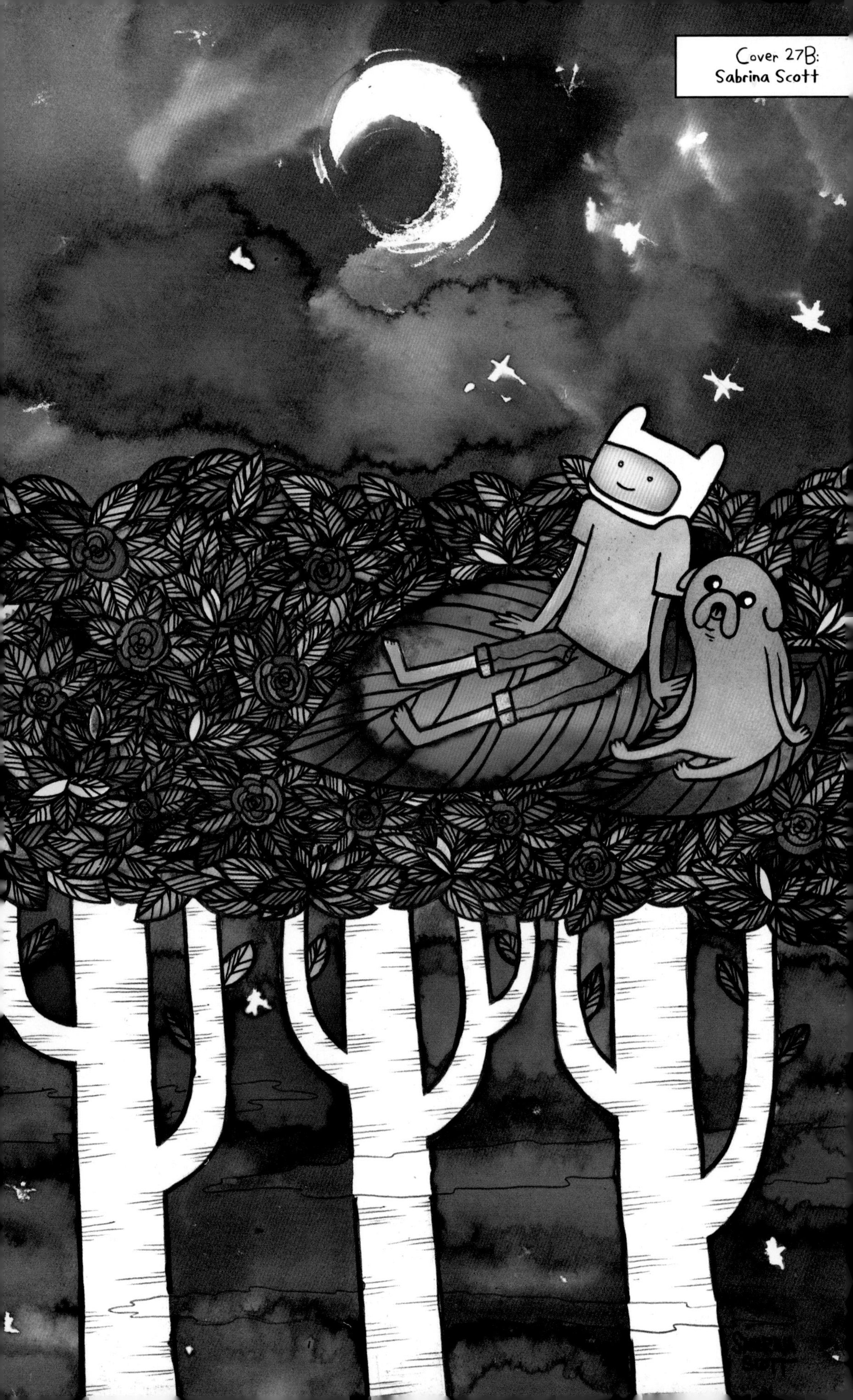

Cover 27B:
Sabrina Scott

Cover 27C:
Tom Hunter

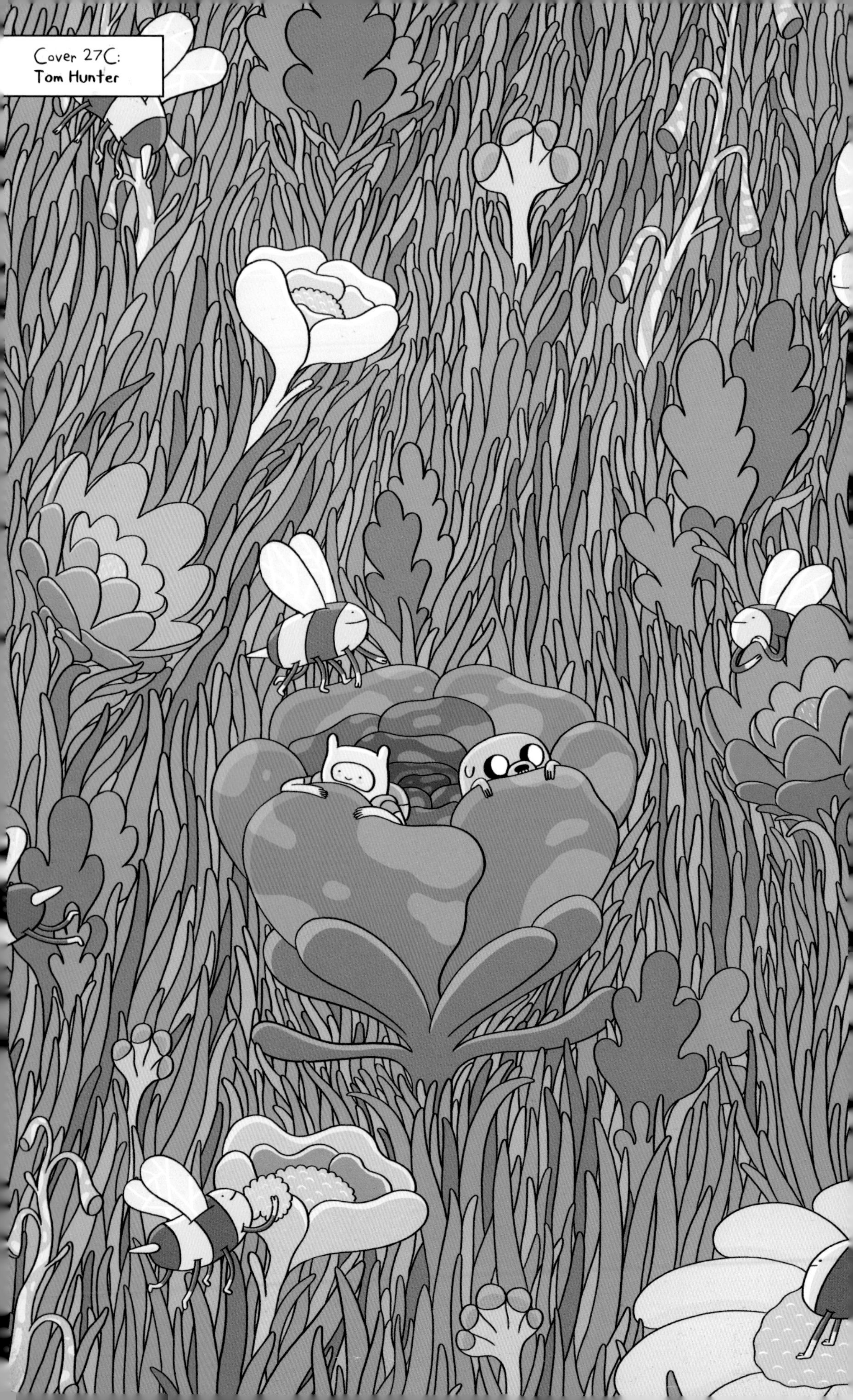

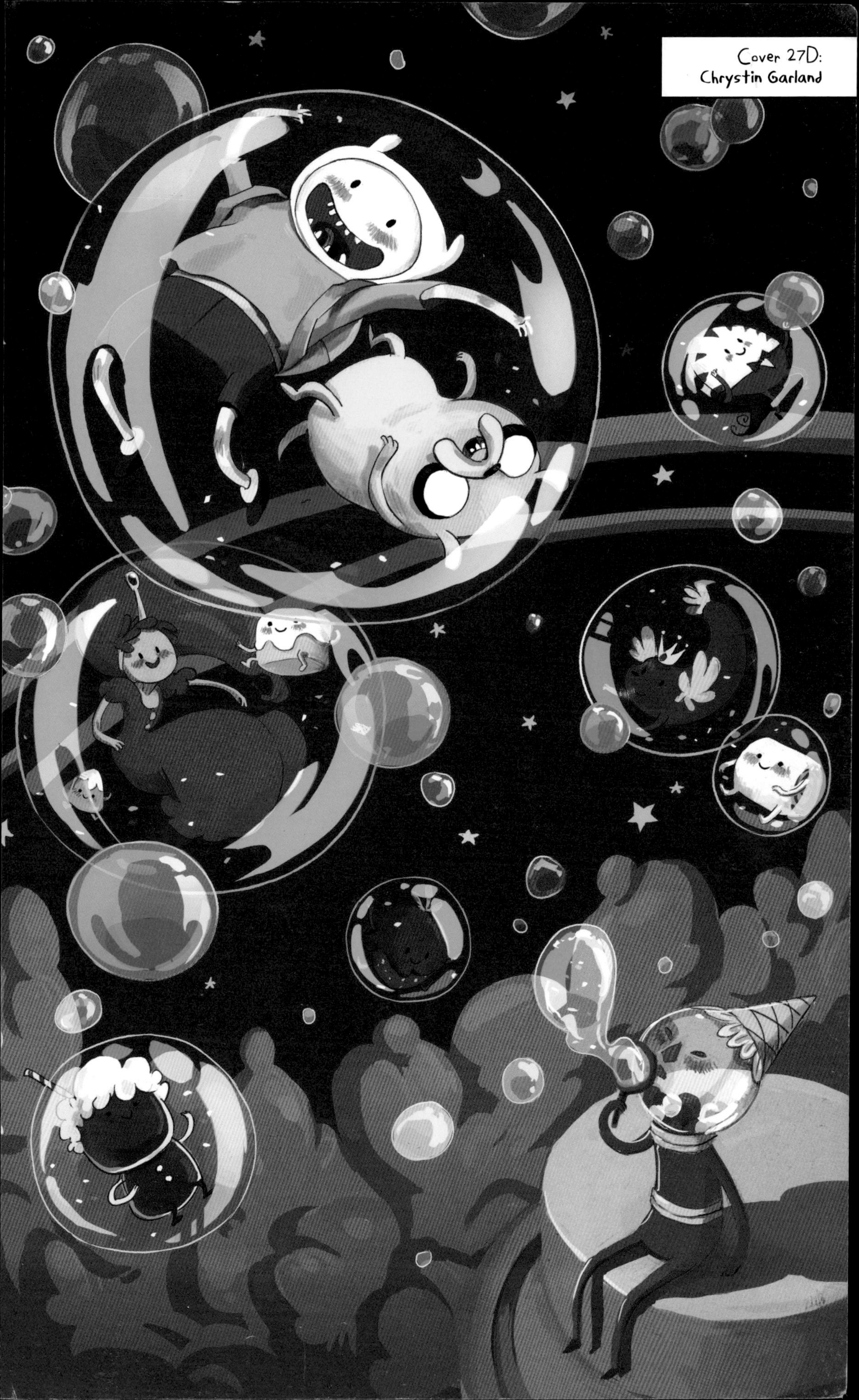

Cover 27D:
Chrystin Garland

Cover 28A:
Mike Holmes

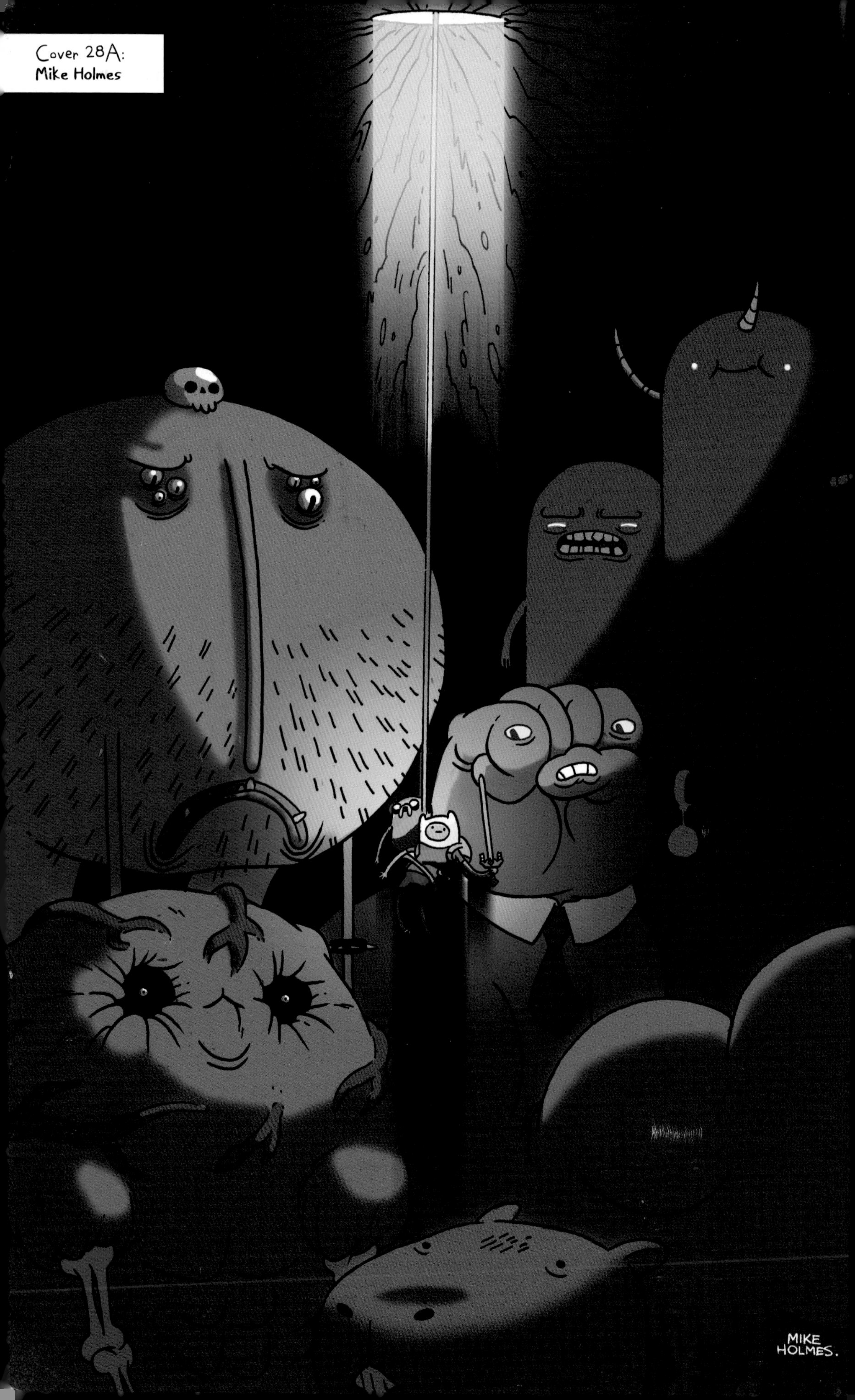
MIKE
HOLMES.

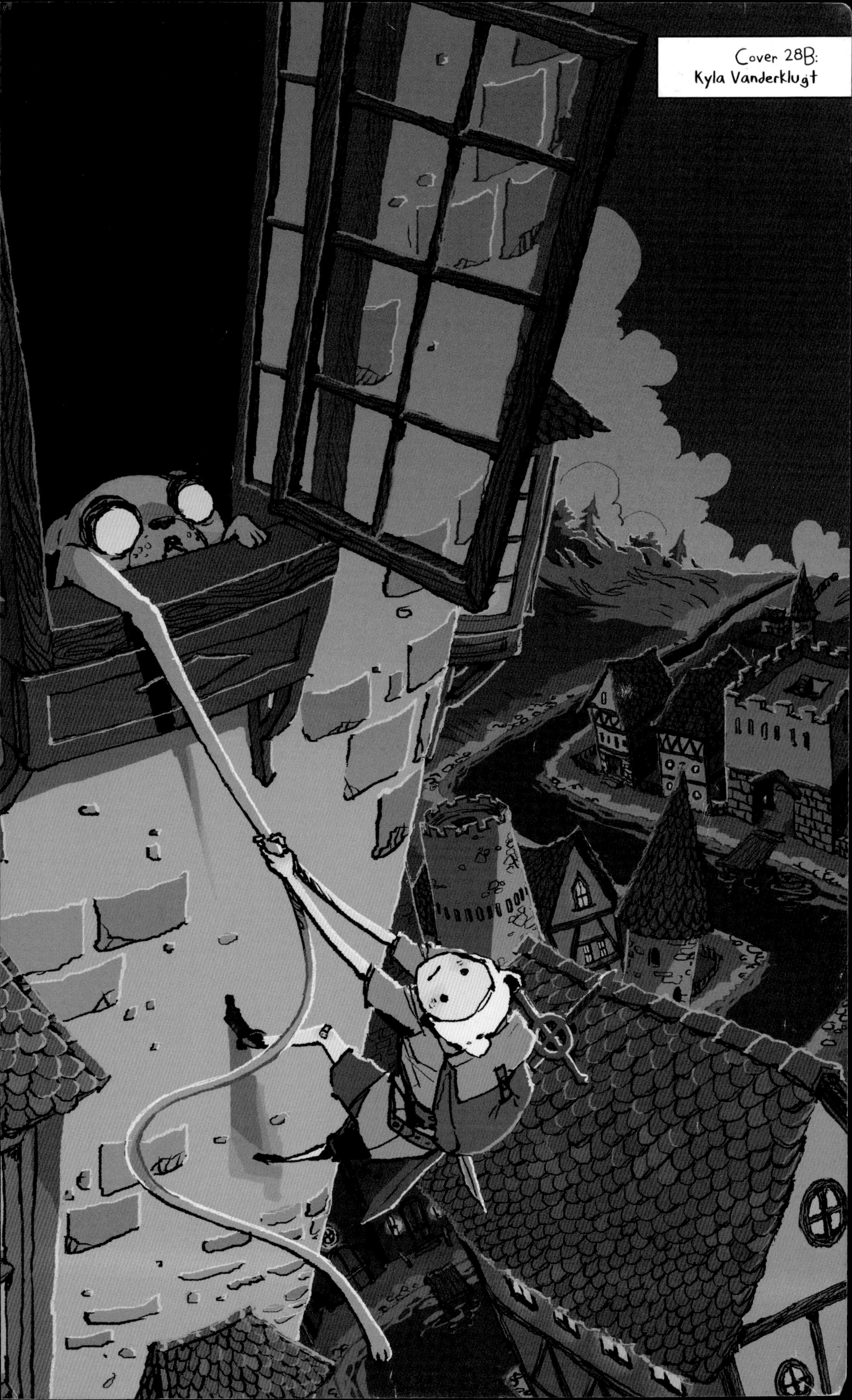

Cover 28B:
Kyla Vanderklugt

Cover 28C:
James Lloyd

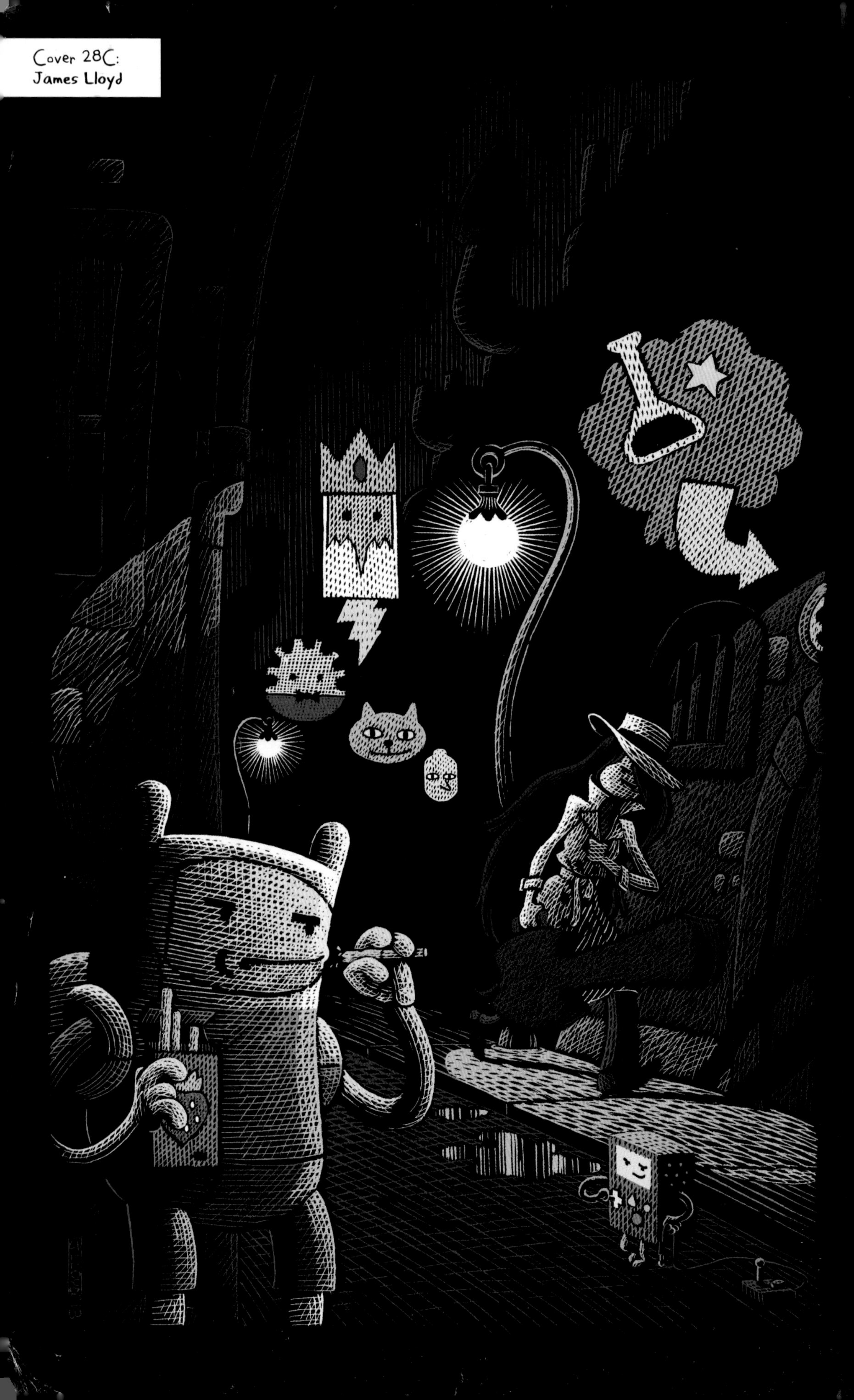

Cover 28D:
Zan Czyzewski

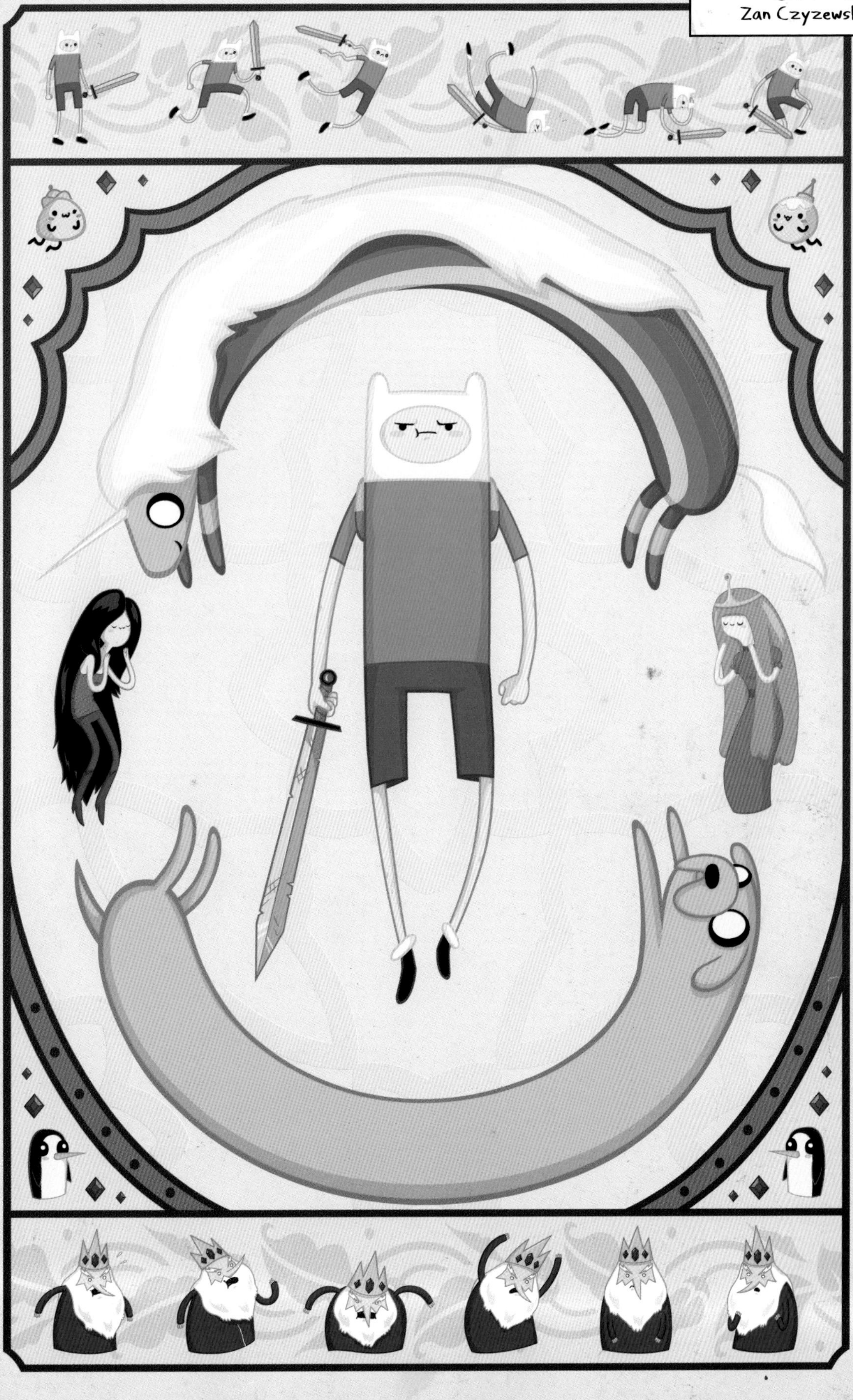

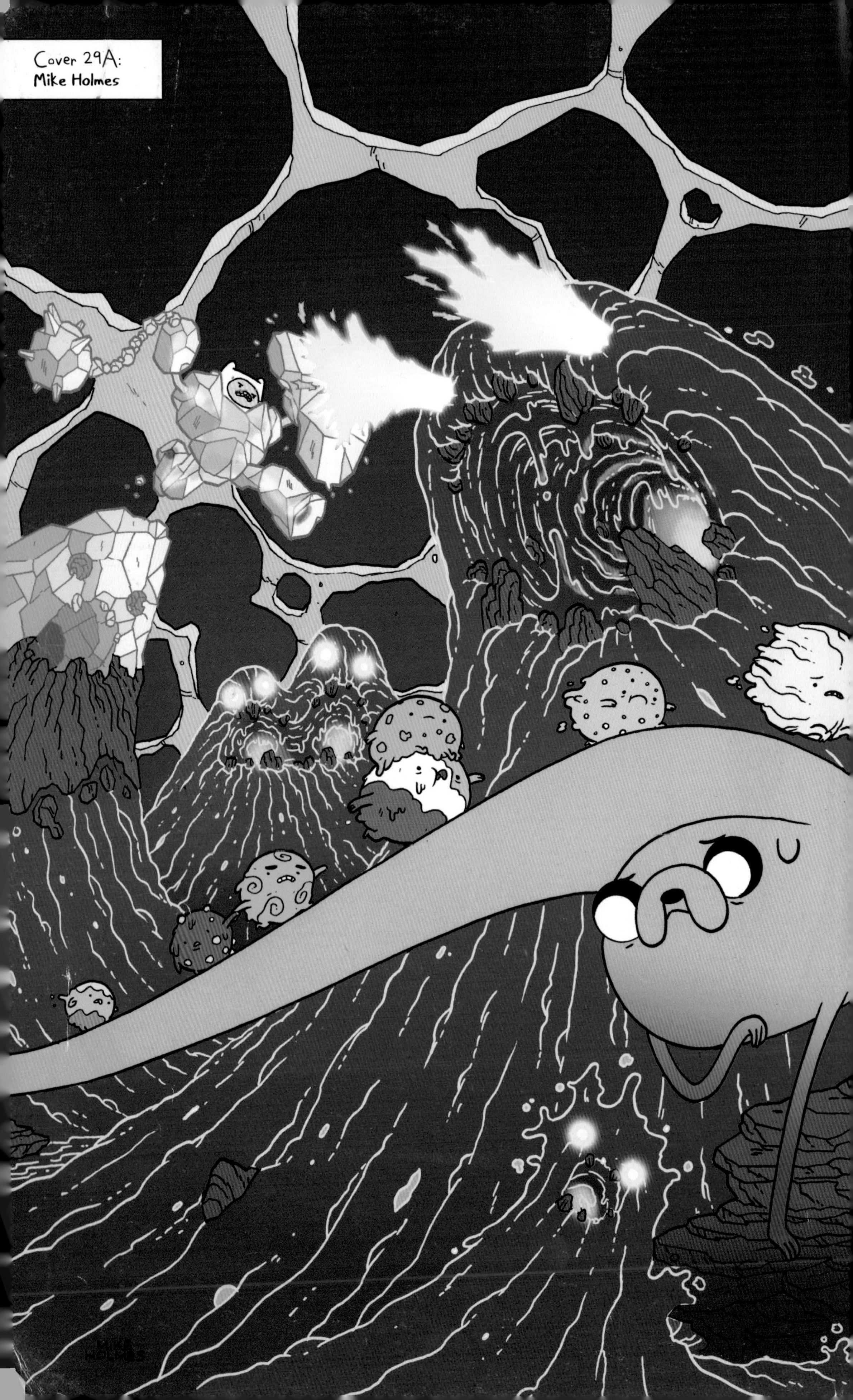

Cover 29A:
Mike Holmes

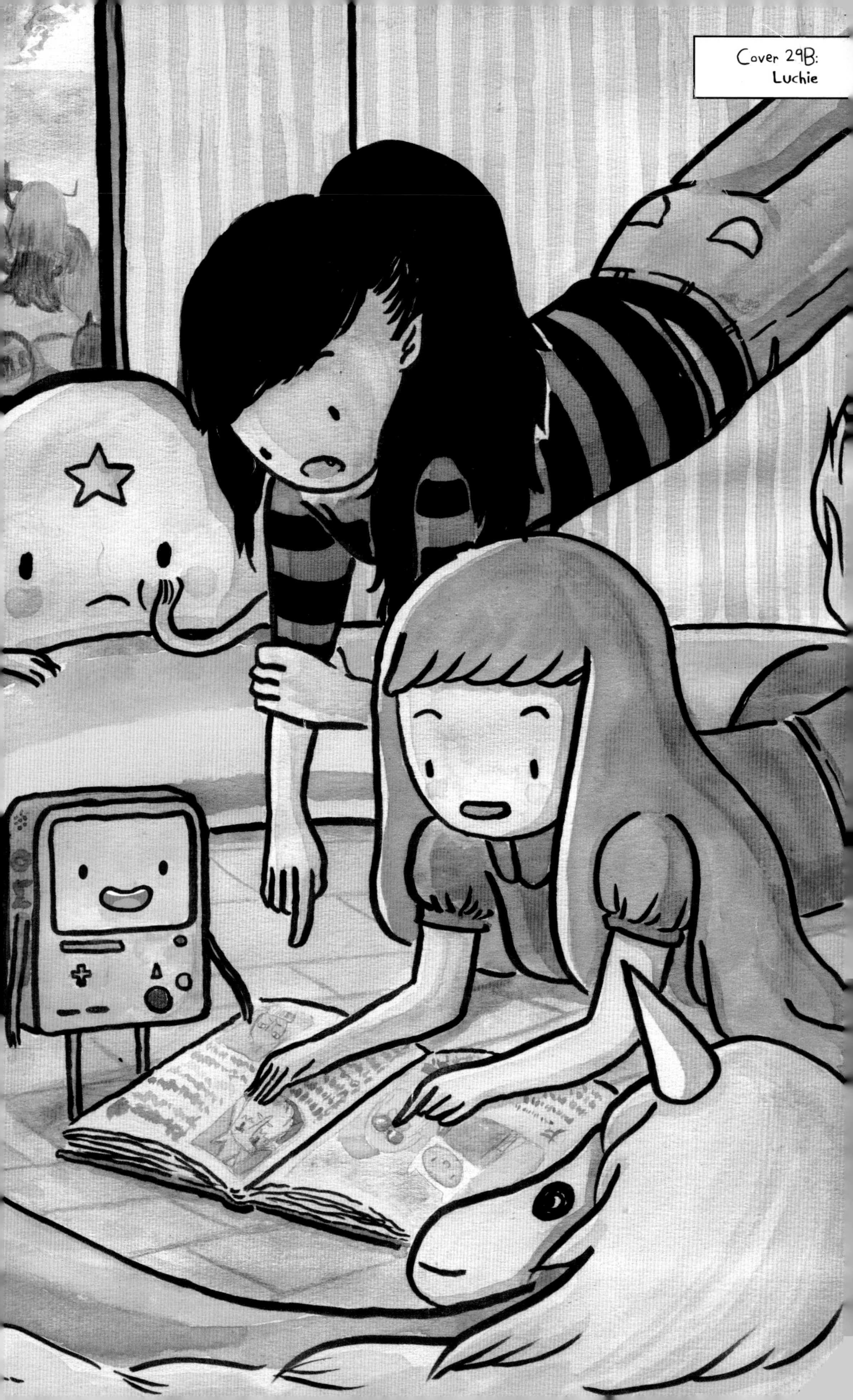

Cover 29B:
Luchie

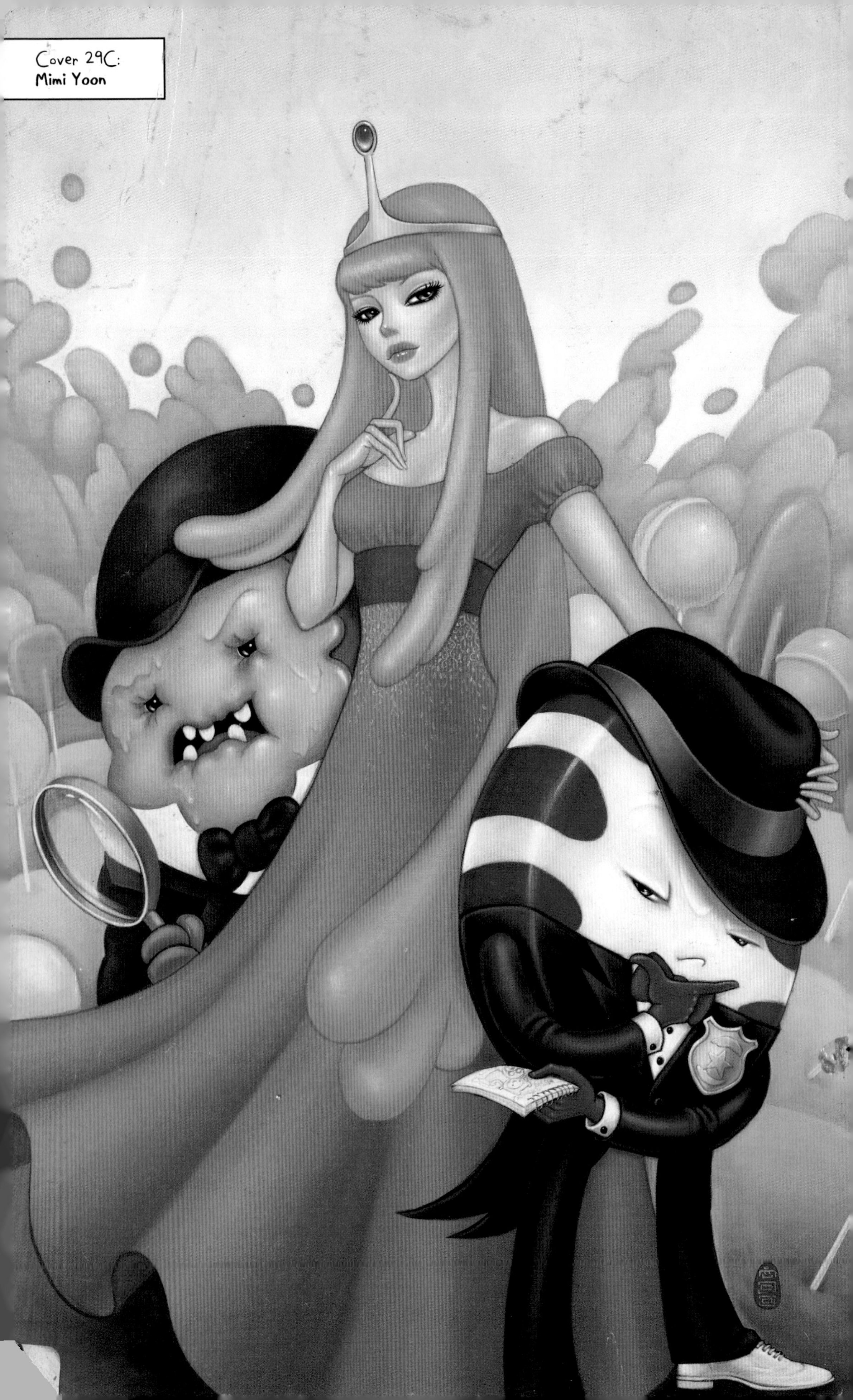

Cover 29C:
Mimi Yoon

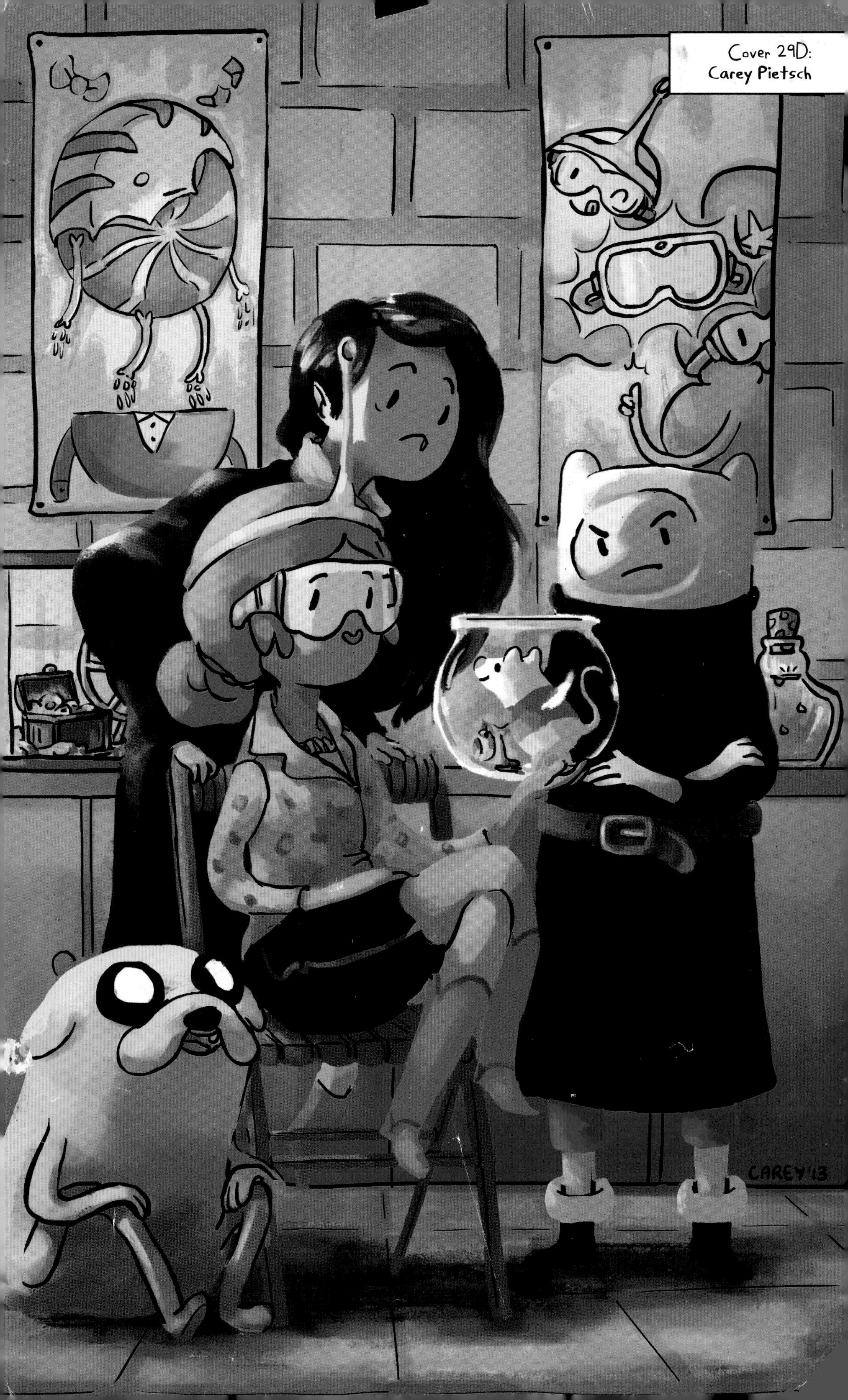
CAREY '13

Cover 29D:
Carey Pietsch